Thomas Hardy

OUTSIDE THE GATES
OF THE WORLD
SELECTED SHORT STORIES

Edited by
JAN JĘDRZEJEWSKI
University of Ulster

With an Introduction by
JOHN BAYLEY
University of Oxford

Series Editor
NORMAN PAGE
University of Nottingham

EVERYMAN
J. M. DENT · LONDON
CHARLES E. TUTTLE
VERMONT

Introduction, notes and critical apparatus
© J. M. Dent 1996

This edition first published in 1996
All rights reserved

J. M. Dent
Orion Publishing Group
Orion House, 5 Upper St Martin's Lane,
London WC2H 9EA
and
Charles E. Tuttle Co., Inc.
28 South Main Street,
Rutland, Vermont 05701, USA

Typeset in Sabon by CentraCet Ltd, Cambridge
Printed in Great Britain by
The Guernsey Press Co. Ltd, Guernsey, C. I.

British Library Cataloguing-in-Publication Data
is available upon request.

ISBN 0 460 87574 4

CONTENTS

NOTE ON THE AUTHOR AND EDITORS

THOMAS HARDY was born in Higher Bockhampton, near Dorchester, in 1840, the first of four children. His father was a stonemason and builder. At sixteen he trained as an architect and in 1862 went to work in London. He wrote poetry but failed to get it published before returning to Bockhampton in 1867.

In 1870 he worked on the restoration of the church at St Juliot in Cornwall, where he met Emma Gifford. They married in 1874. Having financed his novel *Desperate Remedies* (1871), he then lost money on it. *Under the Greenwood Tree* (1872) and *A Pair of Blue Eyes* (1873) followed. *Far from the Madding Crowd*, his first real success, was published in 1874. He published *The Hand of Ethelberta* (1876), *The Return of the Native* (1878) and *The Trumpet-Major* (1880). Moving to London 1878–81, he fell seriously ill between 1880–81. *A Laodicean* (1881) and *Two on a Tower* (1882) were followed by *The Mayor of Casterbridge* (1886) and *The Woodlanders* (1887). In 1883 he settled in Dorchester and moved into the house he had designed, Max Gate, in 1885. His first collection of short stories, *Wessex Tales*, appeared in 1888; three further collections were published between 1891 and 1913. *Tess of the d'Urbervilles* (1891) brought him fame, although its advanced moral stance caused an outcry. After further controversy on the publication of *Jude the Obscure* (1896), he returned to poetry, and only *The Well-Beloved*, written in 1892, appeared later, in 1897.

Wessex Poems, his first book of verse, was published in 1898, and followed by seven further volumes. In 1904–8, *The Dynasts*, an epic drama, was published. Hardy was awarded the Order of Merit in 1910. His wife's death in 1912 inspired some of his greatest poems. He married Florence Dugdale in 1914, and died in 1928.

JOHN BAYLEY has spent his academic career at Oxford, where he was Thomas Warton Professor of English Literature from

1974 to 1992. Among his many publications are *The Romantic Survival* (1956), *Tolstoy and the Novel* (1966), *An Essay on Hardy* (1978), *Shakespeare and Tragedy* (1981), *The Short Story: Henry James to Elizabeth Bowen* (1988), and *Housman's Poems* (1992); his novels include *In Another Country* (1954) and the recently published *Alice* (1994) and *The Queer Captain* (1995).

JAN JĘDRZEJEWSKI is Lecturer in English at the University of Ulster. He has published *Thomas Hardy and the Church* (1996) and papers on George Eliot, Samuel Butler, and the literary relations between the British Isles and Poland; his journalism includes articles and BBC broadcasts, mainly on Northern Ireland.

CHRONOLOGY OF HARDY'S LIFE

Year	Age	Life
1840		Hardy is born 2 June at Higher Bockhampton in the cottage built by his grandfather
1841		Birth of his sister, Mary
1848	8	Attends village school
1849–56	9–16	Attends school in Dorchester
1856	16	Articled to John Hicks, a Dorchester architect
1858	18	About now writes his first surviving poem, 'Domicilium'
1862–7	22–7	Living in London, working as an architect; writes poetry but fails to get it published

CHRONOLOGY OF HIS TIMES

Year	Literary Context	Historical Events
1840		Great Irish famine
		Penny Post is introduced
1842		Chartist riots
1846		Repeal of Corn Laws; Irish Potato Famine
1847	Charlotte Brontë, *Jane Eyre* Emily Brontë, *Wuthering Heights*	Railway reaches Dorchester
1848	Dickens, *Dombey & Son* Thackeray, *Vanity Fair* Pre-Raphaelite Brotherhood active	
1849	Ruskin, *Seven Lamps of Architecture*	
1850	Death of Wordsworth Tennyson becomes Poet Laureate	
1851		The Great Exhibition in London
1853	Arnold, *Poems*	1853–6 The Crimean War
1855	Browning, *Men and Women* Elizabeth Gaskell, *North and South*	
1858	George Eliot, *Scenes of Clerical Life*	
1859	Darwin, *The Origin of Species*	
1860	Collins, *The Woman in White*	
1861	Palgrave's anthology, *The Golden Treasury* *Hymns Ancient and Modern*	American Civil War

Year	Age	Life
1860s		Throughout this decade Hardy steadily loses his religious faith
1865	25	A short fictional piece called 'How I Built Myself a House' is published
1867	27	Returns to Dorset; begins his first novel, *The Poor Man and the Lady*
1868	28	Romantic affair with his cousin, Tryphena Sparks. *The Poor Man and the Lady* is rejected by publishers
1869	29	Works in Weymouth for an architect
1870	30	Meets and falls in love with Emma Lavinia Gifford while at St Juliot in Cornwall planning the restoration of the church
1871	31	*Desperate Remedies*, published anonymously, is a commercial failure
1872	32	Has minor success with *Under the Greenwood Tree*
1873	33	*A Pair of Blue Eyes*, Hardy's first novel to appear as a serial. Becomes a full-time novelist
1874	34	*Far from the Madding Crowd*, his first real success. Marries Emma Gifford. For next nine years they move from one lodging to another
1878	38	*The Return of the Native*. Becomes member of London's Savile Club
1879	39	His short story, 'The Distracted Preacher', is published
1880	40	*The Trumpet-Major*. Is taken ill for several months
1881	41	*A Laodicean*
1882	42	*Two on a Tower*. Visits Paris
1885	45	Moves into Max Gate, house on outskirts of Dorchester. Lives there for the rest of his life
1886	46	*The Mayor of Casterbridge*. Sees Impressionist paintings in London

Year	Literary Context	Historical Events
1863	Death of Thackeray Mill, *Utilitarianism*	
1864	Newman, *Apologia pro Vita Sua*	
1865	Death of Elizabeth Gaskell	
1866	Swinburne, *Poems and Ballads*	
1867	Ibsen, *Peer Gynt*	Second Reform Bill
1868		Gladstone becomes Prime Minister
1869	Mill, *The Subjection of Women*	
1870	Death of Dickens	Franco-Prussian War Education Act brings education for all
1871	Darwin, *The Descent of Man*	Trade Unions legalized
1874		Disraeli becomes Prime Minister The modern bicycle arrives
1876	James's novels begin to be published	
1878		Edison invents the incandescent electric lamp
1879	James Murray becomes editor of what was later to become *The Oxford English Dictionary* Ibsen, *A Doll's House*	
1880	Death of George Eliot Zola, *Nana*	
1881	Revised Version of New Testament	Married Women's Property Act
1882	Deaths of Darwin, D. G. Rossetti and Trollope	Daimler's petrol engine
1885	Birth of D. H. Lawrence	Salisbury becomes Prime Minister
1886	Death of William Barnes, friend of Hardy, poet, philologist, polymath	

Year	Age	Life
1887	47	*The Woodlanders.* Visits France and Italy
1888	48	*Wessex Tales*, his first collection of short stories, and an essay on 'The Profitable Reading of Fiction'
1890	50	An essay, 'Candour in English Fiction'
1891	51	*Tess of the d'Urbervilles; A Group of Noble Dames* (short stories); an essay, 'The Science of Fiction'
1892	52	Death of Hardy's father
1893	53	On visit to Ireland meets Florence Henniker, for whom he developed a great affection
1894	54	*Life's Little Ironies* (short stories)
1895	55	*Jude the Obscure*
1895–6		First collected edition of novels, entitled 'Wessex Novels'
1896	56	Ceases novel-writing and returns to poetry
1897	57	*The Well-Beloved*, much revised after publication as a serial in 1892
1898	58	*Wessex Poems* (51 poems): Hardy's first book of verse, including his own illustrations
1901	61	*Poems of the Past and the Present* (99 poems)
1902	62	Macmillan become his main publishers
1904	64	*The Dynasts*, Part I. Death of his mother, Jemima
1905	65	Receives honorary doctorate from Aberdeen University, the first of several
1906	66	*The Dynasts*, Part II. About now meets Florence Dugdale
1908	68	*The Dynasts*, Part III. Edits a selection of Barnes's verse

Year	Literary Context	Historical Events
1887	Strindberg, *The Father*	
1888	Death of Arnold; birth of T. S. Eliot	
	About now the works of Kipling and Yeats begin to be published	
1889	Deaths of Browning, G. M. Hopkins and Wilkie Collins	
1890	Death of Newman	First underground railway in London
1891	Shaw, *Quintessence of Ibsenism*	
1892	Death of Tennyson	Gladstone Prime Minister
1893	Pinero, *The Second Mrs Tanqueray*	Independent Labour Party set up
1894	Deaths of Stevenson and Pater	Rosebery becomes Prime Minister
1895	Conrad's first novel, *Almayer's Folly*	Freud's first work on psychoanalysis
	Wilde, *The Importance of Being Earnest*	Marconi's 'wireless' telegraphy
1896	Housman, *A Shropshire Lad*	
1898	Wells, *The War of the Worlds*	The Curies discover radium
1899		The Boer War begins
1900	Deaths of Ruskin and Wilde	
1901		Death of Queen Victoria, who is succeeded by Edward VII
1902	Zola dies; Hardy laments his death	Balfour becomes Prime Minister
1903		Wright brothers make first flight in aeroplane with engine
1904	Chekhov, *The Cherry Orchard*	
1906		Liberals win election
1907	Kipling is awarded Nobel Prize	
1908		Asquith becomes Prime Minister

Year	Age	Life
1909	69	*Time's Laughingstocks* (94 poems)
1910	70	Awarded the Order of Merit
1911	71	Ceases spending 'the season' in London
1912	72	Death of his wife, Emma. The Wessex Edition of his works is published by Macmillan
1913	73	*A Changed Man and Other Tales*. Revisits Cornwall and the scenes of his courtship of Emma
1914	74	*Satires of Circumstance* (107 poems). Marries Florence Dugdale
1915	75	Death of his sister, Mary
1916	76	*Selected Poems of Thomas Hardy* edited by Hardy himself
1917	77	*Moments of Vision* (159 poems). Begins to write his autobiography with intention that Florence should publish it under her own name after his death
1919–20	79	A de luxe edition of his work, the Mellstock Edition, is published
1920 onwards	80	Max Gate becomes a place of pilgrimage for hundreds of admirers
1922	82	*Late Lyrics and Earlier* (151 poems)
1923	83	*The Queen of Cornwall* (a poetic play)
1924	84	Hardy's adaptation of *Tess* performed in Dorchester
1925	85	*Human Shows* (152 poems)

Year	Literary Context	Historical Events
1909	Deaths of Swinburne and Meredith	
1910		Death of Edward VII, who is succeeded by George V
1911	Bennett, *Clayhanger* Brooke, *Poems*	
1912		Sinking of *Titanic*
1913	Lawrence, *Sons and Lovers*	First Morris Oxford car
1914	Pound editor of the first anthology of imagist poetry Frost, *North of Boston*	The First World War begins
1915	Virginia Woolf, *The Voyage Out*	
1916	Death of James Lawrence's *The Rainbow* seized by police	Lloyd George becomes Prime Minister
1917		The Russian Revolution
1918	Sassoon, *Counter-Attack* Hopkins, *Poems*	The war ends Women over thirty given the vote
1919		Treaty of Versailles First woman MP
1920	Edward Thomas, *Collected Poems* Owen, *Poems*	First meeting of League of Nations
1922	Eliot, *The Waste Land* Joyce, *Ulysses*	Mussolini comes to power in Italy Women are given equality in divorce proceedings
1924	Forster, *A Passage to India*	Ramsay MacDonald forms first Labour Government Stalin becomes Soviet Dictator
1926	T. E. Lawrence, *Seven Pillars of Wisdom*	The General Strike
1927		Lindbergh makes first crossing of the Atlantic by air

Year	Age	Life
1928	87	Hardy dies on 11 January; part buried in Westminster Abbey, part at the family church at Stinsford. *Winter Words* (105 poems) is published posthumously. *The Early Life of Thomas Hardy*, his disguised autobiography, is published
1930		*The Later Years of Thomas Hardy*, the second volume of the autobiography, is published. *Collected Poems* (918 poems) followed by *Complete Poems* (947 poems) in 1976
1937		Death of Hardy's second wife, Florence

Year	Literary Context	Historical Events
1928	Lawrence's *Lady Chatterley's Lover* privately printed in Florence	

INTRODUCTION

As a form the short story has only recently defined itself. Or perhaps it would be truer to say that only in the present century has criticism been interested in defining it. Certainly Thomas Hardy, the author of the Wessex novels and of many of the finest poems of this century, would not himself have bothered to state in so many words what short stories meant for him, although he produced, in the course of a long and distinguished writing career, some of the most memorable examples of the genre.

Although he was not concerned to be a serious critic, Hardy was a great craftsman. He loved stories, tales and anecdotes drawn from all sources as well as from his native Wessex, and he had an incomparable gift for bringing together a story and a poem. One of his finest tales in verse, 'A Trampwoman's Tragedy', might easily have also been written by him as a prose story. As a craftsman he perceived, in fact, the close relation that can exist between things seen poetically and things seen prosaically as what actually occurred: why, and when, and by whom remembered.

Elizabeth Bowen, one of the best and most sophisticated English short story writers of this century, remarked that every good short story contains in it both the impulse to poetry and the wish to record a historical or a personal moment. The poet Philip Larkin, who produced a memorable novel which in a sense is also both a short story and a poem, observed that the writer in both genres was like a man trying to remember a tune, and finally perhaps contriving to catch it, even if imperfectly, and to set it down.

As poet and as story-teller, as well as one to whom the art of music meant much, Hardy was uniquely endowed in this respect. He would no doubt have understood what Philip Larkin was getting at; and I am fairly sure that he would have admired Larkin's poem-story-novel *A Girl in Winter*. But Hardy, it must be remembered, was also a homely anecdotalist, with a living to earn by writing, and a strong sense of what his audience, or audiences, would enjoy in the way of a tale. He was not consciously concerned to mix poetry into the telling of it, or to aim for the kind of indefinable success aimed for by the more modern and ambitious practitioners of the genre.

In this context it is also significant that Hardy's stories show neither a conscious nor an unconscious development in terms of their outlook, style, and mode of effect. Any of his brief prose fictions could have been written at any time in his working life. In this respect they form a contrast with the stories, say, of Henry James, whose early tales are written very differently from the ones in his later collections. Both James and Hardy were writing originally for periodicals, and the magazines that looked for and published short fictions of all kinds were then numerous and flourishing. But James increasingly came to view his stories as works of art of a special kind, although he sometimes began a story which he subsequently found expanding into a *nouvelle* or full-length novel, while Hardy never deviated from a more homely view of the matter, placing his tales throughout his career where they would be best received, and where they would command the best price.

The stories constituting *Wessex Tales*, his first collection, were, as Hardy tells us in one of his usual brief and not very informative prefaces, 'first collected and published under their present title, in two volumes, in 1888'. His last collection, *A Changed Man*, appeared in 1913, and contains a more than usually heterogeneous assortment of stories of different lengths from different periods, including one of the longest and most inconsequentially charming tales 'The Romantic Adventures of a Milkmaid', which I am particularly glad we have been able to print in this present selection. In the short introduction to *A Changed Man* Hardy speaks of reprinting 'a dozen minor novels' which had previously appeared in magazines. The word he used may be significant, for although 'The Romantic Adventures of a Milkmaid' is indeed the longest, any story by Hardy might be taken, both by him and by his reader, as a minor and miniature novel.

The liveliness and charm of the milkmaid's adventures remind us that the story dates from the time when Hardy's full-length novels, like *Under the Greenwood Tree* and *Far from the*

Madding Crowd, had a natural and spontaneous feel of comedy about them, an atmosphere that would later be darkened in his great and mature, but also more sombre, works. And yet it remains true that at any time of his life Hardy, like most rural narrators, always had a relish for the sad ballad, the unhappy tale, the misfortunes and ironies of life. Had it then been available in translation he would undoubtedly have relished Pushkin's great poem *The Bronze Horseman*, where the poet, in his rhymed introduction, looks back on the occasion of the great flood in St Petersburg in the second decade of the nineteenth century, and, remarking that he is about to bring back memories of it, adds as his climax – 'mine will be a sad tale'. So is Hardy's verse tale, 'A Trampwoman's Tragedy', and many if not most of the prose stories collected in this volume.

And yet not all. Some, and even some of the gloomiest, still have Hardy's lightness and poetic gaiety in touches about them, while the milkmaid's adventures are themselves in the tradition of the happiest sort of pastoral. And while in the later novels, like *The Mayor of Casterbridge*, *Tess of the d'Urbervilles* and *Jude the Obscure*, gloom might be said to take on the aspect of a philosophy, and to go with the view of life Hardy expressed when he coined the Aeschylean-sounding phrase 'the President of the Immortals', Margery Tucker of the 'Romantic Adventures' is in no way subjected to this potentate's dire influence. Tess is herself many things – a symbol, a 'pure woman', a figment of Hardy's own irrepressible tendency to daydream about a Fair Woman, and a 'Not Impossible She' seen on the top of a bus, or as a waitress in a café (the original figure of Tess was glimpsed by him in just such a situation). She is a figure both of power and romance, as well as of social significance. Margery Tucker is none of these things, but benefits from the simple freshness and easiness of Hardy's homely narrative turn, and his unambitious intention in writing the tale. Margery is a milkmaid as Tess was to be, but in this delightful story Hardy had no imaginative compulsion to persecute her as he was both to love and persecute Tess. Aside from the special excitement and ingenuities of her 'romance', Margery experiences no more than the ordinary ups and downs, thrills and disillusionments, which the heroine of a conventional nineteenth-century narrative might expect.

With the 'Noble Dames', who make up the group Hardy

brought out together in 1891, it is a different matter. They are subject not to a general philosophy of sadness, as Tess or Jude will be, but to a whimsical love of the bizarre and the crudely melodramatic in Hardy, which several of his readers and critics have found downright morbid. Critics found it natural to use Hardy as an example when preaching their views on ethics and religion: as an awful example of what was wrong with the modern age. In a study written when he was still a comparatively young man, called *After Strange Gods*, T. S. Eliot denounced for its gloating 'perversity' the story in *A Group of Noble Dames* called 'Barbara of the House of Grebe'. He professed to regard its excessive and unnatural cruelty as typical of the godless world of the late nineteenth century, of which he saw Hardy as one of the main spokesmen and representatives.

The reader of course must judge for himself; but I think that most of us who enjoy Hardy would take all this with a large pinch of salt. It is clear that Hardy was not in any sense in a serious mood when he wrote this story and some others like it: rather, he was indulging his pleasure in grim events of past local history, and what Wordsworth in a poem called 'old unhappy far-off things'. The genre in which he was working is unashamedly one of melodrama and sensation. One of its exponents earlier in the century, Mrs Anna Laetitia Barbauld, had gone so far as to write an essay extolling the genre of the Gothic as intending only to provide 'the pleasure to be extracted from objects of terror'. A comment of Hardy's would seem to confirm this diagnosis in his own case. In response to comments by early reviewers and critics of the collection, that here perhaps he might have gone too far in the direction of purveying morbid thrills, he replied that Gothic heroes, like the well-known villain 'Alonzo the Brave', had been highly popular with the reading public when he was a young man, and that as a youthful reader himself he never wished their deeds of honour and suffering to be in any way played down in the telling.

Of course Hardy was being more than a trifle disingenuous here, as he sometimes could be when defending himself against criticism of his own literary tastes and practices. That there was a real and strong streak of morbidity in Hardy's make-up can hardly be denied; and it hardly emerges at its strongest, or indeed at its most disturbing, in 'Barbara of the House of

Grebe'. Like many descendants of country folk whose lives have for long been rooted in one place, Hardy loved old families whose doings were preserved in county annals; and he took a sly pleasure too in the record of this misdeeds and misfortunes. It was, one might almost say, the duty of the aristocracy to give this sort of entertainment and interest to the lives of the working folk; and though Hardy was not in that sense a working man – his father was an employer of labour and master mason and he himself began his career as an architect – still he identified with the amusements and interests of a wide range of comparatively humble people.

This deeply earthy and rustic nature of Hardy's imagination is nowhere more apparent than in his stories, particularly in *A Group of Noble Dames*. He is telling tales of the great and fashionable in the annals of Wessex for the seeiming benefit of a rural audience, who love to wonder at the doings of the grand folk and to take at the same time an irreverently down-to-earth view of them. The narrations are further dramatized by the nature of the tellers, gathered together as members of a local club – the Maltster, the Rural Dean, the Local Historian and others – each of whom gives an individual flavour, like Chaucer's pilgrims, to the tale that he tells. In this dramatic context it is significant that it is 'the old surgeon' who tells the story of Barbara and her nightmare marriage. A medical man is taking a clinical interest in the sufferings of the wife at the hands of her tyrannical husband: a point which has been ignored by critics of the story's morbidity.

But not all the stories of the group are in this sinister vein. It is a relief to turn to the exciting and attractively straightforward history of 'The Honourable Laura', as recounted by 'the Spark', Hardy's presentation of an elderly roué who has been in his time a man-about-town. He has therefore a natural interest in the time-honoured romantic situation of an eloping couple pursued by the outraged parent, a noble lord from the far north-west of Hardy's Wessex, the Quantock hills in Somerset. In additon to its suitability to the teller, the story contains the same twists of fate and plot which Hardy put in his novels, and the unequalled sense of locality they give the reader: locality dramatized by event, historic or humble. It is worth comparing the way the tale opens with that of two of his novels, *The Return of the Native* and *The Woodlanders*, both of which set the scene in the same terms of a road, a traveller, and a watching figure accustomed, like Hardy himself, to 'notice such things'.

And yet no one, and least of all the author himself, would make any great claims for the stories that he wrote in this genre. From one point of view indeed they are potboilers, anecdotes out of which an author might turn an honest penny. It is this lack of pretension which gives them their special charm. A comparison might well again be made with Pushkin, who in his *Tales of Belkin* produced a collection in a similarly unpretentious vein of entertainment, using the same dramatic device that would be employed by Hardy. One of Pushkin's narrators is a young lady of romantic tastes, and the story she tells of a tryst and encounter, and a wedding in which a stranger finds himself acting the part of bridegroom, was just of the sort that would have appealed to Hardy's own taste in narrative.

For it is worth emphasizing not only that Hardy can be equally at home in a happy tale as in an unhappy one, but that many of his most 'minor' tales have a charm equal to, or even greater than, that of his more famous masterpieces such as 'The Three Strangers' or 'The Withered Arm'. Time-honoured rural anecdotes very often have a touch of the fairy-tale about them. Hardy never recounts such events with tongue in cheek, although both in his verse and his prose he may do so with a good deal of hidden humour. The opening sentence of 'The Romantic Adventures of a Milkmaid' reveals a good deal about the spirit in which its narrative is intended. Not only the decade in which the tale takes place, but the time of day as well – half past four on a spring morning – are disclosed in the initial sentence by the 'testimony of the land-surveyor . . . a gentleman with the faintest curve of humour on his lips'.

Hardy liked to bring his antiquarian interest in the past together with a narrative method of the dramatic sort: with him the two seem natural partners. A particularly evocative tale, or sketch, among the stories in *A Changed Man* is that of the exhumation of 'a tall soldier of old Rome' on the bleak heights of Maiden Castle, the huge and ancient Celtic earthwork that lies just outside Dorchester. Hardy clearly took pleasure in writing of the sense of a furtive joy in a secret archaeological discovery, which he attributes to his shadowy 'companion' in the enterprise of the clandestine 'dig', and the discovery after the companion's death of the little gilt statuette of Mercury, which he had in fact quietly pocketed after its other artefacts were returned to the gravemound.

'The Romantic Adventures of a Milkmaid' is set far later in time, in the early years of the reign of Queen Victoria, when the fashion for Romantic feeling was still running high among the leisured classes. But Hardy gives to his setting here the same unobtrusive awareness of history and locality that he gave to the adventure on the ancient earthwork. Hardy himself was a child at the time of the milkmaid's tale; and he was fascinated by the world of great events as well as by the grand world of society, of which his heroine Margery obtains so vivid a glimpse.

The simplè romantic feelings and yearnings that he never lost were fully developed when he was still a boy. He was the boy who ever afterward recalled with romantic nostalgia Mrs Julia Augusta Martin, the chatelaine of Kingston Maurward, the great house near his family home at Higher Bockhampton. She had been kind to him and had been his first teacher. When she wrote to him after he published *Far from the Madding Crowd*, he even contemplated calling on her at her town house, having last seen her there some twelve years earlier, when he had just arrived in London. Now, however, his courage failed him, and he never saw his old benefactress again. Hardy too was the boy who accompanied his father to all the rustic dances of the neighbourhood, playing the fiddle as his father had taught him. (It is recorded, at least in gossip, that Mrs Hardy, a strong-minded woman, feared that her handsome husband might have his head turned by some country girl on these occasions, and so sent her small eldest child along with him to act as a kind of chaperon. That too would have made a tale from the past, of the kind that Hardy took pleasure in.)

But though the twists and turns of the milkmaid's tale fully explain that curve of humour on the land-surveyor's lips, the implications of the tale are really no laughing matter, as Hardy himself was no doubt well aware. The Baron may be a trifle preposterous as a figure of exoticism and romance: as a catalyst of emotion and desire, and therefore potential disaster, he is very far from being preposterous. Hardy's remarkable powers of intuiting and empathizing with a young woman's feelings are shown in some ways more graphically, even more poignantly, in this light-hearted and artificial tale than they are when the full weight of a mature novel is behind them: and the reason for this may be that so strong an element of the fabulous and fantastic in 'The Romantic Adventures' serves to throw those simple basic emotions into sharp relief. Margery is indeed bewitched, as if by Ariel or by Faust, but her bewitchment is wholly convincing in terms of the quiet life she leads, and the turbulent inner emotions which she feels, and as a young girl is longing to feel. The reader of the story is kept in a genuine suspense until the end. Virginia Woolf remarked that Hardy was the best writer in the world at holding her attention, even in a railway carriage.

The tale might indeed have held her attention, because Hardy has made the artifice of plot serve something much more interesting than a traditional moral dilemma. Fancy Day, the heroine of *Under the Greenwood Tree*, thinks better of her decision to marry the curate instead of her betrothed admirer Dick, the tranter's son. She thinks better of it both out of prudence and out of pity for her young man. No such considerations carry weight with the equally good-hearted Margery. If the Baron asked her to marry him on his deathbed she would have done so; and she would have eloped with him at the end if he had pressed her. She admits this, and the story takes on that atmosphere of 'what might have been' which fascinated Hardy alike in his prose tales and in the terser narrations told in so many of his poems.

That sombre note of 'what might have been' is to be found in several of Hardy's most thoughtful and memorable tales – tales like 'Fellow-Townsmen', 'The Son's Veto', and 'On the Western Circuit'. The last is perhaps the most powerful of all Hardy's stories in its sad implications. The collision is between the Life Force, as it blindly works its way in the life of the illiterate peasant girl, and the young intellectual barrister, the 'end-of-the-age young man' as Hardy calls him, referring to his general belief that the end-product of the nineteenth century was a man worn out by too many doubts and too much thinking. The maid, the mistress, and the young admirer are locked into a relationship that is uncomprehending in more ways than in the fact of Anna's being unable to read, or to reply to her lover's letters.

There is frequently in Hardy's starkest little tales a curious discrepancy between the bleakness of the author's conclusion and the tenderness and sensibility – the strivings and sacrifices of love – which lie in the narrative's texture and background. So it is with 'On the Western Circuit'. The reader may recoil from the sentence near the end in which the author seems to take a pleasure, almost like that of the French realists, in pointing his moral:

> She did not know that before his eyes he beheld as it were a galley, in which he, the fastidious urban, was chained to work for the remainder of his life, with her, the unlettered peasant, chained to his side.

And yet that is far from being the impression the story leaves on us. It contains hope and joy, and all the thoughtless compensations of living, in addition to the sense of waste and despair and 'what might have been'. Hardy in that sense is a peculiar writer, whose perversity in taking consciously the gloomy view is accompanied by the pleasure of the artist and the man in the 'livingness' that the thinker seems to reject.

'The Son's Veto' contains a sharper and more purely social message. Hardy's hostility to clergymen who saw their calling as a means of social advancement and worldly advantage is evident in several of his tales, and more emphatically stated than it is in the novels. Once again the sadness of things and the harshness of social convention are mingled with something touching and tender in the presentation of the mother and her unfortunate suitor.

One of the most insidiously personal stories, though it is lacking in this special and almost invisible dimension of tenderness, is 'An Imaginative Woman'. It has affiliations with Hardy's last and in some ways oddest novel, *The Well-Beloved*; and it probably also reflects his preoccupation in later life with society women like Florence Henniker, who admired him as a writer and poet, perhaps even loved him, but who were not disposed or able to offer him more than their friendship. As a man all too easily given to falling in love, Hardy was greatly unsettled by these relationships and indeed made miserable by them, but as artist he profited from the sense of longing and disquiet they gave him. He frequently entertained quaint ideas about physiognomy, and the transmission of a personal aura or 'family face', and this is made the rather bathetic conclusion of a story which seems to have more in it than so bald an ending allows. Longing and imagination are stronger than the mere effects of physical causes; and as Hardy puts it, 'by a known but inexplicable trick of Nature' there were in the child 'strong traces of resemblance' to the artist the mother had never seen. But perhaps more disturbing than this idea in the story is the sombre undercurrent of marital indifference and disharmony, evident also in 'On the Western Circuit', which produces such unobtrusively resonant moments as a wife and husband 'travelling almost without speaking, under the sense that it was one of those dreary situations occurring in married life which words could not mend . . .'.

The other stories in this selection, 'The Fiddler of the Reels' and those from *Wessex Tales*, show Hardy at his least introspective. Although 'Fellow-Townsmen' suggests Hardy's not infrequent and sombre motif of 'what might have been', it also gives an admirable picture of the seaside town of Bridport, a few miles from Dorchester (Hardy's Casterbridge), as well as offering an exciting narrative that is almost a cliffhanger. The story of 'The Three Strangers' is equally exciting, and told with that impersonal skill, as of a local chronicler, which seems always to have been at Hardy's command. It is heightened too not only by a sense of the past, but of the very special relationship in the locality between past and present, as indicated with particular meaning in the last sentence of the tale: '. . . the arrival of the three strangers at the shepherd's that night, and the details connected therewith, is a story as well-known as ever in the country about Higher Crowstairs'. The reader accepts this to be true, even while knowing with another part of his critical appreciation that the tale is in fact a magnificent variant on an archetypal plot which has been used by chronicles and storytellers worldwide, and no doubt since before the invention of letters.

'The Withered Arm' and 'The Distracted Preacher' are in the same way anecdotes beautifully evoked and fashioned out of hearsay material handed down from the past. A special interest attaches to 'The Distracted Preacher', since it is the first of Hardy's fictions to offer an, as it were, alternative version of the plot, the second striking what he came to consider a truer and more realistic note than the first and more conventional happy ending. But few readers, probably, would wish anything else than that smuggler Lizzy and her young minister should get married; and particularly since they may detect 'the faintest curve of humour' on the author's lips when he gravely informs us that Lizzy in later years 'wrote an excellent tract called *Render Unto Caesar; or, The Repentant Villagers*, in which her own experience was anonymously used as the introductory story'. That mixes just the right note of cheerfulness with the sardonic Hardyesque.

In any case we know from his preface to *Wessex Tales* that the historical smugglers in the case all got off at their trial. But more than thirty years after the tale was written Hardy added the note which tells us that he only used the happy ending, as he said, because 'it was almost *de rigueur* in an English magazine at the time of writing'. The reason he gives may strike us, as Hardy's explanations of his methods are apt to do, as more than a trifle disingenuous, however revealing. He speaks of 'the true incidents of which the tale is a vague and flickering shadow'. In the same spirit Theseus, in Shakespeare's *A Midsummer Night's Dream*, remarks of stage plays that 'the best in this kind are but shadows, and the worst are no worse if imagination do amend them'. With this quotation possibly in mind, or perhaps with some reminiscence of Plato's allegory of the cave, Hardy asserts that where stories are concerned, the plain truth must always be superior to fiction.

In relation to the craft of the story, or indeed to fiction of every sort, this seems a highly dubious proposition. It is of course a pose on the author's part, and an artistically effective one. Somewhat in the modern manner, for example as in John Fowles's novel *The French Lieutenant's Woman*, the reader can choose between the two solutions, and is offered an alternative outcome. One of them, Hardy says, is false, i.e. fictional. But the novelist and story-writer deals in fictions; and fictions, as all writers and their readers know, have their own kind of truth, perhaps even a higher truth. It may certainly seem true that smuggler Owlett and his henchwoman Lizzy are more suited to each other than Lizzy would be to the young minister. And yet, once again, Hardy's fiction gives a kind of tenderness to the relations of the girl and the young clergyman, which may persuade us not only that in their own way they have really fallen in love, but also that their chances in marriage, in their time and society, may be no worse and perhaps even better than those of other couples. Lizzy is a strong-minded young woman after all, and the clergyman a good and honest man.

However that may be, it is not without interest that Hardy

also added the same kind of footnote, or afterthought, to two of his novels – *The Return of the Native* and *The Woodlanders*. In both cases he felt that a more enigmatic, or a more renunciatory, note would have been more appropriate at the end of the novel. We may suspect in each case the influence of the French realists such as Balzac, whom Hardy admired, and his corresponding contempt for the standards of prudish respectability set by English publishers and magazines. Nevertheless it may seem to us in retrospect that his novels are quite sombre enough without the occasional sweetening that the conventions of the time dictated; and that the point of a good story is not what might have happened, or what ought to have happened, but what the author decided should happen. No reader wishes to be left in the air. In any case one of the most famous of the tales here included, 'The Fiddler of the Reels', has a conclusion that is in its way unflinchingly sad enough to suit the most austere taste, although it is also a work of art which eminently requires such an ending, and would not be the masterpiece that it is without it.

JOHN BAYLEY

NOTE ON THE TEXT

The stories included in the present volume were written over a period of almost fifteen years, between 1879 and 1893. All of them were originally published in periodicals, which in some cases involved major bowdlerizations; all subsequently appeared, revised, in the four collections of stories published during Hardy's lifetime (*Wessex Tales* (1888), *A Group of Noble Dames* (1891), *Life's Little Ironies* (1894), '*A Changed Man' and Other Tales* (1913)) and in the later collected editions. The copy-text chosen for this selection is that of the 1912–14 Wessex Edition, which Hardy himself considered definitive and recommended to his readers and critics; the history of the publication of each individual story and the most important textual changes are discussed in the notes. The stories are arranged in chronological order of writing and first publication. Minor alterations have been silently made to modernize and standardize the text in accordance with the Everyman house style.

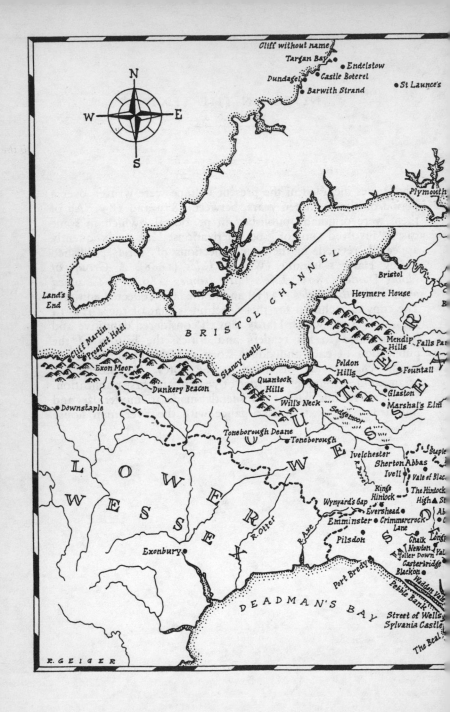

The Wessex of the Novels

OUTSIDE THE GATES
OF THE WORLD

THE DISTRACTED PREACHER

HOW HIS COLD WAS CURED

Something delayed the arrival of the Wesleyan* minister, and a young man came temporarily in his stead. It was on the thirteenth of January 183–* that Mr Stockdale, the young man in question, made his humble entry into the village, unknown, and almost unseen. But when those of the inhabitants who styled themselves of his connection became acquainted with him, they were rather pleased with the substitute than otherwise, though he had scarcely as yet acquired ballast of character sufficient to steady the consciences of the hundred-and-forty Methodists of pure blood who, at this time, lived in Nether-Moynton, and to give in addition supplementary support to the mixed race which went to church in the morning and chapel in the evening,* or when there was a tea – as many as a hundred-and-ten people more, all told, and including the parish-clerk in the winter-time, when it was too dark for the vicar to observe who passed up the street at seven o'clock – which, to be just to him, he was never anxious to do.

It was owing to this overlapping of creeds that the celebrated population-puzzle arose among the denser gentry of the district around Nether-Moynton: how could it be that a parish containing fifteen score of strong full-grown Episcopalians,* and nearly thirteen score of well-matured Dissenters,* numbered barely two-and-twenty score adults in all?

The young man being personally interesting, those with whom he came in contact were content to waive for a while the graver question of his sufficiency. It is said that at this time of his life his eyes were affectionate, though without a ray of levity; that his hair was curly, and his figure tall; that he was, in short, a very lovable youth, who won upon his female hearers as soon as they saw and heard him, and caused them to say, 'Why didn't we know of this before he came, that we might have gi'ed him a warmer welcome!'

The fact was that, knowing him to be only provisionally

selected, and expecting nothing remarkable in his person or doctrine, they and the rest of his flock in Nether-Moynton had felt almost as indifferent about his advent as if they had been the soundest church-going parishioners in the country, and he their true and appointed parson. Thus when Stockdale set foot in the place nobody had secured a lodging for him, and though his journey had given him a bad cold in the head he was forced to attend to that business himself. On inquiry he learnt that the only possible accommodation in the village would be found at the house of one Mrs Lizzy Newberry, at the upper end of the street.

It was a youth who gave this information, and Stockdale asked him who Mrs Newberry might be.

The boy said that she was a widow-woman, who had got no husband, because he was dead. Mr Newberry, he added, had been a well-to-do man enough, as the saying was, and a farmer; but he had gone off in a decline. As regarded Mrs Newberry's serious side, Stockdale gathered that she was one of the trimmers who went to church and chapel both.

'I'll go there,' said Stockdale, feeling that, in the absence of purely sectarian lodgings, he could do no better.

'She's a little particular, and won't hae gover'ment folks, or curates, or the pa'son's friends, or such like,' said the lad dubiously.

'Ah, that may be a promising sign: I'll call. Or no; just you go up and ask first if she can find room for me. I have to see one or two persons on another matter. You will find me down at the carrier's.'

In a quarter of an hour the lad came back, and said that Mrs Newberry would have no objection to accommodate him, whereupon Stockdale called at the house. It stood within a garden-hedge, and seemed to be roomy and comfortable. He saw an elderly woman, with whom he made arrangements to come the same night, since there was no inn in the place, and he wished to house himself as soon as possible; the village being a local centre from which he was to radiate at once to the different small chapels in the neighbourhood. He forthwith sent his luggage to Mrs Newberry's from the carrier's, where he had taken shelter, and in the evening walked up to his temporary home.

As he now lived there, Stockdale felt it unnecessary to knock at the door; and entering quietly he had the pleasure of hearing footsteps scudding away like mice into the back quarters. He advanced to the parlour, as the front room was called, though its stone floor was scarcely disguised by the carpet, which only overlaid the trodden areas, leaving sandy deserts under the furniture. But the room looked snug and cheerful. The firelight shone out brightly, trembling on the bulging mouldings of the table-legs, playing with brass knobs and handles, and lurking in great strength on the under surface of the chimney-piece. A deep armchair, covered with horsehair, and studded with a countless throng of brass nails, was pulled up on one side of the fireplace. The tea-things were on the table, the teapot cover was open, and a little handbell had been laid at that precise point towards which a person seated in the great chair might be expected instinctively to stretch his hand.

Stockdale sat down, not objecting to his experience of the room thus far, and began his residence by tinkling the bell. A little girl crept in at the summons, and made tea for him. Her name, she said, was Marther Sarer, and she lived out there, nodding towards the road and village generally. Before Stockdale had got far with his meal a tap sounded on the door behind him, and on his telling the inquirer to come in, a rustle of garments caused him to turn his head. He saw before him a fine and extremely well-made young woman, with dark hair, a wide, sensible, beautiful forehead, eyes that warmed him before he knew it, and a mouth that was in itself a picture to all appreciative souls.

'Can I get you anything else for tea?' she said, coming forward a step or two, an expression of liveliness on her features, and her hand waving the door by its edge.

'Nothing, thank you,' said Stockdale, thinking less of what he replied than of what might be her relation to the household.

'You are quite sure?' said the young woman, apparently aware that he had not considered his answer.

He conscientiously examined the tea-things, and found them all there. 'Quite sure, Miss Newberry,' he said.

'It is Mrs Newberry,' she said. 'Lizzy Newberry. I used to be Lizzy Simpkins.'

'O, I beg your pardon, Mrs Newberry.' And before he had occasion to say more she left the room.

Stockdale remained in some doubt till Martha Sarah came

to clear the table. 'Whose house is this, my little woman?' said he.

'Mrs Lizzy Newberry's, sir.'

'Then Mrs Newberry is not the old lady I saw this afternoon?'

'No. That's Mrs Newberry's mother. It was Mrs Newberry who comed in to you just by now, because she wanted to see if you was good-looking.'

Later in the evening, when Stockdale was about to begin supper, she came again. 'I have come myself, Mr Stockdale,' she said. The minister stood up in acknowledgment of the honour. 'I am afraid little Marther might not make you understand. What will you have for supper? – there's cold rabbit, and there's a ham uncut.'

Stockdale said he could get on nicely with those viands, and supper was laid. He had no more than cut a slice when tap-tap came to the door again. The minister had already learnt that this particular rhythm in taps denoted the fingers of his enkindling landlady, and the doomed young fellow buried his first mouthful under a look of receptive blandness.

'We have a chicken in the house, Mr Stockdale – I quite forgot to mention it just now. Perhaps you would like Marther Sarer to bring it up?'

Stockdale had advanced far enough in the art of being a young man to say that he did not want the chicken, unless she brought it up herself; but when it was uttered he blushed at the daring gallantry of the speech, perhaps a shade too strong for a serious man and a minister. In three minutes the chicken appeared, but, to his great surprise, only in the hands of Martha Sarah. Stockdale was disappointed, which perhaps it was intended that he should be.

He had finished supper, and was not in the least anticipating Mrs Newberry again that night, when she tapped and entered as before. Stockdale's gratified look told that she had lost nothing by not appearing when expected. It happened that the cold in the head from which the young man suffered had increased with the approach of night, and before she had spoken he was seized with a violent fit of sneezing which he could not anyhow repress.

Mrs Newberry looked full of pity. 'Your cold is very bad tonight, Mr Stockdale.'

Stockdale replied that it was rather troublesome.

'And I've a good mind – ' she added archly, looking at the cheerless glass of water on the table, which the abstemious minister was going to drink.

'Yes, Mrs Newberry?'

'I've a good mind that you should have something more likely to cure it than that cold stuff.'

'Well,' said Stockdale, looking down at the glass, 'as there is no inn here, and nothing better to be got in the village, of course it will do.'

To this she replied, 'There is something better, not far off, though not in the house. I really think you must try it, or you may be ill. Yes, Mr Stockdale, you shall.' She held up her finger, seeing that he was about to speak. 'Don't ask what it is; wait, and you shall see.'

Lizzy went away, and Stockdale waited in a pleasant mood. Presently she returned with her bonnet and cloak on, saying, 'I am so sorry, but you must help me to get it. Mother has gone to bed. Will you wrap yourself up, and come this way, and please bring that cup with you?'

Stockdale, a lonely young fellow, who had for weeks felt a great craving for somebody on whom to throw away superfluous interest, and even tenderness, was not sorry to join her; and followed his guide through the back door, across the garden, to the bottom, where the boundary was a wall. This wall was low, and beyond it Stockdale discerned in the night shades several grey headstones, and the outlines of the church roof and tower.

'It is easy to get up this way,' she said, stepping upon a bank which abutted on the wall; then putting her foot on the top of the stonework, and descending by a spring inside, where the ground was much higher, as is the manner of graveyards to be. Stockdale did the same, and followed her in the dusk across the irregular ground till they came to the tower door, which, when they had entered, she softly closed behind them.

'You can keep a secret?' she said, in a musical voice.

'Like an iron chest!' said he fervently.

Then from under her cloak she produced a small lighted lantern, which the minister had not noticed that she carried at all. The light showed them to be close to the singing-gallery stairs, under which lay a heap of lumber of all sorts, but consisting mostly of decayed framework, pews, panels, and pieces of flooring, that from time to time had been removed from their original fixings in the body of the edifice and replaced by new.

'Perhaps you will drag some of those boards aside?' she said, holding the lantern over her head to light him better. 'Or will you take the lantern while I move them?'

'I can manage it,' said the young man, and acting as she ordered, he uncovered, to his surprise, a row of little barrels bound with wood hoops, each barrel being about as large as the nave* of a heavy waggon-wheel. When they were laid open Lizzy fixed her eyes on him, as if she wondered what he would say.

'You know what they are?' she asked, finding that he did not speak.

'Yes, barrels,' said Stockdale simply. He was an inland man, the son of highly respectable parents, and brought up with a single eye to the ministry; and the sight suggested nothing beyond the fact that such articles were there.

'You are quite right, they are barrels,' she said, in an emphatic tone of candour that was not without a touch of irony.

Stockdale looked at her with an eye of sudden misgiving. 'Not smugglers' liquor?'* he said.

'Yes,' said she. 'They are tubs of spirit that have accidentally floated over in the dark from France.'

In Nether-Moynton and its vicinity at this date people always smiled at the sort of sin called in the outside world illicit trading; and these little kegs of gin and brandy were as well known to the inhabitants as turnips. So that Stockdale's innocent ignorance, and his look of alarm when he guessed the sinister mystery, seemed to strike Lizzy first as ludicrous, and then as very awkward for the good impression that she wished to produce upon him.

'Smuggling is carried on here by some of the people,' she said in a gentle, apologetic voice. 'It has been their practice for generations, and they think it no harm. Now, will you roll out one of the tubs?'

'What to do with it?' said the minister.

'To draw a little from it to cure your cold,' she answered. 'It is so 'nation strong that it drives away that sort of thing in a jiffy. O, it is all right about our taking it. I may have what I like; the owner of the tubs says so. I ought to have had some in the house, and then I shouldn't ha' been put to this trouble; but I drink none myself, and so I often forget to keep it indoors.'

'You are allowed to help yourself, I suppose, that you may not inform where their hiding-place is?'

'Well, no; not that particularly; but I may take any if I want it. So help yourself.'

'I will, to oblige you, since you have a right to it,' murmured the minister; and though he was not quite satisfied with his part in the performance, he rolled one of the 'tubs' out from the corner into the middle of the tower floor. 'How do you wish me to get it out – with a gimlet, I suppose?'

'No, I'll show you,' said his interesting companion; and she held up with her other hand a shoemaker's awl and a hammer. 'You must never do these things with a gimlet, because the wood-dust gets in; and when the buyers pour out the brandy that would tell them that the tub had been broached. An awl makes no dust, and the hole nearly closes up again. Now tap one of the hoops forward.'

Stockdale took the hammer and did so.

'Now make the hole in the part that was covered by the hoop.'

He made the hole as directed. 'It won't run out,' he said.

'O yes it will,' said she. 'Take the tub between your knees, and squeeze the heads; and I'll hold the cup.'

Stockdale obeyed; and the pressure taking effect upon the tub, which seemed to be thin, the spirit spirted out in a stream. When the cup was full he ceased pressing, and the flow immediately stopped. 'Now we must fill up the keg with water,' said Lizzy, 'or it will cluck like forty hens when it is handled, and show that 'tis not full.'

'But they tell you you may take it?'

'Yes, the *smugglers*; but the *buyers* must not know that the smugglers have been kind to me at their expense.'

'I see,' said Stockdale doubtfully. 'I much question the honesty of this proceeding.'

By her direction he held the tub with the hole upwards, and while he went through the process of alternately pressing and ceasing to press, she produced a bottle of water, from which she took mouthfuls, conveying each to the keg by putting her pretty lips to the hole,* where it was sucked in at each recovery of the cask from pressure. When it was again full he plugged the hole, knocked the hoop down to its place, and buried the tub in the lumber as before.

'Aren't the smugglers afraid that you will tell?' he asked, as they recrossed the churchyard.

'O no; they are not afraid of that. I couldn't do such a thing.'

'They have put you into a very awkward corner,' said Stockdale emphatically. 'You must, of course, as an honest person, sometimes feel that it is your duty to inform – really you must.'

'Well, I have never particularly felt it as a duty; and, besides, my first husband – ' She stopped, and there was some confusion in her voice. Stockdale was so honest and unsophisticated that he did not at once discern why she paused: but at last he did perceive that the words were a slip, and that no woman would have uttered 'first husband' by accident unless she had thought pretty frequently of a second. He felt for her confusion, and allowed her time to recover and proceed. 'My husband,' she said, in a self-corrected tone, 'used to know of their doings, and so did my father, and kept the secret. I cannot inform, in fact, against anybody.'

'I see the hardness of it,' he continued, like a man who looked far into the moral of things. 'And it is very cruel that you should be tossed and tantalized between your memories and your conscience. I do hope, Mrs Newberry, that you will soon see your way out of this unpleasant position.'

'Well, I don't just now,' she murmured.

By this time they had passed over the wall and entered the house, where she brought him a glass and hot water, and left him to his own reflections. He looked after her vanishing form, asking himself whether he, as a respectable man, and a minister, and a shining light,* even though as yet only of the halfpenny-candle sort, were quite justified in doing this thing. A sneeze settled the question; and he found that when the fiery liquor was lowered by the addition of twice or thrice the quantity of water, it was one of the prettiest cures for a cold in the head that he had ever known, particularly at this chilly time of the year.

Stockdale sat in the deep chair about twenty minutes sipping and meditating, till he at length took warmer views of things, and longed for the morrow, when he would see Mrs Newberry again. He then felt that, though chronologically at a short distance, it would in an emotional sense be very long before tomorrow came, and walked restlessly round the room. His eye was attracted by a framed and glazed sampler in which a running ornament of fir-trees and peacocks surrounded the following pretty bit of sentiment: –

> Rose-leaves smell when roses thrive,
> Here's my work while I'm alive;
> Rose-leaves smell when shrunk and shed,
> Here's my work when I am dead.

> Lizzy Simpkins. Fear God. Honour the King.
> Aged 11 years.

''Tis hers,' he said to himself. 'Heavens, how I like that name!'

Before he had done thinking that no other name from Abigail to Zenobia* would have suited his young landiady so well, tap-tap came again upon the door; and the minister started as her face appeared yet another time, looking so disinterested that the most ingenious would have refrained from asserting that she had come to affect his feelings by her seductive eyes.

'Would you like a fire in your room, Mr Stockdale, on account of your cold?'

The minister, being still a little pricked in the conscience for countenancing her in watering the spirits, saw here a way to self-chastisement. 'No, I thank you,' he said firmly; 'it is not necessary. I have never been used to one in my life, and it would be giving way to luxury too far.'

'Then I won't insist,' she said, and disconcerted him by vanishing instantly.

Wondering if she was vexed by his refusal, he wished that he had chosen to have a fire, even though it should have scorched him out of bed and endangered his self-discipline for a dozen days. However, he consoled himself with what was in truth a rare consolation for a budding lover, that he was under the same roof with Lizzy; her guest, in fact, to take a poetical view of the term lodger; and that he would certainly see her on the morrow.

The morrow came, and Stockdale rose early, his cold quite gone. He had never in his life so longed for the breakfast hour as he did that day, and punctually at eight o'clock, after a short walk to reconnoitre the premises, he re-entered the door of his dwelling. Breakfast passed, and Martha Sarah attended, but nobody came voluntarily as on the night before to inquire if there were other wants which he had not mentioned, and which she would attempt to gratify. He was disappointed, and went out, hoping to see her at dinner. Dinner time came; he sat down to the meal, finished it, lingered on for a whole hour, although two new teachers were at that moment waiting at the chapel-door to speak to him by appointment. It was useless to wait longer, and he slowly went his way down the lane, cheered by the thought that, after all, he would see her in the evening, and perhaps engage again in the delightful tub-broaching in the neighbouring church tower, which proceeding he resolved to render more moral by steadfastly insisting that no water should be introduced to fill up, though the tub should cluck like all the hens in Christendom. But nothing could disguise the fact that it was a queer business; and his countenance fell when he thought how much more his mind was interested in that matter than in his serious duties.

However, compunction vanished with the decline of day. Night came, and his tea and supper; but no Lizzy Newberry, and no sweet temptations. At last the minister could bear it no longer, and said to his quaint little attendant, 'Where is Mrs Newberry today?' judiciously handing a penny as he spoke.

'She's busy,' said Martha.

'Anything serious happened?' he asked, handing another penny, and revealing yet additional pennies in the background.

'O no – nothing at all!' said she, with breathless confidence. 'Nothing ever happens to her. She's only biding upstairs in bed because 'tis her way sometimes.'

Being a young man of some honour he would not question further, and assuming that Lizzy must have a bad headache, or other slight ailment, in spite of what the girl had said, he went to bed dissatisfied, not even setting eyes on old Mrs Simpkins. 'I said last night that I should see her tomorrow,' he reflected; 'but that was not to be!'

Next day he had better fortune, or worse, meeting her at the foot of the stairs in the morning, and being favoured by a visit or two from her during the day – once for the purpose of making kindly inquiries about his comfort, as on the first evening, and at another time to place a bunch of winter-violets on his table, with a promise to renew them when they drooped. On these occasions there was something in her smile which showed how conscious she was of the effect she produced, though it must be said that it was rather a humorous than a designing consciousness, and savoured more of pride than of vanity.

As for Stockdale, he clearly perceived that he possessed unlimited capacity for backsliding, and wished that tutelary saints* were not denied to Dissenters. He set a watch upon his tongue and eyes for the space of one hour and a half, after which he found it was useless to struggle further, and gave himself up to the situation. 'The other minister will be here in a month,' he said to himself when sitting over the fire. 'Then I shall be off, and she will distract my mind no more! ... And then, shall I go on living by myself for ever? No; when my two years of probation are finished, I shall have a furnished house to live in, with a varnished door and a brass knocker; and I'll march straight back to her, and ask her flat, as soon as the last plate is on the dresser!'

Thus a titillating fortnight was passed by young Stockdale, during which time things proceeded much as such matters have done ever since the beginning of history. He saw the object of attachment several times one day, did not see her at all the next, met her when he least expected to do so, missed her when hints and signs as to where she should be at a given hour almost amounted to an appointment. This mild coquetry was perhaps fair enough under the circumstances of their being so closely lodged, and Stockdale put up with it as philosophically as he was able. Being in her own house she could, after vexing him or disappointing him of her presence, easily win him back by suddenly surrounding him with those little attentions which her position as his landlady put it in her power to bestow. When he had waited indoors half the day to see her, and on finding that she would not be seen, had gone off in a huff to the dreariest and dampest walk he could discover, she would restore equilibrium in the evening with 'Mr Stockdale, I have fancied you must feel draught o' nights from your bedroom window, and so I have been putting up thicker curtains this afternoon while you were out'; or, 'I noticed that you sneezed twice again this morning, Mr Stockdale. Depends upon it that cold is hanging about you yet; I am sure it is – I have thought of it continually; and you must let me make a posset for you.'

Sometimes in coming home he found his sitting-room rearranged, chairs placed where the table had stood, and the table ornamented with the few fresh flowers and leaves that could be obtained at this season, so as to add a novelty to the room. At times she would be standing on a chair outside the house, trying to nail up a branch of the monthly rose which the winter wind had blown down; and of course he stepped forward to assist her, when their hands got mixed in passing the shreds and nails. Thus they became friends again after a disagreement. She would utter on these occasions some pretty and deprecatory remark on the necessity of her troubling him anew; and he would straightway say that he would do a hundred times as much for her if she should so require.

HOW HE SAW TWO OTHER MEN

Matters being in this advancing state, Stockdale was rather surprised one cloudy evening, while sitting in his room, at hearing her speak in low tones of expostulation to some one at the door. It was nearly dark, but the shutters were not yet closed, nor the candles lighted; and Stockdale was tempted to stretch his head towards the window. He saw outside the door a young man in clothes of a whitish colour, and upon reflection judged their wearer to be the well-built and rather handsome miller who lived below. The miller's voice was alternately low and firm, and sometimes it reached the level of positive entreaty; but what the words were Stockdale could in no way hear.

Before the colloquy had ended, the minister's attention was attracted by a second incident. Opposite Lizzy's home grew a clump of laurels, forming a thick and permanent shade. One of the laurel boughs now quivered against the light background of sky, and in a moment the head of a man peered out, and remained still. He seemed to be also much interested in the conversation at the door, and was plainly lingering there to watch and listen. Had Stockdale stood in any other relation to Lizzy than that of a lover, he might have gone out and investigated the meaning of this; but being as yet but an unprivileged ally, he did nothing more than stand up and show himself against the firelight, whereupon the listener disappeared, and Lizzy and the miller spoke in lower tones.

Stockdale was made so uneasy by the circumstance, that as

soon as the miller was gone, he said, 'Mrs Newberry, are you aware that you were watched just now, and your conversation heard?'

'When?' she said.

'When you were talking to that miller. A man was looking from the laurel-tree as jealously as if he could have eaten you.'

She showed more concern than the trifling event seemed to demand, and he added, 'Perhaps you were talking of things you did not wish to be overheard?'

'I was talking only on business,' she said.

'Lizzy, be frank!' said the young man. 'If it was only on business, why should anybody wish to listen to you?'

She looked curiously at him. 'What else do you think it could be, then?'

'Well – the only talk between a young woman and man that is likely to amuse an eavesdropper.'

'Ah yes,' she said, smiling in spite of her preoccupation. 'Well, my cousin Owlett* has spoken to me about matrimony, every now and then, that's true; but he was not speaking of it then. I wish he had been speaking of it, with all my heart. It would have been much less serious for me.'

'O Mrs Newberry!'

'It would. Not that I should ha' chimed in with him, of course. I wish it for other reasons. I am glad, Mr Stockdale, that you have told me of that listener. It is a timely warning, and I must see my cousin again.'

'But don't go away till I have spoken,' said the minister. 'I'll out with it at once, and make no more ado. Let it be Yes or No between us, Lizzy; please do!' And he held out his hand, in which she freely allowed her own to rest, but without speaking.

'You mean Yes by that?' he asked, after waiting a while.

'You may be my sweetheart, if you will.'

'Why not say at once you will wait for me until I have a house and can come back to marry you.'

'Because I am thinking – thinking of something else,' she said with embarrassment. 'It all comes upon me at once, and I must settle one thing at a time.'

'At any rate, dear Lizzy, you can assure me that the miller shall not be allowed to speak to you except on business? You have never directly encouraged him?'

She parried the question by saying, 'You see, he and his party have been in the habit of leaving things on my premises sometimes, and as I have not denied him, it makes him rather forward.'

'Things – what things?'

'Tubs – they are called Things here.'

'But why don't you deny him, my dear Lizzy?'

'I cannot well.'

'You are too timid. It is unfair of him to impose so upon you, and get your good name into danger by his smuggling tricks. Promise me that the next time he wants to leave his tubs here you will let me roll them into the street?'

She shook her head. 'I would not venture to offend the neighbours so much as that,' said she, 'or do anything that would be so likely to put poor Owlett into the hands of the Customs-men.'

Stockdale sighed, and said that he thought hers a mistaken generosity when it extended to assisting those who cheated the king of his dues. 'At any rate, you will let me make him keep his distance as your lover, and tell him flatly that you are not for him?'

'Please not, at present,' she said. 'I don't wish to offend my old neighbours. It is not only Mr Owlett who is concerned.'

'This is too bad,' said Stockdale impatiently.

'On my honour, I won't encourage him as my lover,' Lizzy answered earnestly. 'A reasonable man will be satisfied with that.'

'Well, so I am,' said Stockdale, his countenance clearing.

THE MYSTERIOUS GREATCOAT

Stockdale now began to notice more particularly a feature in the life of his fair landlady, which he had casually observed but scarcely ever thought of before. It was that she was markedly irregular in her hours of rising. For a week or two she would be tolerably punctual, reaching the ground-floor within a few minutes of half-past seven. Then suddenly she would not be visible till twelve at noon, perhaps for three or four days in succession; and twice he had certain proof that she did not leave her room till half-past three in the afternoon. The second time that this extreme lateness came under his notice was on a day when he had particularly wished to consult with her about his future movements; and he concluded, as he always had done, that she had a cold, headache, or other ailment, unless she had kept herself invisible to avoid meeting and talking to him, which he could hardly believe. The former supposition was disproved, however, by her innocently saying, some days later, when they were speaking on a question of health, that she had never had a moment's heaviness, headache, or illness of any kind since the previous January twelvemonth.

'I am glad to hear it,' said he. 'I thought quite otherwise.'

'What, do I look sickly?' she asked, turning up her face to show the impossibility of his gazing on it and holding such a belief for a moment.

'Not at all; I merely thought so from your being sometimes obliged to keep your room through the best part of the day.'

'O, as for that – it means nothing,' she murmured, with a look which some might have called cold, and which was the worst look that he liked to see upon her. 'It is pure sleepiness, Mr Stockdale.'

'Never!'

'It is, I tell you. When I stay in my room till half-past three in the afternoon, you may always be sure that I slept soundly till three, or I shouldn't have stayed there.'

'It is dreadful,' said Stockdale, thinking of the disastrous effects of such indulgence upon the household of a minister, should it become a habit of everyday occurrence.

'But then,' she said, divining his good and prescient thoughts, 'it only happens when I stay awake all night. I don't go to sleep till five or six in the morning sometimes.'

'Ah, that's another matter,' said Stockdale. 'Sleeplessness to such an alarming extent is real illness. Have you spoken to a doctor?'

'O no – there is no need for doing that – it is all natural to me.' And she went away without further remark.

Stockdale might have waited a long time to know the real cause of her sleeplessness, had it not happened that one dark night he was sitting in his bedroom jotting down notes for a sermon, which occupied him perfunctorily for a considerable time after the other members of the household had retired. He did not get to bed till one o'clock. Before he had fallen asleep he

heard a knocking at the front door, first rather timidly performed, and then louder. Nobody answered it, and the person
knocked again. As the house still remained undisturbed, Stockdale got out of bed, went to his window, which overlooked the
door, and opening it, asked who was there.

A young woman's voice replied that Susan Wallis was there,
and that she had come to ask if Mrs Newberry could give her
some mustard to make a plaster with, as her father was taken
very ill on the chest.

The minister, having neither bell nor servant, was compelled
to act in person. 'I will call Mrs Newberry,' he said. Partly
dressing himself, he went along the passage and tapped at
Lizzy's door. She did not answer, and, thinking of her erratic
habits in the matter of sleep, he thumped the door persistently,
when he discovered, by its moving ajar under his knocking, that
it had only been gently pushed to. As there was now a sufficient
entry for the voice, he knocked no longer, but said in firm tones,
'Mrs Newberry, you are wanted.'

The room was quite silent; not a breathing, not a rustle, came
from any part of it. Stockdale now sent a positive shout through
the open space of the door: 'Mrs Newberry!' – still no answer,
or movement of any kind within. Then he heard sounds from
the opposite room, that of Lizzy's mother, as if she had been
aroused by his uproar though Lizzy had not, and was dressing
herself hastily. Stockdale softly closed the younger woman's
door and went on to the other, which was opened by Mrs
Simpkins before he could reach it. She was in her ordinary
clothes, and had a light in her hand.

'What's the person calling about?' she said in alarm.

Stockdale told the girl's errand, adding seriously, 'I cannot
wake Mrs Newberry.'

'It is no matter,' said her mother. 'I can let the girl have what
she wants as well as my daughter.' And she came out of the
room and went downstairs.

Stockdale retired towards his own apartment, saying, however, to Mrs Simpkins from the landing, as if on second
thoughts, 'I suppose there is nothing the matter with Mrs
Newberry, that I could not wake her?'

'O no,' said the old lady hastily. 'Nothing at all.'

Still the minister was not satisfied. 'Will you go in and see?'
he said. 'I should be much more at ease.'

Mrs Simpkins returned up the staircase, went to her daughter's room, and came out again almost instantly. 'There is nothing at all the matter with Lizzy,' she said; and descended again to attend to the applicant, who, having seen the light, had remained quiet during this interval.

Stockdale went into his room and lay down as before. He heard Lizzy's mother open the front door, admit the girl, and then the murmured discourse of both as they went to the store-cupboard for the medicament required. The girl departed, the door was fastened, Mrs Simpkins came upstairs, and the house was again in silence. Still the minister did not fall asleep. He could not get rid of a singular suspicion, which was all the more harassing in being, if true, the most unaccountable thing within his experience. That Lizzy Newberry was in her bedroom when he made such a clamour at the door he could not possibly convince himself, notwithstanding that he had heard her come upstairs at the usual time, go into her chamber, and shut herself up in the usual way. Yet all reason was so much against her being elsewhere, that he was constrained to go back again to the unlikely theory of a heavy sleep, though he had heard neither breath nor movement during a shouting and knocking loud enough to rouse the Seven Sleepers.*

Before coming to any positive conclusion he fell asleep himself, and did not awake till day. He saw nothing of Mrs Newberry in the morning, before he went out to meet the rising sun, as he liked to do when the weather was fine; but as this was by no means unusual, he took no notice of it. At breakfast time he knew that she was not far off by hearing her in the kitchen, and though he saw nothing of her person, that back apartment being rigorously closed against his eyes, she seemed to be talking, ordering, and bustling about among the pots and skimmers in so ordinary a manner, that there was no reason for his wasting more time in fruitless surmise.

The minister suffered from these distractions, and his extemporized sermons were not improved thereby. Already he often said Romans for Corinthians* in the pulpit, and gave out hymns in strange cramped metres, that hitherto had always been skipped, because the congregation could not raise a tune to fit them. He fully resolved that as soon as his few weeks of stay approached their end he would cut the matter short, and commit himself by proposing a definite engagement, repenting at leisure if necessary.

With this end in view, he suggested to her on the evening after her mysterious sleep that they should take a walk together just before dark, the latter part of the proposition being introduced that they might return home unseen. She consented to go; and away they went over a stile, to a shrouded footpath suited for the occasion. But, in spite of attempts on both sides, they were unable to infuse much spirit into the ramble. She looked rather paler than usual, and sometimes turned her head away.

'Lizzy,' said Stockdale reproachfully, when they had walked in silence a long distance.

'Yes,' said she.

'You yawned – much my company is to you!' He put it in that way, but he was really wondering whether her yawn could possibly have more to do with physical weariness from the night before than mental weariness of that present moment. Lizzy apologized, and owned that she was rather tired, which gave him an opening for a direct question on the point; but his modesty would not allow him to put it to her; and he uncomfortably resolved to wait.

The month of February passed with alternations of mud and frost, rain and sleet, east winds and north-westerly gales. The hollow places in the ploughed fields showed themselves as pools of water, which had settled there from the higher levels, and had not yet found time to soak away. The birds began to get lively, and a single thrush came just before sunset each evening, and sang hopefully on the large elm-tree which stood nearest to Mrs Newberry's house. Cold blasts and brittle earth had given place to an oozing dampness more unpleasant in itself than frost; but it suggested coming spring, and its unpleasantness was of a bearable kind.

Stockdale had been going to bring about a practical understanding with Lizzy at least half a dozen times; but, what with the mystery of her apparent absence on the night of the neighbour's call, and her curious way of lying in bed at unaccountable times, he felt a check within him whenever he wanted to speak out. Thus they still lived on as indefinitely affianced lovers, each of whom hardly acknowledged the other's claim to the name of chosen one. Stockdale persuaded himself that his hesitation was owing to the postponement of the ordained minister's arrival, and the consequent delay in his own departure, which did away with all necessity for haste in his courtship; but perhaps it was only that his discretion was reasserting itself, and telling him that he had better get clearer ideas of Lizzy before arranging for the grand contract of his life with her. She, on her part, always seemed ready to be urged further on that question than he had hitherto attempted to go; but she was none the less independent, and to a degree which would have kept from flagging the passion of a far more mutable man.

On the evening of the first of March he went casually into his bedroom about dusk, and noticed lying on a chair a greatcoat, hat, and breeches. Having no recollection of leaving any clothes of his own in that spot, he went and examined them as well as he could in the twilight, and found that they did not belong to him. He paused for a moment to consider how they might have got there. He was the only man living in the house; and yet these were not his garments, unless he had made a mistake. No, they were not his. He called up Martha Sarah.

'How did these things come in my room?' he said, flinging the objectionable articles to the floor.

Martha said that Mrs Newberry had given them to her to brush, and that she had brought them up there thinking they must be Mr Stockdale's, as there was no other gentleman a-lodging there.

'Of course you did,' said Stockdale. 'Now take them down to your mis'ess, and say they are some clothes I have found here and know nothing about.'

As the door was left open he heard the conversation downstairs. 'How stupid!' said Mrs Newberry, in a tone of confusion. 'Why, Marther Sarer, I did not tell you to take 'em to Mr Stockdale's room?'

'I thought they must be his as they was so muddy,' said Martha humbly.

'You should have left 'em on the clothes-horse,' said the young mistress severely; and she came upstairs with the garments on her arm, quickly passed Stockdale's room, and threw them forcibly into a closet at the end of a passage. With this the incident ended and the house was silent again.

There would have been nothing remarkable in finding such clothes in a widow's house had they been clean; or moth-eaten, or creased, or mouldy from long lying by; but that they should be splashed with recent mud bothered Stockdale a good deal.

When a young pastor is in the aspen* stage of attachment, and open to agitation at the merest trifles, a really substantial incongruity of this complexion is a disturbing thing. However, nothing further occurred at that time; but he became watchful, and given to conjecture, and was unable to forget the circumstance.

One morning, on looking from his window, he saw Mrs Newberry herself brushing the tails of a long drab greatcoat, which, if he mistook not, was the very same garment as the one that had adorned the chair of his room. It was densely splashed up to the hollow of the back with neighbouring Nether-Moynton mud, to judge by its colour, the spots being distinctly visible to him in the sunlight. The previous day or two having been wet, the inference was irresistible that the wearer had quite recently been walking some considerable distance about the lanes and fields. Stockdale opened the window and looked out, and Mrs Newberry turned her head. Her face became slowly red; she never had looked prettier, or more incomprehensible. He waved his hand affectionately, and said good-morning; she answered with embarrassment, having ceased her occupation on the instant that she saw him, and rolled up the coat half-cleaned.

Stockdale shut the window. Some simple explanation of her proceeding was doubtless within the bounds of possibility; but he himself could not think of one; and he wished that she had placed the matter beyond conjecture by voluntarily saying something about it there and then.

But, though Lizzy had not offered an explanation at the moment, the subject was brought forward by her at the next time of their meeting. She was chatting to him concerning some other event, and remarked that it happened about the time when she was dusting some old clothes that had belonged to her poor husband.

'You keep them clean out of respect to his memory?' said Stockdale tentatively.

'I air and dust them sometimes,' she said, with the most charming innocence in the world.

'Do dead men come out of their graves and walk in mud?' murmured the minister, in a cold sweat at the deception that she was practising.

'What did you say?' asked Lizzy.

'Nothing, nothing,' said he mournfully. 'Mere words – a phrase that will do for my sermon next Sunday.' It was too plain that Lizzy was unaware that he had seen fresh pedestrian splashes upon the skirts of the tell-tale overcoat, and that she imagined him to believe it had come direct from some chest or drawer.

The aspect of the case was now considerably darker. Stockdale was so much depressed by it that he did not challenge her explanation, or threaten to go off as a missionary to benighted islanders, or reproach her in any way whatever. He simply parted from her when she had done talking, and lived on in perplexity, till by degrees his natural manner became sad and constrained.

AT THE TIME OF THE NEW MOON

The following Thursday was changeable, damp, and gloomy; and the night threatened to be windy and unpleasant. Stockdale had gone away to Knollsea in the morning, to be present at some commemoration service there, and on his return he was met by the attractive Lizzy in the passage. Whether influenced by the tide of cheerfulness which had attended him that day, or by the drive through the open air, or whether from a natural disposition to let bygones alone, he allowed himself to be fascinated into forgetfulness of the greatcoat incident, and upon the whole passed a pleasant evening; not so much in her society as within sound of her voice, as she sat talking in the back parlour to her mother, till the latter went to bed. Shortly after this Mrs Newberry retired, and then Stockdale prepared to go upstairs himself. But before he left the room he remained standing by the dying embers awhile, thinking long of one thing and another; and was only aroused by the flickering of his candle in the socket as it suddenly declined and went out. Knowing that there were a tinder-box, matches, and another candle in his bedroom, he felt his way upstairs without a light. On reaching his chamber he laid his hand on every possible ledge and corner for the tinder-box, but for a long time in vain. Discovering it at length, Stockdale produced a spark, and was kindling the brimstone, when he fancied that he heard a movement in the passage. He blew harder at the lint,* the match flared up, and looking by aid of the blue light through the door, which had been standing open all this time, he was surprised to see a male figure vanishing round the top of the staircase with the evident intention of escaping unobserved. The personage wore the clothes which Lizzy had been brushing, and something in the outline and gait suggested to the minister that the wearer was Lizzy herself.

But he was not sure of this: and, greatly excited, Stockdale determined to investigate the mystery, and to adopt his own way for doing it. He blew out the match without lighting the candle, went into the passage, and proceeded on tiptoe towards Lizzy's room. A faint grey square of light in the direction of the chamber-window as he approached told him that the door was open, and at once suggested that the occupant was gone. He turned and brought down his fist upon the handrail of the staircase: 'It was she; in her late husband's coat and hat!'

Somewhat relieved to find that there was no intruder in the case, yet none the less surprised, the minister crept down the stairs, softly put on his boots, overcoat, and hat, and tried the front door. It was fastened as usual: he went to the back door, found this unlocked, and emerged into the garden. The night was mild and moonless, and rain had lately been falling, though for the present it had ceased. There was a sudden dropping from the trees and bushes every now and then, as each passing wind shook their boughs. Among these sounds Stockdale heard the faint fall of feet upon the road outside, and he guessed from the step that it was Lizzy's. He followed the sound, and, helped by the circumstance of the wind blowing from the direction in which the pedestrian moved, he got nearly close to her, and kept there, without risk of being overheard. While he thus followed her up the street or lane, as it might indifferently be called, there being more hedge than houses on either side, a figure came forward to her from one of the cottage doors. Lizzy stopped; the minister stepped upon the grass and stopped also.

'Is that Mrs Newberry?' said the man who had come out, whose voice Stockdale recognized as that of one of the most devout members of his congregation.

'It is,' said Lizzy.

'I be quite ready – I've been here this quarter-hour.'

'Ah, John,' said she, 'I have bad news; there is danger tonight for our venture.'

'And d'ye tell o't! I dreamed there might be.'

'Yes,' she said hurriedly; 'and you must go at once round to where the chaps are waiting, and tell them they will not be wanted till tomorrow night at the same time. I go to burn the lugger off.'

'I will,' he said; and instantly went off through a gate, Lizzy continuing her way.

On she tripped at a quickening pace till the lane turned into the turnpike-road, which she crossed, and got into the track for Ringsworth. Here she ascended the hill without the least hesitation, passed the lonely hamlet of Holworth, and went down the vale on the other side. Stockdale had never taken any extensive walks in this direction, but he was aware that if she persisted in her course much longer she would draw near to the coast, which was here between two and three miles distant from Nether-Moynton; and as it had been about a quarter-past eleven o'clock when they set out, her intention seemed to be to reach the shore about midnight.

Lizzy soon ascended a small mound, which Stockdale at the same time adroitly skirted on the left; and a dull monotonous roar burst upon his ear. The hillock was about fifty yards from the top of the cliffs, and by day it apparently commanded a full view of the bay. There was light enough in the sky to show her disguised figure against it when she reached the top, where she paused, and afterwards sat down. Stockdale, not wishing on any account to alarm her at this moment, yet desirous of being near her, sank upon his hands and knees, crept a little higher up, and there stayed still.

The wind was chilly, the ground damp, and his position one in which he did not care to remain long. However, before he had decided to leave it, the young man heard voices behind him. What they signified he did not know; but, fearing that Lizzy was in danger, he was about to run forward and warn her that she might be seen, when she crept to the shelter of a little bush which maintained a precarious existence in that exposed spot; and her form was absorbed in its dark and stunted outline as if she had become part of it. She had evidently heard the men as well as he. They passed near him, talking in loud and careless tones, which could be heard above the uninterrupted washings of the sea, and which suggested that they were not engaged in any business at their own risk. This proved to be the fact: some of their words floated across to him, and caused him to forget at once the coldness of his situation.

'What's the vessel?'

'A lugger, about fifty tons.'

'From Cherbourg, I suppose?'

'Yes, 'a b'lieve.'

'But it don't all belong to Owlett?'

'O no. He's only got a share. There's another or two in it – a farmer and such like, but the names I don't know.'

The voices died away, and the heads and shoulders of the men diminished towards the cliff, and dropped out of sight.

'My darling has been tempted to buy a share by that unbeliever Owlett,' groaned the minister, his honest affection for Lizzy having quickened to its intensest point during these moments of risk to her person and name. 'That's why she's here,' he said to himself. 'O, it will be the ruin of her!'

His perturbation was interrupted by the sudden bursting out of a bright and increasing light from the spot where Lizzy was in hiding. A few seconds later, and before it had reached the height of a blaze, he heard her rush past him down the hollow like a stone from a sling, in the direction of home. The light now flared high and wide, and showed its position clearly. She had kindled a bough of furze and stuck it into the bush under which she had been crouching; the wind fanned the flame, which crackled fiercely, and threatened to consume the bush as well as the bough. Stockdale paused just long enough to notice thus much, and then followed rapidly the route taken by the young woman. His intention was to overtake her, and reveal himself as a friend; but run as he would he could see nothing of her. Thus he flew across the open country about Holworth, twisting his legs and ankles in unexpected fissures and descents, till, on coming to the gate between the downs and the road, he was forced to pause to get breath. There was no audible movement either in front or behind him, and he now concluded that she had not outrun him, but that, hearing him at her heels, and believing him one of the excise party, she had hidden herself somewhere on the way, and let him pass by.

He went on at a more leisurely pace towards the village. On reaching the house he found his surmise to be correct, for the gate was on the latch, and the door unfastened, just as he had left them. Stockdale closed the door behind him, and waited silently in the passage. In about ten minutes he heard the same light footstep that he had heard in going out; it paused at the gate, which opened and shut softly, and then the door-latch was lifted, and Lizzy came in.

Stockdale went forward and said at once, 'Lizzy, don't be frightened. I have been waiting up for you.'

She started, though she had recognized the voice. 'It is Mr Stockdale, isn't it?' she said.

'Yes,' he answered, becoming angry now that she was safe indoors, and not alarmed. 'And a nice game I've found you out in tonight. You are in man's clothes, and I am ashamed of you!'

Lizzie could hardly find a voice to answer this unexpected reproach.

'I am only partly in man's clothes,' she faltered, shrinking back to the wall. 'It is only his greatcoat and hat and breeches that I've got on, which is no harm, as he was my own husband; and I do it only because a cloak blows about so, and you can't use your arms. I have got my own dress under just the same – it is only tucked in! Will you go away upstairs and let me pass? I didn't want you to see me at such a time as this!'

'But I have a right to see you! How do you think there can be anything between us now?' Lizzy was silent. 'You are a smuggler,' he continued sadly.

'I have only a share in the run,' she said.

'That makes no difference. Whatever did you engage in such a trade as that for, and keep it such a secret from me all this time?'

'I don't do it always. I only do it in winter-time when 'tis new moon.'

'Well, I suppose that's because it can't be done anywhen else. . . . You have regularly upset me, Lizzy.'

'I am sorry for that,' Lizzy meekly replied.

'Well now,' said he more tenderly, 'no harm is done as yet. Won't you for the sake of me give up this blamable and dangerous practice altogether?'

'I must do my best to save this run,' said she, getting rather husky in the throat. 'I don't want to I give you up – you know that; but I don't want to lose my venture. I don't know what to do now! Why I have kept it so secret from you is that I was afraid you would be angry if you knew.'

'I should think so! I suppose if I had married you without finding this out you'd have gone on with it just the same?'

'I don't know. I did not think so far ahead. I only went tonight to burn the folks off, because we found that the Preventive-men* knew where the tubs were to be landed.'

'It is a pretty mess to be in altogether, is this,' said the distracted young minister. 'Well, what will you do now?'

Lizzie slowly murmured the particulars of their plan, the chief of which were that they meant to try their luck at some other point of the shore the next night; that three landing-places were always agreed upon before the run was attempted, with the understanding that, if the vessel was 'burnt off' from the first point, which was Ringsworth, as it had been by her tonight, the crew should attempt to make the second, which was Lulwind Cove, on the second night; and if there, too, danger threatened, they should on the third night try the third place, which was behind a headland further west.

'Suppose the officers hinder them landing there too?' he said, his attention to this interesting programme displacing for a moment his concern at her share in it.

'Then we shan't try anywhere else all this dark – that's what we call the time between moon and moon – and perhaps they'll string the tubs to a stray-line,* and sink 'em a little-ways from shore, and take the bearings; and then when they have a chance they'll go to creep for 'em.'

'What's that?'

'O, they'll go out in a boat and drag a creeper – that's a grapnel – along the bottom till it catch hold of the stray-line.'

The minister stood thinking; and there was no sound within doors but the tick of the clock on the stairs, and the quick breathing of Lizzy, partly from her walk and partly from agitation, as she stood close to the wall, not in such complete darkness but that he could discern against its whitewashed surface the greatcoat, breeches, and broad hat which covered her.

'Lizzy, all this is very wrong,' he said. 'Don't you remember the lesson of the tribute-money? "Render unto Caesar the things that are Caesar's."* Surely you have heard that read times enough in your growing up?'

'He's dead,' she pouted.

'But the spirit of the text is in force just the same.'

'My father did it, and so did my grandfather, and almost everybody in Nether-Moynton lives by it, and life would be so dull if it wasn't for that, that I should not care to live at all.'

'I am nothing to live for, of course,' he replied bitterly. 'You would not think it worth while to give up this wild business and live for me alone?'

'I have never looked at it like that.'

'And you won't promise and wait till I am ready?'

'I cannot give you my word tonight.' And, looking thoughtfully down, she gradually moved and moved away, going into the adjoining room, and closing the door between them. She remained there in the dark till he was tired of waiting, and had gone up to his own chamber.

Poor Stockdale was dreadfully depressed all the next day by the discoveries of the night before. Lizzy was unmistakably a fascinating young woman, but as a minister's wife she was hardly to be contemplated. 'If I had only stuck to father's little grocery business, instead of going in for the ministry, she would have suited me beautifully!' he said sadly, until he remembered that in that case he would never have come from his distant home to Nether-Moynton, and never have known her.

The estrangement between them was not complete, but it was sufficient to keep them out of each other's company. Once during the day he met her in the garden-path, and said, turning a reproachful eye upon her, 'Do you promise, Lizzie?' But she did not reply. The evening drew on, and he knew well enough that Lizzy would repeat her excursion at night – her half-offended manner had shown that she had not the slightest intention of altering her plans at present. He did not wish to repeat his own share of the adventure; but, act as he would, his uneasiness on her account increased with the decline of day. Supposing that an accident should befall her, he would never forgive himself for not being there to help, much as he disliked the idea of seeming to countenance such unlawful escapades.

As he had expected, she left the house at the same hour at night, this time passing his door without stealth, as if she knew very well that he would be watching, and were resolved to brave his displeasure. He was quite ready, opened the door quickly, and reached the back door almost as soon as she.

'Then you will go, Lizzy?' he said as he stood on the step beside her, who now again appeared as a little man with a face altogether unsuited to his clothes.

'I must,' she said, repressed by his stern manner.

'Then I shall go too,' said he.

'And I am sure you will enjoy it!' she exclaimed in more buoyant tones. 'Everybody does who tries it.'

'God forbid that I should!' he said. 'But I must look after you.'

They opened the wicket and went up the road abreast of each other, but at some distance apart, scarcely a word passing between them. The evening was rather less favourable to smuggling enterprise than the last had been, the wind being lower, and the sky somewhat clear towards the north.

'It is rather lighter,' said Stockdale.

''Tis, unfortunately,' said she. 'But it is only from those few stars over there. The moon was new today at four o'clock, and I expected clouds. I hope we shall be able to do it this dark, for when we have to sink 'em for long it makes the stuff taste bleachy, and folks don't like it so well.'

Her course was different from that of the preceding night, branching off to the left over Lord's Barrow as soon as they had got out of the lane and crossed the highway. By the time they reached Shaldon Down, Stockdale, who had been in perplexed thought as to what he should say to her, decided that he would not attempt expostulation now, while she was excited by the adventure, but wait till it was over, and endeavour to keep her from such practices in future. It occurred to him once or twice, as they rambled on that should they be surprised by the Preventive-guard, his situation would be more awkward than hers, for it would be difficult to prove his true motive in coming to the spot; but the risk was a slight consideration beside his wish to be with her.

They now arrived at a ravine which lay on the outskirts of Shaldon, a village two miles on their way towards the point of the shore they sought. Lizzy broke the silence this time: 'I have to wait here to meet the carriers. I don't know if they have come yet. As I told you, we go to Lulwind Cove tonight, and it is two miles further than Ringsworth.'

It turned out that the men had already come; for while she spoke two or three dozen heads broke the line of the slope, and a company of them at once descended from the bushes where they had been lying in wait. These carriers were men whom Lizzy and other proprietors regularly employed to bring the tubs from the boat to a hiding-place inland. They were all young fellows of Nether-Moynton, Shaldon, and the neighbourhood, quiet and inoffensive persons, even though some held heavy sticks, who simply engaged to carry the cargo for Lizzy and her cousin Owlett, as they would have engaged in any other labour for which they were fairly well paid.

At a word from her they closed in together. 'You had better take it now,' she said to them; and handed to each a packet. It contained six shillings, their remuneration for the night's undertaking, which was paid beforehand without reference to success or failure; but, besides this, they had the privilege of selling as agents when the run was successfully made. As soon as it was done, she said to them, 'The place is the old one, Dagger's Grave, near Lulwind Cove'; the men till that moment not having been told whither they were bound, for obvious reasons. 'Mr Owlett will meet you there,' added Lizzy. 'I shall follow behind, to see that we are not watched.'

The carriers went on, and Stockdale and Mrs Newberry followed at a distance of a stone's throw. 'What do these men do by day?' he said.

'Twelve or fourteen of them are labouring men. Some are brickmakers, some carpenters, some shoemakers, some thatchers. They are all known to me very well. Nine of 'em are of your own congregation.'

'I can't help that,' said Stockdale.

'O, I know you can't. I only told you. The others are more church-inclined, because they supply the pa'son with all the spirits he requires, and they don't wish to show unfriendliness to a customer.'

'How do you choose 'em?' said Stockdale.

'We choose 'em for their closeness, and because they are strong and surefooted, and able to carry a heavy load a long way without being tired.'

Stockdale sighed as she enumerated each particular, for it proved how far involved in the business a woman must be who was so well acquainted with its conditions and needs. And yet he felt more tenderly towards her at this moment than he had felt all the foregoing day. Perhaps it was that her experienced manner and bold indifference stirred his admiration in spite of himself.

'Take my arm, Lizzy,' he murmured.

'I don't want it,' she said. 'Besides, we may never be to each other again what we once have been.'

'That depends upon you,' said he, and they went on again as before.

The hired carriers paced along over Shaldon Down with as little hesitation as if it had been day, avoiding the cart-way, and leaving the village of East Shaldon on the left, so as to reach the crest of the hill at a lonely trackless place not far from the ancient earthwork called Round Pound.* A quarter-hour more of brisk walking brought them within sound of the sea, to the place called Dagger's Grave, not many hundred yards from Lulwind Cove. Here they paused, and Lizzy and Stockdale came up with them, when they went on together to the verge of the cliff. One of the men now produced an iron bar, which he drove firmly into the soil a yard from the edge, and attached to it a rope that he had uncoiled from his body. They all began to descend, partly stepping, partly sliding down the incline, as the rope slipped through their hands.

'You will not go to the bottom, Lizzy?' said Stockdale anxiously.

'No. I stay here to watch,' she said. 'Mr Owlett is down there.'

The men remained quite silent when they reached the shore; and the next thing audible to the two at the top was the dip of heavy oars, and the dashing of waves against a boat's bow. In a moment the keel gently touched the shingle, and Stockdale heard the footsteps of the thirty-six carriers running forwards over the pebbles towards the point of landing.

There was a sousing in the water as of a brood of ducks plunging in, showing that the men had not been particular about keeping their legs, or even their waists, dry from the brine: but it was impossible to see what they were doing, and in a few minutes the shingle was trampled again. The iron bar sustaining the rope, on which Stockdale's hand rested, began to swerve a little, and the carriers one by one appeared climbing up the sloping cliff, dripping audibly as they came, and sustaining themselves by the guide-rope. Each man on reaching the top was seen to be carrying a pair of tubs, one on his back and one on his chest, the two being slung together by cords passing round the chine hoops,* and resting on the carrier's shoulders. Some of the stronger men carried three by putting an extra one on the top behind, but the customary load was a pair, these being quite weighty enough to give their bearer the sensation of having chest and backbone in contact after a walk of four or five miles.

'Where is Mr Owlett?' said Lizzy to one of them.

'He will not come up this way,' said the carrier. 'He's to bide on shore till we be safe off.' Then, without waiting for the rest, the foremost men plunged across the down; and, when the last had ascended, Lizzy pulled up the rope, wound it round her arm, wriggled the bar from the sod, and turned to follow the carriers.

'You are very anxious about Owlett's safety,' said the minister.

'Was there ever such a man!' said Lizzy. 'Why, isn't he my cousin?'

'Yes. Well, it is a bad night's work,' said Stockdale heavily. 'But I'll carry the bar and rope for you.'

'Thank God, the tubs have got so far all right,' said she.

Stockdale shook his head, and, taking the bar, walked by her side towards the downs; and the moan of the sea was heard no more.

'Is this what you meant the other day when you spoke of having business with Owlett?' the young man asked.

'This is it,' she replied. 'I never see him on any other matter.'

'A partnership of that kind with a young man is very odd.'

'It was begun by my father and his, who were brother-laws.'

Her companion could not blind himself to the fact that where tastes and pursuits were so akin as Lizzy's and Owlett's, and where risks were shared, as with them, in every undertaking, there would be a peculiar appropriateness in her answering Owlett's standing question on matrimony in the affirmative. This did not soothe Stockdale, its tendency being rather to stimulate in him an effort to make the pair as inappropriate as possible, and win her away from this nocturnal crew to correctness of conduct and a minister's parlour in some far-removed inland county.

They had been walking near enough to the file of carriers for Stockdale to perceive that, when they got into the road to the village, they split up into two companies of unequal size, each of which made off in a direction of its own. One company, the smaller of the two, went towards the church, and by the time that Lizzy and Stockdale reached their own house these men had scaled the churchyard wall, and were proceeding noiselessly over the grass within.

'I see that Mr Owlett has arranged for one batch to be put in the church again,' observed Lizzy. 'Do you remember my taking you there the first night you came?'

'Yes, of course,' said Stockdale. 'No wonder you had permission to broach the tubs – they were his, I suppose?'

'No, they were not – they were mine; I had permission from myself. The day after that they went several miles inland in a waggon-load of manure, and sold very well.'

At this moment the group of men who had made off to the left some time before began leaping one by one from the hedge opposite Lizzy's house, and the first man, who had no tubs upon his shoulders, came forward.

'Mrs Newberry, isn't it?' he said hastily.

'Yes, Jim,' said she. 'What's the matter?'

'I find that we can't put any in Badger's Clump tonight, Lizzy,' said Owlett. 'The place is watched. We must sling the apple-tree in the orchet if there's time. We can't put any more under the church lumber than I have sent on there, and my mixen* hev already more in en than is safe.'

'Very well,' she said. 'Be quick about it – that's all. What can I do?'

'Nothing at all, please. Ah, it is the minister! – you two that can't do anything had better get indoors and not be zeed.'

While Owlett thus conversed, in a tone so full of contraband anxiety and so free from lover's jealousy, the men who followed him had been descending one by one from the hedge; and it unfortunately happened that when the hindmost took his leap, the cord slipped which sustained his tubs: the result was that both the kegs fell into the road, one of them being stove in by the blow.

"Od drown it all!' said Owlett, rushing back.

'It is worth a good deal, I suppose?' said Stockdale.

'O no – about two guineas and half to us now,' said Lizzy excitedly. 'It isn't that – it is the smell! It is so blazing strong before it has been lowered by water, that it smells dreadfully when spilt in the road like that! I do hope Latimer* won't pass by till it is gone off.'

Owlett and one or two others picked up the burst tub and began to scrape and trample over the spot, to disperse the liquor as much as possible; and then they all entered the gate of Owlett's orchard, which adjoined Lizzy's garden on the right. Stockdale did not care to follow them, for several on recognizing him had looked wonderingly at his presence, though they said nothing. Lizzy left his side and went to the bottom of the garden, looking over the hedge into the orchard, where the men could be dimly seen bustling about, and apparently hiding the tubs. All was done noiselessly, and without a light; and when it was over they dispersed in different directions, those who had taken their cargoes to the church having already gone off to their homes.

Lizzy returned to the garden-gate, over which Stockdale was still abstractedly leaning. 'It is all finished: I am going indoors now,' she said gently. 'I will leave the door ajar for you.'

'O no – you needn't,' said Stockdale; 'I am coming too.'

But before either of them had moved, the faint clatter of horses' hoofs broke upon the ear, and it seemed to come from the point where the track across the down joined the hard road.

'They are just too late!' cried Lizzy exultingly.

'Who?' said Stockdale.

'Latimer, the riding-officer, and some assistant of his. We had better go indoors.'

They entered the house, and Lizzy bolted the door. 'Please don't get a light, Mr Stockdale,' she said.

'Of course I will not,' said he.

'I thought you might be on the side of the king,' said Lizzy, with faintest sarcasm.

'I am,' said Stockdale. 'But, Lizzy Newberry, I love you, and you know it perfectly well; and you ought to know, if you do not, what I have suffered in my conscience on your account these last few days!'

'I guess very well,' she said hurriedly. 'Yet I don't see why. Ah, you are better than I!'

The trotting of the horses seemed to have again died away, and the pair of listeners touched each other's fingers in the cold 'Good-night' of those whom something seriously divided. They were on the landing, but before they had taken three steps apart, the tramp of the horsemen suddenly revived, almost close to the house. Lizzy turned to the staircase window, opened the casement about an inch, and put her face close to the aperture. 'Yes, one of 'em is Latimer,' she whispered. 'He always rides a white horse. One would think it was the last colour for a man in that line.'

Stockdale looked, and saw the white shape of the animal as it passed by; but before the riders had gone another ten yards Latimer reined in his horse, and said something to his companion which neither Stockdale nor Lizzy could hear. Its drift was, however, soon made evident, for the other man stopped also; and sharply turning the horses' heads they cautiously retraced their steps. When they were again opposite Mrs Newberry's garden, Latimer dismounted, and the man on the dark horse did the same.

Lizzy and Stockdale, intently listening and observing the proceedings, naturally put their heads as close as possible to the slit formed by the slightly opened casement; and thus it occurred that at last their cheeks came positively into contact. They went on listening, as if they did not know of the singular incident which had happened to their faces, and the pressure of each to each rather increased than lessened with the lapse of time.

They could hear the Customs-men sniffing the air like hounds as they paced slowly along. When they reached the spot where the tub had burst, both stopped on the instant.

'Ay, ay, 'tis quite strong here,' said the second officer. 'Shall we knock at the door?'

'Well, no,' said Latimer. 'Maybe this is only a trick to put us off the scent. They wouldn't kick up this stink anywhere near their hiding-place. I have known such things before.'

'Anyhow, the things, or some of 'em, must have been brought this way,' said the other.

'Yes,' said Latimer musingly. 'Unless 'tis all done to tole* us the wrong way. I have a mind that we go home for tonight without saying a word, and come the first thing in the morning with more hands. I know they have storages about here, but we can do nothing by this owl's light. We will look round the parish and see if everybody is in bed, John; and if all is quiet, we will do as I say.'

They went on, and the two inside the window could hear them passing leisurely through the whole village, the street of which curved round at the bottom and entered the turnpike-road at another junction. This way the officers followed, and the amble of their horses died quite away.

What will you do?' said Stockdale, withdrawing from his position.

She knew that he alluded to the coming search by the officers, to divert her attention from their own tender incident by the casement, which he wished to be passed over as a thing rather dreamt of than done. 'O, nothing,' she replied, with as much coolness as she could command under her disappointment at his manner. 'We often have such storms as this. You would not be frightened if you knew what fools they are. Fancy riding o' horseback through the place; of course they will hear and see nobody while they make that noise; but they are always afraid to get off, in case some of our fellows should burst out upon 'em, and tie them up to the gate-post, as they have done before now. Good-night, Mr Stockdale.'

She closed the window and went to her room, where a tear fell from her eyes; and that not because of the alertness of the riding-officers.

THE GREAT SEARCH AT NETHER-MOYNTON

Stockdale was so excited by the events of the evening, and the dilemma that he was placed in between conscience and love, that he did not sleep, or even doze, but remained as broadly awake as at noonday. As soon as the grey light began to touch ever so faintly the whiter objects in his bedroom he arose, dressed himself, and went downstairs into the road.

The village was already astir. Several of the carriers had heard the well-known canter of Latimer's horse while they were undressing in the dark that night, and had already communicated with each other and Owlett on the subject. The only doubt seemed to be about the safety of those tubs which had been left under the church gallery-stairs, and after a short discussion at the corner of the mill, it was agreed that these should be removed before it got lighter, and hidden in the middle of a double hedge bordering the adjoining field. However, before anything could be carried into effect, the footsteps of many men were heard coming down the lane from the highway.

'Damn it, here they be,' said Owlett, who, having already drawn the hatch and started his mill for the day, stood stolidly at the mill-door covered with flour, as if the interest of his whole soul was bound up in the shaking walls around him.

The two or three with whom he had been talking dispersed to their usual work, and when the Customs-officers, and the formidable body of men they had hired, reached the village cross, between the mill and Mrs Newberry's house, the village wore the natural aspect of a place beginning its morning labours.

'Now,' said Latimer to his associates, who numbered thirteen men in all, 'what I know is that the things are somewhere in this here place. We have got the day before us, and 'tis hard if we can't light upon 'em and get 'em to Budmouth Custom-house before night. First we will try the fuel-houses, and then we'll work our way into the chimmers,* and then to the ricks and stables, and so creep round. You have nothing but your noses to guide ye, mind, so use 'em today if you never did in your lives before.'

Then the search began. Owlett, during the early part, watched from his mill-window, Lizzy from the door of her house, with the greatest self-possession. A farmer down below, who also had a share in the run, rode about with one eye on his fields and the other on Latimer and his myrmidons,* prepared to put them off the scent if he should be asked a question. Stockdale, who was no smuggler at all, felt more anxiety than the worst of them, and went about his studies with a heavy heart, coming frequently to the door to ask Lizzy some question or other on the consequences to her of the tubs being found.

'The consequences,' she said quietly, 'are simply that I shall lose 'em. As I have none in the house or garden, they can't touch me personally.'

'But you have some in the orchard?'

'Mr Owlett rents that of me, and he lends it to others. So it will be hard to say who put any tubs there if they should be found.'

There was never such a tremendous sniffing known as that which took place in Nether-Moynton parish and its vicinity this day. All was done methodically, and mostly on hands and knees. At different hours of the day they had different plans. From daybreak to breakfast time the officers used their sense of smell in a direct and straightforward manner only, pausing nowhere but at such places as the tubs might be supposed to be secreted in at that very moment, pending their removal on the following night. Among the places tested and examined were: –

Hollow trees	Cupboards	Culverts
Potato-graves	Clock-cases	Hedgerows
Fuel-houses	Chimney-flues	Faggot-ricks
Bedrooms	Rainwater-butts	Haystacks
Apple-lofts	Pigsties	Coppers and ovens.

After breakfast they recommenced with renewed vigour, taking a new line; that is to say, directing their attention to clothes that might be supposed to have come in contact with the tubs in their removal from the shore, such garments being usually tainted with the spirit, owing to its oozing between the staves. They now sniffed at: –

Smock-frocks	Smiths' and shoemakers' aprons
Old shirts and waistcoats	Knee-naps* and hedging-gloves
Coats and hats	Tarpaulins
Breeeches and leggings	Market-cloaks
Women's shawls and gowns	Scarecrows.

And as soon as the midday meal was over, they pushed their search into places where the spirits might have been thrown away in alarm: –

Horse-ponds	Mixens	Sinks in yards
Stable-drains	Wet ditches	Road-scrapings,* and
Cinder-heaps	Cesspools	Back-door gutters.

But still these indefatigable Custom-house men discovered nothing more than the original tell-tale smell in the road opposite Lizzy's house, which even yet had not passed off.

'I'll tell ye what it is, men,' said Latimer, about three o'clock in the afternoon, 'we must begin over again. Find them tubs I will.'

The men, who had been hired for the day, looked at their hands and knees, muddy with creeping on all fours so frequently, and rubbed their noses, as if they had almost had enough of it; for the quantity of bad air which had passed into each one's nostril had rendered it nearly as insensible as a flue. However, after a moment's hesitation, they prepared to start anew, except three, whose power of smell had quite succumbed under the excessive wear and tear of the day.

By this time not a male villager was to be seen in the parish. Owlett was not at his mill, the farmers were not in their fields, the parson was not in his garden, the smith had left his forge, and the wheelwright's shop was silent.

'Where the divil are the folk gone?' said Latimer, waking up to the fact of their absence, and looking round. 'I'll have 'em up for this! Why don't they come and help us? There's not a man about the place but the Methodist parson, and he's an old woman. I demand assistance in the king's name!'

'We must find the jineral public afore we can demand that,' said his lieutenant.

'Well, well, we shall do better without 'em,' said Latimer, who changed his moods at a moment's notice. 'But there's great cause of suspicion in this silence and this keeping out of sight, and I'll bear it in mind. Now we will go across to Owlett's orchard and see what we can find there.'

Stockdale, who heard this discussion from the garden-gate, over which he had been leaning, was rather alarmed, and thought it a mistake of the villagers to keep so completely out of the way. He himself, like the Preventives, had been wondering for the last half-hour what could have become of them. Some labourers were of necessity engaged in distant fields, but the master-workmen should have been at home; though one and all, after just showing themselves at their shops, had apparently gone off for the day. He went in to Lizzy, who sat at a back window sewing, and said, 'Lizzy, where are the men?'

Lizzy laughed. 'Where they mostly are when they're run so hard as this.' She cast her eyes to heaven. 'Up there,' she said.

Stockdale looked up. 'What – on the top of the church tower?' he asked, seeing the direction of her glance.

'Yes.'

'Well, I expect they will soon have to come down,' said he gravely. 'I have been listening to the officers, and they are going to search the orchard over again, and then every nook in the church.'

Lizzy looked alarmed for the first time. 'Will you go and tell our folk?' she said. 'They ought to be let know.' Seeing his conscience struggling within him like a boiling pot, she added, 'No, never mind, I'll go myself.'

She went out, descended the garden, and climbed over the churchyard wall at the same time that the Preventive-men were ascending the road to the orchard. Stockdale could do no less than follow her. By the time that she reached the tower entrance he was at her side, and they entered together.

Nether-Moynton churchtower was, as in many villages, without a turret, and the only way to the top was by going up to the singers' gallery, and thence ascending by a ladder to a square trap-door in the floor of the bell-loft, above which a permanent ladder was fixed, passing through the bells to a hole in the roof. When Lizzy and Stockdale reached the gallery and looked up, nothing but the trap-door and the five holes for the bell-ropes appeared. The ladder was gone.

'There's no getting up,' said Stockdale.

'O yes, there is,' said she. 'There's an eye looking at us at this moment through a knot-hole in that trap-door.'

And as she spoke the trap opened, and the dark line of the ladder was seen descending against the whitewashed wall. When it touched the bottom Lizzy dragged it to its place, and said, 'If you'll go up, I'll follow.'

The young man ascended, and presently found himself among consecrated bells for the first time in his life, nonconformity having been in the Stockdale blood for some generations. He eyed them uneasily, and looked round for Lizzy. Owlett stood here, holding the top of the ladder.

'What, be you really one of us?' said the miller.

'It seems so,' said Stockdale sadly.

'He's not,' said Lizzy who overheard. 'He's neither for nor against us. He'll do us no harm.'

She stepped up beside them, and then they went on to the next stage, which, when they had clambered over the dusty bell-carriages, was of easy ascent, leading towards the hole through which the pale sky appeared, and into the open air. Owlett remained behind for a moment, to pull up the lower ladder.

'Keep down your heads,' said a voice, as soon as they set foot on the flat.

Stockdale here beheld all the missing parishioners, lying on their stomachs on the tower roof, except a few who, elevated on their hands and knees, were peeping through the embrasures of the parapet. Stockdale did the same, and saw the village lying like a map below him, over which moved the figures of the Customs-men, each foreshortened to a crablike object, the crown of his hat forming a circular disc in the centre of him. Some of the men had turned their heads when the young preacher's figure arose among them.

'What, Mr Stockdale?' said Matt Grey, in a tone of surprise.

'I'd as lief that it hadn't been,' said Jim Clarke. 'If the pa'son should see him a-trespassing here in his tower, 'twould be none the better for we, seeing how 'a do hate chapel-members. He'd never buy a tub of us again, and he's as good a customer as we have got this side o' Warm'll.'

'Where is the pa'son?' said Lizzy.

'In his house, to be sure, that he mid see nothing of what's going on – where all good folks ought to be, and this young man likewise.'

'Well, he has brought some news,' said Lizzy. 'They are going to search the orchard and church, can we do anything if they should find?'

'Yes,' said her cousin Owlett. 'That's what we've been talking o', and we have settled our line. Well, be dazed!'

The exclamation was caused by his perceiving that some of the searchers, having got into the orchard, and begun stooping and creeping hither and thither, were pausing in the middle, where a tree smaller than the rest was growing. They drew closer, and bent lower than ever upon the ground.

'O, my tubs!' said Lizzy faintly, as she peered through the parapet at them.

'They have got 'em, 'a b'lieve,' said Owlett.

The interest in the movements of the officers was so keen that not a single eye was looking in any other direction; but at that moment a shout from the church beneath them attracted the attention of the smugglers, as it did also of the party in the orchard, who sprang to their feet and went towards the church-yard wall. At the same time those of the Government men who had entered the church unperceived by the smugglers cried aloud, 'Here be some of 'em at last.'

The smugglers remained in a blank silence, uncertain whether 'some of 'em' meant tubs or men; but again peeping cautiously over the edge of the tower they learnt that tubs were the things descried; and soon these fated articles were brought one by one into the middle of the churchyard from their hiding-place under the gallery-stairs.

'They are going to put 'em on Hinton's vault till they find the rest!' said Lizzy hopelessly. The Customs-men had, in fact, begun to pile up the tubs on a large stone slab which was fixed there; and when all were brought out from the tower, two or three of the men were left standing by them, the rest of the party again proceeding to the orchard.

The interest of the smugglers in the next manoeuvres of their enemies became painfully intense. Only about thirty tubs had been secreted in the lumber of the tower, but seventy were hidden in the orchard, making up all that they had brought ashore as yet, the remainder of the cargo having been tied to a sinker and dropped overboard for another night's operations. The Preven-tives, having re-entered the orchard, acted as if they were positive that here lay hidden the rest of the tubs, which they were determined to find before night fall. They spread themselves out round the field, and advancing on all fours as before, went anew round every apple-tree in the enclosure. The young tree in the middle again led them to pause, and at length the whole company gathered there in a way which signified that a second chain of reasoning had led to the same results as the first.

When they had examined the sod hereabouts for some min-utes, one of the men rose, ran to a disused part of the church where tools were kept, and returned with the sexton's pickaxe and shovel, with which they set to work.

'Are they really buried there?' said the minister, for the grass was so green and uninjured that it was difficult to believe it had been disturbed. The smugglers were too interested to reply, and presently they saw, to their chagrin, the officers stand several on each side of the tree; and, stooping and applying their hands to the soil, they bodily lifted the tree and the turf around it. The apple-tree now showed itself to be growing in a shallow box, with handles for lifting at each of the four sides. Under the site of the tree a square hole was revealed, and an officer went and looked down.

'It is all up now,' said Owlett quietly. 'And now all of ye get down before they notice we are here; and be ready for our next move. I had better bide here till dark, or they may take me on suspicion, as 'tis on my ground. I'll be with ye as soon as daylight begins to pink in.'

'And I?' said Lizzy.

'You please look to the linch-pins and screws; then go indoors and know nothing at all. The chaps will do the rest.'

The ladder was replaced, and all but Owlett descended, the men passing off one by one at the back of the church, and vanishing on their respective errands. Lizzy walked boldly along the street, followed closely by the minister.

'You are going indoors, Mrs Newberry?' he said.

She knew from the words 'Mrs Newberry' that the division between them had widened yet another degree.

'I am not going home,' she said. 'I have a little thing to do before I go in. Martha Sarah will get your tea.'

'O, I don't mean on that account,' said Stockdale. 'What *can* you have to do further in this unhallowed affair?'

'Only a little,' she said.

'What is that? I'll go with you.'

'No, I shall go by myself. Will you please go indoors? I shall be there in less than an hour.'

'You are not going to run any danger, Lizzy?' said the young man, his tenderness reasserting itself.

'None whatever – worth mentioning,' answered she, and went down towards the Cross.

Stockdale entered the garden gate, and stood behind it looking on. The Preventive-men were still busy in the orchard, and at last he was tempted to enter and watch their proceedings. When he came closer he found that the secret cellar, of whose existence he had been totally unaware, was formed by timbers placed across from side to side about a foot under the ground, and grassed over.

The officers looked up at Stockdale's fair and downy countenance, and evidently thinking him above suspicion, went on with their work again. As soon as all the tubs were taken out they began tearing up the turf, pulling out the timbers, and breaking in the sides, till the cellar was wholly dismantled and shapeless, the apple-tree lying with its roots high to the air. But the hole which had in its time held so much contraband merchandise was never completely filled up, either then or afterwards, a depression in the greensward marking the spot to this day.

THE WALK TO WARM'ELL CROSS AND AFTERWARDS

As the goods had all to be carried to Budmouth that night, the next object of the Custom-house officers was to find horses and carts for the journey, and they went about the village for that purpose. Latimer strode hither and thither with a lump of chalk in his hand, marking broad-arrows so vigorously on every vehicle and set of harness that he came across, that it seemed as if he would chalk broad-arrows on the very hedges and roads. The owner of every conveyance so marked was bound to give it up for Government purposes. Stockdale, who had had enough of the scene, turned indoors thoughtful and depressed. Lizzy was already there, having come in at the back, though she had not yet taken off her bonnet. She looked tired, and her mood was not much brighter than his own. They had but little to say to each other; and the minister went away and attempted to read; but at this he could not succeed, and he shook the little bell for tea.

Lizzy herself brought in the tray, the girl having run off into the village during the afternoon, too full of excitement at the proceedings to remember her state of life. However, almost before the sad lovers had said anything to each other, Martha came in in a steaming state.

'O. there's such a stoor, Mrs Newberry and Mr Stockdale! The king's officers can't get the carts ready nohow at all! They pulled Thomas Artnell's, and William Rogers's, and Stephen Sprake's carts into the road, and off came the wheels, and down fell the carts; and they found there was no linch-pins in the arms; and then they tried Samuel Shane's waggon, and found that the screws were gone from he, and at last they looked at the dairyman's cart, and he's got none neither! They have gone now to the blacksmith's to get some made, but he's nowhere to be found!'

Stockdale looked at Lizzy, who blushed very slightly, and went out of the room, followed by Martha Sarah. But before they had got through the passage there was a rap at the front door, and Stockdale recognized Latimer's voice addressing Mrs Newberry, who had turned back.

'For God's sake, Mrs Newberry, have you seen Hardman the blacksmith up this way? If we could get hold of him, we'd e'en a'most drag him by the hair of his head to his anvil, where he ought to be.'

'He's an idle man, Mr Latimer,' said Lizzy archly. 'What do you want him for?'

'Why, there isn't a horse in the place that has got more than three shoes on, and some have only two. The waggon-wheels be without strakes,* and there's no linch-pins to the carts. What with that, and the bother about every set of harness being out of order, we shan't be off before nightfall – upon my soul we shan't. 'Tis a rough lot, Mrs Newberry, that you've got about you here; but they'll play at this game once too often, mark my words they will! There's not a man in the parish that don't deserve to be whipped.'

It happened that Hardman was at that moment a little further up the lane, smoking his pipe behind a holly-bush. When Latimer had done speaking he went on in this direction, and Hardman, hearing the riding-officer's steps, found curiosity too strong for prudence. He peeped out from the bush at the very moment that Latimer's glance was on it. There was nothing left for him to do but to come forward with unconcern.

'I've been looking for you for the last hour!' said Latimer with a glare in his eye.

'Sorry to hear that,' said Hardman. 'I've been out for a stroll, to look for more hid tubs, to deliver 'em up to Gover'ment.'

'O yes, Hardman, we know it,' said Latimer, with withering sarcasm. 'We know that you'll deliver 'em up to Gover'ment.

We know that all the parish is helping us, and have been all day! Now you please walk along with me down to your shop, and kindly let me hire ye in the king's name.'

They went down the lane together; and presently there resounded from the smithy the ring of a hammer not very briskly swung. However, the carts and horses were got into some sort of travelling condition, but it was not until after the clock had struck six, when the muddy roads were glistening under the horizontal light of the fading day. The smuggled tubs were soon packed into the vehicles, and Latimer, with three of his assistants, drove slowly out of the village in the direction of the port of Budmouth, some considerable number of miles distant, the other men of the Preventive-guard being left to watch for the remainder of the cargo, which they knew to have been sunk somewhere between Ringsworth and Lulwind Cove, and to unearth Owlett, the only person clearly implicated by the discovery of the cave.

Women and children stood at the doors as the carts, each chalked with the Government pitchfork, passed in the increasing twilight; and as they stood they looked at the confiscated property with a melancholy expression that told only too plainly the relation which they bore to the trade.

'Well, Lizzy,' said Stockdale, when the crackle of the wheels had nearly died away. 'This is a fit finish to your adventure. I am truly thankful that you have got off without suspicion, and the loss only of the liquor. Will you sit down and let me talk to you?'

'By and by,' she said. 'But I must go out now.'

'Not to that horrid shore again?' he said blankly.

'No, not there. I am only going to see the end of this day's business.'

He did not answer to this, and she moved towards the door slowly, as if waiting for him to say something more.

'You don't offer to come with me,' she added at last. 'I suppose that's because you hate me after all this!'

'Can you say it, Lizzy, when you know I only want to save you from such practices? Come with you! – of course I will, if it is only to take care of you. But why will you go out again?'

'Because I cannot rest indoors. Something is happening, and I must know what. Now, come!' And they went into the dusk together.

When they reached the turnpike-road she turned to the right, and he soon perceived that they were following the direction of the Preventive-men and their load. He had given her his arm, and every now and then she suddenly pulled it back, to signify that he was to halt a moment and listen. They had walked rather quickly along the first quarter of a mile, and on the second or third time of standing still she said, 'I hear them ahead – don't you?'

'Yes,' he said; 'I hear the wheels. But what of that?'

'I only want to know if they get clear away from the neighbourhood.'

'Ah,' said he, a light breaking upon him. 'Something desperate is to be attempted! – and now I remember there was not a man about the village when we left.'

'Hark!' she murmured. The noise of the cartwheels had stopped, and given place to another sort of sound.

''Tis a scuffle!' said Stockdale. 'There'll be murder! Lizzy, let go my arm; I am going on. On my conscience, I must not stay here and do nothing!'

'There'll be no murder, and not even a broken head,' she said. 'Our men are thirty to four of them: no harm will be done at all.'

'Then there *is* an attack!' exclaimed Stockdale; 'and you knew it was to be. Why should you side with men who break the laws like this?'

'Why should you side with men who take from country traders what they have honestly bought wi' their own money in France?' said she firmly.

'They are not honestly bought,' said he.

'They are,' she contradicted. 'I and Mr Owlett and the others paid thirty shillings for every one of the tubs before they were put on board at Cherbourg, and if a king who is nothing to us sends his people to steal our property, we have a right to steal it back again.'

Stockdale did not stop to argue the matter, but went quickly in the direction of the noise, Lizzy keeping at his side. 'Don't you interfere, will you, dear Richard?' she said anxiously, as they drew near. 'Don't let us go any closer: 'tis at Warm'ell Cross where they are seizing 'em. You can do no good, and you may meet with a hard blow!'

'Let us see first what is going on,' he said. But before they had got much further the noise of the cartwheels began again; and Stockdale soon found that they were coming towards him. In another minute the three carts came up, and Stockdale and Lizzy stood in the ditch to let them pass.

Instead of being conducted by four men, as had happened when they went out of the village, the horses and carts were now accompanied by a body of from twenty to thirty, all of whom, as Stockdale perceived to his astonishment, had blackened faces. Among them walked six or eight huge female figures, whom, from their wide strides, Stockdale guessed to be men in disguise. As soon as the party discerned Lizzy and her companion four or five fell back, and when the carts had passed, came close to the pair.

'There is no walking up this way for the present,' said one of the gaunt women, who wore curls a foot long, dangling down the sides of her face, in the fashion of the time. Stockdale recognized this lady's voice as Owlett's.

'Why not?' said Stockdale. 'This is the public highway.'

'Now look here, youngster,' said Owlett. 'O, 'tis the Methodist parson! – what, and Mrs Newberry! Well, you'd better not go up that way, Lizzy. They've all run off, and folks have got their own again.'

The miller then hastened on and joined his comrades. Stockdale and Lizzy also turned back. 'I wish all this hadn't been forced upon us,' she said regretfully. 'But if those Coast-men had got off with the tubs, half the people in the parish would have been in want for the next month or two.'

Stockdale was not paying much attention to her words, and he said, 'I don't think I can go back like this. Those four poor Preventives may be murdered for all I know.'

'Murdered!' said Lizzy impatiently. 'We don't do murder here.'

'Well, I shall go as far as Warm'ell Cross to see,' said Stockdale decisively; and, without wishing her safe home or anything else, the minister turned back. Lizzy stood looking at him till his form was absorbed in the shades; and then, with sadness, she went in the direction of Nether-Moynton.

The road was lonely, and after nightfall at this time of the year there was often not a passer for hours. Stockdale pursued his way without hearing a sound beyond that of his own footsteps; and in due time he passed beneath the trees of the plantation which surrounded the Warm'ell Cross-road. Before he had reached the point of intersection he heard voices from the thicket.

'Hoi-hoi-hoi! Help, help!'

The voices were not at all feeble or despairing, but they were unmistakably anxious. Stockdale had no weapon, and before plunging into the pitchy darkness of the plantation he pulled a stake from the hedge, to use in case of need. When he got among the trees he shouted – 'What's the matter – where are you?'

'Here,' answered the voices; and, pushing through the brambles in that direction, he came near the objects of his search.

'Why don't you come forward?' said Stockdale.

'We be tied to the trees!'

'Who are you?'

'Poor Will Latimer the Customs-officer!' said one plaintively. 'Just come and cut these cords, there's a good man. We were afraid nobody would pass by tonight.'

Stockdale soon loosened them, upon which they stretched their limbs and stood at their ease.

'The rascals!' said Latimer, getting now into a rage, though he had seemed quite meek when Stockdale first came up. ''Tis the same set of fellows. I know they were Moynton chaps to a man.'

'But we can't swear to 'em,' said another. 'Not one of em spoke.'

'What are you going to do?' said Stockdale.

'I'd fain go back to Moynton, and have at 'em again!' said Latimer.

'So would we!' said his comrades.

'Fight till we die!' said Latimer.

'We will, we will!' said his men.

'But,' said Latimer, more frigidly, as they came out of the plantation, 'we don't *know* that these chaps with black faces were Moynton men? And proof is a hard thing.'

'So it is,' said the rest.

'And therefore we won't do nothing at all,' said Latimer, with complete dispassionateness. 'For my part, I'd sooner be them than we. The clitches* of my arms are burning like fire from the cords those two strapping women tied round 'em. My opinion is, now I have had time to think o't, that you may serve your Gover'ment at too high a price. For these two nights and days I have not had an hour's rest; and, please God, here's for home-along.'

The other officers agreed heartily to this course; and, thanking Stockdale for his timely assistance, they parted from him at the Cross, taking themselves the western road, and Stockdale going back to Nether-Moynton.

During that walk the minister was lost in reverie of the most painful kind. As soon as he got into the house, and before entering his own rooms, he advanced to the door of the little back parlour in which Lizzy usually sat with her mother. He found her there alone. Stockdale went forward, and, like a man in a dream, looked down upon the table that stood between him and the young woman, who had her bonnet and cloak still on. As he did not speak, she looked up from her chair at him, with misgiving in her eye.

'Where are they gone?' he then said listlessly.

'Who? – I don't know. I have seen nothing of them since. I came straight in here.'

'If your men can manage to get off with those tubs, it will be a great profit to you, I suppose?'

'A share will be mine, a share my cousin Owlett's, a share to each of the two farmers, and a share divided amongst the men who helped us.'

'And you still think,' he went on slowly, 'that you will not give this business up?'

Lizzy rose, and put her hand upon his shoulder. 'Don't ask that,' she whispered. 'You don't know what you are asking. I must tell you, though I meant not to do it. What I make by that trade is all I have to keep my mother and myself with.'

He was astonished. 'I did not dream of such a thing,' he said. 'I would rather have scraped the roads, had I been you. What is money compared with a clear conscience?'

'My conscience is clear. I know my mother, but the king I have never seen. His dues are nothing to me. But it is a great deal to me that my mother and I should live.'

'Marry me, and promise to give it up. I will keep your mother.'

'It is good of you,' she said, moved a little. 'Let me think of it by myself. I would rather not answer now.'

She reserved her answer till the next day, and came into his room with a solemn face. 'I cannot do what you wished!' she said passionately. 'It is too much to ask. My whole life ha' been

passed in this way.' Her words and manner showed that before
entering she had been struggling with herself in private, and that
the contention had been strong.

Stockdale turned pale, but he spoke quietly. 'Then, Lizzy, we
must part. I cannot go against my principles in this matter, and
I cannot make my profession a mockery. You know how I love
you, and what I would do for you; but this one thing I cannot
do.'

'But why should you belong to that profession?' she burst
out. 'I have got this large house; why can't you marry me, and
live here with us, and not be a Methodist preacher any more? I
assure you, Richard, it is no harm, and I wish you could only
see it as I do! We only carry it on in winter: in summer it is
never done at all. It stirs up one's dull life at this time o' the
year, and gives excitement, which I have got so used to now that
I should hardly know how to do 'ithout it. At nights, when the
wind blows, instead of being dull and stupid, and not noticing
whether it do blow or not, your mind is afield, even if you are
not afield yourself; and you are wondering how the chaps are
getting on; and you walk up and down the room, and look out
o' window, and then you go out yourself, and know your way
about as well by night as by day, and have hairbreadth escapes*
from old Latimer and his fellows, who are too stupid ever to
really frighten us, and only make us a bit nimble.'

'He frightened you a little last night, anyhow: and I would
advise you to drop it before it is worse.'

She shook her head. 'No, I must go on as I have begun. I was
born to it. It is in my blood, and I can't be cured. O, Richard,
you cannot think what a hard thing you have asked, and how
sharp you try me when you put me between this and my love
for 'ee!'

Stockdale was leaning with his elbow on the mantelpiece, his
hands over his eyes. 'We ought never to have met, Lizzy,' he
said. 'It was an ill day for us! I little thought there was anything
so hopeless and impossible in our engagement as this. Well, it is
too late now to regret consequences in this way. I have had the
happiness of seeing you and knowing you at least.'

'You dissent from Church, and I dissent from State,' she said.
'And I don't see why we are not well matched.'

He smiled sadly, while Lizzy remained looking down, her eyes
beginning to overflow.

That was an unhappy evening for both of them, and the days that followed were unhappy days. Both she and he went mechanically about their employments, and his depression was marked in the village by more than one of his denomination with whom he came in contact. But Lizzy, who passed her days indoors, was unsuspected of being the cause: for it was generally understood that a quiet engagement to marry existed between her and her cousin Owlett, and had existed for some time.

Thus uncertainly the week passed on; till one morning Stockdale said to her: 'I have had a letter, Lizzy. I must call you that till I am gone.'

'Gone?' said she blankly.

'Yes,' he said. 'I am going from this place. I felt it would be better for us both that I should not stay after what has happened. In fact, I couldn't stay here, and look on you from day to day, without becoming weak and faltering in my course. I have just heard of an arrangement by which the other minister can arrive here in about a week; and let me go elsewhere.'

That he had all this time continued so firmly fixed in his resolution came upon her as a grievous surprise. 'You never loved me!' she said bitterly.

'I might say the same,' he returned; 'but I will not. Grant me one favour. Come and hear my last sermon on the day before I go.'

Lizzy, who was a churchgoer on Sunday mornings, frequently attended Stockdale's chapel in the evening with the rest of the double-minded; and she promised.

It became known that Stockdale was going to leave, and a good many people outside his own sect were sorry to hear it. The intervening days flew rapidly away, and on the evening of the Sunday which preceded the morning of his departure Lizzy sat in the chapel to hear him for the last time. The little building was full to overflowing, and he took up the subject which all had expected, that of the contraband trade so extensively practised among them. His hearers, in laying his words to their own hearts, did not perceive that they were most particularly directed against Lizzy, till the sermon waxed warm, and Stockdale nearly broke down with emotion. In truth his own earnestness, and her sad eyes looking up at him, were too much for the young man's equanimity. He hardly knew how he ended. He saw Lizzy, as through a mist, turn and go away with the rest of the congregation; and shortly afterwards followed her home.

She invited him to supper, and they sat down alone, her mother having, as was usual with her on Sunday nights, gone to bed early.

'We will part friends, won't we?' said Lizzy, with forced gaiety, and never alluding to the sermon: a reticence which rather disappointed him.

'We will,' he said, with a forced smile on his part; and they sat down.

It was the first meal that they had ever shared together in their lives, and probably the last that they would so share. When it was over, and the indifferent conversation could no longer be continued, he arose and took her hand. 'Lizzy,' he said, 'do you say we must part – do you?'

'You do,' she said solemnly. 'I can say no more.'

'Nor I,' said he. 'If that is your answer, goodbye!'

Stockdale bent over her and kissed her, and she involuntarily returned his kiss. 'I shall go early,' he said hurriedly. 'I shall not see you again.'

And he did leave early. He fancied, when stepping forth into the grey morning light, to mount the van which was to carry him away, that he saw a face between the parted curtains of Lizzy's window, but the light was faint, and the panes glistened with wet; so he could not be sure. Stockdale mounted the vehicle, and was gone; and on the following Sunday the new minister preached in the chapel of the Moynton Wesleyans.

One day, two years after the parting, Stockdale, now settled in a midland town, came into Nether-Moynton by carrier in the original way. Jogging along in the van that afternoon he had put questions to the driver, and the answers that he received interested the minister deeply. The result of them was that he went without the least hesitation to the door of his former lodging. It was about six o'clock in the evening, and the same time of year as when he had left; now, too, the ground was damp and glistening, the west was bright, and Lizzy's snowdrops were raising their heads in the border under the wall.

Lizzy must have caught sight of him from the window, for by the time that he reached the door she was there holding it open: and then, as if she had not sufficiently considered her act of coming out, she drew herself back, saying with some constraint, 'Mr Stockdale!'

'You knew it was,' said Stockdale, taking her hand. 'I wrote to say I should call.'

'Yes, but you did not say when,' she answered.

'I did not. I was not quite sure when my business would lead me to these parts.'

'You only came because business brought you near?'

'Well, that is the fact; but I have often thought I should like to come on purpose to see you. . . . But what's all this that has happened? I told you how it would be, Lizzy, and you would not listen to me.'

'I would not,' she said sadly. 'But I had been brought up to that life; and it was second nature to me. However, it is all over now. The officers have blood-money for taking a man dead or alive, and the trade is going to nothing. We were hunted down like rats.'

'Owlett is quite gone, I hear.'

'Yes. He is in America. We had a dreadful struggle that last time, when they tried to take him. It is a perfect miracle that he lived through it; and it is a wonder that I was not killed. I was shot in the hand. It was not by aim; the shot was really meant for my cousin; but I was behind, looking on as usual, and the bullet came to me. It bled terribly, but I got home without fainting; and it healed after a time. You know how he suffered?'

'No,' said Stockdale. 'I only heard that he just escaped with his life.'

'He was shot in the back; but a rib turned the ball. He was badly hurt. We would not let him be took. The men carried him all night across the meads to Kingsbere, and hid him in a barn, dressing his wound as well as they could, till he was so far recovered as to be able to get about. Then he was caught, and tried with the others at the assizes;* but they all got off.[1] He had given up his mill for some time; and at last he went to Bristol, and took a passage to America, where he's settled.'

'What do you think of smuggling now?' said the minister gravely.

'I own that we were wrong,' said she. 'But I have suffered for

---

[1] See the Preface to *Wessex Tales* (Appendix 2 at the end of this book).

it. I am very poor now, and my mother has been dead these twelve months. . . . But won't you come in, Mr Stockdale?'

Stockdale went in; and it is to be supposed that they came to an understanding; for a fortnight later there was a sale of Lizzy's furniture, and after that a wedding at a chapel in a neighbouring town.

He took her away from her old haunts to the home that he had made for himself in his native county, where she studied her duties as a minister's wife with praiseworthy assiduity. It is said that in after years she wrote an excellent tract called *Render unto Caesar; or, The Repentant Villagers*, in which her own experience was anonymously used as the introductory story. Stockdale got it printed, after making some corrections, and putting in a few powerful sentences of his own; and many hundreds of copies were distributed by the couple in the course of their married life.

NOTE The ending of this story with the marriage of Lizzy and the minister was almost *de rigueur** in an English magazine at the time of writing. But at this late date, thirty years after, it may not be amiss to give the ending that would have been preferred by the writer to the convention used above. Moreover it corresponds more closely with the true incidents* of which the tale is a vague and flickering shadow. Lizzy did not, in fact, marry the minister, but – much to her credit in the author's opinion – stuck to Jim the smuggler, and emigrated with him after their marriage, an expatrial step rather forced upon him by his adventurous antecedents. They both died in Wisconsin between 1850 and 1860. (May 1912.)

FELLOW-TOWNSMEN

The shepherd on the east hill could shout out lambing intelligence to the shepherd on the west hill, over the intervening town chimneys, without great inconvenience to his voice, so nearly did the steep pastures encroach upon the burghers' backyards. And at night it was possible to stand in the very midst of the town and hear from their native paddocks on the lower levels of greensward* the mild lowing of the farmer's heifers, and the profound, warm blowings of breath in which those creatures indulge. But the community which had jammed itself in the valley thus flanked formed a veritable town, with a real mayor and corporation, and a staple manufacture.

During a certain damp evening five-and-thirty years ago, before the twilight was far advanced, a pedestrian of professional appearance, carrying a small bag in his hand and an elevated umbrella, was descending one of these hills by the turnpike-road when he was overtaken by a phaeton.

'Hullo, Downe – is that you?' said the driver of the vehicle, a young man of pale and refined appearance. 'Jump up here with me, and ride down to your door.'

The other turned a plump, cheery, rather self-indulgent face over his shoulder towards the hailer.

'O, good evening, Mr Barnet – thanks,' he said, and mounted beside his acquaintance.

They were fellow-burgesses of the town which lay beneath them, but though old and very good friends they were differently circumstanced. Barnet was a richer man than the struggling young lawyer Downe, a fact which was to some extent perceptible in Downe's manner towards his companion, though nothing of it ever showed in Barnet's manner towards the solicitor. Barnet's position in the town was none of his own making; his father had been a very successful flax-merchant* in the same place, where the trade was still carried on as briskly as the small capacities of its quarters would allow. Having acquired a fair fortune, old Mr Barnet had retired from business, bringing up his son as a gentleman-burgher, and, it must be added, as a well-educated, liberal-minded young man.

'How is Mrs Barnet?' asked Downe.

'Mrs Barnet was very well when I left home,' the other answered constrainedly, exchanging his meditative regard of the horse for one of self-consciousness.

Mr Downe seemed to regret his inquiry, and immediately took up another thread of conversation. He congratulated his friend on his election as a councilman; he thought he had not seen him since that event took place; Mrs Downe had meant to call and congratulate Mrs Barnet, but he feared that she had failed to do so as yet.

Barnet seemed hampered in his replies. 'We should have been glad to see you. I – my wife would welcome Mrs Downe at any time, as you know. . . . Yes, I am a member of the corporation – rather an inexperienced member, some of them say. It is quite true; and I should have declined the honour as premature – having other things on my hands just now, too – if it had not been pressed upon me so very heartily.'

'There is one thing you have on your hands which I can never quite see the necessity for,' said Downe, with good-humoured freedom. 'What the deuce do you want to build that new mansion for, when you have already got such an excellent house as the one you live in?'

Barnet's face acquired a warmer shade of colour; but as the question had been idly asked by the solicitor while regarding the surrounding flocks and fields, he answered after a moment with no apparent embarrassment –

'Well, we wanted to get out of the town, you know; the house I am living in is rather old and inconvenient.'

Mr Downe declared that he had chosen a pretty site for the new building. They would be able to see for miles and miles from the windows. Was he going to give it a name? He supposed so.

Barnet thought not. There was no other house near that was likely to be mistaken for it. And he did not care for a name.

'But I think it has a name!' Downe observed: 'I went past – when was it? – this morning; and I saw something – "Château Ringdale", I think it was, stuck up on a board!'

'It was an idea she – we had for a short time,' said Barnet hastily. 'But we have decided finally to do without a name – at any rate such a name as that. It must have been a week ago that you saw it. It was taken down last Saturday.... Upon that matter I am firm!' he added grimly.

Downe murmured in an unconvinced tone that he thought he had seen it yesterday.

Talking thus they drove into the town. The street was unusually still for the hour of seven in the evening; an increasing drizzle from the sea had prevailed since the afternoon, and now formed a gauze across the yellow lamps, and trickled with a gentle rattle down the heavy roofs of stone tile, that bent the house-ridges hollow-backed with its weight, and in some instances caused the walls to bulge outwards in the upper story. Their route took them past the little town-hall, the Black-Bull Hotel, and onward to the junction of a small street on the right, consisting of a row of those two-and-two windowed brick residences of no particular age, which are exactly alike wherever found, except in the people they contain.

'Wait – I'll drive you up to your door,' said Barnet, when Downe prepared to alight at the corner. He thereupon turned into the narrow street, when the faces of three little girls could be discerned close to the panes of a lighted window a few yards ahead, surmounted by that of a young matron, the gaze of all four being directed eagerly up the empty street. 'You are a fortunate fellow, Downe,' Barnet continued, as mother and children disappeared from the window to run to the door. 'You must be happy if any man is. I would give a hundred such houses as my new one to have a home like yours.'

'Well – yes, we get along pretty comfortably,' replied Downe complacently.

'That house, Downe, is none of my ordering,' Barnet broke out, revealing a bitterness hitherto suppressed, and checking the horse a moment to finish his speech before delivering up his passenger. 'The house I have already is good enough for me, as you supposed. It is my own freehold; it was built by my grandfather, and is stout enough for a castle. My father was born there, lived there, and died there. I was born there, and have always lived there; yet I must needs build a new one.'

'Why do you?' said Downe.

'Why do I? To preserve peace in the household. I do anything for that; but I don't succeed. I was firm in resisting "Château Ringdale", however; not that I would not have put up with the absurdity of the name, but it was too much to have your house christened after Lord Ringdale, because your wife once had a fancy for him. If you only knew everything, you would think all attempt at reconciliation hopeless. In your happy home you have had no such experiences; and God forbid that you ever should. See, here they are all ready to receive you!'

'Of course! And so will your wife be waiting to receive you,' said Downe. 'Take my word for it she will! And with a dinner prepared for you far better than mine.'

'I hope so,' Barnet replied dubiously.

He moved on to Downe's door, which the solicitor's family had already opened. Downe descended, but being encumbered with his bag and umbrella, his foot slipped, and he fell upon his knees in the gutter.

'O, my dear Charles!' said his wife, running down the steps; and, quite ignoring the presence of Barnet, she seized hold of her husband, pulled him to his feet, and kissed him, exclaiming, 'I hope you are not hurt, darling!' The children crowded round, chiming in piteously, 'Poor papa!'

'He's all right,' said Barnet, perceiving that Downe was only a little muddy, and looking more at the wife than at the husband. Almost at any other time – certainly during his fastidious bachelor years – he would have thought her a too demonstrative woman; but those recent circumstances of his own life to which he had just alluded made Mrs Downe's solicitude so affecting that his eye grew damp as he witnessed it. Bidding the lawyer and his family good-night he left them, and drove slowly into the main street towards his own house.

The heart of Barnet was sufficiently impressionable to be influenced by Downe's parting prophecy that he might not be so unwelcome home as he imagined: the dreary night might, at least on this one occasion, make Downe's forecast true. Hence it was in a suspense that he could hardly have believed possible that he halted at his door. On entering his wife was nowhere to be seen, and he inquired for her. The servant informed him that her mistress had the dressmaker with her, and would be engaged for some time.

'Dressmaker at this time of day!'

'She dined early, sir, and hopes you will excuse her joining you this evening.'

'But she knew I was coming tonight?'

'O yes, sir.'

'Go up and tell her I am come.'

The servant did so; but the mistress of the house merely transmitted her former words.

Barnet said nothing more, and presently sat down to his lonely meal, which was eaten abstractedly, the domestic scene he had lately witnessed still impressing him by its contrast with the situation here. His mind fell back into past years upon a certain pleasing and gentle being whose face would loom out of their shades at such times as these. Barnet turned in his chair, and looked with unfocused eyes in a direction southward from where he sat, as if he saw not the room but a long way beyond. 'I wonder if she lives there still!' he said.

He rose with a sudden rebelliousness, put on his hat and coat, and went out of the house, pursuing his way along the glistening pavement while eight o'clock was striking from St Mary's tower, and the apprentices and shopmen were slamming up the shutters from end to end of the town. In two minutes only those shops which could boast of no attendant save the master or the mistress remained with open eyes. These were ever somewhat less prompt to exclude customers than the others: for their owners' ears the closing hour had scarcely the cheerfulness that it possessed for the hired servants of the rest. Yet the night being dreary the delay was not for long, and their windows, too, blinked together one by one.

During this time Barnet had proceeded with decided step in a direction at right angles to the broad main thoroughfare of the town, by a long street leading due southward. Here, though his family had no more to do with the flax manufacture, his own name occasionally greeted him on gates and warehouses, being used allusively by small rising tradesmen as a recommendation, in such words as 'Smith, from Barnet & Co.' – 'Robinson, late manager at Barnet's.' The sight led him to reflect upon his father's busy life, and he questioned if it had not been far happier than his own.

The houses along the road became fewer, and presently open ground appeared between them on either side, the track on the right hand rising to a higher level till it merged in a knoll. On the summit a row of builders' scaffold-poles probed the indistinct sky like spears, and at their bases could be discerned the lower courses of a building lately begun. Barnet slackened his pace and stood for a few moments without leaving the centre of the road, apparently not much interested in the sight, till suddenly his eye was caught by a post in the fore part of the ground bearing a white board at the top. He went to the rails, vaulted over, and walked in far enough to discern painted upon the board 'Château Ringdale'.

A dismal irony seemed to lie in the words, and its effect was to irritate him. Downe, then, had spoken truly. He stuck his umbrella into the sod, and seized the post with both hands, as if intending to loosen and throw it down. Then, like one bewildered by an opposition which would exist none the less though its manifestations were removed, he allowed his arms to sink to his side.

'Let it be,' he said to himself. 'I have declared there shall be peace – if possible.'

Taking up his umbrella he quietly left the enclosure, and went on his way, still keeping his back to the town. He had advanced with more decision since passing the new building, and soon a hoarse murmur rose upon the gloom; it was the sound of the sea. The road led to the harbour, at a distance of a mile from the town, from which the trade of the district was fed. After seeing the obnoxious nameboard Barnet had forgotten to open his umbrella, and the rain tapped smartly on his hat, and occasionally stroked his face as he went on.

Though the lamps were still continued at the roadside they stood at wider intervals than before, and the pavement had given place to rough gravel. Every time he came to a lamp an increasing shine made itself visible upon his shoulders, till at last they quite glistened with wet. The murmur from the shore grew stronger, but it was still some distance off when he paused before one of the smallest of the detached houses by the wayside, standing in its own garden, the latter being divided from the road by a row of wooden palings. Scrutinizing the spot to ensure that he was not mistaken, he opened the gate and gently knocked at the cottage door.

When he had patiently waited minutes enough to lead any man in ordinary cases to knock again, the door was heard to open, though it was impossible to see by whose hand, there being no light in the passage. Barnet said at random, 'Does Miss Savile live here?'

A youthful voice assured him that she did live there, and by a sudden afterthought asked him to come in. It would soon get a light, it said: but the night being wet, mother had not thought it worth while to trim the passage lamp.

'Don't trouble yourself to get a light for me,' said Barnet hastily; 'it is not necessary at all. Which is Miss Savile's sitting-room?'

The young person, whose white pinafore could just be discerned, signified a door in the side of the passage, and Barnet went forward at the same moment, so that no light should fall upon his face. On entering the room he closed the door behind him, pausing till he heard the retreating footsteps of the child.

He found himself in an apartment which was simply and neatly, though not poorly furnished; everything, from the miniature chiffonnier to the shining little daguerreotype which formed the central ornament of the mantelpiece, being in scrupulous order. The picture was enclosed by a frame of embroidered card-board – evidently the work of feminine hands – and it was the portrait of a thin faced, elderly lieutenant in the navy. From behind the lamp on the table a female form now rose into view, that of a young girl, and a resemblance between her and the portrait was early discoverable. She had been so absorbed in some occupation on the other side of the lamp as to have barely found time to realize her visitor's presence.

They both remained standing for a few seconds without speaking. The face that confronted Barnet had a beautiful outline; the Raffaelesque* oval of its contour was remarkable for an English countenance, and that countenance housed in a remote country-road to an unheard-of harbour. But her features did not do justice to this splendid beginning: Nature had recollected that she was not in Italy; and the young lady's lineaments, though not so inconsistent as to make her plain, would have been accepted rather as pleasing than as correct. The preoccupied expression which, like images on the retina,* remained with her for a moment after the state that caused it had ceased, now changed into a reserved, half-proud, and slightly indignant look, in which the blood diffused itself quickly across her cheek, and additional brightness broke the shade of her rather heavy eyes.

'I know I have no business here,' he said, answering the look. 'But I had a great wish to see you, and inquire how you were.

You can give your hand to me, seeing how often I have held it in past days?'

'I would rather forget than remember all that, Mr Barnet,' she answered, as she coldly complied with the request. 'When I think of the circumstances of our last meeting, I can hardly consider it kind of you to allude to such a thing as our past – or, indeed, to come here at all.'

'There was no harm in it surely? I don't trouble you often, Lucy.'

'I have not had the honour of a visit from you for a very long time, certainly, and I did not expect it now,' she said, with the same stiffness in her air. 'I hope Mrs Barnet is very well?'

'Yes, yes!' he impatiently returned. 'At least I suppose so – though I only speak from inference!'

'But she is your wife, sir,' said the young girl tremulously.

The unwonted tones of a man's voice in that feminine chamber had startled a canary that was roosting in its cage by the window; the bird awoke hastily, and fluttered against the bars. She went and stilled it by laying her face against the cage and murmuring a coaxing sound. It might partly have been done to still herself.

'I didn't come to talk of Mrs Barnet,' he pursued; 'I came to talk of you, of yourself alone; to inquire how you are getting on since your great loss.' And he turned towards the portrait of her father.

'I am getting on fairly well, thank you.'

The force of her utterance was scarcely borne out by her look; but Barnet courteously reproached himself for not having guessed a thing so natural; and to dissipate all embarrassment added, as he bent over the table, 'What were you doing when I came? – painting flowers, and by candlelight?'

'O no,' she said, 'not painting them – only sketching the outlines. I do that at night to save time – I have to get three dozen done by the end of the month.'

Barnet looked as if he regretted it deeply. 'You will wear your poor eyes out,' he said, with more sentiment than he had hitherto shown. 'You ought not to do it. There was a time when I should have said you must not. Well – I almost wish I had never seen light with my own eyes when I think of that!'

'Is this a time or place for recalling such matters?' she asked, with dignity. 'You used to have a gentlemanly respect for me, and for yourself. Don't speak any more as you have spoken, and don't come again. I cannot think that this visit is serious, or was closely considered by you.'

'Considered: well, I came to see you as an old and good friend – not to mince matters, to visit a woman I loved. Don't be angry! I could not help doing it, so many things brought you into my mind. . . . This evening I fell in with an acquaintance, and when I saw how happy he was with his wife and family welcoming him home, though with only one-tenth of my income and chances, and thought what might have been in my case, it fairly broke down my discretion, and off I came here. Now I am here I feel that I am wrong to some extent. But the feeling that I should like to see you, and talk of those we used to know in common, was very strong.'

'Before that can be the case a little more time must pass,' said Miss Savile quietly; 'a time long enough for me to regard with some calmness what at present I remember far too impatiently – though it may be you almost forget it. Indeed you must have forgotten it long before you acted as you did.' Her voice grew stronger and more vivacious as she added: 'But I am doing my best to forget it too, and I know I shall succeed from the progress I have made already!'

She had remained standing till now, when she turned and sat down, facing half away from him.

Barnet watched her moodily. 'Yes, it is only what I deserve,' he said. 'Ambition pricked me on* – no, it was not ambition, it was wrongheadedness! Had I but reflected. . . .' He broke out vehemently: 'But always remember this, Lucy: if you had written to me only one little line after that misunderstanding, I declare I should have come back to you. That ruined me!' He slowly walked as far as the little room would allow him to go, and remained with his eyes on the skirting.

'But, Mr Barnet, how could I write to you? There was no opening for my doing so.'

'Then there ought to have been,' said Barnet, turning. 'That was my fault!'

'Well, I don't know anything about that; but as there had been nothing said by me which required any explanation by letter, I did not send one. Everything was so indefinite, and feeling your position to be so much wealthier than mine, I fancied I might have mistaken your meaning. And when I heard of the other lady – a woman of whose family even you might be proud – I thought how foolish I had been, and said nothing.'

'Then I suppose it was destiny – accident – I don't know what, that separated us, dear Lucy. Anyhow you were the woman I ought to have made my wife – and I let you slip, like the foolish man that I was!'

'O, Mr Barnet,' she said, almost in tears, 'don't revive the subject to me; I am the wrong one to console you – think, sir, – you should not be here – it would be so bad for me if it were known!'

'It would – it would, indeed,' he said hastily. 'I am not right in doing this, and I won't do it again.'

'It is a very common folly of human nature, you know, to think the course you did *not* adopt must have been the best,' she continued with gentle solicitude, as she followed him to the door of the room. 'And you don't know that I should have accepted you, even if you had asked me to be your wife.' At this his eye met hers, and she dropped her gaze. She knew that her voice belied her. There was a silence till she looked up to add, in a voice of soothing playfulness, 'My family was so much poorer than yours, even before I lost my dear father, that – perhaps your companions would have made it unpleasant for us on account of my deficiencies.'

'Your disposition would soon have won them round,' said Barnet.

She archly expostulated: 'Now, never mind my disposition; try to make it up with your wife! Those are my commands to you. And now you are to leave me at once.'

'I will. I must make the best of it all, I suppose,' he replied, more cheerfully than he had as yet spoken. 'But I shall never again meet with such a dear girl as you!' And he suddenly opened the door, and left her alone. When his glance again fell on the lamps that were sparsely ranged along the dreary level road, his eyes were in a state which showed straw-like motes of light radiating from each flame into the surrounding air.

On the other side of the way Barnet observed a man under an umbrella, walking parallel with himself. Presently this man left the footway, and gradually converged on Barnet's course. The latter then saw that it was Charlson, a surgeon of the town, who owed him money. Charlson was a man not without ability; yet he did not prosper. Sundry circumstances stood in his way as a medical practitioner: he was needy; he was not a coddle;* he gossiped with men instead of with women; he had married a stranger instead of one of the town young ladies; and he was given to conversational buffoonery. Moreover, his look was quite erroneous. Those only proper features in the family doctor, the quiet eye, and the thin straight passionless lips which never curl in public either for laughter or for scorn, were not his; he had a full-curved mouth, and a bold black eye that made timid people nervous. His companions were what in old times would have been called boon companions – an expression which, though of irreproachable root, suggests fraternization carried to the point of unscrupulousness. All this was against him in the little town of his adoption.

Charlson had been in difficulties, and to oblige him Barnet had put his name to a bill; and, as he had expected, was called upon to meet it when it fell due. It had been only a matter of fifty pounds, which Barnet could well afford to lose, and he bore no ill-will to the thriftless surgeon on account of it. But Charlson had a little too much brazen indifferentism in his composition to be altogether a desirable acquaintance.

'I hope to be able to make that little bill-business right with you in the course of three weeks, Mr Barnet,' said Charlson with hail-fellow friendliness.

Barnet replied good-naturedly that there was no hurry.

This particular three weeks had moved on in advance of Charlson's present with the precision of a shadow for some considerable time.

'I've had a dream,' Charlson continued. Barnet knew from his tone that the surgeon was going to begin his characteristic nonsense, and did not encourage him. 'I've had a dream,' repeated Charlson, who required no encouragement. 'I dreamed that a gentleman, who has been very kind to me, married a haughty lady in haste, before he had quite forgotten a nice little girl he knew before, and that one wet evening, like the present, as I was walking up the harbour-road, I saw him come out of that dear little girl's present abode.'

Barnet glanced towards the speaker. The rays from a neighbouring lamp struck through the drizzle under Charlson's umbrella, so as just to illumine his face against the shade behind, and show that his eye was turned up under the outer corner of its lid, whence it leered with impish jocoseness as he thrust his tongue into his cheek.

'Come,' said Barnet gravely, 'we'll have no more of that.'

'No, no – of course not,' Charlson hastily answered, seeing that his humour had carried him too far, as it had done many times before. He was profuse in his apologies, but Barnet did not reply. Of one thing he was certain – that scandal was a plant of quick root, and that he was bound to obey Lucy's injunction for Lucy's own sake.

He did so, to the letter; and though, as the crocus followed the snowdrop and the daffodil the crocus in Lucy's garden, the harbour-road was a not unpleasant place to walk in, Barnet's feet never trod its stones, much less approached her door. He avoided a saunter that way as he would have avoided a dangerous dram, and took his airings a long distance northward, among severely square and brown ploughed fields, where no other townsman came. Sometimes he went round by the lower lanes of the borough, where the rope-walks stretched in which his family formerly had share, and looked at the rope-makers walking backwards, overhung by apple-trees and bushes, and intruded on by cows and calves, as if trade had established itself there at considerable inconvenience to Nature.

One morning, when the sun was so warm as to raise a steam from the south-eastern slopes of those flanking hills that looked so lovely above the old roofs, but made every low-chimneyed house in the town as smoky as Tophet,* Barnet glanced from the windows of the town-council room for lack of interest in what was proceeding within. Several members of the corporation were present, but there was not much business doing, and in a few minutes Downe came leisurely across to him, saying that he seldom saw Barnet now.

Barnet owned that he was not often present.

Downe looked at the crimson curtain which hung down beside the panes, reflecting its hot hues into their faces, and then out of the window. At that moment there passed along the street a tall commanding lady, in whom the solicitor recognized Barnet's wife. Barnet had done the same thing, and turned away.

'It will be all right some day,' said Downe, with cheering sympathy.

'You have heard, then, of her last outbreak?'

Downe depressed his cheerfulness to its very reverse in a moment. 'No, I have not heard of anything serious,' he said, with as long a face as one naturally round could be turned into at short notice. 'I only hear vague reports of such things.'

'You may think it will be all right,' said Barnet drily. 'But I have a different opinion. . . . No, Downe, we must look the thing in the face. Not poppy nor mandragora* – however, how are your wife and children?'

Downe said that they were all well, thanks; they were out that morning somewhere; he was just looking to see if they were walking that way. Ah, there they were, just coming down the street; and Downe pointed to the figures of two children with a nursemaid, and a lady walking behind them.

'You will come out and speak to her?' he asked.

'Not this morning. The fact is I don't care to speak to anybody just now.'

'You are too sensitive, Mr Barnet. At school I remember you used to get as red as a rose if anybody uttered a word that hurt your feelings.'

Barnet mused. 'Yes,' he admitted, 'there is a grain of truth in that. It is because of that I often try to make peace at home. Life would be tolerable then at any rate, even if not particularly bright.'

'I have thought more than once of proposing a little plan to you,' said Downe with some hesitation. 'I don't know whether it will meet your views, but take it or leave it, as you choose. In fact, it was my wife who suggested it: that she would be very glad to call on Mrs Barnet and get into her confidence. She seems to think that Mrs Barnet is rather alone in the town, and without advisers. Her impression is that your wife will listen to reason. Emily has a wonderful way of winning the hearts of people of her own sex.'

'And of the other sex too, I think. She is a charming woman, and you were a lucky fellow to find her.'

'Well, perhaps I was,' simpered Downe, trying to wear an aspect of being the last man in the world to feel pride. 'However, she will be likely to find out what ruffles Mrs Barnet. Perhaps it is some misunderstanding, you know – something that she is too proud to ask you to explain, or some little thing in your conduct that irritates her because she does not fully comprehend you. The truth is, Emily would have been more ready to make advances if she had been quite sure of her fitness for Mrs Barnet's society, who has of course been accustomed to London people of good position, which made Emily fearful of intruding.'

Barnet expressed his warmest thanks for the well-intentioned proposition. There was reason in Mrs Downe's fear – that he owned. 'But do let her call,' he said. 'There is no woman in England I would so soon trust on such an errand. I am afraid there will not be any brilliant result; still I shall take it as the kindest and nicest thing if she will try it, and not be frightened at a repulse.'

When Barnet and Downe had parted, the former went to the Town Savings-Bank, of which he was a trustee, and endeavoured to forget his troubles in the contemplation of low sums of money, and figures in a network of red and blue lines. He sat and watched the working people making their deposits, to which at intervals he signed his name. Before he left in the afternoon Downe put his head inside the door.

'Emily has seen Mrs Barnet,' he said, in a low voice. 'She has got Mrs Barnet's promise to take her for a drive down to the shore tomorrow, if it is fine. Good afternoon!'

Barnet shook Downe by the hand without speaking, and Downe went away.

The next day was as fine as the arrangement could possibly require. As the sun passed the meridian and declined westward, the tall shadows from the scaffold-poles of Barnet's rising residence streaked the ground as far as to the middle of the highway. Barnet himself was there inspecting the progress of the works for the first time during several weeks. A building in an old-fashioned town five-and-thirty years ago did not, as in the modern fashion, rise from the sod like a booth at a fair. The foundations and lower courses were put in and allowed to settle for many weeks before the superstructure was built up, and a whole summer of drying was hardly sufficient to do justice to the important issues involved. Barnet stood within a window-niche which had as yet received no frame, and thence looked down a slope into the road. The wheels of a chaise were heard, and then his handsome Xantippe,* in the company of Mrs Downe, drove past on their way to the shore. They were driving slowly; there was a pleasing light in Mrs Downe's face, which seemed faintly to reflect itself upon the countenance of her companion – that *politesse du coeur** which was so natural to her having possibly begun already to work results. But whatever the situation, Barnet resolved not to interfere, or do anything to hazard the promise of the day. He might well afford to trust the issue to another when he could never direct it but to ill himself. His wife's clenched rein-hand in its lemon-coloured glove, her stiff erect figure, clad in velvet and lace, and her boldly-outlined face, passed on, exhibiting their owner as one fixed for ever above the level of her companion – socially by her early breeding, and materially by her higher cushion.

Barnet decided to allow them a proper time to themselves, and then stroll down to the shore and drive them home. After lingering on at the house for another hour he started with this intention. A few hundred yards below 'Château Ringdale' stood the cottage in which the late lieutenant's daughter had her lodging. Barnet had not been so far that way for a long time, and as he approached the forbidden ground a curious warmth passed into him, which led him to perceive that, unless he were careful, he might have to fight the battle with himself about Lucy over again. A tenth of his present excuse would, however, have justified him in travelling by that road today.

He came opposite the dwelling, and turned his eyes for a momentary glance into the little garden that stretched from the palings to the door. Lucy was in the enclosure; she was walking and stooping to gather some flowers, possibly for the purpose of painting them, for she moved about quickly, as if anxious to save time. She did not see him; he might have passed unnoticed; but a sensation which was not in strict unison with his previous sentiments that day led him to pause in his walk and watch her. She went nimbly round and round the beds of anemones, tulips, jonquils, polyanthuses, and other old-fashioned flowers, looking a very charming figure in her half-mourning bonnet, and with an incomplete nosegay in her left hand. Raising herself to pull down a lilac blossom she observed him.

'Mr Barnet!' she said, innocently smiling. 'Why, I have been thinking of you many times since Mrs Barnet went by in the pony-carriage, and now here you are!'

'Yes, Lucy,' he said.

Then she seemed to recall particulars of their last meeting, and he believed that she flushed, though it might have been only the fancy of his own super-sensitiveness.

'I am going to the harbour,' he added.

'Are you?' Lucy remarked simply. 'A great many people begin to go there now the summer is drawing on.'

Her face had come more into his view as she spoke, and he noticed how much thinner and paler it was than when he had seen it last. 'Lucy, how weary you look! tell me, can I help you?' he was going to cry out. – 'If I do,' he thought, 'it will be the ruin of us both!' He merely said that the afternoon was fine, and went on his way.

As he went a sudden blast of air came over the hill as if in contradiction to his words, and spoilt the previous quiet of the scene. The wind had already shifted violently, and now smelt of the sea.

The harbour-road soon began to justify its name. A gap appeared in the rampart of hills which shut out the sea, and on the left of the opening rose a vertical cliff, coloured a burning orange by the sunlight, the companion cliff on the right being livid in shade. Between these cliffs, like the Libyan bay which sheltered the shipwrecked Trojans,* was a little haven, seemingly a beginning made by Nature herself of a perfect harbour, which appealed to the passer-by as only requiring a little human industry to finish it and make it famous, the ground on each side as far back as the daisied slopes that bounded the interior valley being a mere layer of blown sand. But the Port-Bredy burgesses a mile inland had, in the course of ten centuries, responded many times to that mute appeal, with the result that the tides had invariably choked up their works with sand and shingle as soon as completed. There were but few houses here: a rough pier, a few boats, some stores, an inn, a residence or two, a ketch unloading in the harbour, were the chief features of the settlement. On the open ground by the shore stood his wife's pony-carriage, empty, the boy in attendance holding the horse.

When Barnet drew nearer, he saw an indigo-coloured spot moving swiftly along beneath the radiant base of the eastern cliff, which proved to be a man in a jersey, running with all his might. He held up his hand to Barnet, as it seemed, and they approached each other. The man was local, but a stranger to him.

'What is it, my man?' said Barnet.

'A terrible calamity!' the boatman hastily explained. Two

ladies had been capsized in a boat – they were Mrs Downe and Mrs Barnet of the old town; they had driven down there that afternoon – they had alighted, and it was so fine, that, after walking about a little while, they had been tempted to go out for a short sail round the cliff. Just as they were putting in to the shore, the wind shifted with a sudden gust, the boat listed over, and it was thought they were both drowned. How it could have happened was beyond his mind to fathom, for John Green knew how to sail a boat as well as any man there.

'Which is the way to the place?' said Barnet.

It was just round the cliff.

'Run to the carriage and tell the boy to bring it to the place as soon as you can. Then go to the Harbour Inn and tell them to ride to town for a doctor. Have they been got out of the water?'

'One lady has.'

'Which?'

'Mrs Barnet. Mrs Downe, it is feared, has fleeted out to sea.'

Barnet ran on to that part of the shore which the cliff had hitherto obscured from his view, and there discerned, a long way ahead, a group of fishermen standing. As soon as he came up one or two recognized him, and, not liking to meet his eye, turned aside with misgiving. He went amidst them and saw a small sailing-boat lying draggled at the water's edge; and, on the sloping shingle beside it, a soaked and sandy woman's form in the velvet dress and yellow gloves of his wife.

All had been done that could be done. Mrs Barnet was in her own house under medical hands, but the result was still uncertain. Barnet had acted as if devotion to his wife were the dominant passion of his existence. There had been much to decide – whether to attempt restoration of the apparently lifeless body as it lay on the shore – whether to carry her to the Harbour Inn – whether to drive with her at once to his own house. The first course, with no skilled help or appliances near at hand, had seemed hopeless. The second course would have occupied nearly as much time as a drive to the town, owing to the intervening ridges of shingle, and the necessity of crossing the harbour by boat to get to the house, added to which much time must have elapsed before a doctor could have arrived down there. By bringing her home in the carriage some precious moments had slipped by; but she had been laid in her own bed in seven minutes, a doctor called to her side, and every possible restorative brought to bear upon her.

At what a tearing pace he had driven up that road, through the yellow evening sunlight, the shadows flapping irksomely into his eyes as each wayside object rushed past between him and the west! Tired workmen with their baskets at their backs had turned on their homeward journey to wonder at his speed. Halfway between the shore and Port-Bredy town he had met Charlson, who had been the first surgeon to hear of the accident. He was accompanied by his assistant in a gig. Barnet had sent on the latter to the coast in case that Downe's poor wife should by that time have been reclaimed from the waves, and had brought Charlson back with him to the house.

Barnet's presence was not needed here, and he felt it to be his next duty to set off at once and find Downe, that no other than himself might break the news to him.

He was quite sure that no chance had been lost for Mrs Downe by his leaving the shore. By the time that Mrs Barnet had been laid in the carriage a much larger group had assembled to lend assistance in finding her friend, rendering his own help superfluous. But the duty of breaking the news was made doubly painful by the circumstance that the catastrophe which had befallen Mrs Downe was solely the result of her own and her husband's loving-kindness towards himself.

He found Downe in his office. When the solicitor comprehended the intelligence he turned pale, stood up, and remained for a moment perfectly still, as if bereft of his faculties; then his shoulders heaved, he pulled out his handkerchief and began to cry like a child. His sobs might have been heard in the next room. He seemed to have no idea of going to the shore, or of doing anything; but when Barnet took him gently by the hand and proposed to start at once, he quietly acquiesced, neither uttering any further word nor making any effort to repress his tears.

Barnet accompanied him to the shore, where, finding that no trace had as yet been seen of Mrs Downe, and that his stay would be of no avail, he left Downe with his friends and the young doctor, and once more hastened back to his own house.

At the door he met Charlson. 'Well!' Barnet said.

'I have just come down,' said the doctor; 'we have done

everything, but without result. I sympathize with you in your bereavement.'

Barnet did not much appreciate Charlson's sympathy, which sounded to his ears as something of a mockery from the lips of a man who knew what Charlson knew about his domestic relations. Indeed there seemed an odd spark in Charlson's full black eye as he said the words; but that might have been imaginary.

'And, Mr Barnet,' Charlson resumed, 'that little matter between us – I hope to settle it finally in three weeks at least.'

'Never mind that now,' said Barnet abruptly. He directed the surgeon to go to the harbour in case his services might even now be necessary there: and himself entered the house.

The servants were coming from his wife's chamber, looking helplessly at each other and at him. He passed them by and entered the room, where he stood regarding the shape on the bed for a few minutes, after which he walked into his own dressing-room adjoining, and there paced up and down. In a minute or two he noticed what a strange and total silence had come over the upper part of the house; his own movements, muffled as they were by the carpet, seemed noisy, and his thoughts to disturb the air like articulate utterances. His eye glanced through the window. Far down the road to the harbour a roof detained his gaze: out of it rose a red chimney, and out of the red chimney a curl of smoke, as from a fire newly kindled. He had often seen such a sight before. In that house lived Lucy Savile; and the smoke was from the fire which was regularly lighted at this time to make her tea.

After that he went back to the bedroom, and stood there some time regarding his wife's silent form. She was a woman some years older than himself, but had not by any means overpassed the maturity of good looks and vigour. Her passionate features, well-defined, firm, and statuesque in life, were doubly so now: her mouth and brow, beneath her purplish black hair, showed only too clearly that the turbulency of character which had made a bear-garden* of his house had been no temporary phase of her existence. While he reflected, he suddenly said to himself, I wonder if all has been done?

The thought was led up to by his having fancied that his wife's features lacked in its completeness the expression which he had been accustomed to associate with the faces of those whose spirits have fled for ever. The effacement of life was not so marked but that, entering uninformed, he might have supposed her sleeping. Her complexion was that seen in the numerous faded portraits by Sir Joshua Reynolds;* it was pallid in comparison with life, but there was visible on a close inspection the remnant of what had once been a flush; the keeping between the cheeks and the hollows of the face being thus preserved, although positive colour was gone. Long orange rays of evening sun stole in through chinks in the blind, striking on the large mirror, and being thence reflected upon the crimson hangings and woodwork of the heavy bedstead, so that the general tone of light was remarkably warm; and it was probable that something might be due to this circumstance. Still the fact impressed him as strange. Charlson had been gone more than a quarter of an hour: could it be possible that he had left too soon, and that his attempts to restore her had operated so sluggishly as only now to have made themselves felt? Barnet laid his hand upon her chest, and fancied that ever and anon a faint flutter of palpitation, gentle as that of a butterfly's wing, disturbed the stillness there – ceasing for a time, then struggling to go on, then breaking down in weakness and ceasing again.

Barnet's mother had been an active practitioner of the healing art among her poorer neighbours, and her inspirations had all been derived from an octavo volume of Domestic Medicine,* which at this moment was lying, as it had lain for many years, on a shelf in Barnet's dressing-room. He hastily fetched it, and there read under the head 'Drowning': –

> Exertions for the recovery of any person who has not been immersed for a longer period than half-an-hour should be continued for at least four hours, as there have been many cases in which returning life has made itself visible even after a longer interval.
>
> Should, however, a weak action of any of the organs show itself when the case seems almost hopeless, our efforts must be redoubled; the feeble spark in this case requires to be solicited; it will certainly disappear under a relaxation of labour.

Barnet looked at his watch; it was now barely two hours and a half from the time when he had first heard of the accident. He threw aside the book and turned quickly to reach a stimulant which had previously been used. Pulling up the blind for more light, his eye glanced out of the window. There he saw that red chimney still smoking cheerily, and that roof, and through the roof that somebody. His mechanical movements stopped, his hand remained on the blindcord, and he seemed to become breathless, as if he had suddenly found himself treading a high rope.

While he stood a sparrow lighted on the window-sill, saw him, and flew away. Next a man and a dog walked over one of the green hills which bulged above the roofs of the town. But Barnet took no notice.

We may wonder what were the exact images that passed through his mind during those minutes of gazing upon Lucy Savile's house, the sparrow, the man and the dog, and Lucy Savile's house again. There are honest men who will not admit to their thoughts, even as idle hypotheses, views of the future that assume as done a deed which they would recoil from doing; and there are other honest men for whom morality ends at the surface of their own heads, who will deliberate what the first will not so much as suppose. Barnet had a wife whose presence distracted his home; she now lay as in death; by merely doing nothing – by letting the intelligence which had gone forth to the world lie undisturbed – he would effect such a deliverance for himself as he had never hoped for, and open up an opportunity of which till now he had never dreamed. Whether the conjuncture had arisen through any unscrupulous, ill-considered impulse of Charlson to help out of a strait the friend who was so kind as never to press him for what was due could not be told; there was nothing to prove it; and it was a question which could never be asked. The triangular situation – himself – his wife – Lucy Savile – was the one clear thing.

From Barnet's actions we may infer that he *supposed* such and such a result, for a moment, but did not deliberate. He withdrew his hazel eyes from the scene without, calmly turned, rang the bell for assistance, and vigorously exerted himself to learn if life still lingered in that motionless frame. In a short time another surgeon was in attendance; and then Barnet's surmise proved to be true. The slow life timidly heaved again; but much care and patience were needed to catch and retain it, and a considerable period elapsed before it could be said with certainty that Mrs Barnet lived. When this was the case, and there was no further room for doubt, Barnet left the chamber. The blue evening smoke from Lucy's chimney had died down to an imperceptible stream, and as he walked about downstairs he murmured to himself, 'My wife was dead, and she is alive again.'*

It was not so with Downe. After three hours' immersion his wife's body had been recovered, life, of course, being quite extinct. Barnet on descending, went straight to his friend's house, and there learned the result. Downe was helpless in his wild grief, occasionally even hysterical. Barnet said little, but finding that some guiding hand was necessary in the sorrow-stricken household, took upon him to supervise and manage till Downe should be in a state of mind to do so for himself.

One September evening, four months later, when Mrs Barnet was in perfect health, and Mrs Downe but a weakening memory, an errand-boy paused to rest himself in front of Mr Barnet's old house, depositing his basket on one of the window-sills. The street was not yet lighted, but there were lights in the house, and at intervals a flitting shadow fell upon the blind at his elbow. Words also were audible from the same apartment, and they seemed to be those of persons in violent altercation. But the boy could not gather their purport, and he went on his way.

Ten minutes afterwards the door of Barnet's house opened, and a tall closely-veiled lady in a travelling-dress came out and descended the freestone steps. The servant stood in the doorway watching her as she went with a measured tread down the street. When she had been out of sight for some minutes Barnet appeared at the door from within.

'Did your mistress leave word where she was going?' he asked.

'No, sir.'

'Is the carriage ordered to meet her anywhere?'

'No, sir.'

'Did she take a latch-key?'

'No, sir.'

Barnet went in again, sat down in his chair, and leaned back. Then in solitude and silence he brooded over the bitter emotions that filled his heart. It was for this that he had gratuitously restored her to life, and made his union with another impossible! The evening drew on, and nobody came to disturb him. At bedtime he told the servants to retire, that he would sit up for Mrs Barnet himself; and when they were gone he leaned his head upon his hand and mused for hours.

The clock struck one, two; still his wife came not, and, with impatience added to depression, he went from room to room till another weary hour had passed. This was not altogether a new experience for Barnet; but she had never before so prolonged her absence. At last he sat down again and fell asleep.

He awoke at six o'clock to find that she had not returned. In searching about the rooms he discovered that she had taken a case of jewels which had been hers before her marriage. At eight a note was brought him; it was from his wife, in which she stated that she had gone by the coach to the house of a distant relative near London, and expressed a wish that certain boxes, articles of clothing, and so on, might be sent to her forthwith. The note was brought to him by a waiter at the Black-Bull Hotel, and had been written by Mrs Barnet immediately before she took her place in the stage.

By the evening this order was carried out, and Barnet, with a sense of relief, walked out into the town. A fair had been held during the day, and the large clear moon which rose over the most prominent hill flung its light upon the booths and standings that still remained in the street, mixing its rays curiously with those from the flaring naphtha lamps. The town was full of country-people who had come in to enjoy themselves, and on this account Barnet strolled through the streets unobserved. With a certain recklessness he made for the harbour-road, and presently found himself by the shore, where he walked on till he came to the spot near which his friend the kindly Mrs Downe had lost her life, and his own wife's life had been preserved. A tremulous pathway of bright moonshine now stretched over the water which had engulfed them, and not a living soul was near.

Here he ruminated on their characters, and next on the young girl in whom he now took a more sensitive interest than at the time when he had been free to marry her. Nothing, so far as he was aware, had ever appeared in his own conduct to show that such an interest existed. He had made it a point of the utmost strictness to hinder that feeling from influencing in the faintest degree his attitude towards his wife; and this was made all the more easy for him by the small demand Mrs Barnet made upon his attentions, for which she ever evinced the greatest contempt; thus unwittingly giving him the satisfaction of knowing that their severance owed nothing to jealousy, or, indeed, to any personal behaviour of his at all. Her concern was not with him or his feelings, as she frequently told him; but that she had, in a moment of weakness, thrown herself away upon a common burgher when she might have aimed at, and possibly brought down, a peer of the realm. Her frequent depreciation of Barnet in these terms had at times been so intense that he was sorely tempted to retaliate on her egotism by owning that he loved at the same low level on which he lived; but prudence had prevailed, for which he was now thankful.

Something seemed to sound upon the shingle behind him over and above the raking of the wave. He looked round, and a slight girlish shape appeared quite close to him. He could not see her face because it was in the direction of the moon.

'Mr Barnet?' the rambler said, in timid surprise. The voice was the voice of Lucy Savile.

'Yes,' said Barnet. 'How can I repay you for this pleasure?'

'I only came because the night was so clear. I am now on my way home.'

'I am glad we have met. I want to know if you will let me do something for you, to give me an occupation, as an idle man? I am sure I ought to help you, for I know you are almost without friends.'

She hesitated. 'Why should you tell me that?' she said.

'In the hope that you will be frank with me.'

'I am not altogether without friends here. But I am going to make a little change in my life – to go out as a teacher of freehand drawing and practical perspective, of course I mean on a comparatively humble scale, because I have not been specially educated for that profession. But I am sure I shall like it much.'

'You have an opening?'

'I have not exactly got it, but I have advertised for one.'

'Lucy, you must let me help you!'

'Not at all.'

'You need not think it would compromise you, or that I am indifferent to delicacy. I bear in mind how we stand. It is very unlikely that you will succeed as teacher of the class you mention, so let me do something of a different kind for you. Say what you would like, and it shall be done.'

'No; if I can't be a drawing-mistress or governess, or something of that sort, I shall go to India and join my brother.'

'I wish I could go abroad, anywhere, everywhere with you, Lucy, and leave this place and its associations for ever!'

She played with the end of her bonnet-string, and hastily turned aside. 'Don't ever touch upon that kind of topic again,' she said, with a quick severity not free from anger. 'It simply makes it impossible for me to see you, much less receive any guidance from you. No, thank you, Mr Barnet; you can do nothing for me at present; and as I suppose my uncertainty will end in my leaving for India, I fear you never will. If ever I think you *can* do anything, I will take the trouble to ask you. Till then, good-bye.'

The tone of her latter words was equivocal, and while he remained in doubt whether a gentle irony was or was not inwrought with their sound, she swept lightly round and left him alone. He saw her form get smaller and smaller along the damp belt of sea-sand between ebb and flood; and when she had vanished round the cliff into the harbour-road he himself followed in the same direction.

That her hopes from an advertisement should be the single thread which held Lucy Savile in England was too much for Barnet. On reaching the town he went straight to the residence of Downe, now a widower with four children. The young motherless brood had been sent to bed about a quarter of an hour earlier, and when Barnet entered he found Downe sitting alone. It was the same room as that from which the family had been looking out for Downe at the beginning of the year, when Downe had slipped into the gutter and his wife had been so enviably tender towards him. The old neatness had gone from the house; articles lay in places which could show no reason for their presence, as if momentarily deposited there some months ago, and forgotten ever since; there were no flowers; things were jumbled together on the furniture which should have been in cupboards; and the place in general had that stagnant, unrenovated air which usually pervades the maimed home of the widower.

Downe soon renewed his customary full-worded lament over his wife, and even when he had worked himself up to tears, went on volubly, as if a listener were a luxury to be enjoyed whenever he could be caught.

'She was a treasure beyond compare, Mr Barnet! I shall never see such another. Nobody now to nurse me – nobody to console me in those daily troubles, you know, Barnet, which makes consolation so necessary to a nature like mine. It would be unbecoming to repine, for her spirit's home was elsewhere – the tender light in her eyes always showed it; but it is a long dreary time that I have before me, and nobody else can ever fill the void left in my heart by her loss – nobody – nobody!' And Downe wiped his eyes again.

'She was a good woman in the highest sense,' gravely answered Barnet, who, though Downe's words drew genuine compassion from his heart, could not help feeling that a tender reticence would have been a finer tribute to Mrs Downe's really sterling virtues than such a second-class lament as this.

'I have something to show you,' Downe resumed, producing from a drawer a sheet of paper on which was an elaborate design for a canopied tomb. 'This has been sent me by the architect, but it is not exactly what I want.'

'You have got Jones to do it, I see, the man who is carrying out my house,' said Barnet, as he glanced at the signature to the drawing.

'Yes, but it is not quite what I want. I want something more striking – more like a tomb I have seen in St Paul's Cathedral. Nothing less will do justice to my feelings, and how far short of them that will fall!'

Barnet privately thought the design a sufficiently imposing one as it stood, even extravagantly ornate; but, feeling that he had no right to criticize, he said gently, 'Downe, should you not live more in your children's lives at the present time, and soften the sharpness of regret for your own past by thinking of their future?'

'Yes, yes; but what can I do more?' asked Downe, wrinkling his forehead hopelessly.

It was with anxious slowness that Barnet produced his reply – the secret object of his visit tonight. 'Did you not say one day that you ought by rights to get a governess for the children?'

Downe admitted that he had said so, but that he could not see his way to it. 'The kind of woman I should like to have,' he said, 'would be rather beyond my means. No; I think I shall send them to school in the town when they are old enough to go out alone.'

'Now, I know of something better than that. The late Lieutenant Savile's daughter, Lucy, wants to do something for herself in the way of teaching. She would be inexpensive, and would answer your purpose as well as anybody for six or twelve months. She would probably come daily if you were to ask her, and so your housekeeping arrangements would not be much affected.'

'I thought she had gone away,' said the solicitor, musing. 'Where does she live?'

Barnet told him, and added that, if Downe should think of her as suitable, he would do well to call as soon as possible, or she might be on the wing. 'If you do see her,' he said, 'it would be advisable not to mention my name. She is rather stiff in her ideas of me, and it might prejudice her against a course if she knew that I recommended it.'

Downe promised to give the subject his consideration, and nothing more was said about it just then. But when Barnet rose to go, which was not till nearly bedtime, he reminded Downe of the suggestion and went up the street to his own solitary home with a sense of satisfaction at his promising diplomacy in a charitable cause.

The walls of his new house were carried up nearly to their full height. By a curious though not infrequent reaction, Barnet's feelings about that unnecessary structure had undergone a change; he took considerable interest in its progress as a long-neglected thing, his wife before her departure having grown quite weary of it as a hobby. Moreover, it was an excellent distraction for a man in the unhappy position of having to live in a provincial town with nothing to do. He was probably the first of his line who had ever passed a day without toil, and perhaps something like an inherited instinct disqualifies such men for a life of pleasant inaction, such as lies in the power of those whose leisure is not a personal accident, but a vast historical accretion which has become part of their natures.

Thus Barnet got into a way of spending many of his leisure hours on the site of the new building, and he might have been seen on most days at this time trying the temper of the mortar by punching the joints with his stick, looking at the grain of a floor-board, and meditating where it grew, or picturing under what circumstances the last fire would be kindled in the at present sootless chimneys. One day when thus occupied he saw three children pass by in the company of a fair young woman, whose sudden appearance caused him to flush perceptibly.

'Ah, she is there,' he thought. 'That's a blessed thing.'

Casting an interested glance over the rising building and the busy workmen, Lucy Savile and the little Downes passed by; and after that time it became a regular though almost unconscious custom of Barnet to stand in the half-completed house and look from the ungarnished windows at the governess as she tripped towards the sea-shore with her young charges, which she was in the habit of doing on most fine afternoons. It was on one of these occasions, when he had been loitering on the first-floor landing, near the hole left for the staircase, not yet erected, that there appeared above the edge of the floor a little hat, followed by a little head.

Barnet withdrew through a doorway, and the child came to the top of the ladder, stepping on to the floor and crying to her sisters and Miss Savile to follow. Another head rose above the floor, and another, and then Lucy herself came into view. The troop ran hither and thither through the empty, shaving-strewn rooms, and Barnet came forward.

Lucy uttered a small exclamation: she was very sorry that she had intruded; she had not the least idea that Mr Barnet was there: the children had come up, and she had followed.

Barnet replied that he was only too glad to see them there. 'And now, let me show you the rooms,' he said.

She passively assented, and he took her round. There was not much to show in such a bare skeleton of a house, but he made the most of it, and explained the different ornamental fittings that were soon to be fixed here and there. Lucy made but few remarks in reply, though she seemed pleased with her visit, and stole away down the ladder, followed by her companions.

After this the new residence became yet more of a hobby for Barnet. Downe's children did not forget their first visit, and when the windows were glazed, and the handsome staircase spread its broad low steps into the hall, they came again, prancing in unwearied succession through every room from ground-floor to attics, while Lucy stood waiting for them at the door. Barnet, who rarely missed a day in coming to inspect progress, stepped out from the drawing-room.

'I could not keep them out,' she said, with an apologetic blush. 'I tried to do so very much: but they are rather wilful, and we are directed to walk this way for the sea air.'

'Do let them make the house their regular playground, and you yours,' said Barnet. 'There is no better place for children to romp and take their exercise in than an empty house, particularly in muddy or damp weather such as we shall get a good deal of now; and this place will not be furnished for a long long time – perhaps never. I am not at all decided about it.'

'O, but it must!' replied Lucy, looking round at the hall. 'The rooms are excellent, twice as high as ours; and the views from the windows are so lovely.'

'I daresay, I daresay,' he said absently.

'Will all the furniture be new?' she asked.

'All the furniture be new – that's a thing I have not thought of. In fact I only come here and look on. My father's house would have been large enough for me, but another person had a voice in the matter, and it was settled that we should build. However, the place grows upon me; its recent associations are cheerful, and I am getting to like it fast.'

A certain uneasiness in Lucy's manner showed that the conversation was taking too personal a turn for her. 'Still, as modern tastes develop, people require more room to gratify them in,' she said, withdrawing to call the children; and serenely bidding him good afternoon she went on her way.

Barnet's life at this period was singularly lonely, and yet he was happier than he could have expected. His wife's estrangement and absence, which promised to be permanent, left him free as a boy in his movements, and the solitary walks that he took gave him ample opportunity for chastened reflection on what might have been his lot if he had only shown wisdom enough to claim Lucy Savile when there was no bar between their lives, and she was to be had for the asking. He would occasionally call at the house of his friend Downe; but there was scarcely enough in common between their two natures to make them more than friends of that excellent sort whose personal knowledge of each other's history and character is always in excess of intimacy, whereby they are not so likely to be severed by a clash of sentiment as in cases where intimacy springs up in excess of knowledge. Lucy was never visible at these times, being either engaged in the school-room, or in taking an airing out of doors; but, knowing that she was now comfortable, and had given up the, to him, depressing idea of going off to the other side of the globe, he was quite content.

The new house had so far progressed that the gardeners were beginning to grass down the front. During an afternoon which he was passing in marking the curve for the carriage-drive, he beheld her coming in boldly towards him from the road. Hitherto Barnet had only caught her on the premises by stealth; and this advance seemed to show that at last her reserve had broken down.

A smile gained strength upon her face as she approached, and it was quite radiant when she came up, and said, without a trace of embarrassment, 'I find I owe you a hundred thanks – and it comes to me quite as a surprise! It was through your kindness that I was engaged by Mr Downe. Believe me, Mr Barnet, I did not know it until yesterday, or I should have thanked you long and long ago!'

'I had offended you – just a trifle – at the time, I think?' said Barnet, smiling, 'and it was best that you should not know.'

'Yes, yes,' she returned hastily. 'Don't allude to that; it is past and over, and we will let it be. The house is finished almost, is it not? How beautiful it will look when the evergreens are grown! Do you call the style Palladian,* Mr Barnet?'

'I – really don't quite know what it is. Yes, it must be Palladian, certainly. But I'll ask Jones, the architect; for, to tell the truth, I had not thought much about the style: I had nothing to do with choosing it, I am sorry to say.'

She would not let him harp on this gloomy refrain, and talked on bright matters till she said, producing a small roll of paper which he had noticed in her hand all the while, 'Mr Downe wished me to bring you this revised drawing of the late Mrs Downe's tomb, while the architect has just sent him. He would like you to look it over.'

The children came up with their hoops, and she went off with them down the harbour-road as usual. Barnet had been glad to get those words of thanks; he had been thinking for many months that he would like her to know of his share in finding her a home such as it was; and what he could not do for himself, Downe had now kindly done for him. He returned to his desolate house with a lighter tread; though in reason he hardly knew why his tread should be light.

On examining the drawing, Barnet found that, instead of the vast altar-tomb and canopy Downe had determined on at their last meeting, it was to be a more modest memorial even than had been suggested by the architect; a coped* tomb of good solid construction, with no useless elaboration at all. Barnet was truly glad to see that Downe had come to reason of his own accord; and he returned the drawing with a note of approval.

He followed up the house-work as before, and as he walked up and down the rooms, occasionally gazing from the windows over the bulging green hills and the quiet harbour that lay between them, he murmured words and fragments of words, which, if listened to, would have revealed all the secrets of his existence. Whatever his reason in going there, Lucy did not call again: the walk to the shore seemed to be abandoned: he must have thought it as well for both that it should be so, for he did not go anywhere out of his accustomed ways to endeavour to discover her.

The winter and the spring had passed, and the house was complete. It was a fine morning in the early part of June, and Barnet, though not in the habit of rising early, had taken a long walk before breakfast; returning by way of the new building. A sufficiently exciting cause of his restlessness today might have been the intelligence which had reached him the night before, that Lucy Savile was going to India after all, and notwithstanding the representations of her friends that such a journey was unadvisable in many ways for an unpractised girl, unless some more definite advantage lay at the end of it than she could show to be the case. Barnet's walk up the slope to the building betrayed that he was in a dissatisfied mood. He hardly saw that the dewy time of day lent an unusual freshness to the bushes and trees which had so recently put on their summer habit of heavy leafage, and made his newly-laid lawn look as well established as an old manorial meadow. The house had been so adroitly placed between six tall elms which were growing on the site beforehand, that they seemed like real ancestral trees; and the rooks, young and old, cawed melodiously to their visitor.

The door was not locked, and he entered. No workmen appeared to be present, and he walked from sunny window to sunny window of the empty rooms, with a sense of seclusion which might have been very pleasant but for the antecedent knowledge that his almost paternal care of Lucy Savile was to be thrown away by her wilfulness. Footsteps echoed through an adjoining room; and bending his eyes in that direction, he perceived Mr Jones, the architect. He had come to look over the building before giving the contractor his final certificate. They walked over the house together. Everything was finished except the papering: there were the latest improvements of the period in bell-hanging, ventilating, smoke-jacks,* fire-grates, and French windows. The business was soon ended, and Jones, having directed Barnet's attention to a book of wall-paper patterns which lay on a bench for his choice, was leaving to keep another engagement, when Barnet said, 'Is the tomb finished yet for Mrs Downe?'

'Well – yes: it is at last,' said the architect, coming back and speaking as if he were in a mood to make a confidence. 'I have had no end of trouble in the matter, and, to tell the truth, I am heartily glad it is over.'

Barnet expressed his surprise. 'I thought poor Downe had given up those extravagant notions of his? Then he has gone back to the altar and canopy after all? Well, he is to be excused, poor fellow!'

'O no – he has not at all gone back to them – quite the reverse,' Jones hastened to say. 'He has so reduced design after design, that the whole thing has been nothing but waste labour for me; till in the end it has become a common headstone, which a mason put up in half a day.'

'A common headstone?' said Barnet.

'Yes. I held out for some time for the addition of a footstone at least. But he said, "O no – he couldn't afford it." '

'Ah, well – his family is growing up, poor fellow, and his expenses are getting serious.'

'Yes, exactly,' said Jones, as if the subject were none of his. And again directing Barnet's attention to the wall-papers, the bustling architect left him to keep some other engagement.

'A common headstone,' murmured Barnet, left again to himself. He mused a minute or two, and next began looking over and selecting from the patterns; but had not long been engaged in the work when he heard another footstep on the gravel without, and somebody enter the open porch.

Barnet went to the door – it was his manservant in search of him.

'I have been trying for some time to find you, sir,' he said. 'This letter has come by the post, and it is marked immediate. And there's this one from Mr Downe, who called just now wanting to see you.' He searched his pocket for the second.

Barnet took the first letter – it had a black border, and bore the London postmark. It was not in his wife's handwriting, or in that of any person he knew; but conjecture soon ceased as he read the page, wherein he was briefly informed that Mrs Barnet had died suddenly on the previous day, at the furnished villa she had occupied near London.

Barnet looked vaguely round the empty hall, at the blank walls, out of the doorway. Drawing a long palpitating breath, and with eyes downcast, he turned and climbed the stairs slowly, like a man who doubted their stability. The fact of his wife having, as it were, died once already, and lived on again, had entirely dislodged the possibility of her actual death from his conjecture. He went to the landing, leant over the balusters,* and after a reverie, of whose duration he had but the faintest notion, turned to the window and stretched his gaze to the cottage further down the road, which was visible from his landing, and from which Lucy still walked to the solicitor's house by a cross path. The faint words that came from his moving lips were simply, 'At last!'

Then, almost involuntarily, Barnet fell down on his knees and murmured some incoherent words of thanksgiving. Surely his virtue in restoring his wife to life had been rewarded! But, as if the impulse struck uneasily on his conscience, he quickly rose, brushed the dust from his trousers, and set himself to think of his next movements. He could not start for London for some hours; and as he had no preparations to make that could not be made in half-an-hour, he mechanically descended and resumed his occupation of turning over the wall-papers. They had all got brighter for him, those papers. It was all changed – who would sit in the rooms that they were to line? He went on to muse upon Lucy's conduct in so frequently coming to the house with the children; her occasional blush in speaking to him; her evident interest in him. What woman can in the long run avoid being interested in a man whom she knows to be devoted to her? If human solicitation could ever effect anything, there should be no going to India for Lucy now. All the papers previously chosen seemed wrong in their shades, and he began from the beginning to choose again.

While entering on the task he heard a forced 'Ahem!' from without the porch, evidently uttered to attract his attention, and footsteps again advancing to the door. His man, whom he had quite forgotten in his mental turmoil, was still waiting there.

'I beg your pardon, sir,' the man said from round the doorway; 'but here's the note from Mr Downe that you didn't take. He called just after you went out, and as he couldn't wait, he wrote this on your study-table.'

He handed in the letter – no black-bordered one now, but a practical-looking note in the well-known writing of the solicitor.

Dear Barnet – it ran – Perhaps you will be prepared for the information I am about to give – that Lucy Savile and myself are going to be married this morning. I have hitherto said nothing as to my intention to any of my friends, for reasons which I am sure you will fully appreciate. The crisis has been brought about by her expressing her intention to join her brother in India. I then discovered that I could not do without her.

It is to be quite a private wedding; but it is my particular wish that you come down here quietly at ten, and go to church with us; it will add greatly to the pleasure I shall experience in the ceremony, and, I believe, to Lucy's also. I have called on you very early to make the request, in the belief that I should find you at home; but you are beforehand with me in your early rising. – Yours sincerely,

C. DOWNE.

'Need I wait, sir?' said the servant after a dead silence.

'That will do, William. No answer,' said Barnet calmly.

When the man had gone Barnet re-read the letter. Turning eventually to the wall-papers, which he had been at such pains to select, he deliberately tore them into halves and quarters, and threw them into the empty fireplace. Then he went out of the house, locked the door, and stood in the front awhile. Instead of returning into the town he went down the harbour-road and thoughtfully lingered about by the sea, near the spot where the body of Downe's late wife had been found and brought ashore.

Barnet was a man with a rich capacity for misery, and there is no doubt that he exercised it to its fullest extent now. The events that had, as it were, dashed themselves together into one half-hour of this day showed that curious refinement of cruelty in their arrangement which often proceeds from the bosom of the whimsical god at other times known as blind Circumstance.* That his few minutes of hope, between the reading of the first and second letters, had carried him to extraordinary heights of rapture was proved by the immensity of his suffering now. The sun blazing into his face would have shown a close watcher that a horizontal line, which had never been seen before, but which was never to be gone thereafter, was somehow gradually forming itself in the smooth of his forehead. His eyes, of a light hazel, had a curious look which can only be described by the word bruised; the sorrow that looked from them being largely mixed with the surprise of a man taken unawares.

The secondary particulars of his present position, too, were odd enough, though for some time they appeared to engage little of his attention. Not a soul in the town knew, as yet, of his wife's death; and he almost owed Downe the kindness of not publishing it till the day was over: the conjuncture, taken with that which had accompanied the death of Mrs Downe, being so singular as to be quite sufficient to darken the pleasure of the impressionable solicitor to a cruel extent, if made known to him. But as Barnet could not set out on his journey to London, where his wife lay, for some hours (there being at this date no railway within a distance of many miles), no great reason existed why he should leave the town.

Impulse in all its forms characterized Barnet, and when he heard the distant clock strike the hour of ten his feet began to carry him up the harbour-road with the manner of a man who must do something to bring himself to life. He passed Lucy Savile's old house, his own now one, and came in view of the church. Now he gave a perceptible start, and his mechanical condition went away. Before the church-gate were a couple of carriages, and Barnet then could perceive that the marriage between Downe and Lucy was at that moment being solemnized within. A feeling of sudden, proud self-confidence, an indocile wish to walk unmoved in spite of grim environments, plainly possessed him, and when he reached the wicket-gate he turned in without apparent effort. Pacing up the paved footway he entered the church and stood for a while in the nave passage. A group of people was standing round the vestry door; Barnet advanced through these and stepped into the vestry.

There they were, busily signing their names. Seeing Downe about to look round Barnet averted his somewhat disturbed face for a second or two; when he turned again front to front he was calm and quite smiling; it was a creditable triumph over himself, and deserved to be remembered in his native town. He greeted Downe heartily, offering his congratulations.

It seemed as if Barnet expected a half-guilty look upon Lucy's face; but no; save the natural flush and flurry engendered by the service just performed, there was nothing whatever in her bearing which showed a disturbed mind: her grey-brown eyes carried in them now as at other times the well-known expression of common-sensed rectitude which never went so far as to touch on hardness. She shook hands with him, and Downe said warmly, 'I wish you could have come sooner: I called on purpose to ask you. You'll drive back with us now?'

'No, no,' said Barnet; 'I am not at all prepared; but I thought I would look in upon you for a moment, even though I had not time to go home and dress. I'll stand back and see you pass out, and observe the effect of the spectacle upon myself as one of the public.'

Then Lucy and her husband laughed, and Barnet laughed and retired; and the quiet little party went gliding down the nave and towards the porch, Lucy's new silk dress sweeping with a smart rustle round the base-mouldings of the ancient font, and Downe's little daughters following in a state of round-eyed interest in their position, and that of Lucy, their teacher and friend.

So Downe was comforted after his Emily's death, which had taken place twelve months, two weeks, and three days before that time.

When the two flys had driven off and the spectators had vanished, Barnet followed to the door, and went out into the sun. He took no more trouble to preserve a spruce exterior; his step was unequal, hesitating, almost convulsive; and the slight changes of colour which went on in his face seemed refracted from some inward flame. In the churchyard he became pale as a summer cloud, and finding it not easy to proceed he sat down on one of the tombstones and supported his head with his hand.

Hard by was a sexton filling up a grave which he had not found time to finish on the previous evening. Observing Barnet, he went up to him, and recognizing him, said, 'Shall I help you home, sir?'

'O no, thank you,' said Barnet, rousing himself and standing up. The sexton returned to his grave, followed by Barnet, who, after watching him awhile, stepped into the grave, now nearly filled, and helped to tread in the earth.

The sexton apparently thought his conduct a little singular, but he made no observation, and when the grave was full,

Barnet suddenly stopped, looked far away, and with a decided step proceeded to the gate and vanished. The sexton rested on his shovel and looked after him for a few moments, and then began banking up the mound.

In those short minutes of treading in the dead man Barnet had formed a design, but what it was the inhabitants of that town did not for some long time imagine. He went home, wrote several letters of business, called on his lawyer, an old man of the same place who had been the legal adviser of Barnet's father before him, and during the evening overhauled a large quantity of letters and other documents in his possession. By eleven o'clock the heap of papers in and before Barnet's grate had reached formidable dimensions, and he began to burn them. This, owing to their quantity, it was not so easy to do as he had expected, and he sat long into the night to complete the task.

The next morning Barnet departed for London, leaving a note for Downe to inform him of Mrs Barnet's sudden death, and that he was gone to bury her; but when a thrice-sufficient time for that purpose had elapsed, he was not seen again in his accustomed walks, or in his new house, or in his old one. He was gone for good, nobody knew whither. It was soon dis-covered that he had empowered his lawyer to dispose of all his property, real and personal, in the borough, and pay in the proceeds to the account of an unknown person at one of the large London banks. The person was by some supposed to be himself under an assumed name; but few, if any, had certain knowledge of that fact.

The elegant new residence was sold with the rest of his possessions; and its purchaser was no other than Downe, now a thriving man in the borough, and one whose growing family and new wife required more roomy accommodation than was afforded by the little house up the narrow side street. Barnet's old habitation was bought by the trustees of the Congregational Baptist body in that town, who pulled down the time-honoured dwelling and built a new chapel on its site. By the time the last hour of that, to Barnet, eventful year had chimed, every vestige of him had disappeared from the precincts of his native place, and the name became extinct in the borough of Pòrt-Bredy, after having been a living force therein for more than two hundred years.

*

Twenty-one years and six months do not pass without setting a mark even upon durable stone and triple brass;* upon humanity such a period works nothing less than transformation. In Barnet's old birthplace vivacious young children with bones like India-rubber had grown up to be stable men and women, men and women had dried in the skin, stiffened, withered, and sunk into decrepitude; while selections from every class had been consigned to the outlying cemetery. Of inorganic differences the greatest was that a railway had invaded the town,* tying it on to a main line at a junction a dozen miles off. Barnet's house on the harbour-road, once so insistently new, had acquired a respectable mellowness, with ivy, Virginia creepers, lichens, damp patches, and even constitutional infirmities of its own like its elder fellows. Its architecture, once so very improved and modern, had already become stale in style, without having reached the dignity of being old-fashioned. Trees about the harbour-road had increased in circumference or disappeared under the saw; while the church had had such a tremendous practical joke played upon it by some facetious restorer* or other as to be scarce recognizable by its dearest old friends.

During this long interval George Barnet had never once been seen or heard of in the town of his fathers.

It was the evening of a market-day, and some half-dozen middle-aged farmers and dairymen were lounging round the bar of the Black-Bull Hotel, occasionally dropping a remark to each other, and less frequently to the two barmaids who stood within the pewter-topped counter in a perfunctory attitude of attention, these latter sighing and making a private observation to one another at odd intervals, on more interesting experiences than the present.

'Days get shorter,' said one of the dairymen, as he looked towards the street, and noticed that the lamplighter was passing by.

The farmers merely acknowledged by their countenances the propriety of this remark, and finding that nobody else spoke, one of the barmaids said 'yes' in a tone of painful duty.

'Come fair-day we shall have to light up before we start for home-along.'*

'That's true,' his neighbour conceded, with a gaze of blankness.

'And after that we shan't see much further difference all's winter.'

The rest were not unwilling to go even so far as this.

The barmaid sighed again, and raised one of her hands from the counter on which they rested to scratch the smallest surface of her face with the smallest of her fingers. She looked towards the door, and presently remarked, 'I think I hear the bus coming in from station.'

The eyes of the dairymen and farmers turned to the glass door dividing the hall from the porch, and in a minute or two the omnibus drew up outside. Then there was a lumbering down of luggage, and then a man came into the hall, followed by a porter with a portmanteau on his poll,* which he deposited on a bench.

The stranger was an elderly person, with curly ashen-white hair, a deeply-creviced outer corner to each eyelid, and a countenance baked by innumerable suns to the colour of terra-cotta, its hue and that of his hair contrasting like heat and cold respectively. He walked meditatively and gently, like one who was fearful of disturbing his own mental equilibrium. But whatever lay at the bottom of his breast had evidently made him so accustomed to its situation there that it caused him little practical inconvenience.

He paused in silence while, with his dubious eyes fixed on the barmaids, he seemed to consider himself. In a moment or two he addressed them, and asked to be accommodated for the night. As he waited he looked curiously round the hall, but said nothing. As soon as invited he disappeared up the staircase, preceded by a chambermaid and candle, and followed by a lad with his trunk. Not a soul had recognized him.

A quarter of an hour later, when the farmers and dairymen had driven off to their homesteads in the country, he came downstairs, took a biscuit and one glass of wine, and walked out into the town, where the radiance from the shop-windows had grown so in volume of late years as to flood with cheerfulness every standing cart, barrow, stall, and idler that occupied the wayside, whether shabby or genteel. His chief interest at present seemed to lie in the names painted over the shop-fronts and on doorways, as far as they were visible; these now differed to an ominous extent from what they had been one-and-twenty years before.

The traveller passed on till he came to the bookseller's, where he looked in through the glass door. A fresh-faced young man was standing behind the counter, otherwise the shop was empty. The grey-haired observer entered, asked for some periodical by way of paying for admission, and with his elbow on the counter began to turn over the pages he had bought, though that he read nothing was obvious.

At length he said, 'Is old Mr Watkins still alive?' in a voice which had a curious youthful cadence in it even now.

'My father is dead, sir,' said the young man.

'Ah, I am sorry to hear it,' said the stranger. 'But it is so many years since I last visited this town that I could hardly expect it should be otherwise.' After a short silence he continued – 'And is the firm of Barnet, Browse, and Company still in existence? – they used to be large flax-merchants and twine-spinners here?'

'The firm is still going on, sir, but they have dropped the name of Barnet. I believe that was a sort of fancy name – at least, I never knew of any living Barnet. 'Tis now Browse and Co.'

'And does Andrew Jones still keep on as architect?'

'He's dead, sir.'

'And the vicar of St Mary's – Mr Melrose?'

'He's been dead a great many years.'

'Dear me!' He paused yet longer, and cleared his voice. 'Is Mr Downe, the solicitor, still in practice?'

'No, sir, he's dead. He died about seven years ago.'

Here it was a longer silence still; and an attentive observer would have noticed that the paper in the stranger's hand increased its imperceptible tremor to a visible shake. That grey-haired gentleman noticed it himself, and rested the paper on the counter. 'Is *Mrs* Downe still alive?' he asked, closing his lips firmly as soon as the words were out of his mouth, and dropping his eyes.

'Yes, sir, she's alive and well. She's living at the old place.'

'In East Street?'*

'O no; at Château Ringdale. I believe it has been in the family for some generations.'

'She lives with her children, perhaps?'

'No; she has no children of her own. There were some Miss Downes; I think they were Mr Downe's daughters by a former wife; but they are married and living in other parts of the town. Mrs Downe lives alone.'

'Quite alone?'

'Yes, sir; quite alone.'

The newly-arrived gentleman went back to the hotel and dined; after which he made some change in his dress, shaved back his beard to the fashion that had prevailed twenty years earlier, when he was young and interesting, and once more emerging, bent his steps in the direction of the harbour-road. Just before getting to the point where the pavement ceased and the houses isolated themselves, he overtook a shambling, stooping, unshaven man, who at first sight appeared like a professional tramp, his shoulders having a perceptible greasiness as they passed under the gaslight. Each pedestrian momentarily turned and regarded the other, and the tramp-like gentleman started back.

'Good – why – is that Mr Barnet? 'Tis Mr Barnet, surely!'

'Yes; and you are Charlson?'

'Yes – ah – you notice my appearance. The Fates have reather ill-used me. By the bye, that fifty pounds. I never paid it, did I? ... But I was not ungrateful!' Here the stooping man laid one hand emphatically on the palm of the other. 'I gave you a chance, Mr George Barnet, which many men would have thought full value received – the chance to marry your Lucy. As far as the world was concerned, your wife was a *drowned woman*, hey?'

'Heaven forbid all that, Charlson!'

'Well, well, 'twas a wrong way of showing gratitude, I suppose. And now a drop of something to drink for old acquaintance' sake! And Mr Barnet, she's again free – there's a chance now if you care for it – ha, ha!' And the speaker pushed his tongue into his hollow cheek and slanted his eye in the old fashion.

'I know all,' said Barnet quickly; and slipping a small present into the hands of the needy, saddening man, he stepped ahead and was soon in the outskirts of the town.

He reached the harbour-road, and paused before the entrance to a well-known house. It was so highly bosomed in trees and shrubs planted since the erection of the building that one would scarcely have recognized the spot as that which had been a mere neglected slope till chosen as a site for a dwelling. He opened the swing-gate, closed it noiselessly, and gently moved into the semicircular drive, which remained exactly as it had been marked out by Barnet on the morning when Lucy Savile ran in to thank him for procuring her the post of governess to Downe's children. But the growth of trees and bushes which revealed itself at every step was beyond all expectation; sun-proof and moon-proof bowers vaulted the walks, and the walls of the house were uniformly bearded with creeping plants as high as the first-floor windows.

After lingering for a few minutes in the dusk of the bending boughs, the visitor rang the door-bell, and on the servant appearing, he announced himself as 'an old friend of Mrs Downe's'.

The hall was lighted, but not brightly, the gas being turned low, as if visitors were rare. There was a stagnation in the dwelling; it seemed to be waiting. Could it really be waiting for him? The partitions which had been probed by Barnet's walking-stick when the mortar was green, were now quite brown with the antiquity of their varnish, and the ornamental woodwork of the staircase, which had glistened with a pale yellow newness when first erected, was now of a rich wine-colour. During the servant's absence the following colloquy could be dimly heard through the nearly closed door of the drawing-room.

'He didn't give his name?'

'He only said "an old friend", ma'am.'

'What kind of gentleman is he?'

'A staidish gentleman, with grey hair.'

The voice of the second speaker seemed to affect the listener greatly. After a pause, the lady said, 'Very well, I will see him.'

And the stranger was shown in face to face with the Lucy who had once been Lucy Savile. The round cheek of that formerly young lady had, of course, alarmingly flattened its curve in her modern representative; a pervasive greyness overspread her once dark-brown hair, like morning rime on heather. The parting down the middle was wide and jagged; once it had been a thin white line, a narrow crevice between two high banks of shade. But there was still enough left to form a handsome knob behind, and some curls beneath inwrought with a few hairs like silver wires were very becoming. In her eyes the only modification was that their originally mild rectitude of expression had become a little more stringent than heretofore. Yet she was still girlish – a girl who had been gratuitously weighted by destiny with a burden of five-and-forty years instead of her proper twenty.

'Lucy, don't you know me?' he said, when the servant had closed the door.

'I knew you the instant I saw you!' she returned cheerfully. 'I don't know why, but I always thought you would come back to your old town again.'

She gave him her hand, and then sat down. 'They said you were dead,' continued Lucy, 'but I never thought so. We should have heard of it for certain if you had been.'

'It is a very long time since we met.'

'Yes; what you must have seen, Mr Barnet, in all these roving years, in comparison with what I have seen in this quiet place!' Her face grew more serious. 'You know my husband has been dead a long time? I am a lonely old woman now, considering what I have been; though Mr Downe's daughters – all married – manage to keep me pretty cheerful.'

And I am a lonely old man, and have been any time these twenty years.'

'But where have you kept yourself? And why did you go off so mysteriously?'

'Well, Lucy, I have kept myself a little in America, and a little in Australia, a little in India, a little at the Cape, and so on; I have not stayed in any place for a long time, as it seems to me, and yet more than twenty years have flown. But when people get to my age two years go like one! – Your second question, why did I go away so mysteriously, is surely not necessary. You guessed why, didn't you?'

'No, I never once guessed,' she said simply; 'nor did Charles, nor did anybody as far as I know.'

'Well, indeed! Now think it over again, and then look at me, and say if you can't guess?'

She looked him in the face with an inquiring smile. 'Surely not because of me?' she said, pausing at the commencement of surprise.

Barnet nodded, and smiled again; but his smile was sadder than hers.

'Because I married Charles?' she asked.

'Yes; solely because you married him on the day I was free to ask you to marry me. My wife died four-and-twenty hours before you went to church with Downe. The fixing of my journey at that particular moment was because of her funeral; but once away I knew I should have no inducement to come back, and took my steps accordingly.'

Her face assumed an aspect of gentle reflection, and she looked up and down his form with great interest in her eyes. 'I never thought of it!' she said. 'I knew, of course, that you had once implied some warmth of feeling towards me, but I concluded that it passed off. And I have always been under the impression that your wife was alive at the time of my marriage. Was it not stupid of me! – But you will have some tea or something? I have never dined late, you know, since my husband's death. I have got into the way of making a regular meal of tea. You will have some tea with me, will you not?'

The travelled man assented quite readily, and tea was brought in. They sat and chatted over the tray, regardless of the flying hour. 'Well, well!' said Barnet presently, as for the first time he leisurely surveyed the room; 'how like it all is, and yet how different! Just where your piano stands was a board on a couple of trestles, bearing the patterns of wall-papers, when I was last here. I was choosing them – standing in this way, as it might be. Then my servant came in at the door, and handed me a note, so. It was from Downe, and announced that you were just going to be married to him. I chose no more wall-papers – tore up all those I had selected, and left the house. I never entered it again till now.'

'Ah, at last I understand it all,' she murmured.

They had both risen and gone to the fireplace. The mantel came almost on a level with her shoulder, which gently rested against it, and Barnet laid his hand upon the shelf close beside her shoulder. 'Lucy,' he said, 'better late than never. Will you marry me now?'

She started back, and the surprise which was so obvious in her wrought even greater surprise in him that it should be so. It was difficult to believe that she had been quite blind to the situation, and yet all reason and common sense went to prove that she was not acting.

'You take me quite unawares by such a question!' she said, with a forced laugh of uneasiness. It was the first time she had shown any embarrassment at all. 'Why,' she added, 'I couldn't marry you for the world.'

'Not after all this! Why not?'

'It is – I would – I really think I may say it – I would upon the whole rather marry you, Mr Barnet, than any other man I have ever met, if I ever dreamed of marriage again. But I don't dream of it – it is quite out of my thoughts; I have not the least intention of marrying again.'

'But – on my account – couldn't you alter your plans a little? Come!'

'Dear Mr Barnet,' she said with a little flutter, 'I would on your account if on anybody's in existence. But you don't know in the least what it is you are asking – such an impracticable thing – I won't say ridiculous, of course, because I see that you are really in earnest, and earnestness is never ridiculous to my mind.'

'Well, yes,' said Barnet more slowly, dropping her hand, which he had taken at the moment of pleading, 'I am in earnest. The resolve, two months ago, at the Cape, to come back once more was, it is true, rather sudden, and as I see now, not well considered. But I am in earnest in asking.'

'And I in declining. With all good feeling and all kindness, let me say that I am quite opposed to the idea of marrying a second time.'

'Well, no harm has been done,' he answered, with the same subdued and tender humorousness that he had shown on such occasions in early life. 'If you really won't accept me, I must put up with it, I suppose.' His eye fell on the clock as he spoke. 'Had you any notion that it was so late?' he asked. 'How absorbed I have been!'

She accompanied him to the hall, helped him to put on his overcoat, and let him out of the house herself.

'Good-night,' said Barnet, on the doorstep, as the lamp shone in his face. 'You are not offended with me? '

'Certainly not. Nor you with me?'

'I'll consider whether I am or not,' he pleasantly replied. 'Good-night.'

She watched him safely through the gate; and when his footsteps had died away upon the road, closed the door softly and returned to the room. Here the modest widow long pondered his speeches, with eyes dropped to an unusually low level. Barnet's urbanity under the blow of her refusal greatly impressed her. After having his long period of probation rendered useless by her decision, he had shown no anger, and had philosophically taken her words as if he deserved no better ones. It was very gentlemanly of him, certainly; it was more than gentlemanly; it was heroic and grand. The more she meditated, the more she questioned the virtue of her conduct in checking him so peremptorily; and went to her bedroom in a mood of dissatisfaction. On looking in the glass she was reminded that there was not so much remaining of her former beauty as to make his frank declaration an impulsive natural homage to her cheeks and eyes; it must undoubtedly have arisen from an old staunch feeling of his, deserving tenderest consideration. She recalled to her mind with much pleasure that he had told her he was staying at the Black-Bull Hotel; so that if, after waiting a day or two, he should not, in his modesty, call again, she might then send him a nice little note. To alter her views for the present was far from her intention; but she would allow herself to be induced to reconsider the case, as any generous woman ought to do.

The morrow came and passed, and Mr Barnet did not drop in. At every knock, light youthful hues flew across her cheek; and she was abstracted in the presence of her other visitors. In the evening she walked about the house, not knowing what to do with herself; the conditions of existence seemed totally different from those which ruled only four-and-twenty short hours ago. What had been at first a tantalizing elusive sentiment was getting acclimatized within her as a definite hope, and her person was so informed by that emotion that she might almost have stood as its emblematical representative by the time the clock struck ten. In short, an interest in Barnet precisely resembling that of her early youth led her present heart to belie her yesterday's words to him, and she longed to see him again.

The next day she walked out early, thinking she might meet him in the street. The growing beauty of her romance absorbed her, and she went from the street to the fields, and from the fields to the shore, without any consciousness of distance, till reminded by her weariness that she could go no further. He had nowhere appeared. In the evening she took a step which under the circumstances seemed justifiable; she wrote a note to him at the hotel, inviting him to tea with her at six precisely, and signing her note 'Lucy'.

In a quarter of an hour the messenger came back. Mr Barnet had left the hotel early in the morning of the day before, but he had stated that he would probably return in the course of the week.

The note was sent back, to be given to him immediately on his arrival.

There was no sign from the inn that this desired event had occurred, either on the next day or the day following. On both nights she had been restless, and had scarcely slept half-an-hour.

On the Saturday, putting off all diffidence, Lucy went herself to the Black-Bull, and questioned the staff closely.

Mr Barnet had cursorily remarked when leaving that he might return on the Thursday or Friday, but they were directed not to reserve a room for him unless he should write.

He had left no address.

Lucy sorrowfully took back her note, went home, and resolved to wait.

She did wait – years and years – but Barnet never reappeared.

THE HONOURABLE LAURA

It was a cold and gloomy Christmas Eve. The mass of cloud overhead was almost impervious to such daylight as still lingered; the snow lay several inches deep upon the ground, and the slanting downfall which still went on threatened to considerably increase its thickness before the morning. The Prospect Hotel, a building standing near the wild north coast of Lower Wessex, looked so lonely and so useless at such a time as this that a passing wayfarer would have been led to forget summer possibilities, and to wonder at the commercial courage which could invest capital, on the basis of the popular taste for the picturesque, in a country subject to such dreary phases. That the district was alive with visitors in August seemed but a dim tradition in weather so totally opposed to all that tempts mankind from home. However, there the hotel stood immovable; and the cliffs, creeks, and headlands which were the primary attractions of the spot, rising in full view on the opposite side of the valley, were now but stern angular outlines, while the townlet in front was tinged over with a grimy dirtiness rather than the pearly grey that in summer lent such beauty to its appearance.

Within the hotel commanding this outlook the landlord walked idly about with his hands in his pockets, not in the least expectant of a visitor, and yet unable to settle down to any occupation which should compensate in some degree for the losses that winter idleness entailed on his regular profession. So little, indeed, was anybody expected, that the coffee-room waiter – a genteel boy, whose plated buttons in summer were as close together upon the front of his short jacket as peas in a pod – now appeared in the back yard, metamorphosed into the unrecognizable shape of a rough country lad in corduroys and hobnailed boots, sweeping the snow away, and talking the local dialect in all its purity, quite oblivious of the new polite accent he had learned in the hot weather from the well-behaved visitors. The front door was closed, and, as if to express still more fully the sealed and chrysalis state of the establishment, a sand-bag was placed at the bottom to keep out the insidious snowdrift, the wind setting in directly from that quarter.

The landlord, entering his own parlour, walked to the large fire which it was absolutely necessary to keep up for his comfort, no such blaze burning in the coffee-room or elsewhere, and after giving it a stir returned to a table in the lobby, whereon lay the visitors' book – now closed and pushed back against the wall. He carelessly opened it; not a name had been entered there since the 19th of the previous November, and that was only the name of a man who had arrived on a tricycle, who, indeed, had not been asked to enter at all.

While he was engaged thus the evening grew darker; but before it was as yet too dark to distinguish objects upon the road winding round the back of the cliffs, the landlord perceived a black spot on the distant white, which speedily enlarged itself and drew near. The probabilities were that this vehicle – for a vehicle of some sort it seemed to be – would pass by and pursue its way to the nearest railway-town as others had done. But, contrary to the landlord's expectation, as he stood conning it through the yet unshuttered windows, the solitary object, on reaching the corner, turned into the hotel-front, and drove up to the door.

It was a conveyance particularly unsuited to such a season and weather, being nothing more substantial than an open basket-carriage* drawn by a single horse. Within sat two persons, of different sexes, as could soon be discerned, in spite of their muffled attire. The man held the reins, and the lady had got some shelter from the storm by clinging close to his side. The landlord rang the hostler's bell to attract the attention of the stable-man, for the approach of the visitors had been deadened to noiselessness by the snow, and when the hostler had come to the horse's head the gentleman and lady alighted, the landlord meeting them in the hall.

The male stranger was a foreign-looking individual of about eight-and-twenty. He was close-shaven, excepting a moustache, his features being good, and even handsome. The lady, who stood timidly behind him, seemed to be much younger – possibly not more than eighteen, though it was difficult to judge either of her age or appearance in her present wrappings.

The gentleman expressed his wish to stay till the morning, explaining somewhat unnecessarily, considering that the house was an inn, that they had been unexpectedly benighted on their drive. Such a welcome being given them as landlords can give in dull times, the latter ordered fires in the drawing and coffee-rooms, and went to the boy in the yard, who soon scrubbed himself up, dragged his disused jacket from its box, polished the buttons with his sleeve, and appeared civilized in the hall. The lady was shown into a room where she could take off her snow-damped garments, which she sent down to be dried, her companion, meanwhile, putting a couple of sovereigns on the table, as if anxious to make everything smooth and comfortable at starting, and requesting that a private sitting-room might be got ready. The landlord assured him that the best upstairs parlour – usually public – should be kept private this evening, and sent the maid to light the candles. Dinner was prepared for them, and, at the gentleman's desire, served in the same apartment; where, the young lady having joined him, they were left to the rest and refreshment they seemed to need.

That something was peculiar in the relations of the pair more than once struck the landlord, though wherein that peculiarity lay it was hard to decide. But that his guest was one who paid his way readily had been proved by his conduct, and dismissing conjectures he turned to practical affairs.

About nine o'clock he re-entered the hall, and, everything being done for the day, again walked up and down, occasionally gazing through the glass door at the prospect without, to ascertain how the weather was progressing. Contrary to prognostication, snow had ceased falling, and, with the rising of the moon, the sky had partially cleared, light fleeces of cloud drifting across the silvery disk. There was every sign that a frost was going to set in later on. For these reasons the distant rising road was even more distinct now between its high banks than it had been in the declining daylight. Not a track or rut broke the virgin surface of the white mantle that lay along it, all marks left by the lately arrived travellers having been speedily obliterated by the flakes falling at the time.

And now the landlord beheld by the light of the moon a sight very similar to that he had seen by the light of day. Again a black spot was advancing down the road that margined the coast. He was in a moment or two enabled to perceive that the present vehicle moved onward at a more headlong pace than the little carriage which had preceded it; next, that it was a brougham drawn by two powerful horses; next, that this carriage, like the former one, was bound for the hotel-door. This desirable feature of resemblance caused the landlord once more to withdraw the sand-bag and advance into the porch.

An old gentleman was the first to alight. He was followed by a young one, and both unhesitatingly came forward.

'Has a young lady, less than nineteen years of age, recently arrived here in the company of a man some years her senior?' asked the old gentleman, in haste. 'A man cleanly shaven for the most part, having the appearance of an opera-singer, and calling himself Signor Smittozzi?'

'We have had arrivals lately,' said the landlord, in the tone of having had twenty at least – not caring to acknowledge the attenuated state of business that afflicted Prospect Hotel in winter.

'And among them can your memory recall two persons such as those I describe? – the man a sort of baritone?'

'There certainly is or was a young couple staying in the hotel; but I could not pronounce on the compass of the gentleman's voice.'

'No, no; of course not. I am quite bewildered. They arrived in a basket-carriage, altogether badly provided?'

'They came in a carriage, I believe, as most of our visitors do.'

'Yes, yes. I must see them at once. Pardon my want of ceremony, and show us in to where they are.'

'But, sir, you forget. Suppose the lady and gentleman I mean are not the lady and gentleman you mean? It would be awkward to allow you to rush in upon them just now while they are at dinner, and might cause me to lose their future patronage.'

'True, true. They may not be the same persons. My anxiety, I perceive, makes me rash in my assumptions!'

'Upon the whole, I think they must be the same, Uncle Quantock,' said the young man, who had not till now spoken. And turning to the landlord: 'You possibly have not such a large assemblage of visitors here, on this somewhat forbidding evening, that you quite forget how this couple arrived, and what the lady wore?' His tone of addressing the landlord had in it a quiet frigidity that was not without irony.

'Ah! what she wore; that's it, James. What did she wear?'

'I don't usually take stock of my guests' clothing,' replied the landlord drily, for the ready money of the first arrival had decidedly biassed him in favour of that gentleman's cause. 'You can certainly see some of it if you want to,' he added carelessly, 'for it is drying by the kitchen fire.'

Before the words were half out of his mouth the old gentleman had exclaimed, 'Ah!' and precipitated himself along what seemed to be the passage to the kitchen; but as this turned out to be only the entrance to a dark china-closet, he hastily emerged again, after a collision with the inn-crockery had told him of his mistake.

'I beg your pardon, I'm sure; but if you only knew my feelings (which I cannot at present explain), you would make allowances. Anything I have broken I will willingly pay for.'

'Don't mention it, sir,' said the landlord. And showing the way, they adjourned to the kitchen without further parley. The eldest of the party instantly seized the lady's cloak, that hung upon a clothes-horse, exclaiming: 'Ah! yes, James, it is hers. I knew we were on their track.'

'Yes, it is hers,' answered the nephew quietly, for he was much less excited than his companion.

'Show us their room at once,' said the uncle.

'William, have the lady and gentleman in the front sitting-room finished dining?'

'Yes, sir, long ago,' said the hundred plated buttons.

'Then show up these gentlemen to them at once. You stay here tonight, gentlemen, I presume? Shall the horses be taken out?'

'Feed the horses and wash their mouths. Whether we stay or not depends upon circumstances,' said the placid younger man, as he followed his uncle and the waiter to the staircase.

'I think, Nephew James,' said the former, as he paused with his foot on the first step – 'I think we had better not be announced, but take them by surprise. She may go throwing herself out of the window, or do some equally desperate thing!'

'Yes, certainly, we'll enter unannounced.' And he called back the lad who preceded them.

'I cannot sufficiently thank you, James, for so effectually aiding me in this pursuit!' exclaimed the old gentleman, taking the other by the hand. 'My increasing infirmities would have hindered my overtaking her tonight, had it not been for your timely aid.'

'I am only too happy, uncle, to have been of service to you in this or any other matter. I only wish I could have accompanied you on a pleasanter journey. However, it is advisable to go up to them at once, or they may hear us.' And they softly ascended the stairs.

On the door being opened a room too large to be comfortable was disclosed, lit by the best branch-candlesticks of the hotel, before the fire of which apartment the truant couple were sitting, very innocently looking over the hotel scrap-book and the album containing views of the neighbourhood. No sooner had the old man entered than the young lady – who now showed herself to be quite as young as described, and remarkably prepossessing as to features – perceptibly turned pale. When the nephew entered she turned still paler, as if she were going to faint. The young man described as an opera-singer rose with grim civility, and placed chairs for his visitors.

'Caught you, thank God!' said the old gentleman breathlessly.

'Yes, worse luck, my lord!' murmured Signor Smittozzi, in native London-English, that distinguished Italian having, in fact, first seen the light as the baby of Mr and Mrs Smith in the vicinity of the City Road.* 'She would have been mine tomorrow. And I think that under the peculiar circumstances it would be wiser – considering how soon the breath of scandal will tarnish a lady's fame – to let her be mine tomorrow, just the same.'

'Never!' said the old man. 'Here is a lady under age, without experience – child-like in her maiden innocence and virtue – whom you have plied* by your vile arts, till this morning at dawn – '

'Lord Quantock, were I not bound to respect your grey hairs – '

'Till this morning at dawn you tempted her away from her father's roof. What blame can attach to her conduct that will not, on a full explanation of the matter, be readily passed over in her and thrown entirely on you? Laura, you return at once with me. I should not have arrived, after all, early enough to deliver you, if it had not been for the disinterestedness of your cousin, Captain Northbrook, who, on my discovering your flight this morning, offered with a promptitude for which I can never sufficiently thank him, to accompany me on my journey,

as the only male relative I have near me. Come, do you hear?
Put on your things; we are off at once.'

'I don't want to go!' pouted the young lady.

'I daresay you don't,' replied her father drily. 'But children
never know what's best for them. So come along, and trust to
my opinion.'

Laura was silent, and did not move, the opera gentleman
looking helplessly into the fire, and the lady's cousin sitting
meditatively calm, as the single one of the four whose position
enabled him to survey the whole escapade with the cool criticism
of a comparative outsider.

'I say to you, Laura, as the father of a daughter under age,
that you instantly come with me. What? Would you compel me
to use physical force to reclaim you?'

'I don't want to return!' again declared Laura.

'It is your duty to return nevertheless, and at once, I inform
you.'

'I don't want to!'

'Now, dear Laura, this is what I say: return with me and your
cousin James quietly, like a good and repentant girl, and nothing
will be said. Nobody knows what has happened as yet, and if
we start at once, we shall be home before it is light tomorrow
morning. Come.'

'I am not obliged to come at your bidding, father, and I would
rather not!'

Now James, the cousin, during this dialogue might have been
observed to grow somewhat restless, and even impatient. More
than once he had parted his lips to speak, but second thoughts
each time held him back. The moment had come, however,
when he could keep silence no longer.

'Come, madam!' he spoke out, 'this farce with your father
has, in my opinion, gone on long enough. Just make no more
ado, and step downstairs with us.'

She gave herself an intractable little twist, and did not reply.

'By the Lord Harry, Laura, I won't stand this!' he said angrily.
'Come, get on your things before I come and compel you. There
is a kind of compulsion to which this talk is child's play. Come,
madam – instantly, I say!'

The old nobleman turned to his nephew and said mildly:
'Leave me to insist, James. It doesn't become you. I can speak to
her sharply enough, if I choose.'

James, however, did not heed his uncle, and went on to the troublesome young woman: 'You say you don't want to come, indeed! A pretty story to tell me, that! Come, march out of the room at once, and leave that hulking fellow for me to deal with afterward. Get on quickly – come!' and he advanced toward her as if to pull her by the hand.

'Nay, nay,' expostulated Laura's father, much surprised at his nephew's sudden demeanour. 'You take too much upon yourself. Leave her to me.'

'I won't leave her to you any longer!'

'You have no right, James, to address either me or her in this way; so just hold your tongue. Come, my dear.'

'I have every right!' insisted James.

'How do you make that out?'

'I have the right of a husband.'

'Whose husband?'

'Hers.'

'What?'

'She's my wife.'

'James!'

'Well, to cut a long story short, I may say that she secretly married me, in spite of your lordship's prohibition, about three months ago. And I must add that, though she cooled down rather quickly, everything went on smoothly enough between us for some time; in spite of the awkwardness of meeting only by stealth. We were only waiting for a convenient moment to break the news to you when this idle Adonis* turned up, and after poisoning her mind against me, brought her into this disgrace.'

Here the operatic luminary, who had sat in rather an abstracted and nerveless attitude till the cousin made his declaration, fired up and cried: 'I declare before Heaven that till this moment I never knew she was a wife! I found her in her father's house an unhappy girl – unhappy, as I believe, because of the loneliness and dreariness of that establishment, and the want of society, and for nothing else whatever. What this statement about her being your wife means I am quite at a loss to understand. Are you indeed married to him, Laura?'

Laura nodded from within her tearful handkerchief. 'It was because of my anomalous position in being privately married to him,' she sobbed, 'that I was unhappy at home – and – and I didn't like him so well as I did at first – and I wished I could get out of the mess I was in! And then I saw you a few times, and when you said, "We'll run off", I thought I saw a way out of it all, and then I agreed to come with you-oo-oo!'

'Well! well! well! And is this true?' murmured the bewildered old nobleman, staring from James to Laura, and from Laura to James, as if he fancied they might be figments of the imagination. 'Is this, then, James, the secret of your kindness to your old uncle in helping him to find his daughter? Good Heavens! What further depths of duplicity are there left for a man to learn!'

'I have married her, Uncle Quantock, as I said,' answered James coolly. 'The deed is done, and can't be undone by talking here.'

'Where were you married?'

'At St Mary's, Toneborough.'

'When?'

'On the 29th of September, during the time she was visiting there.'

'Who married you?'

'I don't know. One of the curates – we were quite strangers to the place. So, instead of my assisting you to recover her, you may as well assist me.'

'Never! never!' said Lord Quantock. 'Madam, and sir, I beg to tell you that I wash my hands of the whole affair. If you are man and wife, as it seems you are, get reconciled as best you may. I have no more to say or do with either of you. I leave you, Laura, in the hands of your husband, and much joy may you bring him; though the situation, I own, is not encouraging.'

Saying this, the indignant speaker pushed back his chair against the table with such force that the candlesticks rocked on their bases, and left the room.

Laura's wet eyes roved from one of the young men to the other, who now stood glaring face to face, and, being much frightened at their aspect, slipped out of the room after her father. Him, however, she could hear going out of the front door, and, not knowing where to take shelter, she crept into the darkness of an adjoining bedroom, and there awaited events with a palpitating heart.

Meanwhile the two men remaining in the sitting-room drew nearer to each other, and the opera-singer broke the silence by saying, 'How could you insult me in the way you did, calling me a fellow, and accusing me of poisoning her mind toward you, when you knew very well I was as ignorant of your relation to her as an unborn babe?'

'O yes, you were quite ignorant; I can believe that readily,' sneered Laura's husband.

'I here call Heaven to witness that I never knew!'

'Recitativo* – the rhythm excellent, and the tone well sustained. Is it likely that any man could win the confidence of a young fool her age, and not get that out of her? Preposterous! Tell it to the most improved new pit-stalls.'

'Captain Northbrook, your insinuations are as despicable as your wretched person!' cried the baritone, losing all patience. And springing forward he slapped the captain in the face with the palm of his hand.

Northbrook flinched but slightly, and calmly using his handkerchief to learn if his nose was bleeding, said, 'I quite expected this insult, so I came prepared.' And he drew forth from a black valise which he carried in his hand a small case of pistols.

The baritone started at the unexpected sight, but recovering from his surprise said, 'Very well, as you will,' though perhaps his tone showed a slight want of confidence.

'Now,' continued the husband, quite confidingly, 'we want no parade, no nonsense, you know. Therefore we'll dispense with seconds?'

The signor slightly nodded.

'Do you know this part of the country well?' Cousin James went on, in the same cool and still manner. 'If you don't, I do. Quite at the bottom of the rocks out there, just beyond the stream which falls over them to the shore, is a smooth sandy space, not so much shut in as to be out of the moonlight; and the way down to it from this side is over steps cut in the cliff; and we can find our way down without trouble. We – we two – will find our way down; but only one of us will find his way up, you understand?'

'Quite.'

'Then suppose we start; the sooner it is over the better. We can order supper before we go out – supper for two; for though we are three at present – '

'Three?'

'Yes; you and I and she – '

'O yes.'

' – We shall be only two by and by; so that, as I say, we will order supper for two; for the lady and *a* gentleman. Whichever comes back alive will tap at her door, and call her in to share the repast with him – she's not off the premises. But we must not alarm her now; and above all things we must not let the inn-people see us go out; it would look so odd for two to go out, and only one come in. Ha! ha!'

'Ha! ha! exactly.'

'Are you ready?'

'Oh – quite.'

'Then I'll lead the way.'

He went softly to the door and downstairs, ordering supper to be ready in an hour, as he had said; then making a feint of returning to the room again, he beckoned to the singer, and together they slipped out of the house by a side door.

The sky was now quite clear, and the wheelmarks of the brougham which had borne away Laura's father, Lord Quantock, remained distinctly visible. Soon the verge of the down was reached, the captain leading the way, and the baritone following silently, casting furtive glances at his companion, and beyond him at the scene ahead. In due course they arrived at the chasm in the cliff which formed the waterfall. The outlook here was wild and picturesque in the extreme, and fully justified the many praises, paintings, and photographic views to which the spot had given birth. What in summer was charmingly green and grey, was now rendered weird and fantastic by the snow.

From their feet the cascade plunged downward almost vertically to a depth of eighty or a hundred feet before finally losing itself in the sand, and though the stream was but small, its impact upon jutting rocks in its descent divided it into a hundred spirts and splashes that sent up a mist into the upper air. A few marginal drippings had been frozen into icicles, but the centre flowed on unimpeded.

The operatic artist looked down as he halted, but his thoughts were plainly not of the beauty of the scene. His companion with the pistols was immediately in front of him, and there was no handrail on the side of the path toward the chasm. Obeying a quick impulse, he stretched out his arm, and with a superhuman thrust sent Laura's husband reeling over. A whirling human shape, diminishing downward in the moon's rays further and further toward invisibility, a smack-smack upon the projecting ledges of rock – at first louder and heavier than that of the brook, and then scarcely to be distinguished from it – then a cessation, then the splashing of the stream as before, and the accompanying murmur of the sea, were all the incidents that disturbed the customary flow of the lofty waterfall.

The singer waited in a fixed attitude for a few minutes, then turning, he rapidly retraced his steps over the intervening upland toward the road, and in less than a quarter of an hour was at the door of the hotel. Slipping quietly in as the clock struck ten, he said to the landlord, over the bar hatchway –

'The bill as soon as you can let me have it, including charges for the supper that was ordered, though we cannot stay to eat it, I am sorry to say.' He added with forced gaiety, 'The lady's father and cousin have thought better of intercepting the marriage, and after quarrelling with each other have gone home independently.'

'Well done, sir!' said the landlord, who still sided with this customer in preference to those who had given trouble and barely paid for baiting the horses. '"Love will find out the way!" as the saying is. Wish you joy, sir!'

Signor Smittozzi went upstairs, and on entering the sitting-room found that Laura had crept out from the dark adjoining chamber in his absence. She looked up at him with eyes red from weeping, and with symptoms of alarm.

'What is it? – where is he?' she said apprehensively.

'Captain Northbrook has gone back. He says he will have no more to do with you.'

'And I am quite abandoned by them! – and they'll forget me, and nobody care about me any more!' She began to cry afresh.

'But it is the luckiest thing that could have happened. All is just as it was before they came disturbing us. But, Laura, you ought to have told me about that private marriage, though it is all the same now; it will be dissolved, of course. You are a wid– virtually a widow.'

'It is no use to reproach me for what is past. What am I to do now?'

'We go at once to Cliff-Martin. The horse has rested thoroughly these last three hours, and he will have no difficulty in doing an additional half-dozen miles. We shall be there before twelve, and there are late taverns in the place, no doubt. There we'll sell both horse and carriage tomorrow morning; and go by the coach to Downstaple. Once in the train we are safe.'

'I agree to anything,' she said listlessly.

In about ten minutes the horse was put in, the bill paid, the lady's dried wraps put round her, and the journey resumed.

When about a mile on their way they saw a glimmering light in advance of them. 'I wonder what that is?' said the baritone, whose manner had latterly become nervous, every sound and sight causing him to turn his head.

'It is only a turnpike,' said she. 'That light is the lamp kept burning over the door.'

'Of course, of course, dearest. How stupid I am!'

On reaching the gate they perceived that a man on foot had approached it, apparently by some more direct path than the roadway they pursued, and was, at the moment they drew up, standing in conversation with the gatekeeper.

'It is quite impossible that he could fall over the cliff by accident or the will of God on such a light night as this,' the pedestrian was saying. 'These two children I tell you of saw two men go along the path toward the waterfall, and ten minutes later only one of 'em came back, walking fast, like a man who wanted to get out of the way because he had done something queer. There is no manner of doubt that he pushed the other man over, and, mark me, it will soon cause a hue and cry for that man.'

The candle shone in the face of the Signor and showed that there had arisen upon it a film of ghastliness. Laura, glancing toward him for a few moments, observed it, till, the gatekeeper having mechanically swung open the gate, her companion drove through, and they were soon again enveloped in the white silence.

Her conductor had said to Laura, just before, that he meant to inquire the way at this turnpike; but he had certainly not done so.

As soon as they had gone a little further the omission, intentional or not, began to cause them some trouble. Beyond the secluded district which they now traversed ran the more frequented road, where progress would be easy, the snow being probably already beaten there to some extent by traffic; but they had not yet reached it, and having no one to guide them their journey began to appear less feasible than it had done before starting. When the little lane which they had entered ascended another hill, and seemed to wind round in a direction contrary to the expected route to Cliff-Martin, the question grew serious.

Ever since overhearing the conversation at the turnpike, Laura had maintained a perfect silence, and had even shrunk somewhat away from the side of her lover.

'Why don't you talk, Laura,' he said with forced buoyancy, 'and suggest the way we should go?'

'O yes, I will,' she responded, a curious fearfulness being audible in her voice.

After this she uttered a few occasional sentences which seemed to persuade him that she suspected nothing. At last he drew rein, and the weary horse stood still.

'We are in a fix,' he said.

She answered eagerly: 'I'll hold the reins while you run forward to the top of the ridge, and see if the road takes a favourable turn beyond. It would give the horse a few minutes' rest, and if you find out no change in the direction, we will retrace this lane, and take the other turning.'

The expedient seemed a good one in the circumstances, especially when recommended by the singular eagerness of her voice; and placing the reins in her hands – a quite unnecessary precaution, considering the state of their hack – he stepped out and went forward through the snow till she could see no more of him.

No sooner was he gone than Laura, with a rapidity which contrasted strangely with her previous stillness, made fast the reins to the corner of the phaeton, and slipping out on the opposite side, ran back with all her might down the hill, till, coming to an opening in the fence, she scrambled through it, and plunged into the copse which bordered this portion of the lane. Here she stood in hiding under one of the large bushes, clinging so closely to its umbrage as to seem but a portion of its mass, and listening intently for the faintest sound of pursuit. But nothing disturbed the stillness save the occasional slipping of gathered snow from the boughs, or the rustle of some wild animal over the crisp flake-bespattered herbage. At length, apparently convinced that her former companion was either unable to find her, or not anxious to do so in the present strange state of affairs, she crept out from the bushes, and in less than an hour found herself again approaching the door of the Prospect Hotel.

As she drew near, Laura could see that, far from being wrapped in darkness, as she might have expected, there were ample signs that all the tenants were on the alert, lights moving about the open space in front. Satisfaction was expressed in her face when she discerned that no reappearance of her baritone and his pony-carriage was causing this sensation; but it speedily gave way to grief and dismay when she saw by the lights the form of a man borne on a stretcher by two others into the porch of the hotel.

'I have caused all this,' she murmured between her quivering lips. 'He has murdered him!' Running forward to the door, she hastily asked of the first person she met if the man on the stretcher was dead.

'No, miss,' said the labourer addressed, eyeing her up and down as an unexpected apparition. 'He is still alive, they say, but not sensible. He either fell or was pushed over the waterfall; 'tis thoughted he was pushed. He is the gentleman who came here just now with the old lord, and went out afterward (as is thoughted) with a stranger who had come a little earlier. Anyhow, that's as I had it.'

Laura entered the house, and acknowledging without the least reserve that she was the injured man's wife, had soon installed herself as head nurse by the bed on which he lay. When the two surgeons who had been sent for arrived, she learnt from them that his wounds were so severe as to leave but a slender hope of recovery, it being little short of miraculous that he was not killed on the spot, which his enemy had evidently reckoned to be the case. She knew who that enemy was, and shuddered.

Laura watched all night, but her husband knew nothing of her presence. During the next day he slightly recognized her, and in the evening was able to speak. He informed the surgeons that, as was surmised, he had been pushed over the cascade by Signor Smittozzi; but he communicated nothing to her who nursed him, not even replying to her remarks; he nodded courteously at any act of attention she rendered, and that was all.

In a day or two it was declared that everything favoured his recovery, notwithstanding the severity of his injuries. Full search was made for Smittozzi, but as yet there was no intelligence of his whereabouts, though the repentant Laura communicated all she knew. As far as could be judged, he had come back to the carriage after searching out the way, and finding the young lady missing, had looked about for her till he was tired; then had driven on to Cliff-Martin, sold the horse and carriage next morning, and disappeared, probably by one of the departing

coaches which ran thence to the nearest station, the only difference from his original programme being that he had gone alone.

During the days and weeks of that long and tedious recovery
Laura watched by her husband's bedside with a zeal and
assiduity which would have considerably extenuated any fault
save one of such magnitude as hers. That her husband did not
forgive her was soon obvious. Nothing that she could do in the
way of smoothing pillows, easing his position, shifting bandages,
or administering draughts, could win from him more than a few
measured words of thankfulness, such as he would probably
have uttered to any other woman on earth who had performed
these particular services for him.

'Dear, dear James,' she said one day, bending her face upon
the bed in an excess of emotion. 'How you have suffered! It has
been too cruel. I am more glad you are getting better than I can
say. I have prayed for it – and I am sorry for what I have done;
I am innocent of the worst, and – I hope you will not think me
so very bad, James!'

'O no. On the contrary, I shall think you very good – as a
nurse,' he answered, the caustic severity of his tone being
apparent through its weakness.

Laura let fall two or three silent tears, and said no more that
day.

Somehow or other Signor Smittozzi seemed to be making
good his escape. It transpired that he had not taken a passage in
either of the suspected coaches, though he had certainly got out
of the county; altogether, the chance of finding him was
problematical.

Not only did Captain Northbrook survive his injuries, but it
soon appeared that in the course of a few weeks he would find
himself little if any the worse for the catastrophe. It could also
be seen that Laura, while secretly hoping for her husband's
forgiveness for a piece of folly of which she saw the enormity
more clearly every day, was in great doubt as to what her future
relations with him would be. Moreover, to add to the compli-
cation, whilst she, as a runaway wife, was unforgiven by her
husband, she and her husband, as a runaway couple, were
unforgiven by her father, who had never once communicated
with either of them since his departure from the inn. But her
immediate anxiety was to win the pardon of her husband, who

possibly might be bearing in mind, as he lay upon his couch, the familiar words of Brabantio, 'She has deceived her father, and may thee.'*

Matters went on thus till Captain Northbrook was able to walk about. He then removed with his wife to quiet apartments on the south coast, and here his recovery was rapid. Walking up the cliffs one day, supporting him by her arm as usual, she said to him, simply, 'James, if I go on as I am going now, and always attend to your smallest want, and never think of anything but devotion to you, will you – try to like me a little?'

'It is a thing I must carefully consider,' he said, with the same gloomy dryness which characterized all his words to her now. 'When I have considered, I will tell you.'

He did not tell her that evening, though she lingered long at her routine work of making his bedroom comfortable, putting the light so that it would not shine into his eyes, seeing him fall asleep, and then retiring noiselessly to her own chamber. When they met in the morning at breakfast, and she had asked him as usual how he had passed the night, she added timidly, in the silence which followed his reply, 'Have you considered?'

'No, I have not considered sufficiently to give you an answer.'

Laura sighed, but to no purpose; and the day wore on with intense heaviness to her, and the customary modicum of strength gained to him.

The next morning she put the same question, and looked up despairingly in his face, as though her whole life hung upon his reply.

'Yes, I have considered,' he said.

'Ah!'

'We must part.'

'O James!'

'I cannot forgive you; no man would. Enough is settled upon you to keep you in comfort, whatever your father may do. I shall sell out, and disappear from this hemisphere.'

'You have absolutely decided?' she asked miserably. 'I have nobody now to c-c-care for – '

'I have absolutely decided,' he shortly returned. 'We had better part here. You will go back to your father. There is no reason why I should accompany you, since my presence would only stand in the way of the forgiveness he will probably grant you if you appear before him alone. We will say farewell to each other in three days from this time. I have calculated on being ready to go on that day.'

Bowed down with trouble she withdrew to her room, and the three days were passed by her husband in writing letters and attending to other business matters, saying hardly a word to her the while. The morning of departure came; but before the horses had been put in to take the severed twain in different directions, out of sight of each other, possibly for ever, the postman arrived with the morning letters.

There was one for the captain; none for her – there were never any for her. However, on this occasion something was enclosed for her in his, which he handed her. She read it and looked up helpless.

'My dear father – is dead!' she said. In a few moments she added, in a whisper, 'I must go to the Manor to bury him. . . . Will you go with me, James?'

He musingly looked out of the window. 'I suppose it is an awkward and melancholy undertaking for a woman alone,' he said coldly. 'Well, well – my poor uncle! – Yes, I'll go with you, and see you through the business.'

So they went off together instead of asunder, as planned. It is unnecessary to record the details of the journey, or of the sad week which followed it at her father's house. Lord Quantock's seat was a fine old mansion standing in its own park, and there were plenty of opportunities for husband and wife either to avoid each other, or to get reconciled if they were so minded, which one of them was at least. Captain Northbrook was not present at the reading of the will. She came to him afterward, and found him packing up his papers, intending to start next morning, now that he had seen her through the turmoil occasioned by her father's death.

'He has left me everything that he could!' she said to her husband. 'James, will you forgive me now, and stay?'

'I cannot stay.'

'Why not?'

'I cannot stay,' he repeated.

'But why?'

'I don't like you.'

He acted up to his word. When she came downstairs the next morning she was told that he had gone.

*

Laura bore her double bereavement as best she could. The vast mansion in which she had hitherto lived, with all its historic contents, had gone to her father's successor in the title; but her own was no unhandsome one. Around lay the undulating park, studded with trees a dozen times her own age; beyond it, the wood; beyond the wood, the farms. All this fair and quiet scene was hers. She nevertheless remained a lonely, repentant, depressed being, who would have given the greater part of everything she possessed to ensure the presence and affection of that husband whose very austerity and phlegm – qualities that had formerly led to the alienation between them – seemed now to be adorable features in his character.

She hoped and hoped again, but all to no purpose. Captain Northbrook did not alter his mind and return. He was quite a different sort of man from one who altered his mind; that she was at last despairingly forced to admit. And then she left off hoping, and settled down to a mechanical routine of existence which in some measure dulled her grief, but at the expense of all her natural animation and the sprightly wilfulness which had once charmed those who knew her, though it was perhaps all the while a factor in the production of her unhappiness.

To say that her beauty quite departed as the years rolled on would be to overstate the truth. Time is not a merciful master, as we all know, and he was not likely to act exceptionally in the case of a woman who had mental troubles to bear in addition to the ordinary weight of years. Be this as it may, eleven other winters came and went, and Laura Northbrook remained the lonely mistress of house and lands without once hearing of her husband. Every probability seemed to favour the assumption that he had died in some foreign land; and offers for her hand were not few as the probability verged on certainty with the long lapse of time. But the idea of remarriage seemed never to have entered her head for a moment. Whether she continued to hope even now for his return could not be distinctly ascertained; at all events she lived a life unmodified in the slightest degree from that of the first six months of his absence.

This twelfth year of Laura's loneliness, and the thirtieth of her life drew on apace, and the season approached that had seen the unhappy adventure for which she so long had suffered. Christmas promised to be rather wet than cold, and the trees on the outskirts of Laura's estate dripped monotonously from day to day upon the turnpike-road which bordered them. On an afternoon in this week between three and four o'clock a hired fly might have been seen driving along the highway at this point, and on reaching the top of the hill it stopped. A gentleman of middle age alighted from the vehicle.

'You need drive no further,' he said to the coachman. 'The rain seems to have nearly ceased. I'll stroll a little way, and return on foot to the inn by dinner time.'

The flyman touched his hat, turned the horse, and drove back as directed. When he was out of sight the gentleman walked on, but he had not gone far before the rain again came down pitilessly, though of this the pedestrian took little heed, going leisurely onward till he reached Laura's park gate, which he passed through. The clouds were thick and the days were short, so that by the time he stood in front of the mansion it was dark. In addition to this his appearance, which on alighting from the carriage had been untarnished, partook now of the character of a drenched wayfarer not too well blessed with this world's goods. He halted for no more than a moment at the front entrance, and going round to the servants' quarter, as if he had a preconceived purpose in so doing, there rang the bell. When a page came to him he inquired if they would kindly allow him to dry himself by the kitchen fire.

The page retired, and after a murmured colloquy returned with the cook, who informed the wet and muddy man that though it was not her custom to admit strangers, she should have no particular objection to his drying himself, the night being so damp and gloomy. Therefore the wayfarer entered and sat down by the fire.

'The owner of this house is a very rich gentleman, no doubt?' he asked, as he watched the meat turning on the spit.

''Tis not a gentleman, but a lady,' said the cook.

'A widow, I presume?'

'A sort of widow. Poor soul, her husband is gone abroad, and has never been heard of for many years.'

'She sees plenty of company, no doubt, to make up for his absence?'

'No, indeed – hardly a soul. Service here is as bad as being in a nunnery.'

In short, the wayfarer, who had at first been so coldly received, contrived by his frank and engaging manner to draw the ladies of the kitchen into a most confidential conversation, in which Laura's history was minutely detailed, from the day of her husband's departure to the present. The salient feature in all their discourse was her unflagging devotion to his memory.

Having apparently learned all that he wanted to know – among other things that she was at this moment, as always, alone – the traveller said he was quite dry; and thanking the servants for their kindness, departed as he had come. On emerging into the darkness he did not, however, go down the avenue by which he had arrived. He simply walked round to the front door. There he rang, and the door was opened to him by a manservant whom he had not seen during his sojourn at the other end of the house.

In answer to the servant's inquiry for his name, he said ceremoniously, 'Will you tell The Honourable Mrs Northbrook that the man she nursed many years ago, after a frightful accident, has called to thank her?'

The footman retreated, and it was rather a long time before any further signs of attention were apparent. Then he was shown into the drawing-room, and the door closed behind him.

On the couch was Laura, trembling and pale. She parted her lips and held out her hands to him, but could not speak. But he did not require speech, and in a moment they were in each other's arms.

Strange news circulated through that mansion and the neighbouring town on the next and following days. But the world has a way of getting used to things, and the intelligence of the return of The Honourable Mrs Northbrook's long-absent husband was soon received with comparative calm.

A few days more brought Christmas, and the forlorn home of Laura Northbrook blazed from basement to attic with light and cheerfulness. Not that the house was overcrowded with visitors, but many were present, and the apathy of a dozen years came at length to an end. The animation which set in thus at the close of the old year did not diminish on the arrival of the new; and by the time its twelve months had likewise run the course of its predecessors, a son had been added to the dwindled line of the Northbrook family.

THE THREE STRANGERS

Among the few features of agricultural England which retain an appearance but little modified by the lapse of centuries, may be reckoned the long, grassy and furzy downs, coombs,* or ewe-leases,* as they are called according to their kind, that fill a large area of certain counties in the south and south-west. If any mark of human occupation is met with hereon, it usually takes the form of the solitary cottage of some shepherd.

Fifty years ago such a lonely cottage stood on such a down, and may possibly be standing there now. In spite of its loneliness, however, the spot, by actual measurement, was not three miles from a county-town. Yet that affected it little. Three miles of irregular upland, during the long inimical seasons, with their sleets, snows, rains, and mists, afford withdrawing space enough to isolate a Timon or a Nebuchadnezzar;* much less, in fair weather, to please that less repellent tribe, the poets, philosophers, artists, and others who 'conceive and meditate of pleasant things'.*

Some old earthen camp or barrow, some clump of trees; at least some starved fragment of ancient hedge is usually taken advantage of in the erection of these forlorn dwellings. But, in the present case, such a kind of shelter had been disregarded. Higher Crowstairs, as the house was called, stood quite detached and undefended. The only reason for its precise situation seemed to be the crossing of two footpaths at right angles hard by, which may have crossed there and thus for a good five hundred years. Hence the house was exposed to the elements on all sides. But, though the wind up here blew unmistakably when it did blow, and the rain hit hard whenever it fell, the various weathers of the winter season were not quite so formidable on the down as they were imagined to be by dwellers on low ground. The raw rimes were not so pernicious as in the hollows, and the frosts were scarcely so severe. When the shepherd and his family who tenanted the house were pitied for their sufferings from the exposure, they said that upon the whole they were less inconvenienced by 'wuzzes and flames' (hoarses and phlegms) than when they had lived by the stream of a snug neighbouring valley.

The night of March 28, 182–, was precisely one of the nights that were wont to call forth these expressions of commiseration. The level rainstorm smote walls, slopes, and hedges like the clothyard shafts of Senlac and Crecy.* Such sheep and outdoor animals as had no shelter stood with their buttocks to the winds; while the tails of little birds trying to roost on some scraggy thorn were blown inside-out like umbrellas. The gable-end of the cottage was stained with wet, and the eavesdroppings flapped against the wall. Yet never was commiseration for the shepherd more misplaced. For that cheerful rustic was entertaining a large party in glorification of the christening of his second girl.

The guests had arrived before the rain began to fall, and they were all now assembled in the chief or living room of the dwelling. A glance into the apartment at eight o'clock on this eventful evening would have resulted in the opinion that it was as cosy and comfortable a nook as could be wished for in boisterous weather. The calling of its inhabitant was proclaimed by a number of highly-polished sheep-crooks without stems that were hung ornamentally over the fireplace, the curl of each shining crook varying from the antiquated type engraved in the patriarchal pictures of old family Bibles to the most approved fashion of the last local sheep-fair. The room was lighted by half-a-dozen candles, having wicks only a trifle smaller than the grease which enveloped them, in candlesticks that were never used but at high-days, holy-days, and family feasts. The lights were scattered about the room, two of them standing on the chimney-piece. This position of candles was in itself significant. Candles on the chimney-piece always meant a party.

On the hearth, in front of a back-brand* to give substance, blazed a fire of thorns, that crackled 'like the laughter of the fool'.*

Nineteen persons were gathered here. Of these, five women, wearing gowns of various bright hues, sat in chairs along the wall; girls shy and not shy filled the window-bench; four men, including Charley Jake the hedge-carpenter, Elijah New the parish-clerk, and John Pitcher, a neighbouring dairyman, the shepherd's father-in-law, lolled in the settle; a young man and maid, who were blushing over tentative *pourparlers** on a life-companionship, sat beneath the corner-cupboard; and an elderly engaged man of fifty or upward moved restlessly about from spots where his betrothed was not to the spot where she was. Enjoyment was pretty general, and so much the more prevailed in being unhampered by conventional restrictions. Absolute confidence in each other's good opinion begat perfect ease, while the finishing stroke of manner, amounting to a truly princely serenity, was lent to the majority by the absence of any expression or trait denoting that they wished to get on in the world, enlarge their minds, or do any eclipsing thing whatever – which nowadays so generally nips the bloom and *bonhomie** of all except the two extremes of the social scale.

Shepherd Fennel had married well, his wife being a dairyman's daughter from a vale at a distance, who brought fifty guineas in her pocket – and kept them there, till they should be required for ministering to the needs of a coming family. This frugal woman had been somewhat exercised as to the character that should be given to the gathering. A sit-still party had its advantages; but an undisturbed position of ease in chairs and settles was apt to lead on the men to such an unconscionable deal of toping* that they would sometimes fairly drink the house dry. A dancing-party was the alternative; but this, while avoiding the foregoing objection on the score of good drink, had a counterbalancing disadvantage in the matter of good victuals; the ravenous appetites engendered by the exercise causing immense havoc in the buttery. Shepherdess Fennel fell back upon the intermediate plan of mingling short dances with short periods of talk and singing, so as to hinder any ungovernable rage in either. But this scheme was entirely confined to her own gentle mind: the shepherd himself was in the mood to exhibit the most reckless phases of hospitality.

The fiddler was a boy of those parts,* about twelve years of age, who had a wonderful dexterity in jigs and reels, though his fingers were so small and short as to necessitate a constant shifting for the high notes, from which he scrambled back to the first position with sounds not of unmixed purity of tone. At seven the shrill tweedle-dee* of this youngster had begun, accompanied by a booming ground-bass from Elijah New, the parish-clerk, who had thoughtfully brought with him his favourite musical instrument, the serpent.* Dancing was instantaneous, Mrs Fennel privately enjoining the players on no account to let the dance exceed the length of a quarter of an hour.

But Elijah and the boy in the excitement of their position quite forgot the injunction. Moreover, Oliver Giles, a man of seventeen, one of the dancers, who was enamoured of his partner, a fair girl of thirty-three rolling years, had recklessly handed a new crown-piece to the musicians, as a bribe to keep going as long as they had muscle and wind. Mrs Fennel, seeing the steam begin to generate on the countenances of her guests, crossed over and touched the fiddler's elbow and put her hand on the serpent's mouth. But they took no notice, and fearing she might lose her character of genial hostess if she were to interfere too markedly, she retired and sat down helpless. And so the dance whizzed on with cumulative fury, the performers moving in their planet-like courses, direct and retrograde, from apogee to perigee, till the hand of the well-kicked clock at the bottom of the room had travelled over the circumference of an hour.

While these cheerful events were in course of enactment within Fennel's pastoral dwelling an incident having considerable bearing on the party had occurred in the gloomy night without. Mrs Fennel's concern about the growing fierceness of the dance corresponded in point of time with the ascent of a human figure to the solitary hill of Higher Crowstairs from the direction of the distant town. This personage strode on through the rain without a pause, following the little-worn path which, further on in its course, skirted the shepherd's cottage.

It was nearly the time of full moon, and on this account, though the sky was lined with a uniform sheet of dripping cloud, ordinary objects out of doors were readily visible. The sad wan light revealed the lonely pedestrian to be a man of supple frame; his gait suggested that he had somewhat passed the period of perfect and instinctive agility, though not so far as to be otherwise than rapid of motion when occasion required. At a rough guess, he might have been about forty years of age. He appeared tall, but a recruiting sergeant, or other person accustomed to the judging of men's heights by the eye, would have discerned that this was chiefly owing to his gauntness, and that he was not more than five-feet-eight or nine.

Notwithstanding the regularity of his tread there was caution in it, as in that of one who mentally feels his way; and despite the fact that it was not a black coat nor a dark garment of any sort that he wore, there was something about him which suggested that he naturally belonged to the black-coated tribes of men. His clothes were of fustian, and his boots hobnailed, yet in his progress he showed not the mud-accustomed bearing of hobnailed and fustianed peasantry.

By the time that he had arrived abreast of the shepherd's premises the rain came down, or rather came along, with yet more determined violence. The outskirts of the little settlement partially broke the force of wind and rain, and this induced him to stand still. The most salient of the shepherd's domestic erections was an empty sty at the forward corner of his hedgeless garden, for in these latitudes the principle of masking the homelier features of your establishment by a conventional frontage was unknown. The traveller's eye was attracted to this small building by the pallid shine of the wet slates that covered it. He turned aside, and, finding it empty, stood under the pent-roof* for shelter.

While he stood the boom of the serpent within the adjacent house, and the lesser strains of the fiddler, reached the spot as an accompaniment to the surging hiss of the flying rain on the sod, its louder beating on the cabbage-leaves of the garden, on the straw hackles of eight or ten beehives just discernible by the path, and its dripping from the eaves into a row of buckets and pans that had been placed under the walls of the cottage. For at Higher Crowstairs, as at all such elevated domiciles, the grand difficulty of housekeeping was an insufficiency of water; and a casual rainfall was utilized by turning out, as catchers, every utensil that the house contained. Some queer stories might be told of the contrivances for economy in suds and dish-waters that are absolutely necessitated in upland habitations during the droughts of summer. But at this season there were no such exigencies; a mere acceptance of what the skies bestowed was sufficient for an abundant store.

At last the notes of the serpent ceased and the house was silent. This cessation of activity aroused the solitary pedestrian from the reverie into which he had lapsed, and, emerging from the shed, with an apparently new intention, he walked up the path to the house-door. Arrived here, his first act was to kneel down on a large stone beside the row of vessels, and to drink a copious draught from one of them. Having quenched his thirst he rose and lifted his hand to knock, but paused with his eye upon the panel. Since the dark surface of the wood revealed absolutely nothing, it was evident that he must be mentally looking through the door, as if he wished to measure thereby all the possibilities that a house of this sort might include, and how they might bear upon the question of his entry.

In his indecision he turned and surveyed the scene around. Not a soul was anywhere visible. The garden-path stretched downward from his feet, gleaming like the track of a snail; the roof of the little well (mostly dry), the well-cover, the top rail of the garden gate, were varnished with the same dull liquid glaze; while, far away in the vale, a faint whiteness of more than usual extent showed that the rivers were high in the meads. Beyond all this winked a few bleared lamplights through the beating drops – lights that denoted the situation of the county-town from which he had appeared to come. The absence of all notes of life in that direction seemed to clinch his intentions, and he knocked at the door.

Within, a desultory chat had taken the place of movement and musical sound. The hedge-carpenter was suggesting a song to the company, which nobody just then was inclined to undertake, so that the knock afforded a not unwelcome diversion.

'Walk in!' said the shepherd promptly.

The latch clicked upward, and out of the night our pedestrian appeared upon the door-mat. The shepherd arose, snuffed two of the nearest candles, and turned to look at him.

Their light disclosed that the stranger was dark in complexion and not unprepossessing as to feature. His hat, which for a moment he did not remove, hung low over his eyes, without concealing that they were large, open, and determined, moving with a flash rather than a glance round the room. He seemed pleased with his survey, and, baring his shaggy head, said, in a rich deep voice, 'The rain is so heavy, friends, that I ask leave to come in and rest awhile.'

'To be sure, stranger,' said the shepherd. 'And faith, you've been lucky in choosing your time, for we are having a bit of a fling for a glad cause – though, to be sure, a man could hardly wish that glad cause to happen more than once a year.'

'Nor less,' spoke up a woman. 'For 'tis best to get your family over and done with, as soon as you can, so as to be all the earlier out of the fag o't.'

'And what may be this glad cause?' asked the stranger.

'A birth and christening,' said the shepherd.

The stranger hoped his host might not be made unhappy either by too many or too few of such episodes, and being invited by a gesture to a pull at the mug, he readily acquiesced. His manner, which, before entering, had been so dubious, was now altogether that of a careless and candid man.

'Late to be traipsing athwart this coomb – hey?' said the engaged man of fifty.

'Late it is, master, as you say. – I'll take a seat in the chimney-corner, if you haves nothing to urge against it, ma'am; for I am a little moist on the side that was next the rain.'

Mrs Shepherd Fennel assented, and made room for the self-invited comer, who, having got completely inside the chimney-corner, stretched out his legs and his arms with the expansiveness of a person quite at home.

'Yes, I am rather cracked in the vamp,'* he said freely, seeing that the eyes of the shepherd's wife fell upon his boots, 'and I am not well fitted either. I have had some rough times lately, and have been forced to pick up what I can get in the way of wearing, but I must find a suit better fit for working-days when I reach home.'

'One of hereabouts?' she inquired.

'Not quite that – further up the country.'

'I thought so. And so be I, and by your tongue you come from my neighbourhood.'

'But you would hardly have heard of me,' he said quickly. 'My time would be long before yours, ma'am, you see.'

This testimony to the youthfulness of his hostess had the effect of stopping her cross-examination.

'There is only one thing more wanted to make me happy,' continued the new-comer. 'And that is a little baccy, which I am sorry to say I am out of.'

'I'll fill your pipe,' said the shepherd.

'I must ask you to lend me a pipe likewise.'

'A smoker, and no pipe about 'ee?'

'I have dropped it somewhere on the road.'

The shepherd filled and handed him a new clay pipe, saying, as he did so, 'Hand me your baccy-box – I'll fill that too, now I am about it.'

The man went through the movement of searching his pockets.

'Lost that too?' said his entertainer, with some surprise.

'I am afraid so,' said the man with some confusion. 'Give it to me in a screw of paper.' Lighting his pipe at the candle with a suction that drew the whole flame into the bowl, he resettled himself in the corner and bent his looks upon the faint steam from his damp legs, as if he wished to say no more.

Meanwhile the general body of guests had been taking little notice of this visitor by reason of an absorbing discussion in which they were engaged with the band about a tune for the next dance. The matter being settled, they were about to stand up when an interruption came in the shape of another knock at the door.

At sound of the same the man in the chimney-corner took up the poker and began stirring the brands as if doing it thoroughly were the one aim of his existence; and a second time the shepherd said, 'Walk in!' In a moment another man stood upon the straw-woven door-mat. He too was a stranger.

This individual was one of a type radically different from the first. There was more of the commonplace in his manner, and a certain jovial cosmopolitanism sat upon his features. He was several years older than the first arrival, his hair being slightly frosted, his eyebrows bristly, and his whiskers cut back from his cheeks. His face was rather full and flabby, and yet it was not altogether a face without power. A few grog-blossoms* marked the neighbourhood of his nose. He flung back his long drab greatcoat, revealing that beneath it he wore a suit of cinder-grey shade throughout, large heavy seals, of some metal or other that would take a polish, dangling from his fob as his only personal ornament. Shaking the water-drops from his low-crowned glazed hat, he said, 'I must ask for a few minutes' shelter, comrades, or I shall be wetted to my skin before I get to Casterbridge.'

'Make yourself at home, master,' said the shepherd, perhaps a trifle less heartily than on the first occasion. Not that Fennel had the least tinge of niggardliness in his composition; but the room was far from large, spare chairs were not numerous, and damp companions were not altogether desirable at close quarters for the women and girls in their bright-coloured gowns.

However, the second comer, after taking off his greatcoat, and hanging his hat on a nail in one of the ceiling-beams as if he had been specially invited to put it there, advanced and sat down at the table. This had been pushed so closely into the chimney-corner, to give all available room to the dancers, that its inner edge grazed the elbow of the man who had ensconced himself by the fire; and thus the two strangers were brought into close companionship. They nodded to each other by way of breaking the ice of unacquaintance, and the first stranger handed his neighbour the family mug – a huge vessel of brown ware, having its upper edge worn away like a threshold by the rub of whole generations of thirsty lips that had gone the way of all flesh,* and bearing the following inscription burnt upon its rotund side in yellow letters: –

THERE IS NO FUN
UNTiLL i CUM.

The other man, nothing loth, raised the mug to his lips, and drank on, and on, and on – till a curious blueness overspread the countenance of the shepherd's wife, who had regarded with no little surprise the first stranger's free offer to the second of what did not belong to him to dispense.

'I knew it!' said the toper to the shepherd with much satisfaction. 'When I walked up your garden before coming in, and saw the hives all of a row, I said to myself, "Where there's bees there's honey, and where there's honey there's mead." But mead of such a truly comfortable sort as this I really didn't expect to meet in my older days.' He took yet another pull at the mug, till it assumed an ominous elevation.

'Glad you enjoy it!' said the shepherd warmly.

'It is goodish mead,' assented Mrs Fennel, with an absence of enthusiasm which seemed to say that it was possible to buy praise for one's cellar at too heavy a price. 'It is trouble enough to make – and really I hardly think we shall make any more. For honey sells well, and we ourselves can make shift with a drop o' small* mead and metheglin* for common use from the comb-washings.'*

'O, but you'll never have the heart!' reproachfully cried the stranger in cinder-grey, after taking up the mug a third time and setting it down empty. 'I love mead, when 'tis old like this, as I love to go to church o' Sundays, or to relieve the needy any day of the week.'

'Ha, ha, ha!' said the man in the chimney-corner, who, in

spite of the taciturnity induced by the pipe of tobacco, could not or would not refrain from this slight testimony to his comrade's humour.

Now the old mead of those days, brewed of the purest first-year or maiden honey, four pounds to the gallon – with its due complement of white of eggs, cinnamon, ginger, cloves, mace, rosemary, yeast, and processes of working, bottling, and cellaring – tasted remarkably strong; but it did not taste so strong as it actually was. Hence, presently, the stranger in cinder-grey at the table, moved by its creeping influence, unbuttoned his waistcoat, threw himself back in his chair, spread his legs, and made his presence felt in various ways.

'Well, well, as I say,' he resumed, 'I am going to Casterbridge, and to Casterbridge I must go. I should have been almost there by this time; but the rain drove me into your dwelling, and I'm not sorry for it.'

'You don't live in Casterbridge?' said the shepherd.

'Not as yet; though I shortly mean to move there.'

'Going to set up in trade, perhaps?'

'No, no,' said the shepherd's wife. 'It is easy to see that the gentleman is rich, and don't want to work at anything.'

The cinder-grey stranger paused, as if to consider whether he would accept that definition of himself. He presently rejected it by answering, 'Rich is not quite the word for me, dame. I do work, and I must work. And even if I only get to Casterbridge by midnight I must begin work there at eight tomorrow morning. Yes, het* or wet, blow or snow, famine or sword,* my day's work tomorrow must be done.'

'Poor man! Then, in spite o' seeming, you be worse off than we?' replied the shepherd's wife.

''Tis the nature of my trade, men and maidens. 'Tis the nature of my trade more than my poverty. . . . But really and truly I must up and off, or I shan't get a lodging in the town.' However, the speaker did not move, and directly added, 'There's time for one more draught of friendship before I go; and I'd perform it at once if the mug were not dry.'

'Here's a mug o' small,' said Mrs Fennel. 'Small, we call it, though to be sure 'tis only the first wash o' the combs.'

'No,' said the stranger disdainfully. 'I won't spoil your first kindness by partaking o' your second.'

'Certainly not,' broke in Fennel. 'We don't increase and

multiply every day, and I'll fill the mug again.' He went away to
the dark place under the stairs where the barrel stood. The
shepherdess followed him.

'Why should you do this?' she said reproachfully, as soon as
they were alone. 'He's emptied it once, though it held enough
for ten people; and now he's not contented wi' the small, but
must needs call for more o' the strong! And a stranger unbe-
known to any of us. For my part, I don't like the look o' the
man at all.'

'But he's in the house, my honey; and 'tis a wet night, and a
christening. Daze* it, what's a cup of mead more or less?
There'll be plenty more next bee-burning.'

'Very well – this time, then,' she answered, looking wistfully
at the barrel. 'But what is the man's calling, and where is he one
of, that he should come in and join us like this?'

'I don't know. I'll ask him again.'

The catastrophe of having the mug drained dry at one pull by
the stranger in cinder-grey was effectually guarded against this
time by Mrs Fennel. She poured out his allowance in a small
cup, keeping the large one at a discreet distance from him. When
he had tossed off his portion the shepherd renewed his inquiry
about the stranger's occupation.

The latter did not immediately reply, and the man in the
chimney-corner, with sudden demonstrativeness, said, 'Anybody
may know my trade – I'm a wheelwright.'

'A very good trade for these parts,' said the shepherd.

'And anybody may know mine – if they've the sense to find it
out,' said the stranger in cinder-grey.

'You may generally tell what a man is by his claws,' observed
the hedge-carpenter, looking at his own hands, 'My fingers be
as full of thorns as an old pin-cushion is of pins.'

The hands of the man in the chimney-corner instinctively
sought the shade, and he gazed into the fire as he resumed his
pipe. The man at the table took up the hedge-carpenter's remark,
and added smartly, 'True; but the oddity of my trade is that,
instead of setting a mark upon me, it sets a mark upon my
customers.'

No observation being offered by anybody in elucidation of
this enigma the shepherd's wife once more called for a song.
The same obstacles presented themselves as at the former time –
one had no voice, another had forgotten the first verse. The

stranger at the table, whose soul had now risen to a good working temperature, relieved the difficulty by exclaiming that, to start the company, he would sing himself. Thrusting one thumb into the arm-hole of his waistcoat, he waved the other hand in the air, and, with an extemporizing gaze at the shining sheep-crooks above the mantelpiece, began: –

> O my trade it is the rarest one,
>> Simple shepherds all –
> My trade is a sight to see;
> For my customers I tie, and take them up on high,
> And waft 'em to a far countree!*

The room was silent when he had finished the verse – with one exception, that of the man in the chimney-corner, who, at the singer's word, 'Chorus!' joined him in a deep bass voice of musical relish –

> And waft 'em to a far countree !

Oliver Giles, John Pitcher the dairyman, the parish-clerk, the engaged man of fifty, the row of young women against the wall, seemed lost in thought not of the gayest kind. The shepherd looked meditatively on the ground, the shepherdess gazed keenly at the singer, and with some suspicion; she was doubting whether this stranger were merely singing an old song from recollection, or was composing one there and then for the occasion. All were as perplexed at the obscure revelation as the guests at Belshazzar's Feast,* except the man in the chimney-corner, who quietly said, 'Second verse, stranger,' and smoked on.

The singer thoroughly moistened himself from his lips inwards, and went on with the next stanza as requested: –

> My tools are but common ones,
>> Simple shepherds all –
> My tools are no sight to see:
> A little hempen string, and a post whereon to swing,
> Are implements enough for me!

Shepherd Fennel glanced round. There was no longer any doubt that the stranger was answering his question rhythmically. The guests one and all started back with suppressed exclamations. The young woman engaged to the man of fifty fainted half-way, and would have proceeded, but finding him wanting in alacrity for catching her she sat down trembling.

'O, he's the – ' whispered the people in the background, mentioning the name of an ominous public officer. 'He's come to do it! 'Tis to be at Casterbridge jail tomorrow – the man for sheep-stealing* – the poor clock-maker we heard of, who used to live away at Shottsford and had no work to do – Timothy Summers, whose family were a-starving, and so he went out of Shottsford by the high-road, and took a sheep in open daylight, defying the farmer and the farmer's wife and the farmer's lad, and every man jack among 'em. He' (and they nodded towards the stranger of the deadly trade) 'is come from up the country to do it because there's not enough to do in his own county-town, and he's got the place here now our own county man's dead; he's going to live in the same cottage under the prison wall.'

The stranger in cinder-grey took no notice of this whispered string of observations, but again wetted his lips. Seeing that his friend in the chimney-corner was the only one who reciprocated his joviality in any way, he held out his cup towards that appreciative comrade, who also held out his own. They clinked together, the eyes of the rest of the room hanging upon the singer's actions. He parted his lips for the third verse; but at that moment another knock was audible upon the door. This time the knock was faint and hesitating.

The company seemed scared; the shepherd looked with consternation towards the entrance, and it was with some effort that he resisted his alarmed wife's deprecatory glance, and uttered for the third time the welcoming words, 'Walk in!'

The door was gently opened, and another man stood upon the mat. He, like those who had preceded him, was a stranger. This time it was a short, small personage, of fair complexion, and dressed in a decent suit of dark clothes.

'Can you tell me the way to – ?' he began: when, gazing round the room to observe the nature of the company amongst whom he had fallen, his eyes lighted on the stranger in cinder-grey. It was just at the instant when the latter, who had thrown his mind into his song with such a will that he scarcely heeded the interruption, silenced all whispers and inquiries by bursting into his third verse: –

> Tomorrow is my working day,
>   Simple shepherds all –
>   Tomorrow is a working day for me:
> For the farmer's sheep is slain, and the lad who did it ta'en,
>   And on his soul may God ha' merc-y!

The stranger in the chimney-corner, waving cups with the singer so heartily that his mead splashed over on the hearth, repeated in his bass voice as before: –

> And on his soul may God ha' merc-y!

All this time the third stranger had been standing in the doorway. Finding now that he did not come forward or go on speaking, the guests particularly regarded him. They noticed to their surprise that he stood before them the picture of abject terror – his knees trembling, his hand shaking so violently that the door-latch by which he supported himself rattled audibly: his white lips were parted, and his eyes fixed on the merry officer of justice in the middle of the room. A moment more and he had turned, closed the door, and fled.

'What a man can it be?' said the shepherd.

The rest, between the awfulness of their late discovery and the odd conduct of this third visitor, looked as if they knew not what to think, and said nothing. Instinctively they withdrew further and further from the grim gentleman in their midst, whom some of them seemed to take for the Prince of Darkness* himself, till they formed a remote circle, an empty space of floor being left between them and him –

> . . . circulus, cujus centrum diabolus.*

The room was so silent – though there were more than twenty people in it – that nothing could be heard but the patter of the rain against the window-shutters, accompanied by the occasional hiss of a stray drop that fell down the chimney into the fire, and the steady puffing of the man in the corner, who had now resumed his pipe of long clay.

The stillness was unexpectedly broken. The distant sound of a gun reverberated through the air – apparently from the direction of the county-town.

'Be jiggered!' cried the stranger who had sung the song, jumping up.

'What does that mean?' asked several.

'A prisoner escaped from the jail – that's what it means.'

All listened. The sound was repeated, and none of them spoke but the man in the chimney-corner, who said quietly, 'I've often been told that in this county they fire a gun at such times; but I never heard it till now.'

'I wonder if it is *my* man?' murmured the personage in cinder-grey.

'Surely it is!' said the shepherd involuntarily. 'And surely we've zeed him! That little man who looked in at the door by now, and quivered like a leaf when he zeed ye and heard your song!'

'His teeth chattered, and the breath went out of his body,' said the dairyman.

'And his heart seemed to sink within him like a stone,' said Oliver Giles.

'And he bolted as if he'd been shot at,' said the hedge-carpenter.

'True – his teeth chattered, and his heart seemed to sink; and he bolted as if he'd been shot at,' slowly summed up the man in the chimney-corner.

'I didn't notice it,' remarked the hangman.

'We were all a-wondering what made him run off in such a fright,' faltered one of the women against the wall, 'and now 'tis explained!'

The firing of the alarm-gun went on at intervals, low and sullenly, and their suspicions became a certainty. The sinister gentleman in cinder-grey roused himself. 'Is there a constable here?' he asked, in thick tones. 'If so, let him step forward.'

The engaged man of fifty stepped quavering out from the wall, his betrothed beginning to sob on the back of the chair.

'You are a sworn constable?'

'I be, sir.'

'Then pursue the criminal at once, with assistance, and bring him back here. He can't have gone far.'

'I will, sir, I will – when I've got my staff. I'll go home and get it, and come sharp here, and start in a body.'

'Staff! – never mind your staff; the man'll be gone!'

'But I can't do nothing without my staff – can I, William, and John, and Charles Jake? No; for there's the king's royal crown a painted on en in yaller and gold, and the lion and the unicorn,* so as when I raise en up and hit my prisoner, 'tis made a lawful blow thereby. I wouldn't 'tempt to take up a man without my staff – no, not I. If I hadn't the law to gie me courage, why, instead o' my taking up him he might take up me!'

'Now, I'm a king's man myself, and can give you authority enough for this,' said the formidable officer in grey. 'Now then, all of ye, be ready. Have ye any lanterns?'

'Yes – have ye any lanterns? – I demand it!' said the constable.

'And the rest of you able-bodied – '

'Able-bodied men – yes – the rest of ye!' said the constable.

'Have you some good stout staves and pitchforks – '

'Staves and pitchforks – in the name o' the law! And take 'em in yer hands and go in quest, and do as we in authority tell ye!'

Thus aroused, the men prepared to give chase. The evidence was, indeed, though circumstantial, so convincing, that but little argument was needed to show the shepherd's guests that after what they had seen it would look very much like connivance if they did not instantly pursue the unhappy third stranger, who could not as yet have gone more than a few hundred yards over such uneven country.

A shepherd is always well provided with lanterns; and, lighting these hastily, and with hurdle-staves in their hands, they poured out of the door, taking a direction along the crest of the hill, away from the town, the rain having fortunately a little abated.

Disturbed by the noise, or possibly by unpleasant dreams of her baptism, the child who had been christened began to cry heart-brokenly in the room overhead. These notes of grief came down through the chinks of the floor to the ears of the women below, who jumped up one by one, and seemed glad of the excuse to ascend and comfort the baby, for the incidents of the last half-hour greatly oppressed them. Thus in the space of two or three minutes the room on the ground-floor was deserted quite.

But it was not for long. Hardly had the sound of footsteps died away when a man returned round the corner of the house from the direction the pursuers had taken. Peeping in at the door, and seeing nobody there, he entered leisurely. It was the stranger of the chimney-corner, who had gone out with the rest. The motive of his return was shown by his helping himself to a cut piece of skimmer-cake* that lay on a ledge beside where he had sat, and which he had apparently forgotten to take with

him. He also poured out half a cup more mead from the quantity
that remained, ravenously eating and drinking these as he stood.
He had not finished when another figure came in just as quietly
– his friend in cinder-grey.

'O – you here?' said the latter, smiling. 'I thought you had
gone to help in the capture.' And this speaker also revealed the
object of his return by looking solicitously round for the
fascinating mug of old mead.

'And I thought you had gone,' said the other, continuing his
skimmer-cake with some effort.

'Well, on second thoughts, I felt there were enough without
me,' said the first confidentially, 'and such a night as it is, too.
Besides, 'tis the business o' the Government to take care of its
criminals – not mine.'

'True; so it is. And I felt as you did, that there were enough
without me.'

'I don't want to break my limbs running over the humps and
hollows of this wild country.'

'Nor I neither, between you and me.'

'These shepherd-people are used to it – simple-minded souls,
you know, stirred up to anything in a moment. They'll have him
ready for me before the morning, and no trouble to me at all.'

'They'll have him, and we shall have saved ourselves all
labour in the matter.'

'True, true. Well, my way is to Casterbridge; and 'tis as much
as my legs will do to take me that far. Going the same way?'

'No, I am sorry to say! I have to get home over there' (he
nodded indefinitely to the right), 'and I feel as you do, that it is
quite enough for my legs to do before bedtime.'

The other had by this time finished the mead in the mug, after
which, shaking hands heartily at the door, and wishing each
other well, they went their several ways.

In the meantime the company of pursuers had reached the
end of the hog's-back elevation which dominated this part of
the down. They had decided on no particular plan of action;
and, finding that the man of the baleful trade was no longer in
their company, they seemed quite unable to form any such plan
now. They descended in all directions down the hill, and
straightway several of the party fell into the snare set by Nature
for all misguided midnight ramblers over this part of the
cretaceous* formation. The 'lanchets', or flint slopes, which

belted the escarpment at intervals of a dozen yards, took the less cautious ones unawares, and losing their footing on the rubbly steep they slid sharply downwards, the lanterns rolling from their hands to the bottom, and there lying on their sides till the horn* was scorched through.

When they had again gathered themselves together the shepherd, as the man who knew the country best, took the lead, and guided them round these treacherous inclines. The lanterns, which seemed rather to dazzle their eyes and warn the fugitive than to assist them in the exploration, were extinguished, due silence was observed; and in this more rational order they plunged into the vale. It was a grassy, briery, moist defile, affording some shelter to any person who had sought it; but the party perambulated it in vain, and ascended on the other side. Here they wandered apart, and after an interval closed together again to report progress. At the second time of closing in they found themselves near a lonely ash, the single tree on this part of the coomb, probably sown there by a passing bird some fifty years before. And here, standing a little to one side of the trunk, as motionless as the trunk itself, appeared the man they were in quest of, his outline being well defined against the sky beyond. The band noiselessly drew up and faced him.

'Your money or your life!' said the constable sternly to the still figure.

'No, no,' whispered John Pitcher. ''Tisn't our side ought to say that. That's the doctrine of vagabonds like him, and we be on the side of the law.'

'Well, well,' replied the constable impatiently; 'I must say something, mustn't I? and if you had all the weight o' this undertaking upon your mind, perhaps you'd say the wrong thing too! – Prisoner at the bar, surrender, in the name of the Father – the Crown, I mane!'

The man under the tree seemed now to notice them for the first time, and, giving them no opportunity whatever for exhibiting their courage, he strolled slowly towards them. He was, indeed, the little man, the third stranger; but his trepidation had in a great measure gone.

'Well, travellers,' he said, 'did I hear ye speak to me?'

'You did: you've got to come and be our prisoner at once!' said the constable. 'We arrest 'ee on the charge of not biding in Casterbridge jail in a decent proper manner to be hung tomorrow morning. Neighbours, do your duty, and seize the culpet!'

On hearing the charge the man seemed enlightened, and, saying not another word, resigned himself with preternatural civility to the search-party, who, with their staves in their hands, surrounded him in all sides, and marched him back towards the shepherd's cottage.

It was eleven o'clock by the time they arrived. The light shining from the open door, a sound of men's voices within, proclaimed to them as they approached the house that some new events had arisen in their absence. On entering they discovered the shepherd's living-room to be invaded by two officers from Casterbridge jail, and a well-known magistrate who lived at the nearest country-seat, intelligence of the escape having become generally circulated.

'Gentlemen,' said the constable, 'I have brought back your man – not without risk and danger; but every one must do his duty! He is inside this circle of able-bodied persons, who have lent me useful aid, considering their ignorance of Crown work. Men, bring forward your prisoner!' And the third stranger was led to the light.

'Who is this?' said one of the officials.

'The man,' said the constable.

'Certainly not,' said the turnkey; and the first corroborated his statement.

'But how can it be otherwise?' asked the constable. 'Or why was he so terrified at sight o' the singing instrument of the law who sat there?' Here he related the strange behaviour of the third stranger on entering the house during the hangman's song.

'Can't understand it,' said the officer coolly. 'All I know is that it is not the condemned man. He's quite a different character from this one; a gauntish fellow, with dark hair and eyes, rather good-looking, and with a musical bass voice that if you heard it once you'd never mistake as long as you lived.'

'Why, souls – 'twas the man in the chimney-corner!'

'Hey – what?' said the magistrate, coming forward after inquiring particulars from the shepherd in the background. 'Haven't you got the man after all?'

'Well, sir,' said the constable, 'he's the man we were in search of, that's true; and yet he's not the man we were in search of. For the man we were in search of was not the man we wanted, sir, if you understand my every-day way; for 'twas the man in the chimney-corner!'

'A pretty kettle of fish altogether!' said the magistrate. 'You had better start for the other man at once.'

The prisoner now spoke for the first time. The mention of the man in the chimney-corner seemed to have moved him as nothing else could do. 'Sir,' he said, stepping forward to the magistrate, 'take no more trouble about me. The time is come when I may as well speak. I have done nothing; my crime is that the condemned man is my brother. Early this afternoon I left home at Shottsford to tramp it all the way to Casterbridge jail to bid him farewell. I was benighted, and called here to rest and ask the way. When I opened the door I saw before me the very man, my brother, that I thought to see in the condemned cell at Casterbridge. He was in this chimney-corner; and jammed close to him, so that he could not have got out if he had tried, was the executioner who'd come to take his life, singing a song about it and not knowing that it was his victim who was close by, joining in to save appearances. My brother threw a glance of agony at me, and I knew he meant, "Don't reveal what you see; my life depends on it." I was so terror-struck that I could hardly stand, and, not knowing what I did, I turned and hurried away.'

The narrator's manner and tone had the stamp of truth, and his story made a great impression on all around. 'And do you know where your brother is at the present time?' asked the magistrate.

'I do not. I have never seen him since I closed this door.'

'I can testify to that, for we've been between ye ever since,' said the constable.

'Where does he think to fly to? – what is his occupation?'

'He's a watch- and clock-maker, sir.'

''A said 'a was a wheelwrights – wicked rogue,' said the constable.

'The wheels of clocks and watches he meant, no doubt,' said Shepherd Fennel. 'I thought his hands were palish for's trade.'

'Well, it appears to me that nothing can be gained by retaining this poor man in custody,' said the magistrate; 'your business lies with the other, unquestionably.'

And so the little man was released off-hand; but he looked nothing the less sad on that account, it being beyond the power of magistrate or constable to raze out the written troubles* in his brain, for they concerned another whom he regarded with more solicitude than himself. When this was done, and the man had gone his way, the night was found to be so far advanced that it was deemed useless to renew the search before the next morning.

Next day, accordingly, the quest for the clever sheep-stealer became general and keen, to all appearance at least. But the intended punishment was cruelly disproportioned to the transgression, and the sympathy of a great many country-folk in that district was strongly on the side of the fugitive. Moreover, his marvellous coolness and daring in hob-and-nobbing with the hangman, under the unprecedented circumstances of the shepherd's party, won their admiration. So that it may be questioned if all those who ostensibly made themselves so busy in exploring woods and fields and lanes were quite so thorough when it came to the private examination of their own lofts and outhouses. Stories were afloat of a mysterious figure being occasionally seen in some old overgrown trackway or other, remote from turnpike-roads; but when a search was instituted in any of these suspected quarters nobody was found. Thus the days and weeks passed without tidings.

In brief, the bass-voiced man of the chimney-corner was never recaptured. Some said that he went across the sea, others that he did not, but buried himself in the depths of a populous city. At any rate, the gentleman in cinder-grey never did his morning's work at Casterbridge, nor met anywhere at all, for business purposes, the genial comrade with whom he had passed an hour of relaxation in the lonely house on the slope of the coomb.

The grass has long been green on the graves of Shepherd Fennel and his frugal wife; the guests who made up the christening party have mainly followed their entertainers to the tomb; the baby in whose honour they all had met is a matron in the sere and yellow leaf.* But the arrival of the three strangers at the shepherd's that night, and the details connected therewith, is a story as well known as ever in the country about Higher Crowstairs.

It was half-past four o'clock (by the testimony of the land-surveyor, my authority for the particulars of this story, a gentleman with the faintest curve of humour on his lips); it was half-past four o'clock on a May morning in the eighteen forties. A dense white fog hung over the Valley of the Exe, ending against the hills on either side.

But though nothing in the vale could be seen from higher ground, notes of differing kinds gave pretty clear indications that bustling life was going on there. This audible presence and visual absence of an active scene had a peculiar effect above the fog level. Nature had laid a white hand over the creatures ensconced within the vale, as a hand might be laid over a nest of chirping birds.

The noises that ascended through the pallid coverlid were perturbed lowings, mingled with human voices in sharps and flats, and the bark of a dog. These, followed by the slamming of a gate, explained as well as eyesight could have done, to any inhabitant of the district, that Dairyman Tucker's under-milker was driving the cows from the meads into the stalls. When a rougher accent joined in the vociferations of man and beast, it would have been realized that the dairy-farmer himself had come out to meet the cows, pail in hand, and white pinafore on; and when, moreover, some women's voices joined in the chorus, that the cows were stalled and proceedings about to commence.

A hush followed, the atmosphere being so stagnant that the milk could be heard buzzing into the pails, together with occasional words of the milkmaids and men.

'Don't ye bide about long upon the road, Margery. You can be back again by skimming-time.'

The rough voice of Dairyman Tucker was the vehicle of this remark. The barton-gate* slammed again, and in two or three minutes a something became visible, rising out of the fog in that quarter.

The shape revealed itself as that of a woman having a young and agile gait. The colours and other details of her dress were then disclosed – a bright pink cotton frock (because winter was over); a small woollen shawl of shepherd's plaid (because summer was not come); a white handkerchief tied over her head-gear, because it was so foggy, so damp, and so early; and a straw bonnet and ribbons peeping from under the handkerchief, because it was likely to be a sunny May day.

Her face was of the hereditary type among families down in these parts: sweet in expression, perfect in hue, and somewhat irregular in feature. Her eyes were of a liquid brown. On her arm she carried a withy basket, in which lay several butter-rolls in an nest of wet cabbage-leaves. She was the 'Margery' who had been told not to 'bide about long upon the road'.

She went on her way across the fields, sometimes above the fog, sometimes below it, not much perplexed by its presence except when the track was so indefinite that it ceased to be a guide to the next stile. The dampness was such that innumerable earthworms lay in couples across the path till, startled even by her light tread, they withdrew suddenly into their holes. She kept clear of all trees. Why was that? There was no danger of lightning on such a morning as this. But though the roads were dry the fog had gathered in the boughs, causing them to set up such a dripping as would go clean through the protecting handkerchief like bullets, and spoil the ribbons beneath. The beech and ash were particularly shunned, for they dripped more maliciously than any. It was an instance of woman's keen appreciativeness of nature's moods and peculiarities: a man crossing those fields might hardly have perceived that the trees dripped at all.

In less than an hour she had traversed a distance of four miles, and arrived at a latticed cottage in a secluded spot. An elderly woman, scarce awake, answered her knocking. Margery delivered up the butter, and said, 'How is granny this morning? I can't stay to go up to her, but tell her I have returned what we owed her.'

Her grandmother was no worse than usual: and receiving back the empty basket the girl proceeded to carry out some intention which had not been included in her orders. Instead of returning to the light labours of skimming-time, she hastened on, her direction being towards a little neighbouring town. Before, however, Margery had proceeded far, she met the postman, laden to the neck with letter-bags, of which he had not yet deposited one.

'Are the shops open yet, Samuel?' she said.

'O no,' replied that stooping pedestrian, not waiting to stand upright. 'They won't be open yet this hour, except the saddler and ironmonger and little tacker-haired* machine-man for the farm folk. They downs their shutters at half-past six, then the baker's at half-past seven, then the draper's at eight.'

'O, the draper's at eight.' It was plain that Margery had wanted the draper's.

The postman turned up a side-path, and the young girl, as though deciding within herself that if she could not go shopping at once she might as well get back for the skimming, retraced her steps.

The public road home from this point was easy but devious. By far the nearest way was by getting over a fence, and crossing the private grounds of a picturesque old country-house, whose chimneys were just visible through the trees. As the house had been shut up for many months, the girl decided to take the straight cut.

She pushed her way through the laurel bushes, sheltering her bonnet with the shawl as an additional safeguard, scrambled over an inner boundary, went along through more shrubberies, and stood ready to emerge upon the open lawn. Before doing so she looked around in the wary manner of a poacher. It was not the first time that she had broken fence in her life; but somehow, and all of a sudden, she had felt herself too near womanhood to indulge in such practices with freedom. However, she moved forth, and the house-front stared her in the face, at this higher level unobscured by fog.

It was a building of the medium size, and unpretending, the façade being of stone; and of the Italian elevation made familiar by Inigo Jones and his school.* There was a doorway to the lawn, standing at the head of a flight of steps. The shutters of the house were closed, and the blinds of the bedrooms drawn down. Her perception of the fact that no crusty caretaker could see her from the windows led her at once to slacken her pace, and stroll through the flower-beds coolly. A house unblinded is a possible spy, and must be treated accordingly; a house with the shutters together is an insensate heap of stone and mortar, to be faced with indifference.

On the other side of the house the greensward* rose to an eminence, whereon stood one of those curious summer shelters sometimes erected on exposed points of view, called an all-the-year-round. In the present case it consisted of four walls radiating from a centre like the arms of a turnstile, with seats in each angle, so that whencesoever the wind came, it was always possible to find a screened corner from which to observe the landscape.

The milkmaid's trackless course led her up the hill and past this erection. At ease as to being watched and scolded as an intruder, her mind flew to other matters; till, at the moment when she was not a yard from the shelter, she heard a foot or feet scraping on the gravel behind it. Someone was in the all-the-year-round, apparently occupying the seat on the other side; as was proved when, on turning, she saw an elbow, a man's elbow, projecting over the edge.

Now the young woman did not much like the idea of going down the hill under the eyes of this person, which she would have to do if she went on, for as an intruder she was liable to be called back and questioned upon her business there. Accordingly she crept softly up and sat in the seat behind, intending to remain there until her companion should leave.

This he by no means seemed in a hurry to do. What could possibly have brought him there, what could detain him there, at six o'clock on a morning of mist when there was nothing to be seen or enjoyed of the vale beneath, puzzled her not a little. But he remained quite still, and Margery grew impatient. She discerned the track of his feet in the dewy grass, forming a line from the house steps, which announced that he was an inhabitant and not a chance passer-by. At last she peeped round.

A fine-framed dark-mustachioed gentleman, in dressing-gown and slippers, was sitting there in the damp without a hat on. With one hand he was tightly grasping his forehead, the other hung over his knee. The attitude bespoke with sufficient clearness a mental condition of anguish. He was quite a different being from any of the men to whom her eyes were accustomed. She had never seen mustachios before, for they were not worn by civilians in Lower Wessex at this date. His hands and his face were white – to her view deadly white – and he heeded nothing outside his own existence. There he remained as motionless as the bushes around him; indeed, he scarcely seemed to breathe.

Having imprudently advanced thus far, Margery's wish was

to get back again in the same unseen manner; but in moving her foot for the purpose it grated on the gravel. He started up with an air of bewilderment, and slipped something into the pocket of his dressing-gown. She was almost certain that it was a pistol. The pair stood looking blankly at each other.

'My Gott, who are you?' he asked sternly, and with not altogether an English articulation. 'What do you do here?'

Margery had already begun to be frightened at her boldness in invading the lawn and pleasure-seat. The house had a master, and she had not known of it. 'My name is Margaret Tucker, sir,' she said meekly. 'My father is Dairyman Tucker. We live at Silverthorn Dairy-house.'

'What were you doing here at this hour of the morning?'

She told him, even to the fact that she had climbed over the fence.

'And what made you peep round at me?'

'I saw your elbow, sir; and I wondered what you were doing?'

'And what was I doing?'

'Nothing. You had one hand on your forehead and the other on your knee. I do hope you are not ill, sir, or in deep trouble?' Margery had sufficient tact to say nothing about the pistol.

'What difference would it make to you if I were ill or in trouble? You don't know me.'

She returned no answer, feeling that she might have taken a liberty in expressing sympathy. But, looking furtively up at him, she discerned to her surprise that he seemed affected by her humane wish, simply as it had been expressed. She had scarcely conceived that such a tall dark man could know what gentle feelings were.

'Well, I am much obliged to you for caring how I am,' said he with a faint smile and an affected lightness of manner which, even to her, only rendered more apparent the gloom beneath. 'I have not slept this past night. I suffer from sleeplessness. Probably you do not.'

Margery laughed a little, and he glanced with interest at the comely picture she presented; her fresh face, brown hair, candid eyes, unpractised manner, country dress, pink hands, empty wicker-basket, and the handkerchief over her bonnet.

'Well,' he said, after his scrutiny, 'I need hardly have asked such a question of one who is Nature's own image.... Ah, but my good little friend,' he added, recurring to his bitter tone and sitting wearily down, 'you don't know what great clouds can hang over some people's lives, and what cowards some men are in face of them. To escape themselves they travel, take picturesque houses, and engage in country sports. But here it is so dreary, and the fog was horrible this morning!'

'Why, this is only the pride of the morning!' said Margery. 'By and by it will be a beautiful day.'

She was going on her way forthwith; but he detained her – detained her with words, talking on every innocent little subject he could think of. He had an object in keeping her there more serious than his words would imply. It was as if he feared to be left alone.

While they still stood, the misty figure of the postman, whom Margery had left a quarter of an hour earlier to follow his sinuous course, crossed the grounds below them on his way to the house. Signifying to Margery by a wave of his hand that she was to step back out of sight, in the hinder* angle of the shelter, the gentleman beckoned to the postman to bring the bag to where he stood. The man did so, and again resumed his journey.

The stranger unlocked the bag and threw it on the seat, having taken one letter from within. This he read attentively, and his countenance changed.

The change was almost phantasmagorial, as if the sun had burst through the fog upon that face: it became clear, bright, almost radiant. Yet it was but a change that may take place in the commonest human being, provided his countenance be not too wooden, or his artifice have not grown to second nature. He turned to Margery, who was again edging off, and, seizing her hand, appeared as though he were about to embrace her. Checking his impulse, he said, 'My guardian child – my good friend – you have saved me!'

'What from?' she ventured to ask.

'That you may never know.'

She thought of the weapon, and guessed that the letter he had just received had effected this change in his mood, but made no observation till he went on to say, 'What did you tell me was your name, dear girl?'

She repeated her name.

'Margaret Tucker.' He stooped, and pressed her hand. 'Sit down for a moment – one moment,' he said, pointing to the end of the seat, and taking the extremest further end for himself, not to discompose her. She sat down.

'It is to ask a question,' he went on, 'and there must be confidence between us. You have saved me from an act of madness! What can I do for you?'

'Nothing, sir.'

'Nothing?'

'Father is very well off, and we don't want anything.'

'But there must be some service I can render, some kindness, some votive offering which I could make, and so imprint on your memory as long as you live that I am not an ungrateful man?'

'Why should you be grateful to me, sir?'

He shook his head. 'Some things are best left unspoken. Now think. What would you like to have best in the world?'

Margery made a pretence of reflecting – then fell to reflecting seriously; but the negative was ultimately as undisturbed as ever: she could not decide on anything she would like best in the world; it was too difficult, too sudden.

'Very well – don't hurry yourself. Think it over all day. I ride this afternoon. You live – where?'

'Silverthorn Dairy-house.'

'I will ride that way homeward this evening. Do you consider by eight o'clock what little article, what little treat, you would most like of any.'

'I will, sir,' said Margery, now warming up to the idea. 'Where shall I meet you? Or will you call at the house, sir?'

'Ah – no. I should not wish the circumstances known out of which our acquaintance rose. It would be more proper – but no.'

Margery, too, seemed rather anxious that he should not call. 'I could come out, sir.' she said. 'My father is odd-tempered, and perhaps – '

It was agreed that she should look over a stile at the top of her father's garden, and that he should ride along a bridle-path outside, to receive her answer. 'Margery,' said the gentleman in conclusion, 'now that you have discovered me under ghastly conditions, are you going to reveal them, and make me an object for the gossip of the curious?'

'No, no sir!' she replied earnestly. 'Why should I do that?'

'You will never tell?'

'Never, never will I tell what has happened here this morning.'

'Neither to your father, nor to your friends, nor to any one?'

'To no one at all,' she said.

'It is sufficient,' he answered. 'You mean what you say, my dear maiden. Now you want to leave me. Good-bye!'

She descended the hill, walking with some awkwardness; for she felt the stranger's eyes were upon her till the fog had enveloped her from his gaze. She took no notice now of the dripping from the trees; she was lost in thought on other things. Had she saved this handsome, melancholy, sleepless, foreign gentleman who had had a trouble on his mind till the letter came? What had he been going to do? Margery could guess that he had meditated death at his own hand. Strange as the incident had been in itself, to her it had seemed stranger even than it was. Contrasting colours heighten each other by being juxtaposed; it is the same with contrasting lives.

Reaching the opposite side of the park there appeared before her for the third time that little old man, the foot-post.* As the turnpike-road ran, the postman's beat was twelve miles a day; six miles out from the town, and six miles back at night. But what with zigzags, devious ways, offsets to country seats, curves to farms, looped courses, and triangles to outlying hamlets, the ground actually covered by him was nearer one-and-twenty miles. Hence it was that Margery, who had come straight, was still abreast of him, despite her long pause.

The weighty sense that she was mixed up in a tragical secret with an unknown and handsome stranger prevented her joining very readily in chat with the postman for some time. But a keen interest in her adventure caused her to respond at once when the bowed man of mails said, 'You hit athwart the grounds of Mount Lodge, Miss Margery, or you wouldn't ha' met me here. Well, somebody hev took the old place at last.'

In acknowledging her route Margery brought herself to ask who the new gentleman might be.

'Guide the girl's heart! What! don't she know? And yet how should ye – he's only just a-come. – Well, nominal, he's a fishing gentleman, come for the summer only. But, more to the subject, he's a foreign noble that's lived in England so long as to be without any true country: some of his letters call him Baron, some Squire, so that 'a must be born to something that can't be earned by elbow-grease and Christian conduct. He was out this

morning a-watching the fog. "Postman," 'a said, "good-morning: give me the bag." O, yes, 'a's a civil genteel nobleman
enough.'

'Took the house for fishing, did he?'

'That's what they say, and as it can be for nothing else I
suppose it's true. But, in final, his health's not good, 'a b'lieve;
he's been living too rithe.* The London smoke got into his
wyndpipe, till 'a couldn't eat. However, I shouldn't mind having
the run of his kitchen.'

'And what is his name?'

'Ah – there you have me! 'Tis a name no man's tongue can
tell, or even woman's, except by pen-and-ink and good scholar-
ship. It begins with X, and who, without the machinery of a
clock in's inside, can speak that? But here 'tis – from his letters.'
The postman with his walking-stick wrote upon the ground.

BARON VON XANTEN

The day, as she had prognosticated, turned out fine; for weather-
wisdom was imbibed with their milk-sops by the children of the
Exe Vale. The impending meeting excited Margery, and she
performed her; duties in her father's house with mechanical
unconsciousness.

Milking, skimming, cheesemaking were done. Her father was
asleep in the settle, the milkmen and maids were gone home to
their cottages, and the clock showed a quarter to eight. She
dressed herself with care, went to the top of the garden, and
looked over the stile. The view was eastward, and a great moon
hung before her in a sky which had not a cloud. Nothing was
moving except on the minutest scale, and she remained leaning
over, the night-hawk sounding his croud* from the bough of an
isolated tree on the open hill side.

Here Margery waited till the appointed time had passed by
three-quarters of an hour; but no Baron came. She had been full
of an idea, and her heart sank with disappointment. Then at last
the pacing of a horse became audible on the soft path without,
leading up from the water-meads, simultaneously with which
she beheld the form of the stranger, riding home, as he had said.

The moonlight so flooded her face as to make her very
conspicuous in the garden-gap. 'Ah, my maiden – what is your
name – Margery!' he said. 'How came you here? But of course I

remember – we were to meet. And it was to be at eight – *proh pudor!** – I have kept you waiting!'

'It doesn't matter, sir. I've thought of something.'

'Thought of something?'

'Yes, sir. You said this morning that I was to think what I would like best in the world, and I have made up my mind.'

'I did say so – to be sure I did,' he replied, collecting his thoughts. 'I remember to have had good reason for gratitude to you.' He placed his hand to his brow, and in a minute alighted, and came up to her with the bridle in his hand. 'I was to give you a treat or present, and you could not think of one. Now you have done so. Let me hear what it is, and I'll be as good as my word.'

'To go to the Yeomanry* Ball that's to be given this month.'

'The Yeomanry Ball – Yeomanry Ball?' he murmured, as if, of all requests in the world, this was what he had least expected. 'Where is what you call the Yeomanry Ball?'

'At Exonbury.'

'Have you ever been to it before?'

'No, sir.'

'Or to any ball?'

'No.'

'But did I not say a gift – a present?'

'Or a treat?'

'Ah, yes, or a treat,' he echoed, with the air of one who finds himself in a slight fix. 'But with whom would you propose to go?'

'I don't know. I have not thought of that yet.'

'You have no friend who could take you, even if I got you an invitation?'

Margery looked at the moon. 'No one who can dance,' she said; adding, with hesitation, 'I was thinking that perhaps – '

'But, my dear Margery,' he said, stopping her, as if he half-divined what her simple dream of a cavalier had been; 'it is very odd that you can think of nothing else than going to a Yeomanry Ball. Think again. You are sure there is nothing else?'

'Quite sure, sir,' she decisively answered. At first nobody would have noticed in that pretty young face any sign of decision; yet it was discoverable. The mouth, though soft, was firm in line; the eyebrows were distinct, and extended near to each other. 'I have thought of it all day,' she continued, sadly.

'Still, sir, if you are sorry you offered me anything, I can let you off.'

'Sorry? – Certainly not, Margery,' he said, rather nettled. 'I'll show you that whatever hopes I have raised in your breast I am honourable enough to gratify. If it lies in my power,' he added with sudden firmness, 'you *shall* go to the Yeomanry Ball. In what building is it to be held?'

'In the Assembly Rooms.'

'And would you be likely to be recognized there? Do you know many people?'

'Not many, sir. None, I may say. I know nobody who goes to balls.'

'Ah, well; you must go, since you wish it; and if there is no other way of getting over the difficulty of having nobody to take you, I'll take you myself. Would you like me to do so? I can dance.'

'O yes, sir; I know that, and I thought you might offer to do it. But would you bring me back again?'

'Of course I'll bring you back. But, by the bye, can *you* dance?'

'Yes.'

'What?'

'Reels, and jigs, and country-dances like the "New-Rigged-Ship" and "Follow-my-Lover", and "Haste-to-the-Wedding", and the "College Hornpipe", and the "Favourite Quickstep", and "Captain White's" dance.'*

'A very good list – a very good! but unluckily I fear they don't dance any of those now. But if you have the instinct we may soon cure your ignorance. Let me see you dance a moment.'

She stood out into the garden-path, the stile being still between them, and seizing a side of her skirt with each hand, performed the movements which are even yet far from uncommon in the dances of the villagers of merry England. But her motions, though graceful, were not precisely those which appear in the figures of a modern ball-room.

'Well, my good friend, it is a very pretty sight,' he said, warming up to the proceedings. 'But you dance too well – you dance all over your person – and that's too thorough a way for the present day. I should say it was exactly how they danced in the time of your poet Chaucer;* but as people don't dance like it now, we must consider. First I must inquire more about this ball, and then I must see you again.'

'If it is a great trouble to you, sir, I – '

'O no, no. I will think it over. So far so good.'

The Baron mentioned an evening and an hour when he would be passing that way again; then mounted his horse and rode away.

On the next occasion, which was just when the sun was changing places with the moon as an illuminator of Silverthorn Dairy, she found him at the spot before her, and unencumbered by a horse. The melancholy that had so weighed him down at their first interview, and had been perceptible at their second, had quite disappeared. He pressed her right hand between both his own across the stile.

'My good maiden, Gott bless you!' said he warmly. 'I cannot help thinking of that morning! I was too much over-shadowed at first to take in the whole force of it. You do not know all; but your presence was a miraculous intervention. Now to more cheerful matters. I have a great deal to tell – that is, if your wish about the ball be still the same?'

'O yes, sir – if you don't object.'

'Never think of my objecting. What I have found out is something which simplifies matters amazingly. In addition to your Yeomanry Ball at Exonbury, there is also to be one in the next county about the same time. This ball is not to be held at the Town Hall of the county town as usual, but at Lord Toneborough's, who is colonel of the regiment, and who, I suppose, wishes to please the yeomen because his brother is going to stand for the county.* Now I find I could take you there very well, and the great advantage of that ball over the Yeomanry Ball in this county is, that there you would be absolutely unknown, and I also. But do you prefer your own neighbourhood?'

'O no, sir. It is a ball I long to see – I don't know what it is like; it does not matter where.'

'Good. Then I shall be able to make much more of you there, where there is no possibility of recognition. That being settled, the next thing is the dancing. Now reels and such things do not do. For think of this – there is a new dance at Almack's* and everywhere else over which the world has gone crazy.'

'How dreadful!'

'Ah – but that is a mere expression – gone mad. It is really an ancient Scythian* dance; but, such is the power of fashion, that, having once been adopted by Society, this dance has made the tour of the Continent in one season.'

'What is its name, sir?'

'The polka.* Young people, who always dance, are ecstatic about it, and old people, who have not danced for years, have begun to dance again on its account. All share the excitement. It arrived in London only some few months ago* – it is now all over the country. Now this is your opportunity, my good Margery. To learn this one dance will be enough. They will dance scarce anything else at that ball. While, to crown all, it is the easiest dance in the world, and as I know it quite well I can practise you in the step. Suppose we try?'

Margery showed some hesitation before crossing the stile: it was a Rubicon* in more ways than one. But the curious reverence which was stealing over her for all that this stranger said and did was too much for prudence. She crossed the stile.

Withdrawing with her to a nook where two high hedges met, and where the grass was elastic and dry, he lightly rested his arm on her waist, and practised with her the new step of fascination. Instead of music he whispered numbers, and she, as may be supposed, showed no slight aptness in following his instructions. Thus they moved round together, the moon-shadows from the twigs racing over their forms as they turned.

The interview lasted about half an hour. Then he somewhat abruptly handed her over the stile and stood looking at her from the other side.

'Well,' he murmured, 'what has come to pass is strange! My whole business after this will be to recover my right mind!'

Margery always declared that there seemed to be some power in the stranger that was more than human, something magical and compulsory, when he seized her and gently trotted her round. But lingering emotions may have led her memory to play pranks with the scene, and her vivid imagination at that youthful age must be taken into account in believing her. However, there is no doubt that the stranger, whoever he might be, and whatever his powers, taught her the elements of modern dancing at a certain interview by moonlight at the top of her father's garden, as was proved by her possession of knowledge on the subject that could have been acquired in no other way.

His was of the first rank of commanding figures, she was one of the most agile of milkmaids, and to casual view it would have seemed all of a piece with Nature's doings that things should go on thus. But there was another side to the case; and whether the strange gentleman were a wild olive tree, or not, it was questionable if the acquaintance would lead to happiness. 'A fleeting romance and a possible calamity': thus it might have been summed up by the practical.

Margery was in Paradise; and yet she was not at this date distinctly in love with the stranger. What she felt was something more mysterious, more of the nature of veneration. As he looked at her across the stile she spoke timidly, on a subject which had apparently occupied her long.

'I ought to have a ball-dress, ought I not, sir?'

'Certainly. And you shall have a ball-dress.'

'Really?'

'No doubt of it. I won't do things by halves for my best friend. I have thought of the ball-dress, and of other things also.'

'And is my dancing good enough?'

'Quite – quite.' He paused, lapsed into thought, and looked at her. 'Margery,' he said, 'do you trust yourself unreservedly to me?'

'O yes, sir,' she replied brightly; 'if I am not too much trouble: if I am good enough to be seen in your society.'

The Baron laughed in a peculiar way. 'Really, I think you may assume as much as that. – However, to business. The ball is on the twenty-fifth, that is next Thursday week; and the only difficulty about the dress is the size. Suppose you lend me this?' And he touched her on the shoulder to signify a tight little jacket she wore.

Margery was all obedience. She took it off and handed it to him. The Baron rolled and compressed it with all his force till it was about as large as an apple-dumpling, and put it into his pocket.

'The next thing,' he said, 'is about getting the consent of your friends to your going. Have you thought of this?'

'There is only my father. I can tell him I am invited to a party, and I don't think he'll mind. Though I would rather not tell him.'

'But it strikes me that you must inform him something of what you intend. I would strongly advise you to do so.' He spoke as if rather perplexed as to the probable custom of the English peasantry in such matters, and added, 'However, it is for you to decide. I know nothing of the circumstances. As to getting to the ball, the plan I have arranged is this. The direction to Lord Toneborough's being the other way from my house, you must meet me at Three-Walks-End in Chillington Wood, two miles or more from here. You know the place? Good. By meeting there we shall save five or six miles of journey – a consideration, as it is a long way. Now, for the last time: are you still firm in your wish for this particular treat and no other? It is not too late to give it up. Cannot you think of something else – something better – some useful household articles you require?'

Margery's countenance, which before had been beaming with expectation, lost its brightness: her lips became close, and her voice broken. 'You have offered to take me, and now – '

'No, no, no,' he said, patting her cheek. 'We will not think of anything else. You shall go.'

But whether the Baron, in naming such a distant spot for the rendezvous, was in hope she might fail him, and so relieve him after all of his undertaking, cannot be said; though it might have been strongly suspected from his manner that he had no great zest for the responsibility of escorting her.

But he little knew the firmness of the young woman he had to deal with. She was one of those soft natures whose power of adhesiveness to an acquired idea seems to be one of the special attributes of that softness. To go to a ball with this mysterious personage of romance was her ardent desire and aim; and none the less in that she trembled with fear and excitement at her position in so aiming. She felt the deepest awe, tenderness, and humility towards the Baron of the strange name; and yet she was prepared to stick to her point.

Thus it was that the afternoon of the eventful day found Margery trudging her way up the slopes from the vale to the place of appointment. She walked to the music of innumerable birds, which increased as she drew away from the open meads towards the groves. She had overcome all difficulties. After thinking out the question of telling or not telling her father, she had decided that to tell him was to be forbidden to go. Her contrivance therefore was this: to leave home this evening on a visit to her invalid grandmother, who lived not far from the Baron's house; but not to arrive at her grandmother's till breakfast time next morning. Who would suspect an intercalated experience of twelve hours with the Baron at a ball? That this piece of deception was indefensible she afterwards owned read-ily enough; but she did not stop to think of it then.

It was sunset within Chillington Wood by the time she reached Three-Walks-End – the converging point of radiating trackways, now floored with a carpet of matted grass, which had never known other scythes than the teeth of rabbits and hares. The twitter overhead had ceased, except from a few braver and larger birds, including the cuckoo, who did not fear night at this pleasant time of year. Nobody seemed to be on the spot when she first drew near, but no sooner did Margery stand at the intersection of the roads than a slight crashing became audible, and her patron appeared. He was so transfigured in dress that she scarcely knew him. Under a light greatcoat, which was flung open, instead of his ordinary clothes he wore a suit of thin black cloth, an open waistcoat with a frill all down his shirt-front, a white tie, shining boots, no thicker than a glove, a coat that made him look like a bird, and a hat that seemed as if it would open and shut like an accordion.

'I am dressed for the ball – nothing worse,' he said, drily smiling. 'So will you be soon.'

'Why did you choose this place for our meeting, sir?' she asked, looking around and acquiring confidence.

'Why did I choose it? Well, because in riding past one day I observed a large hollow tree close by here, and it occurred to me when I was last with you that this would be useful for our purpose. Have you told your father?'

'I have not yet told him, sir.'

'That's very bad of you, Margery. How have you arranged it, then?'

She briefly related her plan, on which he made no comment, but, taking her by the hand as if she were a little child, he led her through the undergrowth to a spot where the trees were older, and standing at wider distances. Among them was the tree he had spoken of – an elm; huge, hollow, distorted, and headless, with a rift in its side.

'Now go inside,' he said, 'before it gets any darker. You will find there everything you want. At any rate, if you do not you must do without it. I'll keep watch; and don't be longer than you can help to be.'

'What am I to do, sir?' asked the puzzled maiden.

'Go inside, and you will see. When you are ready wave your handkerchief at that hole.'

She stooped into the opening. The cavity within the tree formed a lofty circular apartment, four or five feet in diameter, to which daylight entered at the top, and also through a round hole about six feet from the ground, marking the spot at which a limb had been amputated in the tree's prime. The decayed wood of cinnamon-brown, forming the inner surface of the tree, and the warm evening glow, reflected in at the top, suffused the cavity with a faint mellow radiance.

But Margery had hardly given herself time to heed these things. Her eye had been caught by objects of quite another quality. A large white oblong paper box lay against the inside of the tree; over it, on a splinter, hung a small oval looking-glass.

Margery seized the idea in a moment. She pressed through the rift into the tree, lifted the cover of the box, and, behold, there was disclosed within a lovely white apparition in a somewhat flattened state. It was the ball-dress.

This marvel of art was, briefly, a sort of heavenly cobweb. It was a gossamer texture of precious manufacture, artistically festooned in a dozen flounces or more.

Margery lifted it, and could hardly refrain from kissing it. Had any one told her before this moment that such a dress could exist, she would have said, 'No; it's impossible!' She drew back, went forward, flushed, laughed, raised her hands. To say that the maker of that dress had been an individual of talent was simply understatement: he was a genius, and she sunned herself in the rays of his creation.

She then remembered that her friend without had told her to make haste, and she spasmodically proceeded to array herself. In removing the dress she found satin slippers, gloves, a handkerchief nearly all lace, a fan, and even flowers for the hair. 'O, how could he think of it!' she said, clasping her hands and almost crying with agitation. 'And the glass – how good of him!'

Everything was so well prepared, that to clothe herself in these garments was a matter of ease. In a quarter of an hour she was ready, even to shoes and gloves. But what led her more than anything else into admiration of the Baron's foresight was the discovery that there were half-a-dozen pairs each of shoes and gloves, of varying sizes, out of which she selected a fit.

Margery glanced at herself in the mirror, or at as much as she could see of herself: the image presented was superb. Then she hastily rolled up her old dress, put it in the box, and thrust the latter on a ledge as high as she could reach. Standing on tiptoe, she waved the handkerchief through the upper aperture, and bent to the rift to go out.

But what a trouble stared her in the face. The dress was so airy, so fantastical, and so extensive, that to get out in her new clothes by the rift which had admitted her in her old ones was an impossibility. She heard the Baron's steps crackling over the dead sticks and leaves.

'O, sir!' she began in despair.

'What – can't you dress yourself?' he inquired from the back of the trunk.

'Yes; but I can't get out of this dreadful tree!'

He came round to the opening, stooped, and looked in. 'It is obvious that you cannot,' he said, taking in her compass at a glance; and adding to himself, 'Charming! who would have thought that clothes could do so much! – Wait a minute, my little maid: I have it!' he said more loudly.

With all his might he kicked at the sides of the rift, and by that means broke away several pieces of the rotten touchwood.* But, being thinly armed about the feet, he abandoned that process, and went for a fallen branch which lay near. By using the large end as a lever, he tore away pieces of the wooden shell which enshrouded Margery and all her loveliness, till the aperture was large enough for her to pass without tearing her dress. She breathed her relief: the silly girl had begun to fear that she would not get to the ball after all.

He carefully wrapped round her a cloak he had brought with him: it was hooded, and of a length which covered her to the heels.

'The carriage is waiting down the other path,' he said, and gave her his arm. A short trudge over the soft dry leaves brought them to the place indicated. There stood the brougham, the horses, the coachman, all as still as if they were growing on the spot, like the trees. Margery's eyes rose with some timidity to the coachman's figure.

'You need not mind him,' said the Baron. 'He is a foreigner, and heeds nothing.'

In the space of a short minute she was handed inside; the Baron buttoned up his overcoat, and surprised her by mounting with the coachman. The carriage moved off silently over the long grass of the vista, the shadows deepening to black as they proceeded. Darker and darker grew the night as they rolled on; the neighbourhood familiar to Margery was soon left behind, and she had not the remotest idea of the direction they were taking. The stars blinked out, the coachman lit his lamps, and they bowled on again.

In the course of an hour and a half they arrived at a small town, where they pulled up at the chief inn and changed horses; all being done so readily that their advent had plainly been expected. The journey was resumed immediately. Her companion never descended to speak to her; whenever she looked out there he sat upright on his perch, with the mien of a person who had a difficult duty to perform, and who meant to perform it properly at all costs. But Margery could not help feeling a certain dread at her situation – almost, indeed, a wish that she had not come. Once or twice she thought, 'Suppose he is a wicked man, who is taking me off to a foreign country, and will never bring me home again.'

But her characteristic persistence in an original idea sustained her against these misgivings except at odd moments. One incident in particular had given her confidence in her escort: she had seen a tear in his eye when she expressed her sorrow for his troubles. He may have divined that her thoughts would take an uneasy turn, for when they stopped for a moment in ascending a hill he came to the window. 'Are you tired, Margery?' he asked kindly.

'No, sir.'

'Are you afraid?'

'N – no, sir. But it is a long way.'

'We are almost there,' he answered. 'And now, Margery,' he said in a lower tone, 'I must tell you a secret. I have obtained this invitation in a peculiar way. I thought it best for your sake not to come in my own name, and this is how I have managed. A man in this county, for whom I have lately done a service, one whom I can trust, and who is personally as unknown here as you and I, has (privately) transferred his card of invitation to me. So that we go under his name. I explain this that you may not say anything imprudent by accident. Keep your ears open and be cautious.' Having said this the Baron retreated again to his place.

'Then he is a wicked man after all!' she said to herself; 'for he
is going under a false name.' But she soon had the temerity not
to mind it: wickedness of that sort was the one ingredient
required just now to finish him off as a hero in her eyes.

They descended a hill, passed a lodge, then up an avenue; and
presently there beamed upon them the light from other carriages,
drawn up in a file, which moved on by degrees; and at last they
halted before a large arched doorway, round which a group of
people stood.

'We are among the latest arrivals, on account of the distance,'
said the Baron, reappearing. 'But never mind; there are three
hours at least for your enjoyment.'

The steps were promptly flung down, and they alighted. The
steam from the flanks of their swarthy steeds, as they seemed to
her, ascended to the parapet of the porch, and from their nostrils
the hot breath jetted forth like smoke out of volcanoes, attract-
ing the attention of all.

The bewildered Margery was led by the Baron up the steps to
the interior of the house, whence the sounds of music and
dancing were already proceeding. The tones were strange. At
every fourth beat a deep and mighty note throbbed through the
air, reaching Margery's soul with all the force of a blow.

'What is that powerful tune, sir – I have never beard anything
like it?' she said.

'The Drum Polka,' answered the Baron. 'The strange dance I
spoke of and that we practised – introduced from my country
and other parts of the continent.'

Her surprise was not lessened when, at the entrance to the
ball-room, she heard the names of her conductor and herself
announced as 'Mr and Miss Brown'.

However, nobody seemed to take any notice of the announcement, the room beyond being in a perfect turmoil of gaiety, and
Margery's consternation at sailing under false colours subsided.
At the same moment she observed awaiting them a handsome,
dark-haired, rather petite lady in cream-coloured satin. 'Who is
she?' asked Margery of the Baron.

'She is the lady of the mansion,' he whispered. 'She is the wife
of a peer of the realm, the daughter of a marquis, has five
Christian names; and hardly ever speaks to commoners, except
for political purposes.'

'How divine – what joy to be here!' murmured Margery, as she contemplated the diamonds that flashed from the head of her ladyship, who was just inside the ball-room door, in front of a little gilded chair, upon which she sat in the intervals between one arrival and another. She had come down from London at great inconvenience to herself, openly to promote this entertainment.

As Mr and Miss Brown expressed absolutely no meaning to Lady Toneborough (for there were three Browns already present in this rather mixed assembly), and as there was possibly a slight awkwardness in poor Margery's manner, Lady Toneborough touched their hands lightly with the tips of her long gloves, said, 'How d'ye do,' and turned round for more comers.

'Ah, if she only knew we were a rich Baron and his friend, and not Mr and Miss Brown at all, she wouldn't receive us like that, would she?' whispered Margery confidentially.

'Indeed, she wouldn't!' drily said the Baron. 'Now let us drop into the dance at once; some of the people here, you see, dance much worse than you.'

Almost before she was aware she had obeyed his mysterious influence, by giving him one hand, placing the other upon his shoulder, and swinging with him round the room to the steps she had learnt on the sward.

At the first gaze the apartment had seemed to her to be floored with black ice; the figures of the dancers appearing upon it upside down. At last she realized that it was highly-polished oak, but she was none the less afraid to move.

'I am afraid of falling down,' she said.

'Lean on me; you will soon get used to it,' he replied. 'You have no nails in your shoes now, dear.'

His words, like all his words to her, were quite true. She found it amazingly easy in a brief space of time. The floor, far from hindering her, was a positive assistance to one of her natural agility and litheness. Moreover, her marvellous dress of twelve flounces inspired her as nothing else could have done. Externally a new creature, she was prompted to new deeds. To feel as well-dressed as the other women around her is to set any woman at her ease, whencesoever she may have come: to feel much better dressed is to add radiance to that ease.

Her prophet's statement on the popularity of the polka at this juncture was amply borne out. It was among the first seasons of its general adoption in country-houses; the enthusiasm it excited tonight was beyond description, and scarcely credible to the youth of the present day. A new motive power had been introduced into the world of poesy – the polka, as a counterpoise to the new motive power that had been introduced into the world of prose – steam.*

Twenty finished musicians sat in the music gallery at the end, with romantic mop-heads of raven hair, under which their faces and eyes shone like fire under coals.

The nature and object of the ball had led to its being very inclusive. Every rank was there, from the peer to the smallest yeoman, and Margery got on exceedingly well, particularly when the recuperative powers of supper had banished the fatigue of her long drive.

Sometimes she heard people saying, 'Who are they? – brother and sister – father and daughter? And never dancing except with each other – how odd!' But of this she took no notice.

When not dancing the watchful Baron took her through the drawing-rooms and picture galleries adjoining, which tonight were thrown open like the rest of the house; and there, ensconcing her in some curtained nook, he drew her attention to scrapbooks, prints, and albums, and left her to amuse herself with turning them over till the dance in which she was practised should again be called. Margery would much have preferred to roam about during these intervals; but the words the Baron were law, and as he commanded so she acted. In such alternations the evening winged away; till at last came the gloomy words, 'Margery, our time is up.'

'One more – only one!' she coaxed, for the longer they stayed the more freely and gaily moved the dance. This entreaty he granted; but on her asking for yet another, he was inexorable. 'No,' he said. 'We have a long way to go.'

Then she bade adieu to the wondrous scene, looking over her shoulder as they withdrew from the hall; and in a few minutes she was cloaked and in the carriage. The Baron mounted to his seat on the box, where she saw him light a cigar; they plunged under the trees, and she leant back, and gave herself up to contemplate the images that filled her brain. The natural result followed: she fell asleep.

She did not awake till they stopped to change horses, when

she saw against the stars the Baron sitting as erect as ever. 'He watches like the Angel Gabriel,* when all the world is asleep!' she thought.

With the resumption of motion she slept again, and knew no more till he touched her hand and said, 'Our journey is done – we are in Chillington Wood.'

It was almost daylight. Margery scarcely knew herself to be awake till she was out of the carriage and standing beside the Baron, who, having told the coachman to drive on to a certain point indicated, turned to her.

'Now,' he said, smiling, 'run across to the hollow tree; you know where it is. I'll wait as before, while you perform the reverse operation to that you did last night.' She took no heed of the path now, nor regarded whether her pretty slippers became scratched by the brambles or no. A walk of a few steps brought her to the particular tree which she had left about nine hours earlier. It was still gloomy at this spot, the morning not being clear.

She entered the trunk, dislodged the box containing her old clothing, pulled off the satin shoes, and gloves, and dress, and in ten minutes emerged in the cotton gown and shawl of shepherd's plaid.

The Baron was not far off. 'Now you look the milkmaid again,' he said, coming towards her. 'Where is the finery?'

'Packed in the box, sir, as I found it.' She spoke with more humility now. The difference between them was greater than it had been at the ball.

'Good,' he said. 'I must just dispose of it; and then away we go.'

He went back to the tree, Margery following at a little distance. Bringing forth the box, he pulled out the dress as carelessly as if it had been rags. But this was not all. He gathered a few dry sticks, crushed the lovely garment into a loose billowy heap, threw the gloves, fan, and shoes on the top, then struck a light and ruthlessly set fire to the whole.

Margery was agonized. She ran forward; she implored and entreated. 'Please, sir – do spare it – do! My lovely dress – my dear, dear slippers – my fan – it is cruel! Don't burn them, please!'

'Nonsense. We shall have no further use for them if we live a hundred years.'

'But spare a bit of it – one little piece, sir – a scrap of the lace – one bow of the ribbon – the lovely fan – just something!'

But he was as immovable as Rhadamanthus.* 'No,' he said, with a stern gaze of his aristocratic eye. 'It is of no use for you to speak like that. The things are my property. I undertook to gratify you in what you might desire because you had saved my life. To go to a ball, you said. You might much more wisely have said anything else, but no; you said, to go to a ball. Very well – I have taken you to a ball. The clothes were only the means, and I dispose of them my own way. Have I not a right to?'

'Yes, sir,' she said meekly.

He gave the fire a stir. and lace and ribbons, and the twelve flounces, and the embroidery, and all the rest crackled and disappeared. He then put in her hands the butter basket she had brought to take on to her grandmother's, and accompanied her to the edge of the wood, where it merged in the undulating open country in which her granddame* dwelt.

'Now, Margery,' he said, 'here we part. I have performed my contract – at some awkwardness, if I was recognized. But never mind that. How do you feel – sleepy?'

'Not at all, sir,' she said.

'That long nap refreshed you, eh? Now you must make me a promise. That if I require your presence at any time, you will come to me. . . . I am a man of more than one mood,' he went on with sudden solemnity; 'and I may have desperate need of you again, to deliver me from that darkness as of Death which sometimes encompasses me. Promise it, Margery – promise it; that, no matter what stands in the way, you will come to me if I require you.'

'I would have if you had not burnt my pretty clothes!' she pouted.

'Ah – ungrateful!'

'Indeed, then, I will promise, sir,' she said from her heart. 'Wherever I am, if I have bodily strength I will come to you.'

He pressed her hand. 'It is a solemn promise,' he replied. 'Now I must go, for you know your way.'

'I shall hardly believe that it has not been all a dream!' she said, with a childish instinct to cry at his withdrawal. 'There will be nothing left of last night – nothing of my dress, nothing of my pleasure, nothing of the place!'

'You shall remember it in this way,' said he. 'We'll cut our initials on this tree as a memorial, so that whenever you walk this path you will see them.'

Then with a knife he inscribed on the smooth bark of a beech tree the letters M.T., and underneath a large X.

'What, have you no Christian name, sir?' she said.

'Yes, but I don't use it. Now, good-bye, my little friend. – What will you do with yourself today, when you are gone from me?' he lingered to ask.

'Oh – I shall go to my granny's,' she replied with some gloom; 'and have breakfast, and dinner, and tea with her, I suppose; and in the evening I shall go home to Silverthorn Dairy, and perhaps Jim will come to meet me, and all will be the same as usual.'

'Who is Jim?'

'O, he's nobody – only the young man I've got to marry some day.'

'What! you engaged to be married? – Why didn't you tell me this before?'

'I – I don't know, sir.'

'What is the young man's name?'

'James Hayward.'

'What is he?'

'A master lime-burner.'

'Engaged to a master lime-burner, and not a word of this to me! Margery, Margery! when shall a straightforward one of your sex be found! Subtle even in your simplicity! What mischief have you caused me to do, through not telling me this? I wouldn't have so endangered anybody's happiness for a thousand pounds. Wicked girl that you were; why didn't you tell me?'

'I thought I'd better not!' said Margery, beginning to be frightened.

'But don't you see and understand that if you are already the property of a young man, and he were to find out this night's excursion, he may be angry with you and part from you for ever? With him already in the field I had no right to take you at all; he undoubtedly ought to have taken you; which really might have been arranged, if you had not deceived me by saying you had nobody.'

Margery's face wore that aspect of woe which comes from

the repentant consciousness of having been guilty of an enormity. 'But he wasn't good enough to take me, sir!' she said, almost
crying; 'and he isn't absolutely my master until I have married
him, is he?'

'That's a subject I cannot go into. However, we must alter
our tactics. Instead of advising you, as I did at first, to tell of
this experience to your friends, I must now impress on you that
it will be best to keep a silent tongue on the matter – perhaps
for ever and ever. It may come right some day, and you may be
able to say "All's well that ends well." Now, good morning, my
friend. Think of Jim, and forget me.'

'Ah, perhaps I can't do that,' she said, with a tear in her eye,
and a full throat.

'Well – do your best. I can say no more.'

He turned and retreated into the wood, and Margery, sighing,
went on her way.

Between six and seven o'clock in the evening of the same day a
young man descended the hills into the valley of the Exe, at a
point about midway between Silverthorn and the residence of
Margery's grandmother, four miles to the east.

He was a thoroughbred son of the country, as far removed
from what is known as the provincial, as the latter is from the
out-and-out gentleman of culture. His trousers and waistcoat
were of fustian, almost white, but he wore a jacket of old-
fashioned blue West-of-England cloth, so well preserved that
evidently the article was relegated to a box whenever its owner
engaged in such active occupations as he usually pursued. His
complexion was fair, almost florid, and he had scarcely any
beard.

A novel attraction about this young man, which a glancing
stranger would know nothing of, was a rare and curious
freshness of atmosphere that appertained to him, to his clothes,
to all his belongings, even to the room in which he had been
sitting. It might almost have been said that by adding him and
his implements to an overcrowded apartment you made it
healthful. This resulted from his trade. He was a lime-burner;
he handled lime daily; and in return the lime rendered him an
incarnation of salubrity. His hair was dry, fair, and frizzled,
the latter possibly by the operation of the same caustic agent.
He carried as a walking-stick a green sapling, whose growth

had been contorted to a corkscrew pattern by a twining honeysuckle.

As he descended to the level ground of the water-meadows he cast his glance westward, with a frequency that revealed him to be in search of some object in the distance. It was rather difficult to do this, the low sunlight dazzling his eyes by glancing from the river away there, and from the 'carriers' (as they were called) in his path – narrow artificial brooks for conducting the water over the grass. His course was something of a zigzag from the necessity of finding points in these carriers convenient for jumping. Thus peering and leaping and winding, he drew near the Exe, the central river of the miles-long mead.

A moving spot became visible to him in the direction of his scrutiny, mixed up with the rays of the same river. The spot got nearer, and revealed itself to be a slight thing of pink cotton and shepherd's plaid, which pursued a path on the brink of the stream. The young man so shaped his trackless course as to impinge on the path a little ahead of this coloured form, and when he drew near her he smiled and reddened. The girl smiled back to him; but her smile had not the life in it that the young man's had shown.

'My dear Margery – here I am!' he said gladly in an undertone, as with a last leap he crossed the last intervening carrier, and stood at her side.

'You've come all the way from the kiln, on purpose to meet me, and you shouldn't have done it,' she reproachfully returned.

'We finished there at four, so it was no trouble; and if it had been – why, I should ha' come.'

A small sigh was the response.

'What, you are not even so glad to see me as you would be to see your dog or cat?' he continued. 'Come, Mis'ess Margery, this is rather hard. But, by George, how tired you dew look! Why, if you'd been up all night your eyes couldn't be more like tea-saucers. You've walked tew far, that's what it is. The weather is getting warm now, and the air of these low-lying meads is not strengthening in summer. I wish you lived up on higher ground with me, beside the kiln. You'd get as strong as a hoss! Well, there; all that will come in time.'

Instead of saying yes, the fair maid repressed another sigh.

'What, won't it, then?' he said.

'I suppose so,' she answered. 'If it is to be, it is.'

'Well said – very well said, my dear.'

'And if it isn't to be it isn't.'

'What? Who's been putting that into your head? Your grumpy granny, I suppose. However, how is she? Margery, I have been thinking today – in fact, I was thinking it yesterday and all the week – that really we might settle our little business this summer.'

'This summer?' she repeated, with some dismay. 'But the partnership? Remember it was not to be till after that was completed.'

'There I have you!' said he, taking the liberty to pat her shoulder, and the further liberty of advancing his hand behind it to the other. 'The partnership is settled. 'Tis "Vine and Hayward, lime-burners", now, and "Richard Vine" no longer. Yes, Cousin Richard has settled it so, for a time at least, and 'tis to be painted on the carts this week – blue letters – yaller ground. I'll hoss one of 'em, and drive en round to your door as soon as the paint is dry, to show 'ee how it looks?'

'Oh, I am sure you needn't take that trouble, Jim; I can see it quite well enough in my mind,' replied young girl – not without a flitting accent of superiority.

'Hullo,' said Jim, taking her by the shoulders, and looking at her hard. 'What dew that bit of incivility mean? Now, Margery, let's sit down here, and have this cleared.' He rapped with his stick upon the rail of a little bridge they were crossing, and seated himself firmly, leaving a place for her.

'But I want to get home-along, dear Jim,' she coaxed.

'Fidgets.* Sit down, there's a dear. I want a straightforward answer, if you please. In what month, and on what day of the month, will you marry me?'

'O, Jim,' she said, sitting gingerly on the edge, 'that's too plain-spoken for you yet. Before I look at it in that business light I should have to – to – '

'But your father has settled it long ago, and you said it should be as soon as I became a partner. So, dear, you must not mind a plain man wanting a plain answer. Come, name your time.'

She did not reply at once. What thoughts were passing through her brain during the interval? Not images raised by his words, but whirling figures of men and women in red and white and blue, reflected from a glassy floor, in movements timed by the thrilling beats of the Drum Polka. At last she said slowly,

'Jim, you don't know the world, and what a woman's wants can be.'

'But I can make you comfortable. I am in lodgings as yet, but I can have a house for the asking; and as to furniture, you shall choose of the best for yourself – the very best.'

'The best! Far are you from knowing what that is!' said the little woman. 'There be ornaments such as you never dream of; work-tables that would set you in amaze; silver candlesticks, tea- and coffee-pots that would dazzle your eyes: tea-cups, and saucers, gilded all over with guinea-gold;* heavy velvet curtains, gold clocks, pictures, and looking-glasses beyond your very dreams. So don't say I shall have the best.'

'H'm!' said Jim gloomily; and fell into reflection. 'Where did you get those high notions from, Margery?' he presently inquired. 'I'll swear you hadn't got 'em a week ago.' She did not answer, and he added, '*Yew* don't expect to have such things, I hope; deserve them as you may?'

'I was not exactly speaking of what I wanted,' she said severely. 'I said, things a woman *could* want. And since you wish to know what I *can* want to quite satisfy me, I assure you I can want those!'

'You are a pink-and-white conundrum, Margery,' he said; 'and I give you up for tonight. Anybody would think the devil had showed you all the kingdoms of the world since I saw you last!'

She reddened. 'Perhaps he has!' she murmured; then arose, he following her; and they soon reached Margery's home, approaching it from the lower or meadow side – the opposite to that of the garden top, where she had met the Baron.

'You'll come in, won't you, Jim?' she said, with more ceremony than heartiness.

'No – I think not tonight,' he answered. 'I'll consider what you've said.'

'You are very good, Jim,' she returned lightly. 'Good-bye.'

Jim thoughtfully retraced his steps. He was a village character, and he had a villager's simplicity: that is, the simplicity which comes from the lack of a complicated experience. But simple by nature he certainly was not. Among the rank and file of rustics he was quite a Talleyrand,* or rather had been one, till he lost a good deal of his self-command by falling in love.

Now, however, that the charming object of his distraction was out of sight he could deliberate, and measure, and weigh things with some approach to keenness. The substance of his queries was, What change had come over Margery – whence these new notions?

Ponder as he would he could evolve no answer save one, which, eminently unsatisfactory as it was, he felt it would be unreasonable not to accept: that she was simply skittish and ambitious by nature, and would not be hunted into matrimony till he had provided a well-adorned home.

Jim retrod the miles to the kiln, and looked to the fires. The kiln stood in a peculiar, interesting, even impressive spot. It was at the end of a short ravine in a limestone formation, and all around was an open hilly down. The nearest house was that of Jim's cousin and partner, which stood on the outskirts of the down beside the turnpike-road. From this house a little lane wound between the steep escarpments of the ravine till it reached the kiln, which faced down the miniature valley, commanding it as a fort might command a defile.

The idea of a fort in this association owed little to imagination. For on the nibbled green steep above the kiln stood a bygone worn-out specimen of such an erection, huge, impressive, and difficult to scale even now in its decay. It was a British castle or entrenchment, with triple rings of defence, rising roll behind roll, their outlines cutting sharply against the sky, and Jim's kiln nearly undermining their base. When the lime-kiln flared up in the night, which it often did, its fires lit up the front of these ramparts to a great majesty. They were old friends of his, and while keeping up the heat through the long darkness, as it was sometimes his duty to do, he would imagine the dancing lights and shades about the stupendous earthwork to be the forms of those giants who (he supposed) had heaped it up. Often he clambered upon it, and walked about the summit, thinking out the problems connected with his business, his partner, his future, his Margery.

It was what he did this evening, continuing the meditation on the young girl's manner that he had begun upon the road, and still, as then, finding no clue to the change.

While thus engaged he observed a man coming up the ravine to the kiln. Business messages were almost invariably left at the house below, and Jim watched the man with the interest excited by a belief that he had come on a personal matter. On nearer approach Jim recognized him as the gardener at Mount Lodge some miles away. If this meant business, the Baron (of whose arrival Jim had vaguely heard) was a new and unexpected customer.

It meant nothing else, apparently. The man's errand was simply to inform Jim that the Baron required a load of lime for the garden.

'You might have saved yourself trouble by leaving word at Mr Vine's,' said Jim.

'I was to see you personally,' said the gardener, 'and to say that the Baron would like to inquire of you about the different qualities of lime proper for such purposes.'

'Couldn't you tell him yourself?' said Jim.

'He said I was to tell you that,' replied the gardener; 'and it wasn't for me to interfere.'

No motive other than the ostensible one could possibly be conjectured by Jim Hayward at this time; and the next morning he started with great pleasure, in his best business suit of clothes. By eleven o'clock he and his horse and cart had arrived on the Baron's premises, and the lime was deposited where directed; an exceptional spot, just within view of the windows of the south front.

Baron von Xanten, pale and melancholy, was sauntering in the sun on the slope between the house and the all-the-year-round. He looked across to where Jim and the gardener were standing, and the identity of Hayward being established by what he brought, the Baron came down, and the gardener withdrew.

The Baron's first inquiries were, as Jim had been led to suppose they would be, on the exterminating effects of lime upon slugs and snails in its different conditions of slaked and unslaked, ground and in the lump. He appeared to be much interested by Jim's explanations, and eyed the young man closely whenever he had an opportunity.

'And I hope trade is prosperous with you this year,' said the Baron.

'Very, my noble lord,' replied Jim, who, in his uncertainty on the proper method of address, wisely concluded that it was better to err by giving too much honour than by giving too little. 'In short, trade is looking so well that I've become a partner in the firm.'

'Indeed; I am glad to hear it. So now you are settled in life.'

'Well, my lord, I am hardly settled, even now. For I've got to finish it – I mean, to get married.'

'That's an easy matter, compared with the partnership.'

'Now a man might think so, my baron,' said Jim, getting more confidential. 'But the real truth is, 'tis the hardest part of all for me.'

'Your suit prospers, I hope?'

'It don't,' said Jim. 'It don't at all just at present. In short, I can't for the life o' me think what's come over the young woman lately.' And he fell into deep reflection.

Though Jim did not observe it, the Baron's brow became shadowed with self-reproach as he heard those simple words, and his eyes had a look of pity. 'Indeed – since when?' he asked.

'Since yesterday, my noble lord.' Jim spoke meditatively. He was resolving upon a bold stroke. Why not make a confidant of this kind gentleman instead of the parson, as he had intended? The thought was no sooner conceived than acted on. 'My lord,' he resumed, 'I have heard that you are a nobleman of great scope and talent, who has seen more strange countries and characters than I have ever heard of, and know the insides of men well. Therefore I would fain put a question to your noble lordship, if I may so trouble you, and having nobody else in the world who could inform me so trewly.'

'Any advice I can give is at your service, Hayward. What do you wish to know?'

'It is this, my baron. What can I do to bring down a young woman's ambition that's got to such a towering height there's no reaching it or compassing it: how get her to be pleased with me and my station as she used to be when I first knew her?'

'Truly, that's a hard question, my man. What does she aspire to?'

'She's got a craze for fine furniture.'

'How long has she had it?'

'Only just now.'

The Baron seemed still more to experience regret. 'What furniture does she specially covet?' he asked.

'Silver candlesticks, work-tables, looking-glasses, gold tea-things, silver tea-pots, gold clocks, curtains, pictures, and I don't know what all – things I shall never get if I live to be a hundred – not so much that I couldn't raise the money to buy 'em, as that I ought to put it to other uses, or save it for a rainy day.'

'You think the possession of those articles would make her happy?'

'I really think they might, my lord.'

'Good. Open your pocket-book and write as I tell you.'

Jim in some astonishment did as commanded, and elevating his pocket-book against the garden-wall, thoroughly moistened his pencil, and wrote at the Baron's dictation:

'Pair of silver candlesticks: inlaid work-table and work-box: one large mirror: two small ditto: one gilt china tea and coffee service: one silver tea-pot, coffee-pot, sugar-basin, jug, and dozen spoons: French clock: pair of curtains: six large pictures.'

'Now,' said the Baron, 'tear out that leaf and give it to me. Keep a close tongue about this; go home, and don't be surprised at anything that may come to your door.'

'But, my noble lord, you don't mean that your lordship is going to give – '

'Never mind what I am going to do. Only keep your own counsel. I perceive that, though a plain countryman, you are by no means deficient in tact and understanding. If sending these things to you gives me pleasure, why should you object? The fact is, Hayward, I occasionally take an interest in people, and like to do a little for them. I take an interest in you. Now go home, and a week hence invite Marg – the young woman and her father to tea with you. The rest is in your own hands.'

A question often put to Jim in after times was why it had not occurred to him at once that the Baron's liberal conduct must have been dictated by something more personal than sudden spontaneous generosity to him, a stranger. To which Jim always answered that, admitting the existence of such generosity, there had appeared nothing remarkable in the Baron selecting himself as its object. The Baron had told him that he took an interest in him; and self-esteem, even with the most modest, is usually sufficient to override any little difficulty that might occur to an outsider in accounting for a preference. He moreover considered that foreign noblemen, rich and eccentric, might have habits of acting which were quite at variance with those of their English compeers.

So he drove off homeward with a lighter heart than he had known for several days. To have a foreign gentleman take a fancy to him – what a triumph to a plain sort of fellow, who had scarcely expected the Baron to look in his face. It would be a fine story to tell Margery when the Baron gave him liberty to speak out.

Jim lodged at the house of his cousin and partner, Richard Vine, a widower of fifty odd years. Having failed in the development of a household of direct descendants this trades-man had been glad to let his chambers to his much younger relative, when the latter entered on the business of lime manu-facture; and their intimacy had led to a partnership. Jim lived upstairs; his partner lived down, and the furniture of all the rooms was so plain and old-fashioned as to excite the special dislike of Miss Margery Tucker, and even to prejudice her against Jim for tolerating it. Not only were the chairs and tables queer,* but, with due regard to the principle that a man's surroundings should bear the impress of that man's life and occupation, the chief ornaments of the dwelling were a curious collection of calcinations,* that had been discovered from time to time in the lime-kiln – misshapen ingots of strange substance, some of them like Pompeian* remains.

The head of the firm was a quiet-living, narrow-minded, though friendly, man of fifty; and he took a serious interest in Jim's love-suit, frequently inquiring how it progressed, and assuring Jim that if he chose to marry he might have all the upper floor at a low rent, he, Mr Vine, contenting himself entirely with the ground level. It had been so convenient for discussing business matters to have Jim in the same house, that he did not wish any change to be made in consequence of a change in Jim's domestic estate. Margery knew of this wish, and of Jim's concurrent feeling, and did not like the idea at all.

About four days after the young man's interview with the Baron, there drew up in front of Jim's house at noon a waggon laden with cases and packages, large and small. They were all addressed to 'Mr Hayward', and they had come from the largest furnishing warehouses in that part of England.

Three-quarters of an hour were occupied in getting the cases to Jim's rooms. The wary Jim did not show the amazement he felt at his patron's munificence; and presently the senior partner came into the passage, and wondered what was lumbering upstairs.

'O – it's only some things of mine,' said Jim coolly.

'Bearing upon the coming event – eh?' said his partner.

'Exactly,' replied Jim.

Mr Vine, with some astonishment at the number of cases, shortly after went away to the kiln; whereupon Jim shut himself into his rooms, and there he might have been heard ripping up and opening boxes with a cautious hand, afterwards appearing outside the door with them empty, and carrying them off to the outhouse.

A triumphant look lit up his face when, a little later in the afternoon, he sent into the vale to the dairy, and invited Margery and her father to his house to supper.

She was not unsociable that day, and, her father expressing a hard and fast acceptance of the invitation, she perforce agreed to go with him. Meanwhile at home Jim made himself as mysteriously busy as before in those rooms of his, and when his partner returned he too was asked to join in the supper.

At dusk Hayward went to the door, where he stood till he heard the voices of his guests from the direction of the low grounds, now covered with their frequent fleece of fog. The voices grew more distinct, and then on the white surface of the fog there appeared two trunkless heads, from which bodies and a horse and cart gradually extended as the approaching pair rose towards the house.

When they had entered Jim pressed Margery's hand and conducted her up to his rooms, her father waiting below to say a few words to the senior lime-burner.

'Bless me,' said Jim to her, on entering the sitting-room, 'I quite forgot to get a light beforehand; but I'll have one in a jiffy.'

Margery stood in the middle of the dark room, while Jim struck a match; and then the young girl's eyes were conscious of a burst of light, and the rise into being of a pair of handsome silver candlesticks containing two candles that Jim was in the act of lighting.

'Why – where – you have candlesticks like that?' said Margery. Her eyes flew round the room as the growing candle-flames showed other articles. 'Pictures too – and lovely china – why, I knew nothing of this, I declare.'

'Yes – a few things that came to me by accident,' said Jim in quiet tones.

'And a great gold clock under a glass, and a cupid swinging

for a pendulum; and O what a lovely work-table – woods of every colour – and a work-box to match. May I look inside that work-box, Jim? – whose is it?'

'O yes; look at it, of course. It is a poor enough thing, but 'tis mine; and it will belong to the woman I marry, whoever she may be, as well as all the other things here.'

'And the curtains and the looking-glasses: why, I declare I can see myself in a hundred places.'

'That tea-set,' said Jim, placidly pointing to a gorgeous china service and a large silver tea-pot on the side-table, 'I don't use at present, being a bachelor-man; but, says I to myself, "whoever I marry will want some such things for giving her parties; or I can sell 'em" – but I haven't took steps for't yet – '

'Sell 'em – no, I should think not,' said Margery with earnest reproach. 'Why, I hope you wouldn't be so foolish! Why, this is exactly the kind of thing I was thinking of when I told you of the things women could want – of course not meaning myself particularly. I had no idea that you had such valuable – '
Margery was unable to speak coherently, so much was she amazed at the wealth of Jim's possessions.

At this moment her father and the lime-burner came upstairs; and to appear womanly and proper to Mr Vine, Margery repressed the remainder of her surprise. As for the two elderly worthies, it was not till they entered the room and sat down that their slower eyes discerned anything brilliant in the appoint-ments. Then one of them stole a glance at some article, and the other at another; but each being unwilling to express his wonder in the presence of his neighbours, they received the objects before them with quite an accustomed air; the lime-burner inwardly trying to conjecture what all this meant, and the dairyman musing that if Jim's business allowed him to accumu-late at this rate, the sooner Margery became his wife the better. Margery retreated to the work-table, work-box, and tea-service, which she examined with hushed exclamations.

An entertainment thus surprisingly begun could not fail to progress well. Whenever Margery's crusty old father felt the need of a civil sentence, the flash of Jim's fancy articles inspired him to one; while the lime-burner, having reasoned away his first ominous thought that all this had come out of the firm, also felt proud and blithe.

Jim accompanied his dairy friends part of the way home

before they mounted. Her father, finding that Jim wanted to speak to her privately, and that she exhibited some elusiveness, turned to Margery and said, 'Come, come, my lady; no more of this nonsense. You just step behind with that young man, and I and the cart will wait for you.'

Margery, a little scared at her father's peremptoriness, obeyed. It was plain that Jim had won the old man by that night's stroke, if he had not won her.

'I know what you are going to say, Jim,' she began, less ardently now, for she was no longer under the novel influence of the shining silver and glass. 'Well, as you desire it, and as my father desires it, and as I suppose it will be the best course for me, I will fix the day – not this evening, but as soon as I can think it over.'

Notwithstanding a press of business, Jim went and did his duty in thanking the Baron. The latter saw him in his fishing-tackle room, an apartment littered with every appliance that a votary of the rod could require.

'And when is the wedding-day to be, Hayward?' the Baron asked, after Jim had told him that matters were settled.

'It is not quite certain yet, my noble lord,' said Jim cheerfully. 'But I hope 'twill not be long after the time when God A'mighty christens the little apples.'

'And when is that?'

'St Swithin's* – the middle of July. 'Tis to be some time in that month, she tells me.'

When Jim was gone the Baron seemed meditative. He went out, ascended the mount, and entered the weather-screen, where he looked at the seats, as though re-enacting in his fancy the scene of that memorable morning of fog. He turned his eyes to the angle of the shelter, round which Margery had suddenly appeared like a vision, and it was plain that he would not have minded her appearing there then. The juncture had indeed been such an impressive and critical one that she must have seemed rather a heavenly messenger than a passing milk-maid, more especially to a man like the Baron, who, despite the mystery of his origin and life, revealed himself to be a melancholy, emotional character – the Jacques of this forest and stream.*

Behind the mount the ground rose yet higher, ascending to a

plantation which sheltered the house. The Baron strolled up here, and bent his gaze over the distance. The valley of the Exe lay before him, with its shining river, the brooks that fed it, and the trickling springs that fed the brooks. The situation of Margery's house was visible, though not the house itself; and the Baron gazed that way for an infinitely long time, till, remembering himself, he moved on.

Instead of returning to the house he went along the ridge till he arrived at the verge of Chillington Wood, and in the same desultory manner roamed under the trees, not pausing till he had come to Three-Walks-End, and the hollow elm hard by. He peeped in at the rift. In the soft dry layer of touch-wood that floored the hollow Margery's tracks were still visible, as she had made them there when dressing for the ball.

'Little Margery!' murmured the Baron.

In a moment he thought better of this mood, and turned to go home. But behold, a form stood behind him – that of the girl whose name had been on his lips.

She was in utter confusion. 'I – I – did not know you were here, sir!' she began. 'I was out for a little walk.' She could get no further; her eyes filled with tears. That spice of wilfulness, even hardness, which characterized her in Jim's company, magically disappeared in the presence of the Baron.

'Never mind, never mind,' said he, masking under a severe manner whatever he felt. 'The meeting is awkward, and ought not to have occurred, especially if, as I suppose, you are shortly to be married to James Hayward. But it cannot be helped now. You had no idea I was here, of course. Neither had I of seeing you. Remember you cannot be too careful,' continued the Baron, in the same grave tone; 'and I strongly request you as a friend to do your utmost to avoid meetings like this. When you saw me before I turned, why did you not go away?'

'I did not see you, sir. I did not think of seeing you. I was walking this way, and I only looked in to see the tree.'

'That shows you have been thinking of things you should not think of,' returned the Baron. 'Good-morning.'

Margery could answer nothing. A browbeaten glance, almost of misery, was all she gave him. He took a slow step away from her; then turned suddenly back and, stooping, impulsively kissed her cheek, taking her as much by surprise as ever a woman was taken in her life.

Immediately after he went off with a flushed face and rapid strides, which he did not check till he was within his own boundaries.

The haymaking season now set in vigorously, and the weir-hatches were all drawn in the meads to drain off the water. The streams ran themselves dry, and there was no longer any difficulty in walking about among them. The Baron could very well witness from the elevations about his house the activity which followed these preliminaries. The white shirt-sleeves of the mowers glistened in the sun, the scythes flashed, voices echoed, snatches of song floated about, and there were glimpses of red waggon-wheels, purple gowns, and many-coloured handkerchiefs.

The Baron had been told that the haymaking was to be followed by the wedding, and had he gone down the vale to the dairy he would have had evidence to that effect. Dairyman Tucker's house was in a whirlpool of bustle, and among other difficulties was that of turning the cheese-room into a genteel apartment for the time being, and hiding the awkwardness of having to pass through the milk-house to get to the parlour door. These household contrivances appeared to interest Margery much more than the great question of dressing for the ceremony and the ceremony itself. In all relating to that she showed an indescribable backwardness, which later on was well remembered.

'If it were only somebody else, and I was one of the brides-maids, I really think I should like it better!' she murmured one afternoon.

'Away with thee – that's only your shyness!' said one of the milkmaids.

It is said that about this time the Baron seemed to feel the effects of solitude strongly. Solitude revives the simple instincts of primitive man, and lonely country nooks afford rich soil for wayward emotions. Moreover, idleness waters those unconsidered impulses which a short season of turmoil would stamp out. It is difficult to speak with any exactness of the bearing of such conditions on the mind of the Baron – a man of whom so little was ever truly known – but there is no doubt that his mind ran much on Margery as an individual, without reference to her rank or quality, or to the question whether she would marry Jim Hayward that summer. She was the single lovely human thing within his present horizon, for he lived in absolute seclusion; and her image unduly affected him.

But, leaving conjecture, let me state what happened. One Saturday evening, two or three weeks after his accidental meeting with her in the wood, he wrote the note following: –

Dear Margery –

You must not suppose that, because I spoke somewhat severely to you at our chance encounter by the hollow tree, I have any feeling against you. Far from it. Now, as ever, I have the most grateful sense of your considerate kindness to me on a momentous occasion which shall be nameless.

You solemnly promised to come and see me whenever I should send for you. Can you call for five minutes as soon as possible, and disperse those plaguy glooms from which I am so unfortunate as to suffer? If you refuse I will not answer for the consequences. I shall be in the summer shelter of the mount tomorrow morning at half-past ten. If you come I shall be grateful. I have also something for you. – Yours,

X.

In keeping with the tenor of this epistle the desponding, self-oppressed Baron ascended the mount on Sunday morning and sat down. There was nothing here to signify exactly the hour, but before the church bells had begun he heard somebody approaching at the back. The light footstep moved timidly, first to one recess, and then to another; then to the third, where he sat in the shade. Poor Margery stood before him.

She looked worn and weary, and her little shoes and the skirts of her dress were covered with dust. The weather was sultry, the sun being already high and powerful, and rain had not fallen for weeks. The Baron, who walked little, had thought nothing of the effects of this heat and drought in inducing fatigue. A distance which had been but a reasonable exercise on a foggy morning was a drag for Margery now. She was out of breath; and anxiety, even unhappiness, was written on her everywhere.

He rose to his feet and took her hand. He was vexed with himself at sight of her. 'My dear little girl!' he said. 'You are tired – you should not have come.'

'You sent for me, sir; and I was afraid you were ill; and my promise to you was sacred.'

He bent over her, looking upon her downcast face, and still holding her hand; then he dropped it, and took a pace or two backwards.

'It was a whim, nothing more,' he said sadly. 'I wanted to see my little friend, to express good wishes – and to present her with this.' He held forward a small morocco case, and showed her how to open it, disclosing a pretty locket set with pearls. 'It is intended as a wedding present,' he continued. 'To be returned to me again if you do not marry Jim this summer – it is to be this summer, I think?'

'It was, sir,' she said with agitation. 'But it is so no longer. And, therefore, I cannot take this.'

'What do you say?'

'It was to have been today; but now it cannot be.'

'The wedding today – Sunday?' he cried.

'We fixed Sunday not to hinder much time at this busy season of the year,' replied she.

'And have you, then, put it off – surely not?'

'You sent for me, and I have come,' she answered humbly, like an obedient familiar in the employ of some great enchanter. Indeed, the Baron's power over this innocent girl was curiously like enchantment, or mesmeric influence. It was so masterful that the sexual element was almost eliminated. It was that of Prospero over the gentle Ariel.* And yet it was probably only that of the cosmopolite over the recluse, of the experienced man over the simple maid.

'You have come – on your wedding-day! – O Margery, this is a mistake. Of course, you should not have obeyed me, since, though I thought your wedding would be soon, I did not know it was today.'

'I promised you, sir; and I would rather keep my promise to you than be married to Jim.'

'That must not be – the feeling is wrong!' he murmured, looking at the distant hills. 'There seems to be a fate in all this; I get out of the frying-pan into the fire. What a recompense to you for your goodness! The fact is, I was out of health and out of spirits, so I – but no more of that. Now instantly to repair this tremendous blunder that we have made – that's the question.'

After a pause, he went on hurriedly, 'Walk down the hill; get into the road. By that time I shall be there with a phaeton. We may get back in time. What time is it now? If not, no doubt the wedding can be tomorrow; so all will come right again. Don't cry, my dear girl. Keep the locket, of course – you'll marry Jim.'

He hastened down towards the stables, and she went on as directed. It seemed as if he must have put in the horse himself, so quickly did he reappear with the phaeton on the open road. Margery silently took her seat, and the Baron seemed cut to the quick with self-reproach as he noticed the listless indifference with which she acted. There was no doubt that in her heart she had preferred obeying the apparently important mandate that morning to becoming Jim's wife; but there was no less doubt that had the Baron left her alone she would quietly have gone to the altar.

He drove along furiously, in a cloud of dust. There was much to contemplate in that peaceful Sunday morning – the windless trees and fields, the shaking sunlight, the pause in human stir. Yet neither of them heeded, and thus they drew near to the dairy. His first expressed intention had been to go indoors with her, but this he abandoned as impolitic in the highest degree.

'You may be soon enough,' he said, springing down, and helping her to follow. 'Tell the truth: say you were sent for to receive a wedding present – that it was a mistake on my part – a mistake on yours; and I think they'll forgive. . . . And, Margery, my last request to you is this: that if I send for you again, you do not come. Promise solemnly, my dear girl, that any such request shall be unheeded.'

Her lips moved, but the promise was not articulated. 'O, sir, I cannot promise it!' she said at last.

'But you must; your salvation may depend on it!' he insisted almost sternly. 'You don't know what I am.'

'Then, sir, I promise,' she replied. 'Now leave me to myself, please, and I'll go indoors and manage matters.'

He turned the horse and drove away, but only for a little distance. Out of sight he pulled rein suddenly. 'Only to go back and propose it to her, and she'd come!' he murmured.

He stood up in the phaeton, and by this means he could see over the hedge. Margery still sat listlessly in the same place; there was not a lovelier flower in the field. 'No,' he said; 'no, no – never!' He reseated himself, and the wheels sped lightly back over the soft dust to Mount Lodge.

Meanwhile Margery had not moved. If the Baron could dissimulate on the side of severity she could dissimulate on the side of calm. He did not know what had been veiled by the quiet promise to manage matters indoors. Rising at length she first turned away from the house; and by and by, having apparently forgotten till then that she carried it in her hand, she opened the case and looked at the locket. This seemed to give her courage. She turned, set her face towards the dairy in good earnest, and though her heart faltered when the gates came in sight, she kept on and drew near the door.

On the threshold she stood listening. The house was silent. Decorations were visible in the passage, and also the carefully swept and sanded path to the gate, which she was to have trodden as a bride, but the sparrows hopped over it as if it were abandoned; and all appeared to have been checked at its climacteric, like a clock stopped on the strike. Till this moment of confronting the suspended animation of the scene she had not realized the full shock of the convulsion which her disappearance must have caused. It is quite certain – apart from her own repeated assurances to that effect in later years – that in hastening off that morning to her sudden engagement, Margery had not counted the cost of such an enterprise; while a dim notion that she might get back again in time for the ceremony, if the message meant nothing serious, should also be mentioned in her favour. But, upon the whole, she had obeyed the call with an unreasoning obedience worthy of a disciple in primitive times. A conviction that the Baron's life might depend upon her presence – for she had by this time divined the tragical event she had interrupted on the foggy morning – took from her all will to judge and consider calmly. The simple affairs of her and hers seemed nothing beside the possibility of harm to him.

A well-known step moved on the sanded floor within, and she went forward. That she saw her father's face before her, just within the door, can hardly be said: it was rather Reproach and Rage in a human mask.

'What! ye have dared to come back alive, hussy, to look upon the dupery you have practised on honest people! You've mortified us all; I don't want to see 'ee; I don't want to hear 'ee; I don't want to know anything!' He walked up and down the room, unable to command himself. 'Nothing but being dead could have excused 'ee for not meeting and marrying that man this morning; and yet you have the brazen impudence to stand there as well as ever! What be you here for?'

'I've come back to marry Jim, if he wants me to,' she said faintly. 'And if not – perhaps so much the better. I was sent for this morning early. I thought – ' She halted. To say that she had thought a man's death might happen by his own hand if she did not go to him, would never do. 'I was obliged to go,' she said. 'I had given my word.'

'Why didn't you tell us, then, so that the wedding could be put off, without making fools o' us?'

'Because I was afraid you wouldn't let me go, and I had made up my mind to go.'

'To go where?'

She was silent; till she said, 'I will tell Jim all, and why it was; and if he's any friend of mine he'll excuse me.'

'Not Jim – he's no such fool. Jim had put all ready for you, Jim had called at your house, a-dressed up in his new wedding clothes, and a-smiling like the sun; Jim had told the parson, had got the ringers in tow, and the clerk awaiting; and then – you was *gone*! Then Jim turned as pale as rendlewood,* and busted out, "If she don't marry me today," 'a said, "she don't marry me at all! No; let her look elsewhere for a husband. For tew years I've put up with her haughty tricks and her takings," 'a said. "I've droudged and I've traipsed, I've bought and I've sold, all wi' an eye to her; I've suffered horseflesh,"* he says – yes, them was his noble words – "but I'll suffer it no longer. She shall go!" "Jim," says I, "you be a man. If she's alive, I commend 'ee; if she's dead, pity my old age." "She isn't dead," says he; "for I've just heard she was seen walking off across the fields this morning, looking all of a scornful triumph." He turned round and went, and the rest o' the neighbours went; and here be I left to the reproach o't.'

'He was too hasty,' murmured Margery. 'For now he's said this I can't marry him tomorrow, as I might ha' done; and perhaps so much the better.'

'You can be so calm about it, can ye? Be my arrangements nothing, then, that you should break 'em up, and say off hand what wasn't done today might ha' been done tomorrow, and such flick-flack?* Out o' my sight! I won't hear any more. I won't speak to 'ee any more.'

'I'll go away, and then you'll be sorry!'

Very well, go. Sorry – not I.'

He turned and stamped his way into the cheese-room. Margery went upstairs. She too was excited now, and instead of fortifying herself in her bedroom till her father's rage had blown over, as she had often done on lesser occasions, she packed up a bundle of articles, crept down again, and went out of the house. She had a place of refuge in these cases of necessity, and her father knew it, and was less alarmed at seeing her depart than he might otherwise have been. This place was Rook's Gate, the house of her grandmother, who always took Margery's part when that young woman was particularly in the wrong.

The devious way she pursued, to avoid the vicinity of Mount Lodge, was tedious, and she was already weary. But the cottage was a restful place to arrive at, for she was her own mistress there – her grandmother never coming downstairs – and Edy, the woman who lived with and attended her, being a cipher except in muscle and voice. The approach was by a straight open road, bordered by thin lank trees, all sloping away from the south-west wind-quarter,* and the scene bore a strange resemblance to certain bits of Dutch landscape which have been imprinted on the world's eye by Hobbema and his school.*

Having explained to her granny that the wedding was put off, and that she had come to stay, one of Margery's first acts was carefully to pack up the locket and case, her wedding present from the Baron. The conditions of the gift were unfulfilled, and she wished it to go back instantly. Perhaps, in the intricacies of her bosom, there lurked a greater satisfaction with the reason for returning the present than she would have felt just then with a reason for keeping it.

To send the article was difficult. In the evening she wrapped herself up, searched and found a gauze veil that had been used by her grandmother in past years for hiving swarms of bees, buried her face in it, and sallied forth with a palpitating heart till she drew near the tabernacle of her demigod, the Baron. She ventured only to the back-door, where she handed in the parcel addressed to him, and quickly came away.

Now it seems that during the day the Baron had been unable to learn the result of his attempt to return Margery in time for the event he had interrupted. Wishing, for obvious reasons, to avoid direct inquiry by messenger, and being too unwell to go far himself, he could learn no particulars. He was sitting in thought after a lonely dinner when the parcel intimating failure was brought in. The footman whose curiosity had been excited by the mode of its arrival, peeped through the keyhole after closing the door to learn what the packet meant. Directly the Baron had opened it he thrust out his feet vehemently from his chair, and began cursing his ruinous conduct in bringing about such a disaster, for the return of the locket denoted not only no wedding that day, but none tomorrow, or at any time.

'I have done that innocent woman a great wrong!' he murmured. 'Deprived her of, perhaps, her only opportunity of becoming mistress of a happy home!'

A considerable period of inaction followed among all concerned.

Nothing tended to dissipate the obscurity which veiled the life of the Baron. The position he occupied in the minds of the country-folk around was one which combined the mysteriousness of a legendary character with the unobtrusive deeds of a modern gentleman. To this day whoever takes the trouble to go down to Silverthorn in Lower Wessex and make inquiries will find existing there almost a superstitious feeling for the moody, melancholy stranger who resided in the Lodge some forty years ago.

Whence he came, whither he was going, were alike unknown. It was said that his mother had been an English lady of noble family who had married a foreigner not unheard of in circles where men pile up 'the cankered heaps of strange-achieved gold'* – that he had been born and educated in England, taken abroad, and so on. But the facts of a life in such cases are of little account beside the aspect of a life; and hence, though doubtless the years of his existence contained their share of trite and homely circumstance, the curtain which masked all this was never lifted to gratify such a theatre of spectators as those at Silverthorn. Therein lay his charm. His life was a vignette, of which the central strokes only were drawn with any distinctness, the environment shading away to a blank.

He might have been said to resemble that solitary bird, the heron. The still, lonely stream was his frequent haunt; on its banks he would stand for hours with his rod, looking into the water, beholding the tawny inhabitants with the eye of a philosopher, and seeming to say, 'Bite or don't bite – it's all the same to me.' He was often mistaken for a ghost by children; and for a pollard willow by men, when, on their way home in the dusk, they saw him motionless by some rushy bank, unobservant of the decline of day.

Why did he come to fish near Silverthorn? That was never explained. As far as was known he had no relatives near; the fishing there was not exceptionally good; the society thereabout was decidedly meagre. That he had committed some folly or hasty act, that he had been wrongfully accused of some crime, thus rendering his seclusion from the world desirable for a while, squared very well with his frequent melancholy. But such as he was there he lived, well supplied with fishing-tackle, and tenant of a furnished house, just suited to the requirements of such an eccentric being as he.

Margery's father, having privately ascertained that she was living with her grandmother, and getting into no harm, refrained from communicating with her, in the hope of seeing her contrite at his door. It had, of course, become known about Silverthorn that at the last moment Margery refused to wed Hayward, by absenting herself from the house. Jim was pitied, yet not pitied much, for it was said that he ought not to have been so eager for a woman who had shown no anxiety for him.

And where was Jim himself? It must not be supposed that that tactician had all this while withdrawn from mortal eye to tear his hair in silent indignation and despair. He had, in truth, merely retired up the lonesome defile between the downs to his smouldering kiln, and the ancient ramparts above it; and there, after his first hours of natural discomposure, he quietly waited for overtures from the possibly repentant Margery. But no overtures arrived, and then he meditated anew on the absorbing problem of her skittishness, and how to set about another campaign for her conquest, notwithstanding his late disastrous failure. Why had he failed? To what was her strange conduct owing? That was the thing which puzzled him.

He had made no advance in solving the riddle when, one morning, a stranger appeared on the down above him, looking as if he had lost his way. The man had a good deal of black hair below his felt hat, and carried under his arm a case containing a musical instrument. Descending to where Jim stood, he asked if

there were not a short cut across that way to Tivworthy, where
a fête was to be held.

'Well, yes, there is,' said Jim. 'But 'tis an enormous distance
for 'ee.'

'O yes,' replied the musician. 'I wish to intercept the carrier
on the highway.'

The nearest way was precisely in the direction of Rook's Gate,
where Margery, as Jim knew, was staying. Having some time to
spare, Jim was strongly impelled to make a kind act to the lost
musician a pretext for taking observations in that neighbourhood; and telling his acquaintance that he was going the same
way, he started without further ado.

They skirted the long length of meads, and in due time arrived
at the back of Rook's Gate, where the path joined the high road.
A hedge divided the public way from the cottage garden. Jim
drew up at this point and said, 'Your road is straight on: I turn
back here.'

But the musician was standing fixed, as if in great perplexity.
Thrusting his hand into his forest of black hair, he murmured,
'Surely it is the same – surely!'

Jim, following the direction of his neighbour's eyes, found
them to be fixed on a figure till that moment hidden from
himself – Margery Tucker – who was crossing the garden to an
opposite gate with a little cheese in her arms, her head thrown
back, and her face quite exposed.

'What of her?' said Jim.

'Two months ago I formed one of the band at the Yeomanry
Ball given by Lord Toneborough in the next county. I saw that
young lady dancing the polka there in robes of gauze and lace.
Now I see her carry a cheese!'

'Never!' said Jim incredulously.

'But I do not mistake. I say it is so!'

Jim ridiculed the idea; the bandsman protested, and was about
to lose his temper, when Jim gave in with the good-nature of a
person who can afford to despise opinions; and the musician
went his way.

As he dwindled out of sight Jim began to think more carefully
over what he had said. The young man's thoughts grew quite to
an excitement, for there came into his mind the Baron's extraordinary kindness in regard to furniture, hitherto accounted for
by the assumption that the nobleman had taken a fancy to him.

Could it be, among all the amazing things of life, that the Baron was at the bottom of this mischief, and that he had amused himself by taking Margery to a ball?

Doubts and suspicions which distract some lovers to imbecility only served to bring out Jim's great qualities. Where he trusted he was the most trusting fellow in the world; where he doubted he could be guilty of the slyest strategy. Once suspicious, he became one of those subtle, watchful characters who, without integrity, make good thieves; with a little, good jobbers; with a little more, good diplomatists. Jim was honest, and he considered what to do.

Retracing his steps, he peeped again. She had gone in; but she would soon reappear, for it could be seen that she was carrying little new cheeses one by one to a spring-cart and horse tethered outside the gate – her grandmother, though not a regular dairy-woman, still managing a few cows by means of a man and maid. With the lightness of a cat Jim crept round to the gate, took a piece of chalk from his pocket, and wrote upon the boarding 'The Baron'. Then he retreated to the other side of the garden where he had just watched Margery.

In due time she emerged with another little cheese, came on to the garden-door, and glanced upon the chalked words which confronted her. She started; the cheese rolled from her arms to the ground, and broke into pieces like a pudding.

She looked fearfully round, her face burning like sunset, and, seeing nobody, stooped to pick up the flaccid lumps. Jim, with a pale face, departed as invisibly as he had come. He had proved the bandsman's tale to be true. On his way back he formed a resolution. It was to beard the lion in his den – to call on the Baron.

Meanwhile Margery had recovered her equanimity, and gathered up the broken cheese. But she could by no means account for the handwriting. Jim was just the sort of fellow to play her such a trick at ordinary times, but she imagined him to be far too incensed against her to do it now; and she suddenly wondered if it were any sort of signal from the Baron himself.

Of him she had lately heard nothing. If ever monotony pervaded a life it pervaded hers at Rook's Gate; and she had begun to despair of any happy change. But it is precisely when the social atmosphere seems stagnant that great events are brewing. Margery's quiet was broken first, as we have seen, by a slight start, only sufficient to make her drop a cheese; and then by a more serious matter.

She was inside the same garden one day when she heard two watermen talking without. The conversation was to the effect that the strange gentleman who had taken Mount Lodge for the season was seriously ill.

'How ill?' cried Margery through the hedge, which screened her from recognition.

'Bad abed,' said one of the watermen.

'Inflammation of the lungs,' said the other.

'Got wet, fishing,' the first chimed in.

Margery could gather no more. An ideal admiration rather than any positive passion existed in her breast for the Baron: she had of late seen too little of him to allow any incipient views of him as a lover to grow to formidable dimensions. It was an extremely romantic feeling, delicate as an aroma, capable of quickening to an active principle, or dying to 'a painless sympathy',* as the case might be.

This news of his illness, coupled with the mysterious chalking on the gate, troubled her, and revived his image much. She took to walking up and down the garden-paths, looking into the hearts of flowers, and not thinking what they were. His last request had been that she was not to go to him if he should send for her; and now she asked herself, was the name on the gate a hint to enable her to go without infringing the letter of her promise? Thus unexpectedly had Jim's manoeuvre operated.

Ten days passed. All she could hear of the Baron were the same words, 'Bad abed,' till one afternoon, after a gallop of the physician to the Lodge, the tidings spread like lightning that the Baron was dying.

Margery distressed herself with the question whether she might be permitted to visit him and say her prayers at his bedside; but she feared to venture; and thus eight-and-forty hours slipped away, and the Baron still lived. Despite her shyness and awe of him she had almost made up her mind to call when, just at dusk on that October evening, somebody came to the door and asked for her.

She could see the messenger's head against the low new moon. He was a manservant. He said he had been all the way to her father's, and had been sent thence to her here. He simply brought a note, and, delivering it into her hands, went away.

> Dear Margery Tucker – ran the note – They say I am not likely to live, so I want to see you. Be here at eight o'clock this evening. Come quite alone to the side-door, and tap four times softly. My trusty man will admit you. The occasion is an important one. Prepare yourself for a solemn ceremony, which I wish to have performed while it lies in my power.
>
> VON XANTEN.

Margery's face flushed up, and her neck and arms glowed in sympathy. The quickness of youthful imagination, and the assumptiveness of woman's reason, sent her straight as an arrow his thought: 'He wants to marry me!'

She had heard of similar strange proceedings, in which the orange-flower and the sad cypress were intertwined.* People sometimes wished on their deathbeds, from motives of esteem, to form a legal tie which they had not cared to establish as a domestic one during their active life.

For a few minutes Margery could hardly be called excited; she was excitement itself. Between surprise and modesty she blushed and trembled by turns. She became grave, sat down in the solitary room, and looked into the fire. At seven o'clock she rose resolved, and went quite tranquilly upstairs, where she speedily began to dress.

In making this hasty toilet nine-tenths of her care were given to her hands. The summer had left them slightly brown, and she held them up and looked at them with some misgiving, the fourth finger of her left hand more especially. Hot washings and cold washings, certain products from bee and flower known only to country girls, everything she could think of, were used upon those little sunburnt hands, till she persuaded herself that they were really as white as could be wished by a husband with a hundred titles. Her dressing completed, she left word with Edy that she was going for a long walk, and set out in the direction of Mount Lodge.

She no longer tripped like a girl, but walked like a woman. While crossing the park she murmured 'Baroness von Xanten' in a pronunciation of her own. The sound of that title caused her such agitation that she was obliged to pause, with her hand upon her heart.

The house was so closely neighboured by shrubberies on three of its sides that it was not till she had gone nearly round it that she found the little door. The resolution she had been an hour in forming failed her when she stood at the portal. While pausing for courage to tap, a carriage drove up to the front entrance a little way off, and peeping round the corner she saw alight a clergyman, and a gentleman in whom Margery fancied that she recognized a well-known solicitor from the neighbouring town. She had no longer any doubt of the nature of the ceremony proposed. 'It is sudden – but I must obey him!' she murmured; and tapped four times.

The door was opened so quickly that the servant must have been standing immediately inside. She thought him the man who had driven them to the ball – the silent man who could be trusted. Without a word he conducted her up the back staircase, and through a door at the top, into a wide corridor. She was asked to wait in a little dressing-room, where there was a fire, and an old metal-framed looking-glass over the mantelpiece, in which she caught sight of herself. A red spot burnt in each of her cheeks; the rest of her face was pale; and her eyes were like diamonds of the first water.

Before she had been seated many minutes the man came back noiselessly, and she followed him to a door covered by a red and black curtain, which he lifted, and ushered her into a large chamber. A screened light stood on a table before her, and on her left the hangings of a tall, dark, four-post bedstead obstructed her view of the centre of the room. Everything here seemed of such a magnificent type to her eyes that she felt confused, diminished to half her height, half her strength, half her prettiness. The man who had conducted her retired at once, and some one came softly round the angle of the bed-curtains. He held out his hand kindly – rather patronisingly: it was the solicitor whom she knew by sight. This gentleman led her forward, as if she had been a lamb rather than a woman, till the occupant of the bed was revealed.

The Baron's eyes were closed, and her entry had been so noiseless that he did not open them. The pallor of his face nearly matched the white bed-linen, and his dark hair and heavy black moustache were like dashes of ink on a clean page. Near him sat the parson and another gentleman, whom she afterwards learnt to be a London physician; and on the parson whispering a few words the Baron opened his eyes. As soon as he saw her he smiled faintly, and held out his hand.

Margery would have wept for him, if she had not been too overawed and palpitating to do anything. She quite forgot what she had come for, shook hands with him mechanically, and could hardly return an answer to his weak 'Dear Margery, you see how I am – how are you?'

In preparing for marriage she had not calculated on such a scene as this. Her affection for the Baron had too much of the vague in it to afford her trustfulness now. She wished she had not come. On a sign from the Baron the lawyer brought her a chair, and the oppressive silence was broken by the Baron's words.

'I am pulled down to death's door, Margery,' he said; 'and I suppose I soon shall pass through. . . . My peace has been much disturbed in this illness, for just before it attacked me I received – that present you returned, from which, and in other ways, I learnt that you had lost your chance of marriage. . . . Now it was I who did the harm, and you can imagine how the news has affected me. It has worried me all the illness through, and I cannot dismiss my error from my mind. . . . I want to right the wrong I have done you before I die. Margery, you have always obeyed me, and, strange as the request may be, will you obey me now?'

She whispered, 'Yes.'

'Well, then,' said the Baron, 'these three gentlemen are here for a special purpose: one helps the body – he's called a physician; another helps the soul – he's a parson; the other helps the understanding – he's a lawyer. They are here partly on my account, and partly on yours.'

The speaker then made a sign to the lawyer, who went out of the door. He came back almost instantly, but not alone. Behind him, dressed up in his best clothes, with a flower in his buttonhole and a bridegroom's air, walked – Jim.

Margery could hardly repress a scream. As for flushing and blushing, she had turned hot and turned pale so many times already during the evening, that there was really now nothing of that sort left for her to do; and she remained in complexion much as before. O, the mockery of it! That secret dream – that sweet word 'Baroness!' – which had sustained her all the way along. Instead of a Baron there stood Jim, white-waistcoated, demure, every hair in place, and, if she mistook not, even a deedy* spark in his eye.

Jim's surprising presence on the scene may be briefly accounted for. His resolve to seek an explanation with the Baron at all risks had proved unexpectedly easy: the interview had at once been granted, and then, seeing the crisis at which matters stood, the Baron had generously revealed to Jim the whole of his indebtedness to and knowledge of Margery. The truth of the Baron's statement, the innocent nature as yet of the acquaint-anceship, his sorrow for the rupture he had produced, was so evident that, far from having any further doubts of his patron, Jim frankly asked his advice on the next step to be pursued. At this stage the Baron fell ill, and, desiring much to see the two young people united before his death, he had sent anew to Hayward, and proposed the plan which they were now about to attempt – a marriage at the bedside of the sick man by special licence.* The influence at Lambeth* of some friends of the Baron's, and the charitable bequests of his late mother to several deserving Church funds, were generally supposed to be among the reasons why the application for the licence was not refused.

This, however, is of small consequence. The Baron probably knew, in proposing this method of celebrating the marriage, that his enormous power over her would outweigh any senti-mental obstacles which she might set up – inward objections that, without his presence and firmness, might prove too much for her acquiescence. Doubtless he foresaw, too, the advantage of getting her into the house before making the individuality of her husband clear to her mind.

Now, the Baron's conjectures were right as to the event, but wrong as to the motives. Margery was a perfect little dissembler on some occasions, and one of them was when she wished to hide any sudden mortification that might bring her into ridicule. She had no sooner recovered from her first fit of discomfiture than pride bade her suffer anything rather than reveal her absurd disappointment. Hence the scene progressed as follows:

'Come here, Hayward,' said the invalid. Hayward came near. The Baron, holding her hand in one of his own, and her lover's in the other, continued, 'Will you, in spite of your recent vexation with her, marry her now if she does not refuse?'

'I will, sir,' said Jim promptly.

'And Margery, what do you say? It is merely a setting of things right. You have already promised this young man to be his wife, and should, of course, perform your promise. You don't dislike Jim?'

'O no, sir,' she said, in a low, dry voice.

'I like him better than I can tell you,' said the Baron. 'He is an honourable man, and will make you a good husband. You must remember that marriage is a life contract, in which general compatibility of temper and worldly position is of more import-ance than fleeting passion, which never long survives. Now, will you, at my earnest request, and before I go to the South of Europe to die, agree to make this good man happy? I have expressed your views on the subject, haven't I, Hayward?'

'To a T, sir,' said Jim emphatically, with a motion of raising his hat to his influential ally, till he remembered he had no hat on. 'And, though I could hardly expect Margery to gie in for my asking, I feels she ought to gie in for yours.'

'And you accept him, my little friend?'

'Yes, sir,' she murmured, 'if he'll agree to a thing or two.'

'Doubtless he will – what are they?'

'That I shall not be made to live with him till I am in the mind for it; and that my having him shall be kept unknown for the present.'

'Well, what do you think of it, Hayward?'

'Anything that you or she may wish I'll do, my noble lord,' said Jim.

'Well, her request is not unreasonable, seeing that the proceed-ings are, on my account, a little hurried. So we'll proceed. You rather expected this, from my allusion to a ceremony in my note, did you not, Margery?'

'Yes, sir,' said she, with an effort.

'Good; I thought so; you looked so little surprised.'

We now leave the scene in the bedroom for a spot not many yards off.

When the carriage seen by Margery at the door was driving up to Mount Lodge it arrested the attention, not only of the young girl, but of a man who had for some time been moving slowly about the opposite lawn, engaged in some operation while he smoked a short pipe. A short observation of his doings would have shown that he was sheltering some delicate plants from an expected frost, and that he was the gardener. When the light at the door fell upon the entering forms of parson and lawyer – the former a stranger, the latter known to him – the gardener walked thoughtfully round the house. Reaching the small side-entrance he was further surprised to see it noiselessly open to a young woman, in whose momentarily illumined features he discerned those of Margery Tucker.

Altogether there was something curious in this. The man returned to the lawn front, and perfunctorily went on putting shelters over certain plants, though his thoughts were plainly otherwise engaged. On the grass his footsteps were noiseless, and the night moreover being still, he could presently hear a murmuring from the bedroom window over his head.

The gardener took from a tree a ladder that he had used in nailing that day, set it under the window, and ascended half-way, hoodwinking his conscience by seizing a nail or two with his hand and testing their twig-supporting powers. He soon heard enough to satisfy him. The words of a church-service in the strange parson's voice were audible in snatches through the blind: they were words he knew to be part of the solemnization of matrimony, such as 'wedded wife', 'richer for poorer', and so on; the less familiar parts being a more or less confused sound.

Satisfied that a wedding was in progress there, the gardener did not for a moment dream that one of the contracting parties could be other than the sick Baron. He descended the ladder and again walked round the house, waiting only till he saw Margery emerge from the same little door; when, fearing that he might be discovered, he withdrew in the direction of his own cottage.

This building stood at the lower corner of the garden, and as soon as the gardener entered he was accosted by a handsome woman in a widow's cap, who called him father, and said that supper had been ready for a long time. They sat down, but during the meal the gardener was so abstracted and silent that his daughter put her head winningly to one side and said, 'What is it, father dear?'

'Ah – what is it?' cried the gardener. 'Something that makes very little difference to me, but may be of great account to you, if you play your cards well. *There's been a wedding at the Lodge tonight!*' He related to her, with a caution to secrecy, all that he had heard and seen.

'We are folk that have got to get their living,' he said, 'and such ones mustn't tell tales about their betters – Lord forgive the mockery of the word! – but there's something to be made of it. She's a nice maid; so, Harriet, do you take the first chance you get for honouring her, before others know what has happened. Since this is done so privately it will be kept private for some time – till after his death, no question; when I expect she'll take this house for herself, and blaze out* as a widow-lady ten thousand pound strong. You being a widow, she may make you her company-keeper; and so you'll have a home by a little contriving.'

While this conversation progressed at the gardener's Margery was on her way out of the Baron's house. She was, indeed, married. But, as we know, she was not married to the Baron. The ceremony over she seemed but little discomposed, and expressed a wish to return alone as she had come. To this, of course, no objection could be offered under the terms of the agreement, and wishing Jim a frigid good-bye, and the Baron a very quiet farewell, she went out by the door which had admitted her. Once safe and alone in the darkness of the park she burst into tears, which dropped upon the grass as she passed along. In the Baron's room she had seemed scared and helpless; now her reason and emotions returned. The farther she got away from the glamour of that room, and the influence of its occupant, the more she became of opinion that she had acted foolishly. She had disobediently left her father's house, to obey him here. She had pleased everybody but herself.

However, thinking was now too late. How she got into her grandmother's house she hardly knew; but without a supper, and without confronting either her relative or Edy, she went to bed.

On going out into the garden next morning, with a strange sense of being another person than herself, she beheld Jim leaning mutely over the gate.

He nodded. 'Good morning, Margery,' he said civilly.

'Good morning,' said Margery in the same tone.

'I beg your pardon,' he continued. 'But which way was you going this morning?'

'I am not going anywhere just now, thank you. But I shall go to my father's by and by with Edy.' She went on with a sigh, 'I have done what he has all along wished, that is, married you; and there's no longer reason for enmity atween him and me.'

'Trew – trew. Well, as I am going the same way, I can give you a lift in the trap, for the distance is long.'

'No, thank you – I am used to walking,' she said.

They remained in silence, the gate between them, till Jim's convictions would apparently allow him to hold his peace no longer. 'This is a bad job!' he murmured.

'It is,' she said, as one whose thoughts have only too readily been identified. 'How I came to agree to it is more than I can tell!' And tears began rolling down her cheeks.

'The blame is more mine than yours, I suppose,' he returned. 'I ought to have said No, and not backed up the gentleman in carrying out this scheme. 'Twas his own notion entirely, as perhaps you know. I should never have thought of such a plan; but he said you'd be willing, and that it would be all right; and I was too ready to believe him.'

'The thing is, how to remedy it,' said she bitterly. 'I believe, of course, in your promise to keep this private, and not to trouble me by calling.'

'Certainly,' said Jim. 'I don't want to trouble you. As for that, why, my dear Mrs Hayward – '

'Don't Mrs Hayward me!' said Margery sharply. 'I won't be Mrs Hayward!'

Jim paused. 'Well, you are she by law, and that was all I meant,' he said mildly.

'I said I would acknowledge no such thing, and I won't. A thing can't be legal when it's against the wishes of the persons the laws are made to protect. So I beg you not to call me that any more.'

'Very well, Miss Tucker,' said Jim deferentially. 'We can live on exactly as before. We can't marry anybody else, that's true; but beyond that there's no difference, and no harm done. Your father ought to be told, I suppose, even if nobody else is? It will partly reconcile him to you, and make your life smoother.'

Instead of directly replying, Margery exclaimed in a low voice:

'O, it is a mistake – I didn't see it all, owing to not having time to reflect! I agreed, thinking that at least I should get reconciled to father by the step. But perhaps he would as soon have me not married at all as married and parted. I must ha' been enchanted – bewitched – when I gave my consent to this! I only did it to please that dear good dying nobleman – though why he should have wished it so much I can't tell!'

'Nor I neither,' said Jim. 'Yes, we've been fooled into it, Margery,' he said, with extraordinary gravity. 'He's had his way wi' us, and now we've got to suffer for it. Being a gentleman of patronage, and having bought several loads of lime o' me, and having given me all that splendid furniture, I could hardly refuse – '

'What, did he give you that?'

'Ay, sure – to help me win ye.'

Margery covered her face with her hands; whereupon Jim stood up from the gate and looked critically at her. ''Tis a footy* plot between you two men to – snare me!' she exclaimed. 'Why should you have done it – why should he have done it – when I've not deserved to be treated so. He bought the furniture, did he! O, I've been taken in – I've been wronged!' The grief and vexation of finding that long ago, when fondly believing the Baron to have lover-like feelings himself for her, he was still conspiring to favour Jim's suit, was more than she could endure.

Jim with distant courtesy waited, nibbling a straw, till her paroxysm was over. 'One word, Miss Tuck – Mrs – Margery,' he then recommenced gravely. 'You'll find me man enough to respect your wish, and to leave you to yourself – for ever and ever, if that's all. But I've just one word of advice to render 'ee. That is, that before you go to Silverthorn Dairy yourself you let me drive ahead and call on your father. He's friends with me, and he's not friends with you. I can break the news, a little at a time, and I think I can gain his good will for you now, even though the wedding be no natural wedding at all. At any count, I can hear what he's got to say about 'ee, and come back here and tell 'ee.'

She nodded a cool assent to this, and he left her strolling about the garden in the sunlight while he went on to reconnoitre as agreed. It must not be supposed that Jim's dutiful echoes of Margery's regret at her precipitate marriage were all gospel; and there is no doubt that his private intention, after telling the dairy-farmer what had happened, was to ask his temporary assent to her caprice, till, in the course of time, she should be reasoned out of her whims and induced to settle down with Jim in a natural manner. He had, it it true, been somewhat nettled by her firm objection to him, and her keen sorrow for what she had done to please another; but he hoped for the best.

But, alas for the astute Jim's calculations! He drove on to the dairy, whose white walls now gleamed in the morning sun; made fast the horse to a ring in the wall, and entered the barton. Before knocking, he perceived the dairyman walking across from a gate in the other direction, as if he had just come in. Jim went over to him. Since the unfortunate incident on the morning of the intended wedding they had merely been on nodding terms, from a sense of awkwardness in their relations.

'What – is that thee?' said Dairyman Tucker, in a voice which unmistakably startled Jim by its abrupt fierceness. 'A pretty fellow thou be'st!'

It was a bad beginning for the young man's life as a son-in-law, and augured ill for the delicate consultation he desired.

'What's the matter?' said Jim.

'Matter! I wish some folks would burn their lime without burning other folks' property along wi' it. You ought to be ashamed of yourself. You call yourself a man, Jim Hayward, and an honest lime-burner, and a respectable, market-keeping Christen, and yet at six o'clock this morning, instead o' being where you ought to ha' been – at your work, there was neither vell or mark* o' thee to be seen!'

'Faith, I don't know what you are raving at,' said Jim.

'Why – the sparks from thy couch-heap blew over upon my hay-rick, and the rick's burnt to ashes; and all to come out o' my well-squeezed pocket. I'll tell thee what it is, young man. There's no business in thee. I've known Silverthorn folk, quick and dead, for the last couple-o'-score year, and I've never knew one so three-cunning* for harm as thee, my gentleman lime-burner; and I reckon it one o' the luckiest days o' my life when I 'scaped having thee in my family. That maid of mine was right; I was wrong. She seed thee to be a drawlacheting* rogue, and 'twas her wisdom to go off that morning and get rid o' thee. I commend her for't, and I'm going to fetch her home tomorrow.'

'You needn't take the trouble. She's coming home-along tonight of her own accord. I have seen her this morning, and she told me so.'

'So much the better. I'll welcome her warm. Nation! I'd sooner see her married to the parish fool than thee. Not you – you don't care for my hay. Tarrying about where you shouldn't be – in bed, no doubt; that's what you was a-doing. Now, don't you darken my doors again, and the sooner you be off my bit o' ground the better I shall be pleased.'

Jim looked, as he felt, stultified. If the rick had been really destroyed, a little blame certainly attached to him, but he could not understand how it had happened. However, blame or none, it was clear he could not, with any self-respect, declare himself to be this peppery old gaffer's son-in-law in the face of such an attack as this.

For months – almost years – the one transaction that had seemed necessary to compose these two families satisfactorily was Jim's union with Margery. No sooner had it been completed than it appeared on all sides as the gravest mishap for both. Stating coldly that he would discover how much of the accident was to be attributed to his negligence, and pay the damage, he went out of the barton, and returned the way he had come.

Margery had been keeping a look-out for him, particularly wishing him not to enter the house, lest others should see the seriousness of their interview; and as soon as she heard wheels she went to the gate, which was out of view.

'Surely father has been speaking roughly to you!' she said, on seeing his face.

'Not the least doubt that he have,' said Jim.

'But is he still angry with me?'

'Not in the least. He's waiting to welcome 'ee.'

'Ah! because I've married you.'

'Because he thinks you have *not* married me! He's jawed* me up hill and down. He hates me; and for your sake I have not explained a word.'

Margery looked towards home with a sad, severe gaze. 'Mr Hayward,' she said, 'we have made a great mistake, and we are in a strange position.'

'True, but I'll tell you what, mistress – I won't stand – ' He stopped suddenly. 'Well, well; I've promised!' he quietly added.

'We must suffer for our mistake,' she went on. 'The way to suffer least is to keep our own counsel on what happened last evening, and not to meet. I must now return to my father.'

He inclined his head in indifferent assent, and she went indoors, leaving him there.

*

Margery returned home, as she had decided, and resumed her old life at Silverthorn. And seeing her father's animosity towards Jim, she told him not a word of the marriage.

Her inner life, however, was not what it once had been. She had suffered a mental and emotional displacement – a shock, which had set a shade of astonishment on her face as a permanent thing.

Her indignation with the Baron for collusion with Jim, at first bitter, lessened with the lapse of a few weeks, and at length vanished in the interest of some tidings she received one day.

The Baron was not dead, but he was no longer at the Lodge. To the surprise of the physicians, a sufficient improvement had taken place in his condition to permit of his removal before the cold weather came. His desire for removal had been such, indeed, that it was advisable to carry it out at almost any risk. The plan adopted had been to have him borne on men's shoulders in a sort of palanquin to the shore near Idmouth, a distance of several miles, where a yacht lay awaiting him. By this means the noise and jolting of a carriage, along irregular bye-roads, were avoided. The singular procession over the fields took place at night, and was witnessed by but few people, one being a labouring man, who described the scene to Margery. When the seaside was reached a long, narrow gangway was laid from the deck of the yacht to the shore, which was so steep as to allow the yacht to lie quite near. The men, with their burden, ascended by the light of lanterns, the sick man was laid in the cabin, and, as soon as his bearers had returned to the shore, the gangway was removed, a rope was heard skirring* over wood in the darkness, the yacht quivered, spread her woven wings to the air, and moved away. Soon she was but a small shapeless phantom upon the wide breast of the sea.

It was said that the yacht was bound for Algiers.

When the inimical autumn and winter weather came on, Margery wondered if he were still alive. The house being shut up, and the servants gone, she had no means of knowing, till, on a particular Saturday, her father drove her to Exonbury market. Here, in attending to his business, he left her to herself for a while. Walking in a quiet street in the professional quarter of the town, she saw coming towards her the solicitor who had been present at the wedding, and who had acted for the Baron in various small local matters during his brief residence at the Lodge.

She reddened to peony hues, averted her eyes, and would have passed him. But he crossed over and barred the pavement, and when she met his glance he was looking with friendly severity at her. The street was quiet, and he said in a low voice, 'How's the husband?'

'I don't know, sir,' said she.

'What – and are your stipulations about secrecy and separate living still in force?'

'They will always be,' she replied decisively. 'Mr Hayward and I agreed on the point, and we have not the slightest wish to change the arrangement.'

'H'm. Then 'tis Miss Tucker to the world; Mrs Hayward to me and one or two others only?'

Margery nodded. Then she nerved herself by an effort, and, though blushing painfully, asked, 'May I put one question, sir? Is the Baron dead?'

'He is dead to you and to all of us. Why should you ask?'

'Because, if he's alive, I am sorry I married James Hayward. If he is dead I do not much mind my marriage.'

'I repeat, he is dead to you,' said the lawyer emphatically. 'I'll tell you all I know. My professional services for him ended with his departure from this country; but I think I should have heard from him if he had been alive still. I have not heard at all: and this, taken in connection with the nature of his illness, leaves no doubt in my mind that he is dead.'

Margery sighed, and thanking the lawyer she left him with a tear for the Baron in her eye. After this incident she became more restful; and the time drew on for her periodical visit to her grandmother.

A few days subsequent to her arrival her aged relative asked her to go with a message to the gardener at Mount Lodge (who still lived on there, keeping the grounds in order for the landlord). Margery hated that direction now, but she went. The Lodge, which she saw over the trees, was to her like a skull from which the warm and living flesh had vanished. It was twilight by the time she reached the cottage at the bottom of the Lodge garden, and, the room being illuminated within, she saw through the window a woman she had never seen before. She was dark, and rather handsome, and when Margery knocked she opened the door. It was the gardener's widowed daughter, who had been advised to make friends with Margery.

She now found her opportunity. Margery's errand was soon completed, the young widow, to her surprise, treating her with preternatural respect, and afterwards offering to accompany her home. Margery was not sorry to have a companion in the gloom, and they walked on together. The widow, Mrs Peach, was demonstrative and confidential, and told Margery all about herself. She had come quite recently to live with her father – during the Baron's illness, in fact – and her husband had been captain of a ketch.

'I saw you one morning, ma'am,' she said. 'But you didn't see me. It was when you were crossing the hill in sight of the Lodge. You looked at it, and sighed. 'Tis the lot of widows to sigh, ma'am, is it not?'

'Widows – yes, I suppose; but what do you mean?'

Mrs Peach lowered her voice. 'I can't say more, ma'am, with proper respect. But there seems to be no question of the poor Baron's death; and though these foreign princes can take (as my poor husband used to tell me) what they call left-handed wives, and leave them behind when they go abroad, widowhood is widowhood, left-handed or right. And really, to be the left-handed wife of a foreign baron is nobler than to be married all round to a common man. You'll excuse my freedom, ma'am; but being a widow myself, I have pitied you from my heart; so young as you are, and having to keep it a secret, and (excusing me) having no money out of his vast riches because 'tis swllowed up by Baroness Number One.'

Now Margery did not understand a word more of this than the bare fact that Mrs Peach suspected her to be the Baron's undowered widow, and such was the milkmaid's nature that she did not deny the widow's impeachment. The latter continued –

'But ah, ma'am, all your troubles are straight backward in your memory – while I have troubles before as well as grief behind.'

'What may they be, Mrs Peach?' inquired Margery, with an air of the Baroness.

The other dropped her voice to revelation tones: 'I have been forgetful enough of my first man to lose my heart to a second!'

'You shouldn't do that – it is wrong. You should control your feelings.'

'But how am I to control my feelings?'

'By going to your dead husband's grave, and things of that sort.'

'Do you go to your dead husband's grave?'

'How can I go to Algiers?'

'Ah – too true! Well, I've tried everything to cure myself – read the words against it, gone to the Table* the first Sunday of every month, and all sorts. But, avast,* my shipmate! – as my poor man used to say – there 'tis just the same. In short, I've made up my mind to encourage the new one. 'Tis flattering that I, a new-comer, should have been found out by a young man so soon.'

'Who is he?' said Margery listlessly.

'A master lime-burner.'

'A master lime-burner?'

'That's his profession. He's a partner-in-co., doing very well indeed.'

'But what's his name?'

'I don't like to tell you his name, for, though 'tis night, that covers all shame-facedness, my face is as hot as a 'Talian iron,* I declare! Do you just feel it.'

Margery put her hand on Mrs Peach's face, and sure enough, hot it was. 'Does he come courting?' she asked quickly.

'Well – only in the way of business. He never comes unless lime is wanted in the neighbourhood. He's in the Yeomanry, too, and will look very fine when he comes out in regimentals for drill in May.'

'Oh – in the Yeomanry,' Margery said, with a slight relief. 'Then it can't – is he a young man?'

'Yes, junior partner-in-co.'

The description had an odd resemblance to Jim, of whom Margery had not heard a word for months. He had promised silence and absence, and had fulfilled his promise literally, with a gratuitous addition that was rather amazing, if indeed it were Jim whom the widow loved. One point in the description puzzled Margery: Jim was not in the Yeomanry, unless, by a surprising development of enterprise, he had entered it recently.

At parting Margery said, with an interest quite tender, 'I should like to see you again, Mrs Peach, and hear of your attachment. When can you call?'

'Oh – any time, dear Baroness, I'm sure – if you think I am good enough.'

'Indeed, I do, Mrs Peach. Come as soon as you've seen the lime-burner again.'

Seeing that Jim lived several miles from the widow, Margery was rather surprised, and even felt a slight sinking of the heart, when her new acquaintance appeared at her door so soon as the evening of the following Monday. She asked Margery to walk out with her, which the young woman readily did.

'I am come at once,' said the widow breathlessly, as soon as they were in the lane, 'for it is so exciting that I can't keep it. I must tell it to somebody, if only a bird, or a cat, or a garden snail.'

'What is it?' asked her companion.

'I've pulled grass from my husband's grave to cure it – wove the blades into true lover's knots; took off my shoes upon the sod*; but, avast, my shipmate! – '

'Upon the sod – why?'

'To feel the damp earth he's in, and make the sense of it enter my soul. But no. It has swelled to a head; he is going to meet me at the Yeomanry Review.'

'The master lime-burner?'

The widow nodded.

'When is it to be?'

'Tomorrow. He looks so lovely in his accoutrements! He's such a splendid soldier; that was the last straw that kindled my soul to say yes. He's home from Exonbury for a night between the drills,' continued Mrs Peach. 'He goes back tomorrow morning for the Review, and when it's over he's going to meet me. . . . But, guide my heart, there he is!'

Her exclamation had rise in the sudden appearance of a brilliant red uniform through the trees, and the tramp of a horse carrying the wearer thereof. In another half-minute the military gentleman would have turned the corner, and faced them.

'He'd better not see me; he'll think I know too much,' said Margery precipitately. 'I'll go up here.'

The widow, whose thoughts had been of the same cast, seemed much relieved to see Margery disappear in the planta-tion, in the midst of a spring chorus of birds. Once among the trees, Margery turned her head, and, before she could see the rider's person she recognized the horse as Tony, the lightest of three that Jim and his partner owned, for the purpose of carting out lime to their customers.

Jim, then, had joined the Yeomanry since his estrangement from Margery. A man who had worn the young Queen Victoria's uniform* for seven days only could not be expected to look as if it were part of his person, in the manner of long-trained soldiers; but he was a well-formed young fellow, and of an age when few positions came amiss to one who has the capacity to adapt himself to circumstances.

Meeting the blushing Mrs Peach (to whom Margery in her mind sternly denied the right to blush at all), Jim alighted and moved on with her, probably at Mrs Peach's own suggestion; so that what they said, how long they remained together, and how they parted, Margery knew not. She might have known some of these things by waiting; but the presence of Jim had bred in her heart a sudden disgust for the widow, and a general sense of discomfiture. She went away in an opposite direction, turning her head and saying to the unconscious Jim, 'There's a fine rod in pickle for you, my gentleman, if you carry out that pretty scheme!'

Jim's military *coup** had decidedly astonished her. What he might do next she could not conjecture. The idea of his doing anything sufficiently brilliant to arrest her attention would have seemed ludicrous, had not Jim, by entering the Yeomanry, revealed a capacity for dazzling exploits which made it unsafe to predict any limitation to his powers.

Margery was now excited. The daring of the wretched Jim in bursting into scarlet amazed her as much as his doubtful acquaintanceship with the demonstrative Mrs Peach. To go to that Review, to watch the pair, to eclipse Mrs Peach in brilliancy, to meet and pass them in withering contempt – if she only could do it! But, alas! she was a forsaken woman. 'If the Baron were alive, or in England,' she said to herself (for sometimes she thought he might possibly be alive), 'and he were to take me to this Review, wouldn't I show that forward Mrs Peach what a lady is like, and keep among the select company, and not mix with the common people at all!'

It might at first sight be thought that the best course for Margery at this juncture would have been to go to Jim, and nip the intrigue in the bud without further scruple. But her own declaration in after days was that whoever could say that was far from realizing her situation. It was hard to break such ice as divided their two lives now, and to attempt it at that moment was a too humiliating proclamation of defeat. The only plan she could think of – perhaps not a wise one in the circumstances – was to go to the Review herself, and be the gayest there.

A method of doing this with some propriety soon occurred to her. She dared not ask her father, who scorned to waste time in sight-seeing, and whose animosity towards Jim knew no abatement; but she might call on her old acquaintance, Mr Vine, Jim's partner, who would probably be going with the rest of the holiday-folk, and ask if she might accompany him in his spring-trap. She had no sooner perceived the feasibility of this, through her being at her grandmother's, than she decided to meet with the old man early the next morning.

In the meantime Jim and Mrs Peach had walked slowly along the road together, Jim leading the horse, and Mrs Peach informing him that her father, the gardener, was at Jim's village farther on, and that she had come to meet him. Jim, for reasons of his own, was going to sleep at his partner's that night, and thus their route was the same. The shades of eve closed in upon them as they walked, and by the time they reached the lime-kiln, which it was necessary to pass to get to the village, it was quite dark. Jim stopped at the kiln, to see if matters had progressed rightly in his seven days' absence, and Mrs Peach, who stuck to him like a teazle, stopped also, saying she would wait for her father there.

She held the horse while he ascended to the top of the kiln. Then rejoining her, and not quite knowing what to do, he stood beside her looking at the flames, which tonight burnt up brightly, shining a long way into the dark air, even up to the ramparts of the earthwork above them, and overhead into the bosoms of the clouds.

It was during this proceeding that a carriage, drawn by a pair of dark horses, came along the turnpike-road. The light of the kiln caused the horses to swerve a little, and the occupant of the carriage looked out. He saw the bluish, lightning-like flames from the limestone, rising from the top of the furnace, and hard by the figures of Jim Hayward, the widow, and the horse, standing out with spectral distinctness against the mass of night behind. The scene wore the aspect of some unholy assignation in Pandaemonium,* and it was all the more impressive from the fact that both Jim and the woman were quite unconscious of the striking spectacle they presented. The gentleman in the carriage watched them till he was borne out of sight.

Having seen to the kiln, Jim and the widow walked on again, and soon Mrs Peach's father met them, and relieved Jim of the lady. When they had parted, Jim, with an expiration not unlike a breath of relief, went on to Mr Vine's, and, having put the horse into the stable, entered the house. His partner was seated at the table, solacing himself after the labours of the day by luxurious alternations between a long clay pipe and a mug of perry.

'Well,' said Jim eagerly, 'what's the news – how do she take it?'

'Sit down – sit down,' said Vine. ''Tis working well; not but that I deserve something o' thee for the trouble I've had in watching her. The soldiering was a fine move; but the woman is a better! – who invented it?'

'I myself,' said Jim modestly.

'Well; jealousy is making her rise like a thunderstorm, and in a day or two you'll have her for the asking, my sonny. What's the next step?'

'The widow is getting rather a weight upon a feller, worse luck,' said Jim. 'But I must keep it up until tomorrow, at any rate. I have promised to see her at the Review, and now the great thing is that Margery should see we a-smiling together – I in my full-dress uniform and clinking arms o' war. 'Twill be a good strong sting, and will end the business, I hope. Couldn't you manage to put the hoss in and drive her there? She'd go if you were to ask her.'

'With all my heart,' said Mr Vine, moistening the end of a new pipe in his perry. 'I can call at her grammer's for her – 'twill be all in my way.'

Margery duly followed up her intention by arraying herself the next morning in her loveliest guise, and keeping watch for Mr Vine's appearance upon the high road, feeling certain that his would form one in the procession of carts and carriages which set in towards Exonbury that day. Jim had gone by at a very early hour, and she did not see him pass. Her anticipation was verified by the advent of Mr Vine about eleven o'clock, dressed to his highest effort; but Margery was surprised to find that, instead of her having to stop him, he pulled in towards the gate of his own accord. The invitation planned between Jim and the old man on the previous night was now promptly given, and, as may be supposed, as promptly accepted. Such a strange coincidence she had never before known. She was quite ready, and they drove onward at once.

The Review was held on some high ground a little way out of the city, and her conductor suggested that they should put up the horse at the inn, and walk to the field – a plan which pleased her well, for it was more easy to take preliminary observations on foot without being seen herself than when sitting elevated in a vehicle.

They were just in time to secure a good place near the front, and in a few minutes after their arrival the reviewing officer came on the ground. Margery's eye had rapidly run over the troop in which Jim was enrolled, and she discerned him in one of the ranks, looking remarkably new and bright, both as to uniform and countenance. Indeed, if she had not worked herself into such a desperate state of mind she would have felt proud of him then and there. His shapely upright figure was quite noteworthy in the row of rotund yeomen on his right and left; while his charger Tony expressed by his bearing, even more than Jim, that he knew nothing about lime-carts whatever, and everything about trumpets and glory. How Jim could have scrubbed Tony to such shining blackness she could not tell, for the horse in his natural state was ingrained with lime-dust, that burnt the colour out of his coat as it did out of Jim's hair. Now he pranced martially, and was a war-horse every inch of him.

Having discovered Jim her next search was for Mrs Peach, and, by dint of some oblique glancing Margery indignantly discovered the widow in the most forward place of all, her head and bright face conspicuously advanced; and, what was more shocking, she had abandoned her mourning for a violet drawn-bonnet and a gay spencer,* together with a parasol luxuriously fringed in a way Margery had never before seen. 'Where did she get the money?' said Margery, under her breath. 'And to forget that poor sailor so soon!'

These general reflections were precipitately postponed by her discovering that Jim and the widow were perfectly alive to each other's whereabouts, and in the interchange of telegraphic signs of affection, which on the latter's part took the form of a playful fluttering of her handkerchief or waving of her parasol. Richard Vine had placed Margery in front of him, to protect her from the crowd, as he said, he himself surveying the scene over her bonnet. Margery would have been even more surprised than she was if she had known that Jim was not only aware of Mrs Peach's presence, but also of her own, the treacherous Mr Vine having drawn out his flame-coloured handkerchief and waved it to Jim over the young woman's head as soon as they had taken up their position.

'My partner makes a tidy soldier, eh – Miss Tucker?' said the senior lime-burner. 'It is my belief as a Christian that he's got a party here that he's making signs to – that handsome figure o' fun straight over-right* him.'

'Perhaps so,' she said.

'And it's growing warm between 'em if I don't mistake,' continued the merciless Vine.

Margery was silent, biting her lip; and the troops being now set in motion, all signalling ceased for the present between soldier Hayward and his pretended sweetheart.

'Have you a piece of paper that I could make a memorandum on, Mr Vine?' asked Margery.

Vine took out his pocket-book and tore a leaf from it, which he handed her with a pencil.

'Don't move from here – I'll return in a minute,' she continued, with the innocence of a woman who means mischief. And, withdrawing herself to the back, where the grass was clear, she pencilled down the words –

JIM'S MARRIED.

Armed with this document she crept into the throng behind the unsuspecting Mrs Peach, slipped the paper into her pocket on the top of her handkerchief, and withdrew unobserved, rejoining Mr Vine with a bearing of *nonchalance**.

By and by the troops were in different order, Jim taking a left-hand position almost close to Mrs Peach. He bent down and said a few words to her. From her manner of nodding assent it was surely some arrangement about a meeting by and by when Jim's drill was over, and Margery was more certain of the fact when, the Review having ended, and the people having strolled off to another part of the field where sports were to take place, Mrs Peach tripped away in the direction of the city.

'I'll just say a word to my partner afore he goes off the ground, if you'll spare me a minute,' said the old lime-burner. 'Please stay here till I'm back again.' He edged along the front till he reached Jim.

'How is she?' said the latter.

'In a trimming sweat,' said Mr Vine. 'And my counsel to 'ee is to carry this larry* no further. 'Twill do no good. She's as ready to make friends with 'ee as any wife can be; and more showing off can only do harm.'

'But I must finish off with a spurt,' said Jim. 'And this is how I am going to do it. I have arranged with Mrs Peach that, as soon as we soldiers have entered the town and been dismissed, I'll meet her there. It is really to say good-bye, but she don't know that; and I wanted it to look like a 'lopement to Margery's eyes. When I'm clear of Mrs Peach I'll come back here and make it up with Margery on the spot. But don't say I'm coming, or she may be inclined to throw off again. Just hint to her that I may be meaning to be off to London with the widow.'

The old man still insisted that this was going too far.

'No, no, it isn't,' said Jim. 'I know how to manage her. 'Twill just mellow her heart nicely by the time I come back. I must bring her down real tender, or 'twill all fail.'

His senior reluctantly gave in and returned to Margery. A short time afterwards the Yeomanry band struck up, and Jim with the regiment followed towards Exonbury.

'Yes, yes; they are going to meet,' said Margery to herself, perceiving that Mrs Peach had so timed her departure as to be in the town at Jim's dismounting.

'Now we will go and see the games,' said Mr Vine; 'they are really worth seeing. There's greasy poles, and jumping in sacks, and other trials of the intellect, that nobody ought to miss who wants to be abreast of his generation.'

Margery felt so indignant at the apparent assignation, which seemed about to take place despite her anonymous writing, that she helplessly assented to go anywhere, dropping behind Vine, that he might not see her mood.

Jim followed out his programme with literal exactness. No sooner was the troop dismissed in the city than he sent Tony to stable and joined Mrs Peach, who stood on the edge of the pavement expecting him. But this acquaintance was to end: he meant to part from her for ever and in the quickest time, though civilly; for it was important to be with Margery as soon as possible. He had nearly completed the manoeuvre to his satisfaction when, in drawing her handkerchief from her pocket to wipe the tears from her eyes, Mrs Peach's hand grasped the paper, which she read at once.

'What! is that true?' she said, holding it out to Jim.

Jim started and admitted that it was, beginning an elaborate explanation and apologies. But Mrs Peach was thoroughly roused, and then overcome. 'He's married, he's married!' she said, and swooned, or feigned to swoon, so that Jim was obliged to support her.

'He's married, he's married!' said a boy hard by who watched the scene with interest.

'He's married, he's married!' said a hilarious group of other boys near, with smiles several inches broad, and shining teeth; and so the exclamation echoed down the street.

Jim cursed his ill-luck; the loss of time that this dilemma entailed grew serious; for Mrs Peach was now in such a hysterical state that he could not leave her with any good grace or feeling. It was necessary to take her to a refreshment room, lavish restoratives upon her, and altogether to waste nearly half an hour. When she had kept him as long as she chose, she forgave him; and thus at last he got away, his heart swelling with tenderness towards Margery. He at once hurried up the street to effect the reconciliation with her.

'How shall I do it?' he said to himself. 'Why, I'll step round to her side, fish for her hand, draw it through my arm as if I wasn't aware of it. Then she'll look in my face, I shall look in hers, and we shall march off the field triumphant, and the thing will be done without takings or tears.'

He entered the field and went straight as an arrow to the place appointed for the meeting. It was at the back of a refreshment tent outside the mass of spectators, and divided from their view by the tent itself. He turned the corner of the canvas, and there beheld Vine at the indicated spot. But Margery was not with him.

Vine's hat was thrust back into his poll. His face was pale, and his manner bewildered. 'Hullo? what's the matter?' said Jim. 'Where's my Margery?'

'You've carried this footy game too far, my man!' exclaimed Vine, with the air of a friend who has 'always told you so'. 'You ought to have dropped it several days ago, when she would have come to 'ee like a cooing dove. Now this is the end o't!'

'Hey! what, my Margery? Has anything happened, for God's sake?'

'She's gone.'

'Where to?'

'That's more than earthly man can tell! I never see such a thing! 'Twas a stroke o' the black art – as if she were sperrited away. When we got to the games I said – mind, you told me to! – I said, "Jim Hayward thinks o' going off to London with that widow woman" – mind you told me to! She showed no wonderment, though a' seemed very low. Then she said to me, "I don't like standing here in this slummocky* crowd. I shall feel more at home among the gentlepeople." And then she went to where the carriages were drawn up, and near her there was a grand coach, a-blazing with lions and unicorns, and hauled by two coal-black horses. I hardly thought much of it then, and by degrees lost sight of her behind it. Presently the other carriages moved off, and I thought still to see her standing there. But no, she had vanished; and then I saw the grand coach rolling away, and glimpsed Margery in it, beside a fine dark gentleman with black mustachios, and a very pale prince-like face. As soon as the horses got into the hard road they rattled on like hell-and-skimmer,* and went out of sight in the dust, and – that's all. If you'd come back a little sooner you'd ha' caught her.'

Jim had turned whiter than his pipeclay. 'O, this is too bad – too bad!' he cried in anguish, striking his brow. 'That paper and that fainting woman kept me so long. Who could have done it? But 'tis my fault. I've stung her too much. I shouldn't have carried it so far.'

'You shouldn't – just what I said,' replied his senior.

'She thinks I've gone off with that cust* widow; and to spite me she's gone off with the man! Do you know who that stranger wi' the lions and unicorns is? Why, 'tis that foreigner who calls himself a Baron, and took Mount Lodge for six months last year to make mischief – a villain! O, my Margery – that it should come to this! She's lost, she's ruined! – Which way did they go?'

Jim turned to follow in the direction indicated, when, behold, there stood at his back her father, Dairyman Tucker.

'Now look here, young man,' said Dairyman Tucker. 'I've just heard all that wailing – and straightway will ask 'ee to stop it sharp. 'Tis like your brazen impudence to teave* and wail when you be another woman's husband; yes, faith, I see'd her a-fainting in yer arms when you wanted to get away from her, and honest folk a-standing round who knew you'd married her, and said so. I heard it, thou you didn't see me. "He's married!" says they. Some sly register-office business, no doubt; but sly doings will out. As for Margery – who's to be called higher titles in these parts hencefor'ard – I'm her father, and I say it's all right what she's done. Don't I know private news, hey? Haven't I just learnt that secret weddings of high people can happen at expected deathbeds by special licence, as well as low people at registrars' offices? And can't husbands come back and claim their own when they choose? Begone, young man, and leave noblemen's wives alone; and I thank God I shall be rid of a numskull!'

Swift words of explanation rose to Jim's lips, but they paused there and died. At that last moment he could not, as Margery's husband, announce Margery's shame and his own, and transform her father's triumph to wretchedness at a blow.

'I – I – must leave here,' he stammered. Going from the place in an opposite course to that of the fugitives, he doubled when out of sight, and in an incredibly short space had entered the town. Here he made inquiries for the emblazoned carriage, and gained from one or two persons a general idea of its route. They thought it had taken the highway to London. Saddling poor Tony before he had half eaten his corn, Jim galloped along the same road.

Now Jim was quite mistaken in supposing that by leaving the field in a roundabout manner he had deceived Dairyman Tucker as to his object. That astute old man immediately divined that Jim was meaning to track the fugitives, in ignorance (as the dairyman supposed) of their lawful relation. He was soon assured of the fact, for, creeping to a remote angle of the field, he saw Jim hastening into the town. Vowing vengeance on the young lime-burner for his mischievous interference between a nobleman and his secretly-wedded wife, the dairy-farmer determined to balk him.

Tucker had ridden on to the Review ground, so that there was no necessity for him, as there had been for poor Jim, to re-enter the town before starting. The dairyman hastily untied his

mare from the row of other horses, mounted, and descended to
a bridle-path which would take him obliquely into the London
road a mile or so ahead. The old man's route being along one
side of an equilateral triangle, while Jim's was along two sides
of the same, the former was at the point of intersection long
before Hayward.

Arrived here, the dairyman pulled up and looked around. It
was a spot at which the highway forked; the left arm, the more
important, led on through Sherton Abbas and Melchester to
London; the right to Idmouth and the coast. Nothing was visible
on the white track to London; but on the other there appeared
the back of a carriage, which rapidly ascended a distant hill and
vanished under the trees. It was the Baron's who, according to
the sworn information of the gardener at Mount Lodge, had
made Margery his wife.

The carriage having vanished, the dairyman gazed in the
opposite direction, towards Exonbury. Here he beheld Jim in
his regimentals, laboriously approaching on Tony's back.

Soon he reached the forking roads, and saw the dairyman by
the wayside. But Jim did not halt. Then the dairyman practised
the greatest duplicity of his life.

'Right along the London road, if you want to catch 'em!' he
said.

'Thank 'ee, dairyman, thank 'ee!' cried Jim, his pale face
lighting up with gratitude, for he believed that Tucker had learnt
his mistake from Vine, and had come to his assistance. Without
drawing rein he diminished along the road not taken by the
flying pair. The dairyman rubbed his hands with delight, and
returned to the city as the cathedral clock struck five.

Jim pursued his way through the dust, up hill and down hill;
but never saw ahead of him the vehicle of his search. That
vehicle was passing along a diverging way at a distance of many
miles from where he rode. Still he sped onwards, till Tony
showed signs of breaking down; and then Jim gathered from
inquiries he made that he had come the wrong way. It burst
upon his mind that the dairyman, still ignorant of the truth, had
misinformed him. Heavier in his heart than words can describe
he turned Tony's drooping head, and resolved to drag his way
home.

But the horse was now so jaded that it was impossible to
proceed far. Having gone about half a mile back he came again

to a small roadside hamlet and inn, where he put up Tony for a rest and feed. As for himself, there was no quiet in him. He tried to sit and eat in the inn kitchen; but he could not stay there. He went out, and paced up and down the road.

Standing in sight of the white way by which he had come he beheld advancing towards him the horses and carriage he sought, now black and daemonic against the slanting fires of the western sun.

The why and wherefore of this sudden appearance he did not pause to consider. His resolve to intercept the carriage was instantaneous. He ran forward, and doggedly waiting barred the way to the advancing equipage.

The Baron's coachman shouted, but Jim stood firm as a rock, and on the former attempting to push past him Jim drew his sword, resolving to cut the horses down rather than be displaced. The animals were thrown nearly back upon their haunches, and at this juncture a gentleman looked out of the window. It was the Baron himself.

'Who's there?' he inquired.

'James Hayward!' replied the young man fiercely, 'and he demands his wife.'

The Baron leapt out, and told the coachman to drive back out of sight and wait for him.

'I was hastening to find you,' he said to Jim. 'Your wife is where she ought to be, and where you ought to be also – by your own fireside. Where's the other woman?'

Jim, without replying, looked incredulously into the carriage as it turned. Margery was certainly not there. 'The other woman is nothing to me,' he said bitterly. 'I used her to warm up Margery: I have now done with her. The question I ask, my lord, is, what business had you with Margery today?'

'My business was to help her to regain the husband she had seemingly lost. I saw her; she told me you had eloped by the London road with another. I, who have – mostly – had her happiness at heart, told her I would help her to follow you if she wished. She gladly agreed; we drove after, but could hear no tidings of you in front of us. Then I took her – to your house – and there she awaits you. I promised to send you to her if human effort could do it, and was tracking you for that purpose.'

'Then you've been a-pursuing after me?'

'You and the widow.'

'And I've been pursuing after you and Margery! . . . My noble lord, your actions seem to show that I ought to believe you in this; and when you say you've her happiness at heart, I don't forget that you've formerly proved it to be so. Well, Heaven forbid that I should think wrongfully of you if you don't deserve it! A mystery to me you have always been, my noble lord, and in this business more than in any.'

'I am glad to hear you say no worse. In one hour you'll have proof of my conduct – good and bad. Can I do anything more? Say the word, and I'll try.'

Jim reflected. 'Baron,' he said, 'I am a plain man, and wish only to lead a quiet life with my wife, as a man should. You have great power over her – power to any extent, for good or otherwise. If you command her anything on earth, righteous or questionable, that she'll do. So that, since you ask me if you can do more for me, I'll answer this, you can promise never to see her again. I mean no harm, my lord; but your presence can do no good; you will trouble us. If I return to her, will you for ever stay away?'

'Hayward,' said the Baron, 'I swear to you that I will disturb you and your wife by my presence no more.' And he took Jim's hand, and pressed it within his own upon the hilt of Jim's sword.

In relating this incident to the present narrator Jim used to declare that, to his fancy, the ruddy light of the setting sun burned with more then earthly fire on the Baron's face as the words were spoken; and that the ruby flash of his eye in the same light was what he never witnessed before nor since in the eye of mortal man. After this there was nothing more to do or say in that place. Jim accompanied his never-to-be-forgotten acquaintance to the carriage, closed the door after him, waved his hat to him, and from that hour he and the Baron met not again on earth.

A few words will suffice to explain the fortunes of Margery while the foregoing events were in action elsewhere. On leaving her companion Vine she had gone distractedly among the carriages, the rather to escape his observation than of any set purpose. Standing here she thought she heard her name pro-nounced, and turning, saw her foreign friend, whom she had supposed to be, if not dead, a thousand miles off. He beckoned, and she went close. 'You are ill – you are wretched,' he said, looking keenly in her face. 'Where's your husband?'

She told him her sad suspicion that Jim had run away from her. The Baron reflected, and inquired a few other particulars of her late life. Then he said, 'You and I must find him. Come with me.' At this word of command from the Baron she had entered the carriage as docilely as a child, and there she sat beside him till he chose to speak, which was not till they were some way out of the town, at the forking ways, and the Baron had discovered that Jim was certainly not, as they had supposed, making off from Margery along that particular branch of the fork that led to London.

'To pursue him in this way is useless, I perceive,' he said. 'And the proper course now is that I should take you to his house. That done I will return, and bring him to you if mortal persuasion can do it.'

'I didn't want to go to his house without him, sir,' said she, tremblingly.

'Didn't want to!' he answered. 'Let me remind you, Margery Hayward, that your place is in your husband's house. Till you are there you have no right to criticize his conduct, however wild it may be. Why have you not been there before?'

'I don't know, sir,' she murmured, her tears falling silently upon her hand.

'Don't you think you ought to be there?'

She did not answer.

'Of course you ought.'

Still she did not speak.

The Baron sank into silence, and allowed his eye to rest on her. What thoughts were all at once engaging his mind after those moments of reproof? Margery had given herself into his hands without a remonstrance. Her husband had apparently deserted her. She was absolutely in his power, and they were on the high road.

That his first impulse in inviting her to accompany him had been the legitimate one denoted by his words cannot reasonably be doubted. That his second was otherwise soon became revealed, though not at first to her, for she was too bewildered to notice where they were going. Instead of turning and taking the road to Jim's, the Baron, as if influenced suddenly by her reluctance to return thither if Jim was playing truant, signalled to the coachman to take the branch road to the right, as her father had discerned.

They soon approached the coast near Idmouth. The carriage stopped. Margery awoke from her reverie.

'Where are we?' she said, looking out of the window, with a start. Before her was an inlet of the sea, and in the middle of the inlet rode a yacht, its masts repeating as if from memory the rocking they had practised in their native forest.

'At a little sea-side nook, where my yacht lies at anchor,' he said tentatively. 'Now, Margery, in five minutes we can be aboard, and in half-an-hour we can be sailing away all the world over. Will you come?'

'I cannot decide,' she said, in low tones.

'Why not?'

'Because – '

Then on a sudden Margery seemed to see all contingencies: she became white as a fleece, and a bewildered look came into her eyes. With clasped hands she leant on the Baron.

Baron von Xanten observed her distracted look, averted his face, and coming to a decision opened the carriage door, quickly mounted outside, and in a second or two the carriage left the shore behind, and ascended the road by which it had come.

In about an hour they reached Jim Hayward's home. The Baron alighted, and spoke to her through the window. 'Margery, can you forgive a lover's bad impulse, which I swear was unpremeditated?' he asked. 'If you can, shake my hand.'

She did not do it, but eventually allowed him to help her out of the carriage. He seemed to feel the awkwardness keenly; and seeing it, she said, 'Of course I forgive you, sir, for I felt for a moment as you did. Will you send my husband to me?'

'I will, if any man can,' said he. 'Such penance is milder than I deserve! God bless you and give you happiness! I shall never see you again!' He turned, entered the carriage, and was gone; and having found out Jim's course, came up with him upon the road as described.

In due time the latter reached his lodging at his partner's. The woman who took care of the house in Vine's absence at once told Jim that a lady who had come in a carriage was waiting for him in his sitting-room. Jim proceeded thither with agitation, and beheld, shrinkingly ensconced in the large slippery chair, and surrounded by the brilliant articles that had so long awaited her, his long-estranged wife.

Margery's eyes were round and fear-stricken. She essayed to speak, but Jim, strangely enough, found the readier tongue then. 'Why did I do it, you would ask,' he said. 'I cannot tell. Do you forgive my deception? O Margery – you are my Margery still! But how could you trust yourself in the Baron's hands this afternoon, without knowing him better?'

'He said I was to come, and I went,' she said, as well as she could for tearfulness.

'You obeyed him blindly.'

'I did. But perhaps I was not justified in doing it.'

'I don't know,' said Jim musingly. 'I think he's a good man.' Margery did not explain.* And then a sunnier mood succeeded her tremblings and tears, till old Mr Vine came into the house below, and Jim went down to declare that all was well, and sent off his partner to break the news to Margery's father, who as yet remained unenlightened.

The dairyman bore the intelligence of his daughter's untitled state as best he could, and punished her by not coming near her for several weeks, though at last he grumbled his forgiveness, and made up matters with Jim. The handsome Mrs Peach vanished to Plymouth, and found another sailor, not without a reasonable complaint against Jim and Margery both that she had been unfairly used.

As for the mysterious gentleman who had exercised such an influence over their lives, he kept his word, and was a stranger to Lower Wessex thenceforward. Baron or no Baron, English-man or foreigner, he had shown a genuine interest in Jim, and real sorrow for a certain reckless phase of his acquaintance with Margery. That he had a more tender feeling toward the young girl than he wished her or any one else to perceive there could be no doubt. That he was strongly tempted at times to adopt other than conventional courses with regard to her is also clear, particularly at that critical hour when she rolled along the high road with him in the carriage, after turning from the fancied pursuit of Jim. But at other times he schooled impassioned sentiments into fair conduct, which even erred on the side of harshness. In after years there was a report that another attempt on his life with a pistol, during one of those fits of moodiness to which he seemed constitutionally liable, had been effectual; but nobody in Silverthorn was in a position to ascertain the truth.

There he is still regarded as one who had something about him magical and unearthly. In his mystery let him remain; for a man, no less than a landscape, who awakens an interest under uncertain lights and touches of unfathomable shade, may cut but a poor figure in a garish noontide shine.

When she heard of his mournful death Margery sat in her nursing-chair, gravely thinking for nearly ten minutes, to the total neglect of her infant in the cradle. Jim, from the other side of the fireplace, said, 'You are sorry enough for him, Margery. I am sure of that.'

'Yes, yes,' she murmured, 'I am sorry.' After a moment she added: 'Now that he's dead I'll make a confession, Jim, that I have never made to a soul. If he had pressed me – which he did not – to go with him when I was in the carriage that night beside his yacht, I would have gone. And I was disappointed that he did not press me.'

'Suppose he were to suddenly appear now, and say in a voice of command, "Margery, come with me!"'

'I believe I should have no power to disobey,' she returned, with a mischievous look. 'He was like a magician to me. I think he was one. He could move me as a loadstone moves a speck of steel. . . . Yet no,' she added, hearing the infant cry, 'he would not move me now. It would be so unfair to baby.'

'Well,' said Jim, with no great concern (for '*la jalousie rétrospective*,' as George Sand calls it,* had nearly died out of him), 'however he might move 'ee, my love, he'll never come. He swore it to me: and he was a man of his word.'

A TRYST AT AN ANCIENT EARTHWORK

At one's every step forward it rises higher against the south sky, with an obtrusive personality that compels the senses to regard it and consider. The eyes may bend in another direction, but never without the consciousness of its heavy, high-shouldered presence at its point of vantage. Across the intervening levels the gale races in a straight line from the fort, as if breathed out of it hitherward. With the shifting of the clouds the faces of the steeps vary in colour and in shade, broad lights appearing where mist and vagueness had prevailed, dissolving in their turn into melancholy grey, which spreads over and eclipses the luminous bluffs. In this so-thought immutable spectacle all is change.

Out of the invisible marine region on the other side birds soar suddenly into the air, and hang over the summits of the heights with the indifference of long familiarity. Their forms are white against the tawny concave of cloud, and the curves they exhibit in their floating signify that they are seagulls which have journeyed inland from expected stress of weather. As the birds rise behind the fort, so do the clouds rise behind the birds, almost, as it seems, stroking with their bagging bosoms the uppermost flyers.

The profile of the whole stupendous ruin, as seen at a distance of a mile eastward, is cleanly cut as that of a marble inlay. It is varied with protuberances, which from hereabouts have the animal aspect of warts, wens, knuckles, and hips. It may indeed be likened to an enormous many-limbed organism of an antediluvian* time partaking of the cephalopod* in shape – lying lifeless, and covered with a thin green cloth, which hides its substance, while revealing its contour. This dull green mantle of herbage stretches down towards the levels, where the ploughs have essayed for centuries to creep up near and yet nearer to the base of the castle, but have always stopped short before reaching it. The furrows of these environing attempts show themselves distinctly, bending to the incline as they trench upon it; mounting in steeper curves, till the steepness baffles them, and their parallel threads show like the striae* of waves pausing on the curl. The peculiar place of which these are some of the features is 'Mai-Dun', 'The Castle of the Great Hill', said to be the Dunium of Ptolemy,* the capital of the Durotriges,* which eventually came into Roman occupation, and was finally deserted on their withdrawal from the island.

The evening is followed by a night on which an invisible moon bestows a subdued, yet pervasive light – without radiance, as without blackness. From the spot whereon I am ensconced in a cottage, a mile away, the fort has now ceased to be visible; yet, as by day, to anybody whose thoughts have been engaged with it and its barbarous grandeurs of past time the form asserts its existence behind the night gauzes as persistently as if it had a voice. Moreover, the south-west wind continues to feed the intervening arable flats with vapours brought directly from its sides.

The midnight hour for which there has been occasion to wait at length arrives, and I journey towards the stronghold in obedience to a request urged earlier in the day. It concerns an appointment, which I rather regret my decision to keep now that night is come. The route thither is hedgeless and treeless – I need not add deserted. The moonlight is sufficient to disclose the pale riband-like surface of the way as it trails along between the expanses of darker fallow. Though the road passes near the fortress it does not conduct directly to its fronts. As the place is without an inhabitant, so it is without a trackway. So presently leaving the macadamized road to pursue its course elsewhither, I step off upon the fallow, and plod stumblingly across it. The castle looms out of the shade by degrees, like a thing waking up and asking what I want there. It is now so enlarged by nearness that its whole shape cannot be taken in at one view. The ploughed ground ends as the rise sharpens, the sloping basement of grass begins, and I climb upward to invade Mai-Dun.

Impressive by day as this largest Ancient-British work in the kingdom undoubtedly is, its impressiveness is increased now. After standing still and spending a few minutes in adding its age to its size, and its size to its solitude, it becomes appallingly mournful in its growing closeness. A squally wind blows in the face with an impact which proclaims that the vapours of the air sail low tonight. The slope that I so laboriously clamber up the wind skips sportively down. Its track can be discerned even in this light by the undulations of the withered grass-bents – the only produce of this upland summit except moss. Four minutes of ascent, and a vantage-ground of some sort is gained. It is only the crest of the outer rampart. Immediately within this a chasm gapes; its bottom is imperceptible, but the counterscarp slopes not too steeply to admit of a sliding descent if cautiously performed. The shady bottom, dank and chilly, is thus gained, and reveals itself as a kind of winding lane, wide enough for a waggon to pass along, floored with rank herbage, and trending away, right and left, into obscurity, between the concentric walls of earth. The towering closeness of these on each hand, their impenetrability, and their ponderousness, are felt as a physical pressure. The way is now up the second of them, which stands steeper and higher than the first. To turn aside, as did Christian's companion, from such a Hill Difficulty,* is the more natural tendency; but the way to the interior is upward. There is, of course, an entrance to the fortress; but that lies far off on the other side. It might possibly have been the wiser course to seek for easier ingress there.

However, being here, I ascend the second acclivity. The grass stems – the grey beard of the hill – sway in a mass close to my stooping face. The dead heads of these various grasses – fescues, fox-tails, and ryes – bob and twitch as if pulled by a string underground. From a few thistles a whistling proceeds; and even the moss speaks, in its humble way, under the stress of the blast.

That the summit of the second line of defence has been gained is suddenly made known by a contrasting wind from a new quarter, coming over with the curve of a cascade. These novel gusts raise a sound from the whole camp or castle, playing upon it bodily as upon a harp. It is with some difficulty that a foothold can be preserved under their sweep. Looking aloft for a moment I perceive that the sky is much more overcast than it has been hitherto, and in a few instants a dead lull in what is now a gale ensues with almost preternatural abruptness. I take advantage of this to sidle down the second counterscarp,* but by the time the ditch is reached the lull reveals itself to be but the precursor of a storm. It begins with a heave of the whole atmosphere, like the sigh of a weary strong man on turning to recommence unusual exertion, just as I stand here in the second fosse. That which now radiates from the sky upon the scene is not so much light as vaporous phosphorescence.

The wind, quickening, abandons the natural direction it has pursued on the open upland, and takes the course of the gorge's length, rushing along therein helter-skelter, and carrying thick rain upon its back. The rain is followed by hailstones which fly through the defile in battalions – rolling, hopping, ricochetting, snapping, clattering down the shelving banks in an undefinable haze of confusion. The earthen sides of the fosse seem to quiver under the drenching onset, though it is practically no more to them than the blows of Thor* upon the giant of Jotun-land.* It is impossible to proceed further till the storm somewhat abates, and I draw up behind a spur of the inner scarp, where possibly a barricade stood two thousand years ago; and thus await events.

The roar of the storm can be heard travelling the complete circuit of the castle – a measured mile – coming round at intervals like a circumambulating column of infantry. Doubtless such a column has passed this way in its time, but the only columns which enter in these latter days are the columns of sheep and oxen that are sometimes seen here now; while the only semblance of heroic voices heard are the utterances of such, and of the many winds which make their passage through the ravines.

The expected lightning radiates round, and a rumbling as from its subterranean vaults – if there are any – fills the castle. The lightning repeats itself, and, coming after the aforesaid thoughts of martial men, it bears a fanciful resemblance to swords moving in combat. It has the very brassy hue of the ancient weapons that here were used. The so sudden entry upon the scene of this metallic flame is as the entry of a presiding exhibitor who unrolls the maps, uncurtains the pictures, unlocks the cabinets, and effects a transformation by merely exposing the materials of his science, unintelligibly cloaked till then. The abrupt configuration of the bluffs and mounds is now for the first time clearly revealed – mounds whereon, doubtless, spears and shields have frequently lain while their owners loosened their sandals and yawned and stretched their arms in the sun. For the first time, too, a glimpse is obtainable of the true entrance used by its occupants of old, some way ahead.

There, where all passage has seemed to be inviolably barred by an almost vertical façade, the ramparts are found to overlap each other like loosely clasped fingers, between which a zigzag path may be followed – a cunning construction that puzzles the uninformed eye. But its cunning, even where not obscured by dilapidation, is now wasted on the solitary forms of a few wild badgers, rabbits, and hares. Men must have often gone out by those gates in the morning to battle with the Roman legions under Vespasian;* some to return no more, others to come back at evening, bringing with them the noise of their heroic deeds. But not a page, not a stone, has preserved their fame.

Acoustic perceptions multiply tonight. We can almost hear the stream of years that have borne those deeds away from us. Strange articulations seem to float on the air from that point, the gateway, where the animation in past times must frequently have concentrated itself at hours of coming and going, and general excitement. There arises an ineradicable fancy that they are human voices; if so, they must be the lingering air-borne vibrations of conversations uttered at least fifteen hundred years ago. The attention is attracted from mere nebulous imaginings about yonder spot by a real moving of something close at hand.

I recognize by the now moderate flashes of lightning, which are sheet-like and nearly continuous, that it is the gradual elevation of a small mound of earth. At first no larger than a man's fist it reaches the dimensions of a hat, then sinks a little and is still. It is but the heaving of a mole who chooses such weather as this to work in from some instinct that there will be nobody abroad to molest him. As the fine earth lifts and lifts and falls loosely aside fragments of burnt clay roll out of it – clay that once formed part of cups or other vessels used by the inhabitants of the fortress.

The violence of the storm has been counterbalanced by its transitoriness. From being immersed in well-nigh solid media of cloud and hail shot with lightning, I find myself uncovered of the humid investiture and left bare to the mild gaze of the moon, which sparkles now on every wet grass-blade and frond of moss.

But I am not yet inside the fort, and the delayed ascent of the third and last escarpment is now made. It is steeper than either. The first was a surface to walk up, the second to stagger up, the third can only be ascended on the hands and toes. On the summit obtrudes the first evidence which has been met with in these precincts that the time is really the nineteenth century; it is in the form of a white notice-board on a post, and the wording can just be discerned by the rays of the setting moon:

> CAUTION. – Any Person found removing Relics, Skeletons, Stones, Pottery, Tiles, or other Material from this Earthwork, or cutting up the Ground, will be Prosecuted as the Law directs.

Here one observes a difference underfoot from what has gone before: scraps of Roman tile and stone chippings protrude through the grass in meagre quantity, but sufficient to suggest that masonry stood on the spot. Before the eye stretches under the moonlight the interior of the fort. So open and so large is it as to be practically an upland plateau, and yet its area lies wholly within the walls of what may be designated as one building. It is a long-violated retreat; all its corner-stones, plinths, and architraves* were carried away to build neighbouring villages even before mediaeval or modern history began. Many a block which once may have helped to form a bastion here rests now in broken and diminished shape as part of the chimney-corner of some shepherd's cottage within the distant horizon, and the corner-stones of this heathen altar may form the base-course of some adjoining village church.

Yet the very bareness of these inner courts and wards, their condition of mere pasturage, protects what remains of them as no defences could do. Nothing is left visible that the hands can seize on or the weather overturn, and a permanence of general outline at least results, which no other condition could ensure.

The position of the castle on this isolated hill bespeaks deliberate and strategic choice exercised by some remote mind capable of prospective reasoning to a far extent. The natural configuration of the surrounding country and its bearing upon such a stronghold were obviously long considered and viewed mentally before its extensive design was carried into execution. Who was the man that said, 'Let it be built here!' – not on that hill yonder, or on that ridge behind, but on this best spot of all? Whether he were some great one of the Belgae,* or of the Durotriges, or the travelling engineer of Britain's united tribes, must for ever remain time's secret; his form cannot be realized, nor his countenance, nor the tongue that he spoke, when he set down his foot with a thud and said, 'Let it be here!'

Within the innermost enclosure, though it is so wide that at a superficial glance the beholder has only a sense of standing on a breezy down, the solitude is rendered yet more solitary by the knowledge that between the benighted sojourner herein and all kindred humanity are those three concentric walls of earth which no being would think of scaling on such a night as this, even were he to hear the most pathetic cries issuing hence that could be uttered by a spectre-chased soul. I reach a central mound or platform – the crown and axis of the whole structure. The view from here by day must be of almost limitless extent. On this raised floor, daïs, or rostrum, harps have probably twanged more or less tuneful notes in celebration of daring, strength, or cruelty; of worship, superstition, love, birth, and death; of simple loving-kindness* perhaps never. Many a time must the king or leader have directed his keen eyes hence across the open lands towards the ancient road, the Icening Way,* still visible in the distance, on the watch for armed companies approaching either to succour or to attack.

I am startled by a voice pronouncing my name. Past and present have become so confusedly mingled under the associations of the spot that for a time it has escaped my memory that this mound was the place agreed on for the aforesaid appointment. I turn and behold my friend. He stands with a dark lantern in his hand and a spade and light pickaxe over his shoulder. He expresses both delight and surprise that I have come. I tell him I had set out before the bad weather began.

He, to whom neither weather, darkness, nor difficulty seems to have any relation or significance, so entirely is his soul wrapt up in his own deep intentions, asks me to take the lantern and accompany him. I take it and walk by his side. He is a man about sixty, small in figure, with grey old-fashioned whiskers cut to the shape of a pair of crumb-brushes. He is entirely in black broadcloth – or rather, at present, black and brown, for he is bespattered with mud from his heels to the crown of his low hat. He has no consciousness of this – no sense of anything but his purpose, his ardour for which causes his eyes to shine like those of a lynx, and gives his motions all the elasticity of an athlete's.

'Nobody to interrupt us at this time of night!' he chuckles with fierce enjoyment.

We retreat a little way and find a sort of angle, an elevation in the sod, a suggested squareness amid the mass of irregularities around. Here, he tells me, if anywhere, the king's house stood. Three months of measurement and calculation have confirmed him in this conclusion.

He requests me now to open the lantern, which I do, and the light streams out upon the wet sod. At last divining his proceedings I say that I had no idea, in keeping the tryst, that he was going to do more at such an unusual time than meet me for a meditative ramble through the stronghold. I ask him why, having a practicable object, he should have minded interruptions and not have chosen the day? He informs me, quietly pointing to his spade, that it was because his purpose is to dig, then signifying with a grim nod the gaunt notice-post against the sky beyond. I inquire why, as a professed and well-known antiquary with capital letters at the tail of his name, he did not obtain the necessary authority, considering the stringent penalties for this sort of thing; and he chuckles fiercely again with suppressed delight, and says, 'Because they wouldn't have given it!'

He at once begins cutting up the sod, and, as he takes the pickaxe to follow on with, assures me that, penalty or no penalty, honest men or marauders, he is sure of one thing, that we shall not be disturbed at our work till after dawn.

I remember to have heard of men who, in their enthusiasm for some special science, art, or hobby, have quite lost the moral sense which would restrain them from indulging it illegitimately; and I conjecture that here, at last, is an instance of such an one. He probably guesses the way my thoughts travel, for he stands up and solemnly asserts that he has a distinctly justifiable intention in this matter; namely, to uncover, to search, to verify a theory or displace it, and to cover up again. He means to take away nothing – not a grain of sand. In this he says he sees no such monstrous sin. I inquire if this is really a promise to me? He repeats that it is a promise, and resumes digging. My contribution to the labour is that of directing the light constantly upon the hole. When he has reached something more than a foot deep he digs more cautiously, saying that, be it much or little there, it will not lie far below the surface; such things never are deep. A few minutes later the point of the pickaxe clicks upon a stony substance. He draws the implement out as feelingly as if it had entered a man's body. Taking up the spade he shovels with care, and a surface, level as an altar, is presently disclosed. His eyes flash anew; he pulls handfuls of grass and mops the surface clean, finally rubbing it with his handkerchief. Grasping the lantern from my hand he holds it close to the ground, when the rays reveal a complete mosaic – a pavement of minute tesserae* of many colours, of intricate pattern, a work of much art, of much time, and of much industry. He exclaims in a shout that he knew it always – that it is not a Celtic stronghold exclusively, but also a Roman; the former people having probably contributed little more than the original framework which the latter took and adapted till it became the present imposing structure.

I ask, What if it is Roman?

A great deal, according to him. That it proves all the world to be wrong in this great argument, and himself alone to be right! Can I wait while he digs further?

I agree – reluctantly; but he does not notice my reluctance. At an adjoining spot he begins flourishing the tools anew with the skill of a navvy, this venerable scholar with letters after his name. Sometimes he falls on his knees, burrowing with his hands in the manner of a hare, and where his old-fashioned broadcloth touches the sides of the hole it gets plastered with the damp earth. He continually murmurs to himself how import-ant, how very important, this discovery is! He draws out an object; we wash it in the same primitive way by rubbing it with the wet grass, and it proves to be a semi-transparent bottle of iridescent beauty, the sight of which draws groans of luxurious sensibility from the digger. Further and further search brings out a piece of a weapon. It is strange indeed that by merely peeling off a wrapper of modern accumulations we have lowered ourselves into an ancient world. Finally a skeleton is uncovered, fairly perfect. He lays it out on the grass, bone to its bone.

My friend says the man must have fallen fighting here, as this is no place of burial. He turns again to the trench, scrapes, feels, till from a corner he draws out a heavy lump – a small image four or five inches high. We clean it as before. It is a statuette, apparently of gold, or more probably, of bronze-gilt – a figure of Mercury,* obviously, its head being surmounted with the petasus or winged hat, the usual accessory of that deity. Further inspection reveals the workmanship to be of good finish and detail, and, preserved by the limy earth, to be as fresh in every line as on the day it left the hands of its artificer.

We seem to be standing in the Roman Forum* and not on a hill in Wessex. Intent upon this truly valuable relic of the old empire of which even this remote spot was a component part, we do not notice what is going on in the present world till reminded of it by the sudden renewal of the storm. Looking up I perceive that the wide extinguisher of cloud has again settled down upon the fortress-town, as if resting upon the edge of the inner rampart, and shutting out the moon. I turn my back to the tempest, still directing the light across the hole. My companion digs on unconcernedly; he is living two thousand years ago, and despises things of the moment as dreams. But at last he is fairly beaten, and standing up beside me looks round on what he has done. The rays of the lantern pass over the trench to the tall skeleton stretched upon the grass on the other side. The beating rain has washed the bones clean and smooth, and the forehead, cheek-bones, and two-and-thirty teeth of the skull glisten in the candle-shine as they lie.

This storm, like the first, is of the nature of a squall, and it ends as abruptly as the other. We dig no further. My friend says that it is enough – he has proved his point. He turns to replace the bones in the trench and covers them. But they fall to pieces under his touch: the air has disintegrated them, and he can only sweep in the fragments. The next act of his plan is more than difficult, but is carried out. The treasures are inhumed again in their respective holes: they are not ours. Each deposition seems to cost him a twinge; and at one moment I fancied I saw him slip his hand into his coat pocket.

'We must re-bury them *all*,' say I.

'O yes,' he answers with integrity. 'I was wiping my hand.'

The beauties of the tesselated floor of the governor's house are once again consigned to darkness; the trench is filled up; the sod laid smoothly down; he wipes the perspiration from his forehead with the same handkerchief he had used to mop the skeleton and tesserae clean; and we make for the eastern gate of the fortress.

Dawn bursts upon us suddenly as we reach the opening. It comes by the lifting and thinning of the clouds that way till we are bathed in a pink light. The direction of his homeward journey is not the same as mine, and we part under the outer slope.

Walking along quickly to restore warmth I muse upon my eccentric friend, and cannot help asking myself this question: Did he really replace the gilded image of the god Mercurius with the rest of the treasures? He seemed to do so; and yet I could not testify to the fact. Probably, however, he was as good as his word.

*

It was thus I spoke to myself, and so the adventure ended. But one thing remains to be told, and that is concerned with seven years after. Among the effects of my friend, at that time just deceased, was found, carefully preserved, a gilt statuette representing Mercury, labelled 'Debased Roman'. No record was attached to explain how it came into his possession. The figure was bequeathed to the Casterbridge Museum.

THE WITHERED ARM *

A LORN MILKMAID

It was an eighty-cow dairy, and the troop of milkers, regular and supernumerary, were all at work; for, though the time of year was as yet but early April, the feed lay entirely in water-meadows,* and the cows were 'in full pail'. The hour was about six in the evening, and three-fourths of the large, red, rectangular animals having been finished off, there was opportunity for a little conversation.

'He do bring home his bride tomorrow, I hear. They've come as far as Anglebury today.'

The voice seemed to proceed from the belly of the cow called Cherry, but the speaker was a milking-woman, whose face was buried in the flank of that motionless beast.

'Hav' anybody seen her?' said another.

There was a negative response from the first. 'Though they say she's a rosy-cheeked, tisty-tosty* little body enough,' she added; and as the milkmaid spoke she turned her face so that she could glance past her cow's tail to the other side of the barton,* where a thin, fading woman of thirty milked somewhat apart from the rest.

'Years younger than he, they say,' continued the second, with also a glance of reflectiveness in the same direction.

'How old do you call him, then?'

'Thirty or so.'

'More like forty,' broke in an old milkman near, in a long white pinafore or 'wropper', and with the brim of his hat tied down, so that he looked like a woman. ''A was born before our Great Weir was builded, and I hadn't man's wages when I laved* water there.'

The discussion waxed so warm that the purr of the milk streams became jerky, till a voice from another cow's belly cried with authority, 'Now then, what the Turk* do it matter to us about Farmer Lodge's age, or Farmer Lodge's new mis'ess? I shall have to pay him nine pound a year for the rent of every one of these milchers,* whatever his age or hers. Get on with your work, or 'twill be dark afore we have done. The evening is pinking in a'ready.' This speaker was the dairyman himself, by whom the milkmaids and men were employed.

Nothing more was said publicly about Farmer Lodge's wedding, but the first woman murmured under her cow to her next neighbour, "Tis hard for *she*,' signifying the thin worn milkmaid aforesaid.

'O no,' said the second. 'He ha'n't spoke to Rhoda Brook for years.'

When the milking was done they washed their pails and hung them on a many-forked stand made as usual of the peeled limb of an oak-tree, set upright in the earth, and resembling a colossal antlered horn. The majority then dispersed in various directions homeward. The thin woman who had not spoken was joined by a boy of twelve or thereabout, and the twain went away up the field also.

Their course lay apart from that of the others, to a lonely spot high above the water-meads, and not far from the border of Egdon Heath, whose dark countenance was visible in the distance as they drew nigh to their home.

'They've just been saying down in barton that your father brings his young wife home from Anglebury tomorrow,' the woman observed. 'I shall want to send you for a few things to market, and you'll be pretty sure to meet 'em.'

'Yes, mother,' said the boy. 'Is father married then?'

'Yes. . . . You can give her a look, and tell me what she's like, if you do see her.'

'Yes, mother.'

'If she's dark or fair, and if she's tall – as tall as I. And if she seems like a woman who has ever worked for a living, or one that has been always well off, and has never done anything, and shows marks of the lady on her, as I expect she do.'

'Yes.'

They crept up the hill in the twilight and entered the cottage. It was built of mud-walls, the surface of which had been washed by many rains into channels and depressions that left none of the original flat face visible; while here and there in the thatch above a rafter showed like a bone protruding through the skin.

She was kneeling down in the chimney-corner, before two

pieces of turf laid together with the heather inwards, blowing at the red-hot ashes with her breath till the turves flamed. The radiance lit her pale cheek, and made her dark eyes, that had once been handsome, seem handsome anew. 'Yes,' she resumed, 'see if she is dark or fair, and if you can, notice if her hands be white; if not, see if they look as though she had ever done housework, or are milker's hands like mine.'

The boy again promised, inattentively this time, his mother not observing that he was cutting a notch with his pocket-knife in the beech-backed chair.

THE YOUNG WIFE

The road from Anglebury to Holmstoke is in general level; but there is one place where a sharp ascent breaks its monotony. Farmers homeward-bound from the former market-town, who trot all the rest of the way, walk their horses up this short incline.

The next evening while the sun was yet bright a handsome new gig, with a lemon-coloured body and red wheels, was spinning westward along the level highway at the heels of a powerful mare. The driver was a yeoman in the prime of life, cleanly shaven like an actor, his face being toned to that bluish-vermilion hue which so often graces a thriving farmer's features when returning home after successful dealings in the town. Beside him sat a woman, many years his junior – almost, indeed, a girl. Her face too was fresh in colour, but it was of a totally different quality – soft and evanescent, like the light under a heap of rose-petals.

Few people travelled this way, for it was not a main road; and the long white riband of gravel that stretched before them was empty, save of one small scarce-moving speck, which presently resolved itself into the figure of a boy, who was creeping on at a snail's pace, and continually looking behind him – the heavy bundle he carried being some excuse for, if not the reason of, his dilatoriness. When the bouncing gig-party slowed at the bottom of the incline above mentioned, the pedestrian was only a few yards in front. Supporting the large bundle by putting one hand on his hip, he turned and looked straight at the farmer's wife as though he would read her through and through, pacing along abreast of the horse.

The low sun was full in her face, rendering every feature, shade, and contour distinct, from the curve of her little nostril to the colour of her eyes. The farmer, though he seemed annoyed at the boy's persistent presence, did not order him to get out of the way; and thus the lad preceded them, his hard gaze never leaving her, till they reached the top of the ascent, when the farmer trotted on with relief in his lineaments – having taken no outward notice of the boy whatever.

'How that poor lad stared at me!' said the young wife.

'Yes, dear; I saw that he did.'

'He is one of the village, I suppose?'

'One of the neighbourhood. I think he lives with his mother a mile or two off.'

'He knows who we are, no doubt?'

'O yes. You must expect to be stared at just at first, my pretty Gertrude.'

'I do – though I think the poor boy may have looked at us in the hope we might relieve him of his heavy load, rather than from curiosity.'

'O no,' said her husband off-handedly. 'These country lads will carry a hundredweight once they get it on their backs; besides his pack had more size than weight in it. Now, then, another mile and I shall be able to show you our house in the distance – if it is not too dark before we get there.' The wheels spun round, and particles flew from their periphery as before, till a white house of ample dimensions revealed itself, with farm-buildings and ricks at the back.

Meanwhile the boy had quickened his pace, and turning up a bye-lane some mile and half short of the white farmstead, ascended towards the leaner pastures, and so on to the cottage of his mother.

She had reached home after her day's milking at the outlying dairy, and was washing cabbage at the doorway in the declining light. 'Hold up the net a moment,' she said, without preface, as the boy came up.

He flung down his bundle, held the edge of the cabbage-net, and as she filled its meshes with the dripping leaves she went on, 'Well, did you see her?'

'Yes; quite plain.'

'Is she ladylike?'

'Yes; and more. A lady complete.'

'Is she young?'

'Well, she's growed up, and her ways be quite a woman's.'

'Of course. What colour is her hair and face?'

'Her hair is lightish, and her face as comely as a live doll's.'

'Her eyes, then, are not dark like mine?'

'No – of a bluish turn, and her mouth is very nice and red; and when she smiles, her teeth show white.'

'Is she tall?' said the woman sharply.

'I couldn't see. She was sitting down.'

'Then do you go to Holmstoke church tomorrow morning: she's sure to be there. Go early and notice her walking in, and come home and tell me if she's taller than I.'

'Very well, mother. But why don't you go and see for yourself?'

'*I* go to see her! I wouldn't look up at her if she were to pass my window this instant. She was with Mr Lodge, of course. What did he say or do?'

'Just the same as usual.'

'Took no notice of you?'

'None.'

Next day the mother put a clean shirt on the boy, and started him off for Holmstoke church. He reached the ancient little pile when the door was just being opened, and he was the first to enter. Taking his seat by the font, he watched all the parishioners file in. The well-to-do Farmer Lodge came nearly last; and his young wife, who accompanied him, walked up the aisle with the shyness natural to a modest woman who had appeared thus for the first time. As all other eyes were fixed upon her, the youth's stare was not noticed now.

When he reached home his mother said, 'Well?' before he had entered the room.

'She is not tall. She is rather short,' he replied.

'Ah!' said his mother, with satisfaction.

'But she's very pretty – very. In fact, she's lovely.' The youthful freshness of the yeoman's wife had evidently made an impression even on the somewhat hard nature of the boy.

'That's all I want to hear,' said his mother quickly. 'Now, spread the table-cloth. The hare you wired is very tender; but mind that nobody catches you. – You've never told me what sort of hands she had.'

'I have never seen 'em. She never took off her gloves.'

'What did she wear this morning?'

'A white bonnet and a silver-coloured gownd*. It whewed* and whistled so loud when it rubbed against the pews that the lady coloured up more than ever for very shame at the noise, and pulled it in to keep it from touching; but when she pushed into her seat, it whewed more than ever. Mr Lodge, he seemed pleased, and his waistcoat stuck out, and his great golden seals hung like a lord's; but she seemed to wish her noisy gownd anywhere but on her.'

'Not she! However, that will do now.'

These descriptions of the newly-married couple were continued from time to time by the boy at his mother's request, after any chance encounter he had had with them. But Rhoda Brook, though she might easily have seen young Mrs Lodge for herself by walking a couple of miles, would never attempt an excursion towards the quarter where the farmhouse lay. Neither did she, at the daily milking in the dairyman's yard on Lodge's outlying second farm, ever speak on the subject of the recent marriage. The dairyman, who rented the cows of Lodge, and knew perfectly the tall milkmaid's history, with manly kindliness always kept the gossip in the cow-barton from annoying Rhoda. But the atmosphere thereabout was full of the subject during the first days of Mrs Lodge's arrival; and from her boy's description and the casual words of the other milkers, Rhoda Brook could raise a mental image of the unconscious Mrs Lodge that was realistic as a photograph.

A VISION

One night, two or three weeks after the bridal return, when the boy was gone to bed, Rhoda sat a long time over the turf ashes that she had raked out in front of her to extinguish them. She contemplated so intently the new wife, as presented to her in her mind's eye over the embers, that she forgot the lapse of time. At last, wearied with her day's work, she too retired.

But the figure which had occupied her so much during this and the previous days was not to be banished at night. For the first time Gertrude Lodge visited the supplanted woman in her dreams. Rhoda Brook dreamed – since her assertion that she really saw, before falling asleep, was not to be believed – that the young wife, in the pale silk dress and white bonnet, but with features shockingly distorted, and wrinkled as by age, was sitting upon her chest as she lay. The pressure of Mrs Lodge's person grew heavier; the blue eyes peered cruelly into her face; and then the figure thrust forward its left hand mockingly, so as to make the wedding-ring it wore glitter in Rhoda's eyes. Maddened mentally, and nearly suffocated by pressure, the sleeper struggled; the incubus, still regarding her, withdrew to the foot of the bed, only, however, to come forward by degrees, resume her seat, and flash her left hand as before.

Gasping for breath, Rhoda, in a last desperate effort, swung out her right hand, seized the confronting spectre by its obtrusive left arm, and whirled it backward to the floor, starting up herself as she did so with a low cry.

'O, merciful heaven!' she cried, sitting on the edge of the bed in a cold sweat; 'that was not a dream – she was here!'

She could feel her antagonist's arm within her grasp even now – the very flesh and bone of it, as it seemed. She looked on the floor whither she had whirled the spectre, but there was nothing to be seen.

Rhoda Brook slept no more that night, and when she went milking at the next dawn they noticed how pale and haggard she looked. The milk that she drew quivered into the pail; her hand had not calmed even yet, and still retained the feel of the arm. She came home to breakfast as wearily as if it had been suppertime.

'What was that noise in your chimmer,* mother, last night?' said her son. 'You fell off the bed, surely?'

'Did you hear anything fall? At what time?'

'Just when the clock struck two.'

She could not explain, and when the meal was done went silently about her household work, the boy assisting her, for he hated going afield on the farms, and she indulged his reluctance. Between eleven and twelve the garden-gate clicked, and she lifted her eyes to the window. At the bottom of the garden, within the gate, stood the woman of her vision. Rhoda seemed transfixed.

'Ah, she said she would come!' exclaimed the boy, also observing her.

'Said so – when? How does she know us?'

'I have seen and spoken to her. I talked to her yesterday.'

'I told you,' said the mother, flushing indignantly, 'never to speak to anybody in that house, or go near the place.'

'I did not speak to her till she spoke to me. And I did not go near the place. I met her in the road.'

'What did you tell her?'

'Nothing. She said, "Are you the poor boy who had to bring the heavy load from market?" And she looked at my boots, and said they would not keep my feet dry if it came on wet, because they were so cracked. I told her I lived with my mother, and we had enough to do to keep ourselves, and that's how it was; and she said then, "I'll come and bring you some better boots, and see your mother." She gives away things to other folks in the meads besides us.'

Mrs Lodge was by this time close to the door – not in her silk, as Rhoda had dreamt of in the bed-chamber, but in a morning hat, and gown of common light material, which became her better than silk. On her arm she carried a basket.

The impression remaining from the night's experience was still strong. Brook had almost expected to see the wrinkles, the scorn, and the cruelty on her visitor's face. She would have escaped an interview, had escape been possible. There was, however, no backdoor to the cottage, and in an instant the boy had lifted the latch to Mrs Lodge's gentle knock.

'I see I have come to the right house,' said she, glancing at the lad, and smiling. 'But I was not sure till you opened the door.'

The figure and action were those of the phantom; but her voice was so indescribably sweet, her glance so winning, her smile so tender, so unlike that of Rhoda's midnight visitant, that the latter could hardly believe the evidence of her senses. She was truly glad that she had not hidden away in sheer aversion, as she had been inclined to do. In her basket Mrs Lodge brought the pair of boots that she had promised to the boy, and other useful articles.

At these proofs of a kindly feeling towards her and hers Rhoda's heart reproached her bitterly. This innocent young thing should have her blessing and not her curse. When she left them a light seemed gone from the dwelling. Two days later she came again to know if the boots fitted; and less than a fortnight after that paid Rhoda another call. On this occasion the boy was absent.

'I walk a good deal,' said Mrs Lodge, 'and your house is the nearest outside our own parish. I hope you are well. You don't look quite well.'

Rhoda said she was well enough; and, indeed, though the paler of the two, there was more of the strength that endures in her well-defined features and large frame than in the soft-cheeked young woman before her. The conversation became quite confidential as regarded their powers and weaknesses; and when Mrs Lodge was leaving, Rhoda said, 'I hope you will find this air agree with you, ma'am, and not suffer from the damp of the water-meads.'

The younger one replied that there was not much doubt of it, her general health being usually good. 'Though, now you remind me,' she added, 'I have one little ailment which puzzles me. It is nothing serious, but I cannot make it out.'

She uncovered her left hand and arm; and their outline confronted Rhoda's gaze as the exact original of the limb she had beheld and seized in her dream. Upon the pink round surface of the arm were faint marks of an unhealthy colour, as if produced by a rough grasp. Rhoda's eyes became riveted on the discolorations; she fancied that she discerned in them the shape of her own four fingers.

'How did it happen?' she said mechanically.

'I cannot tell,' replied Mrs Lodge, shaking her head. 'One night when I was sound asleep, dreaming I was away in some strange place, a pain suddenly shot into my arm there, and was so keen as to awaken me. I must have struck it in the daytime, I suppose, though I don't remember doing so.' She added, laughing, 'I tell my dear husband that it looks just as if he had flown into a rage and struck me there. O, I daresay it will soon disappear.'

'Ha, ha! Yes. . . . On what night did it come?'

Mrs Lodge considered, and said it would be a fortnight ago on the morrow. 'When I awoke I could not remember where I was,' she added, 'till the clock striking two reminded me.'

She had named the night and the hour of Rhoda's spectral encounter, and Brook felt like a guilty thing.* The artless disclosure startled her; she did not reason on the freaks of coincidence; and all the scenery of that ghastly night returned with double vividness to her mind.

'O, can it be,' she said to herself, when her visitor had departed, 'that I exercise a malignant power over people against my own will?' She knew that she had been slyly called a witch since her fall; but never having understood why that particular stigma had been attached to her, it had passed disregarded. Could this be the explanation, and had such things as this ever happened before?

A SUGGESTION

The summer drew on, and Rhoda Brook almost dreaded to meet Mrs Lodge again, notwithstanding that her feeling for the young wife amounted well-nigh to affection. Something in her own individuality seemed to convict Rhoda of crime. Yet a fatality sometimes would direct the steps of the latter to the outskirts of Holmstoke whenever she left her house for any other purpose than her daily work; and hence it happened that their next encounter was out of doors. Rhoda could not avoid the subject which had so mystified her, and after the first few words she stammered, 'I hope your – arm is well again. ma'am?' She had perceived with consternation that Gertrude Lodge carried her left arm stiffly.

'No; it is not quite well. Indeed it is no better at all; it is rather worse. It pains me dreadfully sometimes.'

'Perhaps you had better go to a doctor, ma'am.'

She replied that she had already seen a doctor. Her husband had insisted upon her going to one. But the surgeon had not seemed to understand the afflicted limb at all; he had told her to bathe it in hot water, and she had bathed it, but the treatment had done no good.

'Will you let me see it?' said the milkwoman.

Mrs Lodge pushed up her sleeve and disclosed the place, which was a few inches above the wrist. As soon as Rhoda Brook saw it, she could hardly preserve her composure. There was nothing of the nature of a wound, but the arm at that point had a shrivelled look, and the outline of the four fingers appeared more distinct than at the former time. Moreover, she fancied that they were imprinted in precisely the relative position of her clutch upon the arm in the trance; the first finger towards Gertrude's wrist, and the fourth towards her elbow.

What the impress resembled seemed to have struck Gertrude herself since their last meeting. 'It looks almost like finger-marks,' she said; adding with a faint laugh, 'my husband says it is as if some witch, or the devil himself, had taken hold of me there, and blasted the flesh.'

Rhoda shivered. 'That's fancy,' she said hurriedly. 'I wouldn't mind it, if I were you.'

'I shouldn't so much mind it,' said the younger, with hesitation, 'if – if I hadn't a notion that it makes my husband – dislike me – no, love me less. Men think so much of personal appearance.'

'Some do – he for one.'

'Yes; and he was very proud of mine, at first.'

'Keep your arm covered from his sight.'

'Ah – he knows the disfigurement is there!' She tried to hide the tears that filled her eyes.

'Well, ma'am, I earnestly hope it will go away soon.'

And so the milkwoman's mind was chained anew to the subject by a horrid sort of spell as she returned home. The sense of having been guilty of an act of malignity increased, affect as she might to ridicule her superstition. In her secret heart Rhoda did not altogether object to a slight diminution of her successor's beauty, by whatever means it had come about; but she did not wish to inflict upon her physical pain. For though this pretty young woman had rendered impossible any reparation which Lodge might have made Rhoda for his past conduct, everything like resentment at the unconscious usurpation had quite passed away from the elder's mind.

If the sweet and kindly Gertrude Lodge only knew of the dream-scene in the bed-chamber, what would she think? Not to inform her of it seemed treachery in the presence of her friendliness; but tell she could not of her own accord – neither could she devise a remedy.

She mused upon the matter the greater part of the night; and the next day, after the morning milking, set out to obtain another glimpse of Gertrude Lodge if she could, being held to her by a gruesome fascination. By watching the house from a distance the milkmaid was presently able to discern the farmer's wife in a ride she was taking alone – probably to join her husband in some distant field. Mrs Lodge perceived her, and cantered in her direction.

'Good morning, Rhoda!' Gertrude said, when she had come up. 'I was going to call.'

Rhoda noticed that Mrs Lodge held the reins with some difficulty.

'I hope – the bad arm,' said Rhoda.

'They tell me there is possibly one way by which I might be able to find out the cause, and so perhaps the cure, of it,' replied the other anxiously. 'It is by going to some clever man over in Egdon Heath. They did not know if he was still alive – and I cannot remember his name at this moment; but they said that you knew more of his movements than anybody else hereabout, and could tell me if he were still to be consulted. Dear me – what was his name? But you know.'

'Not Conjuror Trendle?'* said her thin companion, turning pale.

'Trendle – yes. Is he alive?'

'I believe so,' said Rhoda, with reluctance.

'Why do you call him conjuror?'

'Well – they say – they used to say he was a – he had powers other folks have not.'

'O, how could my people be so superstitious as to recommend a man of that sort! I thought they meant some medical man. I shall think no more of him.'

Rhoda looked relieved, and Mrs Lodge rode on. The milk-woman had inwardly seen, from the moment she heard of her having been mentioned as a reference for this man, that there must exist a sarcastic feeling among the work-folk that a sorceress would know the whereabouts of the exorcist. They suspected her, then. A short time ago this would have given no concern to a woman of her common sense. But she had a haunting reason to be superstitious now; and she had been seized with sudden dread that this Conjuror Trendle might name her as the malignant influence which was blasting the fair person of Gertrude, and so lead her friend to hate her for ever, and to treat her as some fiend in human shape.

But all was not over. Two days after, a shadow intruded into the window-pattern thrown on Rhoda Brook's floor by the afternoon sun. The woman opened the door at once, almost breathlessly.

'Are you alone?' said Gertrude. She seemed to be no less harassed and anxious than Brook herself.

'Yes,' said Rhoda.

'The place on my arm seems worse, and troubles me!' the young farmer's wife went on. 'It is so mysterious! I do hope it will not be an incurable wound. I have again been thinking of what they said about Conjuror Trendle. I don't really believe in such men, but I should not mind just visiting him, from curiosity – though on no account must my husband know. Is it far to where he lives?'

'Yes – five miles,' said Rhoda backwardly. 'In the heart of Egdon.'

'Well, I should have to walk. Could not you go with me to show me the way – say tomorrow afternoon?'

'O, not I; that is – ,' the milkwoman murmured, with a start of dismay. Again the dread seized her that something to do with her fierce act in the dream might be revealed, and her character in the eyes of the most useful friend she had ever had be ruined irretrievably.

Mrs Lodge urged, and Rhoda finally assented, though with much misgiving. Sad as the journey would be to her, she could not conscientiously stand in the way of a possible remedy for her patron's strange affliction. It was agreed that, to escape suspicion of their mystic intent, they should meet at the edge of the heath at the corner of a plantation which was visible from the spot where they now stood.

CONJUROR TRENDLE

By the next afternoon Rhoda would have done anything to escape this inquiry. But she had promised to go. Moreover, there was a horrid fascination at times in becoming instrumental in throwing such possible light on her own character as would reveal her to be something greater in the occult world than she had ever herself suspected.

She started just before the time of day mentioned between them, and half-an-hour's brisk walking brought her to the south-eastern extension of the Egdon tract of country, where the fir plantation was. A slight figure, cloaked and veiled, was already there. Rhoda recognized, almost with a shudder, that Mrs Lodge bore her left arm in a sling.

They hardly spoke to each other, and immediately set out on their climb into the interior of this solemn country, which stood high above the rich alluvial soil they had left half-an-hour before. It was a long walk; thick clouds made the atmosphere dark, though it was as yet only early afternoon; and the wind howled dismally over the slopes of the heath – not improbably the same heath which had witnessed the agony of the Wessex King Ina, presented to after-ages as Lear.* Gertrude Lodge talked most, Rhoda replying with monosyllabic preoccupation. She had a strange dislike to walking on the side of her companion where hung the afflicted arm, moving round to the other when inadvertently near it. Much heather had been brushed by their feet when they descended upon a cart-track, beside which stood the house of the man they sought.

He did not profess his remedial practices openly, or care anything about their continuance, his direct interests being those of a dealer in furze, turf, 'sharp sand',* and other local products. Indeed, he affected not to believe largely in his own powers, and when warts that had been shown him for cure miraculously disappeared – which it must be owned they infallibly did – he would say lightly, 'O, I only drink a glass of grog upon 'em at your expense – perhaps it's all chance,' and immediately turn the subject.

He was at home when they arrived, having in fact seen them descending into his valley. He was a grey-bearded man, with a reddish face, and he looked singularly at Rhoda the first moment he beheld her. Mrs Lodge told him her errand; and then with words of self-disparagement he examined her arm.

'Medicine can't cure it,' he said promptly. ''Tis the work of an enemy.'

Rhoda shrank into herself, and drew back.

'An enemy? What enemy?' asked Mrs Lodge.

He shook his head. 'That's best known to yourself,' he said. 'If you like, I can show the person to you, though I shall not myself know who it is. I can do no more; and don't wish to do that.'

She pressed him; on which he told Rhoda to wait outside

where she stood, and took Mrs Lodge into the room. It opened immediately from the door; and, as the latter remained ajar, Rhoda Brook could see the proceedings without taking part in them. He brought a tumbler from the dresser, nearly filled it with water, and fetching an egg, prepared it in some private way; after which he broke it on the edge of the glass so that the white went in and the yolk remained. As it was getting gloomy, he took the glass and its contents to the window, and told Gertrude to watch the mixture closely. They leant over the table together, and the milkwoman could see the opaline* hue of the egg-fluid changing form as it sank in the water, but she was not near enough to define the shape that it assumed.

'Do you catch the likeness of any face or figure as you look?' demanded the conjuror of the young woman.

She murmured a reply, in tones so low as to be inaudible to Rhoda, and continued to gaze intently into the glass. Rhoda turned, and walked a few steps away.

When Mrs Lodge came out, and her face was met by the light, it appeared exceedingly pale – as pale as Rhoda's – against the sad dun shades of the upland's garniture.* Trendle shut the door behind her, and they at once started homeward together. But Rhoda perceived that her companion had quite changed.

'Did he charge much?' she asked tentatively.

'O no – nothing. He would not take a farthing,' said Gertrude.

'And what did you see?' inquired Rhoda.

'Nothing I – care to speak of.' The constraint in her manner was remarkable; her face was so rigid as to wear an oldened aspect, faintly suggestive of the face in Rhoda's bed-chamber.

'Was it you who first proposed coming here?' Mrs Lodge suddenly inquired, after a long pause. 'How very odd, if you did!'

'No. But I am not sorry we have come, all things considered,' she replied. For the first time a sense of triumph possessed her, and she did not altogether deplore that the young thing at her side should learn that their lives had been antagonized by other influences than their own.

The subject was no more alluded to during the long and dreary walk home. But in some way or other a story was whispered about the many-dairied lowland that winter that Mrs Lodge's gradual loss of the use of her left arm was owing to her being 'overlooked'* by Rhoda Brook. The latter kept her own counsel about the incubus, but her face grew sadder and thinner; and in the spring she and her boy disappeared from the neighbourhood of Holmstoke.

A SECOND ATTEMPT

Half a dozen years passed away, and Mr and Mrs Lodge's married experience sank into prosiness, and worse. The farmer was usually gloomy and silent: the woman whom he had wooed for her grace and beauty was contorted and disfigured in the left limb; moreover, she had brought him no child, which rendered it likely that he would be the last of a family who had occupied that valley for some two hundred years. He thought of Rhoda Brook and her son; and feared this might be a judgment from heaven upon him.

The once blithe-hearted and enlightened Gertrude was changing into an irritable, superstitious woman, whose whole time was given to experimenting upon her ailment with every quack remedy she came across. She was honestly attached to her husband, and was ever secretly hoping against hope to win back his heart again by regaining some at least of her personal beauty. Hence it arose that her closet was lined with bottles, packets, and ointment-pots of every description – nay, bunches of mystic herbs, charms, and books of necromancy, which in her school-girl time she would have ridiculed as folly.

'Damned if you won't poison yourself with these apothecary messes and witch mixtures some time or other,' said her husband, when his eye chanced to fall upon the multitudinous array.

She did not reply, but turned her sad, soft glance upon him in such heart-swollen reproach that he looked sorry for his words, and added, 'I only meant it for your good, you know, Gertrude.'

'I'll clear out the whole lot, and destroy them,' said she huskily, 'and try such remedies no more!'

'You want somebody to cheer you,' he observed. 'I once thought of adopting a boy; but he is too old now. And he is gone away I don't know where.'

She guessed to whom he alluded; for Rhoda Brook's story had in the course of years become known to her; though not a word had ever passed between her husband and herself on the subject. Neither had she ever spoken to him of her visit to Conjuror Trendle, and of what was revealed to her, or she thought was revealed to her, by that solitary heathman.

She was now five-and-twenty; but she seemed older. 'Six years of marriage, and only a few months of love,' she sometimes whispered to herself. And then she thought of the apparent cause, and said, with a tragic glance at her withering limb, 'If I could only again be as I was when he first saw me!'

She obediently destroyed her nostrums and charms; but there remained a hankering wish to try something else – some other sort of cure altogether. She had never revisited Trendle since she had been conducted to the house of the solitary by Rhoda against her will; but it now suddenly occurred to Gertrude that she would, in a last desperate effort at deliverance from this seeming curse, again seek out the man, if he yet lived. He was entitled to a certain credence, for the indistinct form he had raised in the glass had undoubtedly resembled the only woman in the world who – as she now knew, though not then – could have a reason for bearing her ill-will. The visit should be paid.

This time she went alone, though she nearly got lost on the heath, and roamed a considerable distance out of her way. Trendle's house was reached at last, however: he was not indoors, and instead of waiting at the cottage, she went to where his bent figure was pointed out to her at work a long way off. Trendle remembered her, and laying down the handful of furze-roots which he was gathering and throwing into a heap, he offered to accompany her in her homeward direction, as the distance was considerable and the days were short. So they walked together, his head bowed nearly to the earth, and his form of a colour with it.

'You can send away warts and other excrescences, I know,' she said; 'why can't you send away this?' And the arm was uncovered.

'You think too much of my powers!' said Trendle; 'and I am old and weak now, too. No, no; it is too much for me to attempt in my own person. What have ye tried?'

She named to him some of the hundred medicaments and counterspells which she had adopted from time to time. He shook his head.

'Some were good enough,' he said approvingly; 'but not many

of them for such as this. This is of the nature of a blight, not of the nature of a wound; and if you ever do throw it off, it will be all at once.'

'If I only could!'

'There is only one chance of doing it known to me. It has never failed in kindred afflictions, – that I can declare. But it is hard to carry out, and especially for a woman.'

'Tell me!' said she.

'You must touch with the limb the neck of a man who's been hanged.'

She started a little at the image he had raised.

'Before he's cold – just after he's cut down,' continued the conjuror impassively.

'How can that do good?'

'It will turn the blood and change the constitution. But, as I say, to do it is hard. You must go to the jail when there's a hanging, and wait for him when he's brought off the gallows. Lots have done it, though perhaps not such pretty women as you. I used to send dozens for skin complaints. But that was in former times. The last I sent was in '13 – near twelve years ago.'

He had no more to tell her; and, when he had put her into a straight track homeward, turned and left her, refusing all money as at first.

A RIDE

The communication sank deep into Gertrude's mind. Her nature was rather a timid one; and probably of all remedies that the white wizard could have suggested there was not one which would have filled her with so much aversion as this, not to speak of the immense obstacles in the way of its adoption.

Casterbridge, the county-town, was a dozen or fifteen miles off; and though in those days, when men were executed for horse-stealing, arson, and burglary,* an assize* seldom passed without a hanging, it was not likely that she could get access to the body of the criminal unaided. And the fear of her husband's anger made her reluctant to breathe a word of Trendle's suggestion to him or to anybody about him.

She did nothing for months, and patiently bore her disfigurement as before. But her woman's nature, craving for renewed love, through the medium of renewed beauty (she was but twenty-five), was ever stimulating her to try what, at any rate, could hardly do her any harm. 'What came by a spell will go by a spell surely,' she would say. Whenever her imagination pictured the act she shrank in terror from the possibility of it: then the words of the conjuror, 'It will turn your blood,' were seen to be capable of a scientific no less than a ghastly interpretation; the mastering desire returned, and urged her on again.

There was at this time but one county paper, and that her husband only occasionally borrowed. But old-fashioned days had old-fashioned means, and news was extensively conveyed by word of mouth from market to market, or from fair to fair, so that, whenever such an event as an execution was about to take place, few within a radius of twenty miles were ignorant of the coming sight; and, so far as Holmstoke was concerned, some enthusiasts had been known to walk all the way to Casterbridge and back in one day, solely to witness the spectacle. The next assizes were in March; and when Gertrude Lodge heard that they had been held, she inquired stealthily at the inn as to the result, as soon as she could find opportunity.

She was, however, too late. The time at which the sentences were to be carried out had arrived, and to make the journey and obtain admission at such short notice required at least her husband's assistance. She dared not tell him, for she had found by delicate experiment that these smouldering village beliefs made him furious if mentioned, partly because he half entertained them himself. It was therefore necessary to wait for another opportunity.

Her determination received a fillip from learning that two epileptic children had attended from this very village of Holmstoke many years before with beneficial results, though the experiment had been strongly condemned by the neighbouring clergy. April, May, June, passed; and it is no overstatement to say that by the end of the last-named month Gertrude well-nigh longed for the death of a fellow-creature. Instead of her formal prayers each night, her unconscious prayer was, 'O Lord, hang some guilty or innocent person soon!'

This time she made earlier inquiries, and was altogether more systematic in her proceedings. Moreover, the season was summer, between the haymaking and the harvest, and in the leisure thus afforded him her husband had been holiday-taking away from home.

The assizes were in July, and she went to the inn as before. There was to be one execution – only one – for arson.

Her greatest problem was not how to get to Casterbridge, but what means she should adopt for obtaining admission to the jail. Though access for such purposes had formerly never been denied, the custom had fallen into desuetude; and in contemplating her possible difficulties, she was again almost driven to fall back upon her husband. But, on sounding him about the assizes, he was so uncommunicative, so more than usually cold, that she did not proceed, and decided that whatever she did she would do alone.

Fortune, obdurate hitherto, showed her unexpected favour. On the Thursday before the Saturday fixed for the execution, Lodge remarked to her that he was going away from home for another day or two on business at a fair, and that he was sorry he could not take her with him.

She exhibited on this occasion so much readiness to stay at home that he looked at her in surprise. Time had been when she would have shown deep disappointment at the loss of such a jaunt. However, he lapsed into his usual taciturnity, and on the day named left Holmstoke.

It was now her turn. She at first had thought of driving, but on reflection held that driving would not do, since it would necessitate her keeping to the turnpike-road, and so increase by tenfold the risk of her ghastly errand being found out. She decided to ride, and avoid the beaten track, notwithstanding that in her husband's stables there was no animal just at present which by any stretch of imagination could be considered a lady's mount, in spite of his promise before marriage to always keep a mare for her. He had, however, many cart-horses, fine ones of their kind; and among the rest was a serviceable creature, an equine Amazon,* with a back as broad as a sofa, on which Gertrude had occasionally taken an airing when unwell. This horse she chose.

On Friday afternoon one of the men brought it round. She was dressed, and before going down looked at her shrivelled arm. 'Ah!' she said to it, 'if it had not been for you this terrible ordeal would have been saved me!'

When strapping up the bundle in which she carried a few

articles of clothing, she took occasion to say to the servant, 'I take these in case I should not get back tonight from the person I am going to visit. Don't be alarmed if I am not in by ten, and close up the house as usual. I shall be at home tomorrow for certain.' She meant then to tell her husband privately: the deed accomplished was not like the deed projected. He would almost certainly forgive her.

And then the pretty palpitating Gertrude Lodge went from her husband's homestead; but though her goal was Casterbridge she did not take the direct route thither through Stickleford. Her cunning course at first was in precisely the opposite direction. As soon as she was out of sight, however, she turned to the left, by a road which led into Egdon, and on entering the heath wheeled round, and set out in the true course, due westerly. A more private way down the county could not be imagined; and as to direction, she had merely to keep her horse's head to a point a little to the right of the sun. She knew that she would light upon a furze-cutter or cottager of some sort from time to time, from whom she might correct her bearing.

Though the date was comparatively recent, Egdon was much less fragmentary in character than now. The attempts – successful and otherwise – at cultivation on the lower slopes, which intrude and break up the original heath into small detached heaths, had not been carried far; Enclosure Acts* had not taken effect, and the banks and fences which now exclude the cattle of those villagers who formerly enjoyed rights of commonage* thereon, and the carts of those who had turbary* privileges which kept them in firing all the year round, were not erected. Gertrude, therefore, rode along with no other obstacles than the prickly furze-bushes, the mats of heather, the white water-courses, and the natural steeps and declivities of the ground.

Her horse was sure, if heavy-footed and slow, and though a draught animal, was easy-paced; had it been otherwise, she was not a woman who could have ventured to ride over such a bit of country with a half-dead arm. It was therefore nearly eight o'clock when she drew rein to breathe her bearer on the last outlying high point of heath-land towards Casterbridge, previous to leaving Egdon for the cultivated valleys.

She halted before a pool called Rushy-pond, flanked by the ends of two hedges; a railing ran through the centre of the pond, dividing it in half. Over the railing she saw the low green country; over the green trees the roofs of the town; over the roofs a white flat façade, denoting the entrance to the county jail. On the roof of this front specks were moving about; they seemed to be workmen erecting something. Her flesh crept. She descended slowly, and was soon amid cornfields and pastures. In another half-hour, when it was almost dusk, Gertrude reached the White Hart, the first inn of the town on that side.

Little surprise was excited by her arrival; farmers' wives rode on horseback then more than they do now; though, for that matter, Mrs Lodge was not imagined to be a wife at all; the innkeeper supposed her some harum-skarum young woman who had come to attend 'hang-fair'* next day. Neither her husband nor herself ever dealt in Casterbridge market, so that she was unknown. While dismounting she beheld a crowd of boys standing at the door of a harness-maker's shop just above the inn, looking inside it with deep interest.

'What is going on there?' she asked of the ostler.

'Making the rope for tomorrow.'

She throbbed responsively, and contracted her arm.

''Tis sold by the inch afterwards,' the man continued. 'I could get you a bit, miss, for nothing, it you'd like?'

She hastily repudiated any such wish, all the more from a curious creeping feeling that the condemned wretch's destiny was becoming interwoven with her own; and having engaged a room for the night, sat down to think.

Up to this time she had formed but the vaguest notions about her means of obtaining access to the prison. The words of the cunning-man returned to her mind. He had implied that she should use her beauty, impaired though it was, as a pass-key. In her inexperience she knew little about jail functionaries; she had heard of a high-sheriff and an under-sheriff, but dimly only. She knew, however, that there must be a hangman, and to the hangman she determined to apply.

A WATER-SIDE HERMIT

At this date, and for several years after, there was a hangman to almost every jail. Gertrude found, on inquiry, that the Caster-bridge official dwelt in a lonely cottage by a deep slow river flowing under the cliff on which the prison buildings were situate – the stream being the self-same one, though she did not know it, which watered the Stickleford and Holmstoke meads lower down in its course.

Having changed her dress, and before she had eaten or drunk – for she could not take her ease till she had ascertained some particulars – Gertrude pursued her way by a path along the water-side to the cottage indicated. Passing thus the outskirts of the jail, she discerned on the level roof over the gateway three rectangular lines against the sky, where the specks had been moving in her distant view; she recognized what the erection was, and passed quickly on. Another hundred yards brought her to the executioner's house, which a boy pointed out. It stood close to the same stream, and was hard by a weir, the waters of which emitted a steady roar.

While she stood hesitating the door opened, and an old man came forth shading a candle with one hand. Locking the door on the outside, he turned to a flight of wooden steps fixed against the end of the cottage, and began to ascend them, this being evidently the staircase to his bedroom. Gertrude hastened forward, but by the time she reached the foot of the ladder he was at the top. She called to him loudly enough to be heard above the roar of the weir; he looked down and said, 'What d'ye want here?'

'To speak to you a minute.'

The candlelight, such as it was, fell upon her imploring, pale, upturned face, and Davies* (as the hangman was called) backed down the ladder. 'I was just going to bed,' he said; '"Early to bed and early to rise," but I don't mind stopping a minute for such a one as you. Come into house.' He reopened the door, and preceded her to the room within.

The implements of his daily work, which was that of a jobbing gardener, stood in a corner, and seeing probably that she looked rural, he said, 'If you want me to undertake country work I can't come, for I never leave Casterbridge for gentle nor simple – not I. My real calling is officer of justice,' he added formally.

'Yes, yes! That's it. Tomorrow!'

'Ah! I thought so. Well, what's the matter about that? 'Tis no use to come here about the knot – folks do come continually, but I tell 'em one knot is as merciful as another if ye keep it under the ear. Is the unfortunate man a relation; or, I should say, perhaps' (looking at her dress) 'a person who's been in your employ?'

'No. What time is the execution?'

'The same as usual – twelve o'clock, or as soon after as the London mail-coach gets in. We always wait for that, in case of a reprieve.'

'O – a reprieve – I hope not!' she said involuntarily.

'Well, – hee, hee! – as a matter of business, so do I! But still, if ever a young fellow deserved to be let off, this one does; only just turned eighteen, and only present by chance when the rick was fired. Howsomever, there's not much risk of it, as they are obliged to make an example of him, there having been so much destruction of property that way lately.'

'I mean,' she explained, 'that I want to touch him for a charm, a cure of an affliction, by the advice of a man who has proved the virtue of the remedy.'

'O yes, miss! Now I understand. I've had such people come in past years. But it didn't strike me that you looked of a sort to require blood-turning. What's the complaint? The wrong kind for this, I'll be bound.'

'My arm.' She reluctantly showed the withered skin.

'Ah! – 'tis all a-scram!'* said the hangman, examining it.

'Yes,' said she.

'Well,' he continued, with interest, 'that *is* the class o' subject, I'm bound to admit! I like the look of the wownd; it is truly as suitable for the cure as any I ever saw. 'Twas a knowing-man that sent 'ee, whoever he was.'

'You can contrive for me all that's necessary?' she said breathlessly.

'You should really have gone to the governor of the jail, and your doctor with 'ee, and given your name and address – that's how it used to be done, if I recollect. Still, perhaps, I can manage it for a trifling fee.'

'O, thank you! I would rather do it this way, as I should like it kept private.'

'Lover not to know, eh?'

'No – husband.'

'Aha! Very well. I'll get 'ee a touch of the corpse.'

'Where is it now?' she said, shuddering.

'It? – *he*, you mean; he's living yet. Just inside that little small winder up there in the glum.'* He signified the jail on the cliff above.

She thought of her husband and her friends. 'Yes, of course,' she said; 'and how am I to proceed?'

He took her to the door. 'Now, do you be waiting at the little wicket in the wall, that you'll find up there in the lane, not later than one o'clock. I will open it from the inside, as I shan't come home to dinner till he's cut down. Good-night. Be punctual; and if you don't want anybody to know 'ee, wear a veil. Ah – once I had such a daughter as you!'

She went away, and climbed the path above, to assure herself that she would be able to find the wicket next day. Its outline was soon visible to her – a narrow opening in the outer wall of the prison precincts. The steep was so great that, having reached the wicket, she stopped a moment to breathe; and, looking back upon the water-side cot, saw the hangman again ascending his outdoor staircase. He entered the loft or chamber to which it led, and in a few minutes extinguished his light.

The town clock struck ten, and she returned to the White Hart as she had come.

A RENCOUNTER

It was one o'clock on Saturday. Gertrude Lodge, having been admitted to the jail as above described, was sitting in a waiting-room within the second gate, which stood under a classic archway of ashlar,* then comparatively modern, and bearing the inscription, 'COVNTY JAIL: 1793'. This had been the façade she saw from the heath the day before. Near at hand was a passage to the roof on which the gallows stood.

The town was thronged, and the market suspended; but Gertrude had seen scarcely a soul. Having kept her room till the hour of the appointment, she had proceeded to the spot by a way which avoided the open space below the cliff where the spectators had gathered; but she could, even now, hear the multitudinous babble of their voices, out of which rose at intervals the hoarse croak of a single voice uttering the words, 'Last dying speech and confession!' There had been no reprieve, and the execution was over; but the crowd still waited to see the body taken down.

Soon the persistent woman heard a trampling overhead, then a hand beckoned to her, and, following directions, she went out and crossed the inner paved court beyond the gatehouse, her knees trembling so that she could scarcely walk. One of her arms was out of its sleeve, and only covered by her shawl.

On the spot at which she had now arrived were two trestles, and before she could think of their purpose she heard heavy feet descending stairs somewhere at her back. Turn her head she would not, or could not, and, rigid in this position, she was conscious of a rough coffin passing her shoulder, borne by four men. It was open, and in it lay the body of a young man, wearing the smockfrock of a rustic, and fustian breeches. The corpse had been thrown into the coffin so hastily that the skirt of the smockfrock was hanging over. The burden was temporarily deposited on the trestles.

By this time the young woman's state was such that a grey mist seemed to float before her eyes, on account of which, and the veil she wore, she could scarcely discern anything: it was as though she had nearly died, but was held up by a sort of galvanism.

'Now!' said a voice close at hand, and she was just conscious that the word had been addressed to her.

By a last strenuous effort she advanced, at the same time hearing persons approaching behind her. She bared her poor curst arm; and Davies, uncovering the face of the corpse, took Gertrude's hand, and held it so that her arm lay across the dead man's neck, upon a line the colour of an unripe blackberry, which surrounded it.

Gertrude shrieked: 'the turn o' the blood,' predicted by the conjuror, had taken place. But at that moment a second shriek rent the air of the enclosure: it was not Gertrude's, and its effect upon her was to make her start round.

Immediately behind her stood Rhoda Brook, her face drawn, and her eyes red with weeping. Behind Rhoda stood Gertrude's own husband; his countenance lined, his eyes dim, but without a tear.

'D—n you! what are you doing here?' he said hoarsely.

'Hussy – to come between us and our child now!' cried Rhoda. 'This is the meaning of what Satan showed me in the vision! You are like her at last!' And clutching the bare arm of the younger woman, she pulled her unresistingly back against the wall. Immediately Brook had loosened her hold the fragile young Gertrude slid down against the feet of her husband. When he lifted her up she was unconscious.

The mere sight of the twain had been enough to suggest to her that the dead young man was Rhoda's son. At that time the relatives of an executed convict had the privilege of claiming the body for burial, if they chose to do so; and it was for this purpose that Lodge was awaiting the inquest with Rhoda. He had been summoned by her as soon as the young man was taken in the crime, and at different times since; and he had attended in court during the trial. This was the 'holiday' he had been indulging in of late. The two wretched parents had wished to avoid exposure; and hence had come themselves for the body, a waggon and sheet for its conveyance and covering being in waiting outside.

Gertrude's case was so serious that it was deemed advisable to call to her the surgeon who was at hand. She was taken out of the jail into the town; but she never reached home alive. Her delicate vitality, sapped perhaps by the paralyzed arm, collapsed under the double shock that followed the severe strain, physical and mental, to which she had subjected herself during the previous twenty-four hours. Her blood had been 'turned' indeed – too far. Her death took place in the town three days after.

Her husband was never seen in Casterbridge again; once only in the old market-place at Anglebury, which he had so much frequented, and very seldom in public anywhere. Burdened at first with moodiness and remorse, he eventually changed for the better, and appeared as a chastened and thoughtful man. Soon after attending the funeral of his poor young wife he took steps towards giving up the farms in Holmstoke and the adjoining parish, and, having sold every head of his stock, he went away to Port-Bredy, at the other end of the county, living there in solitary lodgings till his death two years later of a painless decline.* It was then found that he had bequeathed the whole of his not inconsiderable property to a reformatory for boys, subject to the payment of a small annuity to Rhoda Brook, if she could be found to claim it.

For some time she could not be found; but eventually she reappeared in her old parish, – absolutely refusing, however, to have anything to do with the provision made for her. Her monotonous milking at the dairy was resumed, and followed for many long years, till her form became bent, and her once abundant dark hair white and worn away at the forehead – perhaps by long pressure against the cows. Here, sometimes, those who knew her experiences would stand and observe her, and wonder what sombre thoughts were beating inside that impassive, wrinkled brow, to the rhythm of the alternating milk-streams.

BARBARA OF THE HOUSE OF GREBE

It was apparently an idea, rather than a passion, that inspired Lord Uplandtowers' resolve to win her. Nobody ever knew when he formed it, or whence he got his assurance of success in the face of her manifest dislike of him. Possibly not until after that first important act of her life which I shall presently mention. His matured and cynical doggedness at the age of nineteen, when impulse mostly rules calculation, was remarkable, and might have owed its existence as much to his succession to the earldom and its accompanying local honours in childhood, as to the family character; an elevation which jerked him into maturity, so to speak, without his having known adolescence. He had only reached his twelfth year when his father, the fourth Earl, died, after a course of the Bath waters.

Nevertheless, the family character had a great deal to do with it. Determination was hereditary in the bearers of that escutcheon; sometimes for good, sometimes for evil.

The seats of the two families were about ten miles apart, the way between them lying along the now old, then new, turnpike-road connecting Havenpool and Warborne with the city of Melchester; a road which, though only a branch from what was known as the Great Western Highway,* is probably, even at present, as it has been for the last hundred years, one of the finest examples of a macadamized turnpike-track that can be found in England.

The mansion of the Earl, as well as that of his neighbour, Barbara's father, stood back about a mile from the highway, with which each was connected by an ordinary drive and lodge. It was along this particular highway that the young Earl drove on a certain evening at Christmastide some twenty years before the end of the last century, to attend a ball at Chene Manor, the home of Barbara and her parents Sir John and Lady Grebe. Sir John's was a baronetcy created a few years before the breaking out of the Civil War,* and his lands were even more extensive than those of Lord Uplandtowers himself, comprising this Manor of Chene, another on the coast near, half the Hundred of Cockdene,* and well-enclosed lands in several other parishes, notably Warborne and those contiguous. At this time Barbara was barely seventeen, and the ball is the first occasion on which we have any tradition of Lord Uplandtowers attempting tender relations with her; it was early enough, God knows.

An intimate friend – one of the Drenkhards* – is said to have dined with him that day, and Lord Uplandtowers had, for a wonder, communicated to his guest the secret design of his heart.

'You'll never get her – sure; you'll never get her!' this friend had said at parting. 'She's not drawn to your lordship by love: and as for thought of a good match, why, there's no more calculation in her than in a bird.'

'We'll see,' said Lord Uplandtowers impassively.

He no doubt thought of his friend's forecast as he travelled along the highway in his chariot; but the sculptural repose of his profile against the vanishing daylight on his right hand would have shown his friend that the Earl's equanimity was undisturbed. He reached the solitary wayside tavern called Lornton Inn – the rendezvous of many a daring poacher for operations in the adjoining forest; and he might have observed, if he had taken the trouble, a strange post-chaise standing in the halting-space before the inn. He duly sped past it, and half-an-hour after through the little town of Warborne. Onward, a mile further, was the house of his entertainer.

At this date it was an imposing edifice – or, rather, congeries* of edifices – as extensive as the residence of the Earl himself, though far less regular. One wing showed extreme antiquity, having huge chimneys, whose substructures projected from the external walls like towers; and a kitchen of vast dimensions, in which (it was said) breakfasts had been cooked for John of Gaunt.* Whilst he was yet in the forecourt he could hear the rhythm of French horns and clarionets, the favourite instruments of those days at such entertainments.

Entering the long parlour, in which the dance had just been opened by Lady Grebe with a minuet – it being now seven o'clock, according to the tradition – he was received with a welcome befitting his rank, and looked round for Barbara. She was not dancing, and seemed to be preoccupied – almost, indeed, as though she had been waiting for him. Barbara at this time was a good and pretty girl, who never spoke ill of any one, and hated other pretty women the very least possible. She did not refuse him for the country-dance which followed, and soon after was his partner in a second.

The evening wore on, and the horns and clarionets tootled merrily. Barbara evinced towards her lover neither distinct preference nor aversion; but old eyes would have seen that she pondered something. However, after supper she pleaded a headache, and disappeared. To pass the time of her absence, Lord Uplandtowers went into a little room adjoining the long gallery, where some elderly ones were sitting by the fire – for he had a phlegmatic dislike of dancing for its own sake, – and, lifting the window-curtains, he looked out of the window into the park and wood, dark now as a cavern. Some of the guests appeared to be leaving even so soon as this, two lights showing themselves as turning away from the door and sinking to nothing in the distance.

His hostess put her head into the room to look for partners for the ladies, and Lord Uplandtowers came out. Lady Grebe informed him that Barbara had not returned to the ball-room: she had gone to bed in sheer necessity.

'She has been so excited over the ball all day,' her mother continued, 'that I feared she would be worn out early. . . . But sure, Lord Uplandtowers, you won't be leaving yet?'

He said that it was near twelve o'clock, and that some had already left.

'I protest nobody has gone yet,' said Lady Grebe.

To humour her he stayed till midnight, and then set out. He had made no progress in his suit; but he had assured himself that Barbara gave no other guest the preference, and nearly everybody in the neighbourhood was there.

"Tis only a matter of time,' said the calm young philosopher.

The next morning he lay till near ten o'clock, and he had only just come out upon the head of the staircase when he heard hoofs upon the gravel without; in a few moments the door had been opened, and Sir John Grebe met him in the hall, as he set foot on the lowest stair.

'My lord – where's Barbara – my daughter?'

Even the Earl of Uplandtowers could not repress amazement. 'What's the matter, my dear Sir John,' says he.

The news was startling, indeed. From the Baronet's disjointed explanation Lord Uplandtowers gathered that after his own and the other guests' departure Sir John and Lady Grebe had gone to rest without seeing any more of Barbara; it being understood by them that she had retired to bed when she sent word to say that she could not join the dancers again. Before then she had told her maid that she would dispense with her services for this night; and there was evidence to show that the young lady had never lain down at all, the bed remaining unpressed. Circumstances seemed to prove that the deceitful girl had feigned indisposition to get an excuse for leaving the ball-room, and that she had left the house within ten minutes, presumably during the first dance after supper.

'I saw her go,' said Lord Uplandtowers.

'The devil you did!' says Sir John.

'Yes.' And he mentioned the retreating carriage-lights, and how he was assured by Lady Grebe that no guest had departed.

'Surely that was it!' said the father. 'But she's not gone alone, d'ye know!'

'Ah – who is the young man?'

'I can on'y guess. My worst fear is my most likely guess. I'll say no more. I thought – yet I would not believe – it possible that you was the sinner. Would that you had been! But 'tis t'other, 'tis t'other, by Heaven! I must e'en up and after 'em!'

'Whom do you suspect?'

Sir John would not give a name, and, stultified rather than agitated, Lord Uplandtowers accompanied him back to Chene. He again asked upon whom were the Baronet's suspicions directed; and the impulsive Sir John was no match for the insistence of Uplandtowers.

He said at length, 'I fear 'tis Edmond Willowes.'

'Who's he?'

'A young fellow of Shottsford-Forum – a widow-woman's son,' the other told him, and explained that Willowes's father, or grandfather, was the last of the old glass-painters in that place, where (as you may know) the art lingered on when it had died out in every other part of England.

'By God that's bad – mighty bad!' said Lord Uplandtowers, throwing himself back in the chaise in frigid despair.

They despatched emissaries in all directions; one by the Melchester Road, another by Shottsford-Forum, another coastwards.

But the lovers had a ten-hours' start; and it was apparent that sound judgment had been exercised in choosing as their time of flight the particular night when the movements of a strange carriage would not be noticed, either in the park or on the neighbouring highway, owing to the general press of vehicles. The chaise which had been seen waiting at Lornton Inn was, no doubt, the one they had escaped in; and the pair of heads which had planned so cleverly thus far had probably contrived marriage ere now.

The fears of her parents were realized. A letter sent by special messenger from Barbara, on the evening of that day, briefly informed them that her lover and herself were on the way to London, and before this communication reached her home they would be united as husband and wife. She had taken this extreme step because she loved her dear Edmond as she could love no other man, and because she had seen closing round her the doom of marriage with Lord Uplandtowers, unless she put that threatened fate out of possibility by doing as she had done. She had well considered the step beforehand, and was prepared to live like any other country-townsman's wife if her father repudiated her for her action.

'Damn her!' said Lord Uplandtowers, as he drove homeward that night. 'Damn her for a fool!' – which shows the kind of love he bore her.

Well; Sir John had already started in pursuit of them as a matter of duty, driving like a wild man to Melchester, and thence by the direct highway to the capital. But he soon saw that he was acting to no purpose; and by and by, discovering that the marriage had actually taken place, he forebore all attempts to unearth them in the City, and returned and sat down with his lady to digest the event as best they could.

To proceed against this Willowes for the abduction of our heiress was, possibly, in their power; yet, when they considered the now unalterable facts, they refrained from violent retribution. Some six weeks passed, during which time Barbara's parents, though they keenly felt her loss, held no communication with the truant, either for reproach or condonation. They continued to think of the disgrace she had brought upon herself; for, though the young man was an honest fellow, and the son of an honest father, the latter had died so early, and his widow had had such struggles to maintain herself, that the son was very imperfectly educated. Moreover, his blood was, as far as they knew, of no distinction whatever, whilst hers, through her mother, was compounded of the best juices of ancient baronial distillation, containing tinctures of Maundeville, and Mohun, and Syward, and Peverell, and Culliford, and Talbot, and Plantagenet, and York, and Lancaster,* and God knows what besides, which it was a thousand pities to throw away.

The father and mother sat by the fireplace that was spanned by the four-centred arch bearing the family shields on its haunches,* and groaned aloud – the lady more than Sir John.

'To think this should have come upon us in our old age!' said he.

'Speak for yourself!' she snapped through her sobs, 'I am only one-and-forty! . . . Why didn't ye ride faster and overtake 'em!'

In the meantime the young married lovers, caring no more about their blood than about ditch-water, were intensely happy – happy, that is, in the descending scale which, as we all know, Heaven in its wisdom has ordained for such rash cases; that is to say, the first week they were in the seventh heaven, the second in the sixth, the third week temperate, the fourth reflective, and so on; a lover's heart after possession being comparable to the earth in its geologic stages, as described to us sometimes by our worthy President;* first a hot coal, then a warm one, then a cooling cinder, then chilly – the simile shall be pursued no further. The long and the short of it was that one day a letter, sealed with their daughter's own little seal, came into Sir John and Lady Grebe's hands; and, on opening it, they found it to contain an appeal from the young couple to Sir John to forgive them for what they had done, and they would fall on their naked knees and be most dutiful children for evermore.

Then Sir John and his lady sat down again by the fireplace with the four-centred arch, and consulted, and re-read the letter. Sir John Grebe, if the truth must be told, loved his daughter's happiness far more, poor man, than he loved his name and lineage; he recalled to his mind all her little ways, gave vent to a sigh; and, by this time acclimatized to the idea of the marriage, said that what was done could not be undone, and that he supposed they must not be too harsh with her. Perhaps Barbara and her husband were in actual need; and how could they let their only child starve?

A slight consolation had come to them in an unexpected manner. They had been credibly informed that an ancestor of plebeian Willowes was once honoured with intermarriage with a scion of the aristocracy who had gone to the dogs. In short, such is the foolishness of distinguished parents, and sometimes of others also, that they wrote that very day to the address Barbara had given them, informing her that she might return home and bring her husband with her; they would not object to see him, would not reproach her, and would endeavour to welcome both, and to discuss with them what could best be arranged for their future.

In three or four days a rather shabby post-chaise drew up at the door of Chene Manor-house, at sound of which the tender-hearted baronet and his wife ran out as if to welcome a prince and princess of the blood. They were overjoyed to see their spoilt child return safe and sound – though she was only Mrs Willowes, wife of Edmond Willowes of nowhere. Barbara burst into penitential tears, and both husband and wife were contrite enough, as well they might be, considering that they had not a guinea to call their own.

When the four had calmed themselves, and not a word of chiding had been uttered to the pair, they discussed the position soberly, young Willowes sitting in the background with great modesty till invited forward by Lady Grebe in no frigid tone.

'How handsome he is!' she said to herself. 'I don't wonder at Barbara's craze for him.'

He was, indeed, one of the handsomest men who ever set his lips on a maid's. A blue coat, murrey* waistcoat, and breeches of drab* set off a figure that could scarcely be surpassed. He had large dark eyes, anxious now, as they glanced from Barbara to her parents and tenderly back again to her; observing whom, even now in her trepidation, one could see why the *sang-froid** of Lord Uplandtowers had been raised to more than lukewarmness. Her fair young face (according to the tale handed down by old women) looked out from under a grey conical hat, trimmed with white ostrich-feathers, and her little toes peeped from a buff petticoat worn under a puce gown. Her features were not regular: they were almost infantine, as you may see from miniatures in possession of the family, her mouth showing much sensitiveness, and one could be sure that her faults would not lie on the side of bad temper unless for urgent reasons.

Well, they discussed their state as became them, and the desire of the young couple to gain the goodwill of those upon whom they were literally dependent for everything induced them to agree to any temporizing measure that was not too irksome. Therefore, having been nearly two months united, they did not oppose Sir John's proposal that he should furnish Edmond Willowes with funds sufficient for him to travel a year on the Continent in the company of a tutor, the young man undertaking to lend himself with the utmost diligence to the tutor's instructions, till he became polished outwardly and inwardly to the degree required in the husband of such a lady as Barbara. He was to apply himself to the study of languages, manners, history, society, ruins, and everything else that came under his eyes, till he should return to take his place without blushing by Barbara's side.

'And by that time,' said worthy Sir John, 'I'll get my little place out at Yewsholt ready for you and Barbara to occupy on your return. The house is small and out of the way; but it will do for a young couple for a while.'

'If 'twere no bigger than a summer-house it would do!' says Barbara.

'If 'twere no bigger than a sedan-chair!' says Willowes. 'And the more lonely the better.'

'We can put up with the loneliness,' said Barbara, with less zest. 'Some friends will come, no doubt.'

All this being laid down, a travelled tutor was called in – a man of many gifts and great experience, – and on a fine morning away tutor and pupil went. A great reason urged against Barbara accompanying her youthful husband was that his attentions to her would naturally be such as to prevent his zealously applying every hour of his time to learning and seeing – an argument of wise prescience, and unanswerable. Regular days for letter-writing were fixed, Barbara and her Edmond exchanged their last kisses at the door, and the chaise swept under the archway into the drive.

He wrote to her from Le Havre, as soon as he reached that port, which was not for seven days, on account of adverse winds; he wrote from Rouen, and from Paris; described to her his sight of the King and Court at Versailles,* and the wonderful marble-work and mirrors in that palace; wrote next from Lyons; then, after a comparatively long interval, from Turin, narrating his fearful adventures in crossing Mont Cenis* on mules, and how he was overtaken with a terrific snowstorm, which had well-nigh been the end of him, and his tutor, and his guides. Then he wrote glowingly of Italy; and Barbara could see the development of her husband's mind reflected in his letters month by month; and she much admired the forethought of her father in suggesting this education for Edmond. Yet she sighed sometimes – her husband being no longer in evidence to fortify her in her choice of him – and timidly dreaded what mortifications might be in store for her by reason of this *mésalliance*.* She went out very little; for on the one or two occasions on which she had shown herself to former friends she noticed a distinct difference in their manner, as though they should say, 'Ah, my happy swain's wife; you're caught!'

Edmond's letters were as affectionate as ever; even more affectionate, after a while, than hers were to him. Barbara observed this growing coolness in herself; and like a good and honest lady was horrified and grieved, since her only wish was to act faithfully and uprightly. It troubled her so much that she prayed for a warmer heart, and at last wrote to her husband to beg him, now that he was in the land of Art, to send her his portrait, ever so small, that she might look at it all day and every day, and never for a moment forget his features.

Willowes was nothing loth, and replied that he would do more than she wished: he had made friends with a sculptor in Pisa, who was much interested in him and his history; and he had commissioned this artist to make a bust of himself in marble, which when finished he would send her. What Barbara had wanted was something immediate; but she expressed no objection to the delay; and in his next communication Edmond told her that the sculptor, of his own choice, had decided to extend the bust to a full-length statue, so anxious was he to get a specimen of his skill introduced to the notice of the English aristocracy. It was progressing well, and rapidly.

Meanwhile, Barbara's attention began to be occupied at home with Yewsholt Lodge, the house that her kind-hearted father was preparing for her residence when her husband returned. It was a small place on the plan of a large one – a cottage built in the form of a mansion, having a central hall with a wooden gallery running round it, and rooms no bigger than closets to support this introduction. It stood on a slope so solitary, and surrounded by trees so dense, that the birds who inhabited the boughs sang at strange hours, as if they hardly could distinguish night from day.

During the progress of repairs at this bower Barbara frequently visited it. Though so secluded by the dense growth, it was near the high road, and one day while looking over the fence she saw Lord Uplandtowers riding past. He saluted her courteously, yet with mechanical stiffness, and did not halt. Barbara went home, and continued to pray that she might never cease to love her husband. After that she sickened, and did not come out of doors again for a long time.

The year of education had extended to fourteen months, and the house was in order for Edmond's return to take up his abode there with Barbara, when, instead of the accustomed letter for her, came one to Sir John Grebe in the handwriting of the said tutor, informing him of a terrible catastrophe that had occurred to them at Venice. Mr Willowes and himself had attended the theatre one night during the Carnival* of the preceding week, to witness the Italian comedy, when, owing to the carelessness of one of the candle-snuffers, the theatre had caught fire, and been burnt to the ground. Few persons had lost their lives, owing to the superhuman exertions of some of the audience in getting out the senseless sufferers; and, among them all, he who had risked his own life the most heroically was Mr Willowes. In re-entering for the fifth time to save his fellow-creatures some fiery beams had fallen upon him, and he had been given up for lost. He was, however, by the blessing of Providence, recovered, with the life still in him, though he was fearfully burnt; and by almost a miracle he seemed likely to survive, his constitution being wondrously sound. He was, of course, unable to write, but he was receiving the attention of several skilful surgeons. Further report would be made by the next mail or by private hand.

The tutor said nothing in detail of poor Willowes's sufferings, but as soon as the news was broken to Barbara she realized how intense they must have been, and her immediate instinct was to rush to his side, though, on consideration, the journey seemed impossible to her. Her health was by no means what it had been, and to post across Europe at that season of the year, or to traverse the Bay of Biscay in a sailing-craft, was an undertaking that would hardly be justified by the result. But she was anxious to go till, on reading to the end of the letter, her husband's tutor was found to hint very strongly against such a step if it should be contemplated, this being also the opinion of the surgeons. And though Willowes's comrade refrained from giving his reasons, they disclosed themselves plainly enough in the sequel.

The truth was that the worst of the wounds resulting from the fire had occurred to his head and face – that handsome face which had won her heart from her, – and both the tutor and the surgeons knew that for a sensitive young woman to see him before his wounds had healed would cause more misery to her by the shock than happiness to him by her ministrations.

Lady Grebe blurted out what Sir John and Barbara had thought, but had had too much delicacy to express.

'Sure, 'tis mighty hard for you, poor Barbara, that the one little gift he had to justify your rash choice of him – his wonderful good looks – should be taken away like this, to leave 'ee no excuse at all for your conduct in the world's eyes. . . . Well, I wish you'd married t'other – that do I!' And the lady sighed.

'He'll soon get right again,' said her father soothingly.

Such remarks as the above were not often made; but they were frequent enough to cause Barbara an uneasy sense of self-stultification. She determined to hear them no longer; and the house at Yewsholt being ready and furnished, she withdrew thither with her maids, where for the first time she could feel mistress of a home that would be hers and her husband's exclusively, when he came.

After long weeks Willowes had recovered sufficiently to be able to write himself, and slowly and tenderly he enlightened her upon the full extent of his injuries. It was a mercy, he said, that he had not lost his sight entirely; but he was thankful to say that he still retained full vision in one eye, though the other was dark for ever. The sparing manner in which he meted out particulars of his condition told Barbara how appalling had been his experience. He was grateful for her assurance that nothing could change her; but feared she did not fully realize that he was so sadly disfigured as to make it doubtful if she would recognize him. However, in spite of all, his heart was as true to her as it ever had been.

Barbara saw from his anxiety how much lay behind. She replied that she submitted to the decrees of Fate, and would welcome him in any shape as soon as he could come. She told him of the pretty retreat in which she had taken up her abode, pending their joint occupation of it, and did not reveal how much she had sighed over the information that all his good looks were gone. Still less did she say that she felt a certain strangeness in awaiting him, the weeks they had lived together having been so short by comparison with the length of his absence.

Slowly drew on the time when Willowes found himself well enough to come home. He landed at Southampton, and posted thence towards Yewsholt. Barbara arranged to go out to meet him as far as Lornton Inn – the spot between the Forest and the Chase at which he had waited for night on the evening of their elopement. Thither she drove at the appointed hour in a little pony-chaise, presented her by her father on her birthday for her especial use in her new house; which vehicle she sent back on arriving at the inn, the plan agreed upon being that she should perform the return journey with her husband in his hired coach.

There was not much accommodation for a lady at this wayside tavern; but, as it was a fine evening in early summer, she did not mind – walking about outside, and straining her eyes along the highway for the expected one. But each cloud of dust that enlarged in the distance and drew near was found to disclose a conveyance other than his post-chaise. Barbara remained till the appointment was two hours passed, and then began to fear that owing to some adverse wind in the Channel he was not coming that night.

While waiting she was conscious of a curious trepidation that was not entirely solicitude, and did not amount to dread; her tense state of incertitude bordered both on disappointment and on relief. She had lived six or seven weeks with an imperfectly educated yet handsome husband whom now she had not seen for seventeen months, and who was so changed physically by an accident that she was assured she would hardly know him. Can we wonder at her compound state of mind?

But her immediate difficulty was to get away from Lornton Inn, for her situation was becoming embarrassing. Like too many of Barbara's actions, this drive had been undertaken without much reflection. Expecting to wait no more than a few minutes for her husband in his post-chaise, and to enter it with him, she had not hesitated to isolate herself by sending back her own little vehicle. She now found that, being so well known in this neighbourhood, her excursion to meet her long-absent husband was exciting great interest. She was conscious that more eyes were watching her from the inn-windows than met her own gaze. Barbara had decided to get home by hiring whatever kind of conveyance the tavern afforded, when, straining her eyes for the last time over the now darkening highway, she perceived yet another dust-cloud drawing near. She paused; a chariot ascended to the inn, and would have passed had not its occupant caught sight of her standing expectantly. The horses were checked on the instant.

'You here – and alone, my dear Mrs Willowes?' said Lord Uplandtowers, whose carriage it was.

She explained what had brought her into this lonely situation; and, as he was going in the direction of her own home, she accepted his offer of a seat beside him. Their conversation was embarrassed and fragmentary at first; but when they had driven a mile or two she was surprised to find herself talking earnestly and warmly to him: her impulsiveness was in truth but the natural consequence of her late existence – a somewhat desolate one by reason of the strange marriage she had made; and there is no more indiscreet mood than that of a woman surprised into talk who has long been imposing upon herself a policy of reserve. Therefore her ingenuous heart rose with a bound into her throat when, in response to his leading questions, or rather hints, she allowed her troubles to leak out of her. Lord Uplandtowers took her quite to her own door, although he had driven three miles out of his way to do so; and in handing her down she heard from him a whisper of stern reproach: 'It need not have been thus if you had listened to me!'

She made no reply, and went indoors. There, as the evening wore away, she regretted more and more that she had been so friendly with Lord Uplandtowers. But he had launched himself upon her so unexpectedly: if she had only foreseen the meeting with him, what a careful line of conduct she would have marked out! Barbara broke into a perspiration of disquiet when she thought of her unreserve, and, in self-chastisement, resolved to sit up till midnight on the bare chance of Edmond's return; directing that supper should be laid for him, improbable as his arrival till the morrow was.

The hours went past, and there was dead silence in and round about Yewsholt Lodge, except for the soughing of the trees; till, when it was near upon midnight, she heard the noise of hoofs and wheels approaching the door. Knowing that it could only be her husband, Barbara instantly went into the hall to meet him. Yet she stood there not without a sensation of faintness, so many were the changes since their parting! And, owing to her casual encounter with Lord Uplandtowers, his voice and image still remained with her, excluding Edmond, her husband, from the inner circle of her impressions.

But she went to the door, and the next moment a figure stepped inside, of which she knew the outline, but little besides. Her husband was attired in a flapping black cloak and slouched hat, appearing altogether as a foreigner, and not as the young English burgess who had left her side. When he came forward into the light of the lamp, she perceived with surprise, and almost with fright, that he wore a mask. At first she had not noticed this – there being nothing in its colour which would lead a casual observer to think he was looking on anything but a real countenance.

He must have seen her start of dismay at the unexpectedness of his appearance, for he said hastily: 'I did not mean to come in to you like this – I thought you would have been in bed. How good you are, dear Barbara!' He put his arm round her, but he did not attempt to kiss her.

'O Edmond – it *is* you? – it must be?' she said, with clasped hands, for though his figure and movement were almost enough to prove it, and the tones were not unlike the old tones, the enunciation was so altered as to seem that of a stranger.

'I am covered like this to hide myself from the curious eyes of the inn-servants and others,' he said, in a low voice. 'I will send back the carriage and join you in a moment.'

'You are quite alone?'

'Quite. My companion stopped at Southampton.'

The wheels of the post-chaise rolled away as she entered the dining-room, where the supper was spread; and presently he rejoined her there. He had removed his cloak and hat, but the mask was still retained; and she could now see that it was of special make, of some flexible material like silk, coloured so as to represent flesh; it joined naturally to the front hair, and was otherwise cleverly executed.

'Barbara – you look ill,' he said, removing his glove, and taking her hand.

'Yes – I have been ill,' said she.

'Is this pretty little house ours?'

'O – yes.' She was hardly conscious of her words, for the hand he had ungloved in order to take hers was contorted, and had one or two of its fingers missing; while through the mask she discerned the twinkle of one eye only.

'I would give anything to kiss you, dearest, now at this moment!' he continued, with mournful passionateness. 'But I cannot – in this guise. The servants are abed, I suppose?'

'Yes,' said she. 'But I can call them? You will have some supper?'

He said he would have some, but that it was not necessary to call anybody at that hour. Thereupon they approached the table, and sat down, facing each other.

Despite Barbara's scared state of mind, it was forced upon her notice that her husband trembled, as if he feared the impression he was producing, or was about to produce, as much as, or more than, she. He drew nearer, and took her hand again.

'I had this mask made at Venice,' he began, in evident embarrassment. 'My darling Barbara – my dearest wife – do you think you – will mind when I take it off? You will not dislike me – will you?'

'O Edmond, of course I shall not mind,' said she. 'What has happened to you is our misfortune; but I am prepared for it.'

'Are you sure you are prepared?'

'O yes! You are my husband.'

'You really feel quite confident that nothing external can affect you?' he said again, in a voice rendered uncertain by his agitation.

'I think I am – quite,' she answered faintly.

He bent his head. 'I hope, I hope you are,' he whispered.

In the pause which followed, the ticking of the clock in the hall seemed to grow loud; and he turned a little aside to remove the mask. She breathlessly awaited the operation, which was one of some tediousness, watching him one moment, averting her face the next; and when it was done she shut her eyes at the dreadful spectacle that was revealed. A quick spasm of horror had passed through her; but though she quailed she forced herself to regard him anew, repressing the cry that would naturally have escaped from her ashy lips. Unable to look at him longer, Barbara sank down on the floor beside her chair, covering her eyes.

'You cannot look at me!' he groaned in a hopeless way. 'I am too terrible an object even for you to bear! I knew it; yet I hoped against it. O, this is a bitter fate – curse the skill of those Venetian surgeons who saved me alive! ... Look up, Barbara,' he continued beseechingly; 'view me completely; say you loathe me, if you do loathe me, and settle the case between us for ever!'

His unhappy wife pulled herself together for a desperate strain. He was her Edmond; he had done her no wrong; he had suffered. A momentary devotion to him helped her, and lifting her eyes as bidden she regarded this human remnant, this *écorché*,* a second time. But the sight was too much. She again involuntarily looked aside and shuddered.

'Do you think you can get used to this?' he said. 'Yes or no! Can you bear such a thing of the charnel-house near you? Judge for yourself, Barbara. Your Adonis,* your matchless man, has come to this!'

The poor lady stood beside him motionless, save for the restlessness of her eyes. All her natural sentiments of affection and pity were driven clean out of her by a sort of panic; she had just the same sense of dismay and fearfulness that she would have had in the presence of an apparition She could nohow fancy this to be her chosen one – the man she had loved; he was metamorphosed to a specimen of another species. 'I do not loathe you,' she said with trembling. 'But I am so horrified – so overcome! Let me recover myself. Will you sup now? And while you do so may I go to my room to – regain my old feeling for you? I will try, if I may leave you awhile? Yes, I will try!'

Without waiting for an answer from him, and keeping her gaze carefully averted, the frightened woman crept to the door and out of the room. She heard him sit down to the table, as if to begin supper; though, Heaven knows, his appetite was slight enough after a reception which had confirmed his worst surmises. When Barbara had ascended the stairs and arrived in her chamber she sank down, and buried her face in the coverlet of the bed.

Thus she remained for some time. The bed-chamber was over the dining-room, and presently as she knelt Barbara heard Willowes thrust back his chair, and rise to go into the hall. In five minutes that figure would probably come up the stairs and confront her again; it, – this new and terrible form, that was not her husband's. In the loneliness of this night, with neither maid nor friend beside her, she lost all self-control, and at the first sound of his footstep on the stairs, without so much as flinging a cloak round her, she flew from the room, ran along the gallery to the back staircase, which she descended, and, unlocking the back door, let herself out. She scarcely was aware what she had done till she found herself in the greenhouse, crouching on a flower-stand.

Here she remained, her great timid eyes strained through the glass upon the garden without, and her skirts gathered up, in fear of the field-mice which sometimes came there. Every moment she dreaded to hear footsteps which she ought by law to have longed for, and a voice that should have been as music to her soul. But Edmond Willowes came not that way. The nights were getting short at this season, and soon the dawn appeared, and the first rays of the sun. By daylight she had less fear than in the dark. She thought she could meet him, and accustom herself to the spectacle.

So the much-tried young woman unfastened the door of the hot-house, and went back by the way she had emerged a few hours ago. Her poor husband was probably in bed and asleep, his journey having been long; and she made as little noise as possible in her entry. The house was just as she had left it, and she looked about in the hall for his cloak and hat, but she could not see them; nor did she perceive the small trunk which had been all that he brought with him, his heavier baggage having been left at Southampton for the road-waggon. She summoned courage to mount the stairs; the bedroom-door was open as she had left it. She fearfully peeped round; the bed had not been pressed. Perhaps he had lain down on the dining-room sofa. She descended and entered; he was not there. On the table beside his unsoiled plate lay a note, hastily written on the leaf of a pocket-book. It was something like this:

My Ever-Beloved Wife. – The effect that my forbidding appearance has produced upon you was one which I foresaw as quite possible. I hoped against it, but foolishly so. I was aware that no *human* love could survive such a catastrophe. I confess I thought yours *divine*; but, after so long an absence, there could not be left sufficient warmth to overcome the too natural first aversion. It was an experiment, and it has failed. I do not blame you; perhaps, even, it is better so. Good-bye. I leave England for one year. You will see me again at the expiration of that time, if I live. Then I will ascertain your true feeling; and, if it be against me, go away for ever.

E. W.

On recovering from her surprise, Barbara's remorse was such that she felt herself absolutely unforgivable. She should have regarded him as an afflicted being, and not have been this slave to mere eyesight, like a child. To follow him and entreat him to return was her first thought. But on making inquiries she found that nobody had seen him: he had silently disappeared.

More than this, to undo the scene of last night was impossible. Her terror had been too plain, and he was a man unlikely to be coaxed back by her efforts to do her duty. She went and confessed to her parents all that had occurred; which, indeed, soon became known to more persons than those of her own family.

The year passed, and he did not return; and it was doubted if he were alive. Barbara's contrition for her unconquerable repugnance was now such that she longed to build a church-aisle, or erect a monument, and devote herself to deeds of charity for the remainder of her days. To that end she made inquiry of the excellent parson under whom she sat on Sundays, at a vertical distance of a dozen feet. But he could only adjust his wig and tap his snuff-box; for such was the lukewarm state of religion in those days, that not an aisle, steeple, porch, east window, Ten-Commandment board, lion-and-unicorn,* or brass candlestick, was required anywhere at all in the neighbourhood as a votive offering from a distracted soul – the last century contrasting greatly in this respect with the happy times in which we live,* when urgent appeals for contributions to such objects pour in by every morning's post, and nearly all churches have been made to look like new pennies. As the poor lady could not ease her conscience this way, she determined at least to be charitable, and soon had the satisfaction of finding her porch thronged every morning by the raggedest, idlest, most drunken, hypocritical, and worthless tramps in Christendom.

But human hearts are as prone to change as the leaves of the creeper on the wall, and in the course of time, hearing nothing of her husband, Barbara could sit unmoved whilst her mother and friends said in her hearing, 'Well, what has happened is for the best.' She began to think so herself, for even now she could not summon up that lopped and mutilated form without a shiver, though whenever her mind flew back to her early wedded days, and the man who had stood beside her then, a thrill of tenderness moved her, which if quickened by his living presence might have become strong. She was young and inexperienced, and had hardly on his late return grown out of the capricious fancies of girlhood.

But he did not come again, and when she thought of his word that he would return once more, if living, and how unlikely he was to break his word, she gave him up for dead. So did her parents; so also did another person – that man of silence, of irresistible incisiveness, of still countenance, who was as awake as seven sentinels when he seemed to be as sound asleep as the figures on his family monument. Lord Uplandtowers, though not yet thirty, had chuckled like a caustic fogey of threescore when he heard of Barbara's terror and flight at her husband's return, and of the latter's prompt departure. He felt pretty sure, however, that Willowes, despite his hurt feelings, would have reappeared to claim his bright-eyed property if he had been alive at the end of the twelve months.

As there was no husband to live with her, Barbara had relinquished the house prepared for them by her father, and taken up her abode anew at Chene Manor, as in the days of her girlhood. By degrees the episode with Edmond Willowes seemed but a fevered dream, and as the months grew to years Lord Uplandtowers' friendship with the people at Chene – which had somewhat cooled after Barbara's elopement – revived considerably, and he again became a frequent visitor there. He could not make the most trivial alteration or improvement at Knollingwood Hall, where he lived, without riding off to consult with his friend Sir John at Chene; and thus putting himself frequently under her eyes, Barbara grew accustomed to him, and talked to him as freely as to a brother. She even began to look up to him as a person of authority, judgment, and prudence; and though his severity on the bench towards poachers, smugglers, and turnip-stealers was matter of common notoriety, she trusted that much of what was said might be misrepresentation.

Thus they lived on till her husband's absence had stretched to years, and there could be no longer any doubt of his death. A passionless manner of renewing his addresses seemed no longer out of place in Lord Uplandtowers. Barbara did not love him, but hers was essentially one of those sweet-pea or with-wind natures which require a twig of stouter fibre than its own to hang upon and bloom. Now, too, she was older, and admitted to herself that a man whose ancestor had run scores of Saracens through and through in fighting for the site of the Holy Sepulchre* was a more desirable husband, socially considered, than one who could only claim with certainty to know that his father and grandfather were respectable burgesses.

Sir John took occasion to inform her that she might legally consider herself a widow; and, in brief, Lord Uplandtowers carried his point with her, and she married him, though he could never get her to own that she loved him as she had loved Willowes. In my childhood I knew an old lady whose mother saw the wedding, and she said that when Lord and Lady Uplandtowers drove away from her father's house in the evening it was in a coach-and-four, and that my lady was dressed in green and silver, and wore the gayest hat and feather that ever were seen; though whether it was that the green did not suit her complexion, or otherwise, the Countess looked pale, and the reverse of blooming. After their marriage her husband took her to London, and she saw the gaieties of a season there; then they returned to Knollingwood Hall, and thus a year passed away.

Before their marriage her husband had seemed to care but little about her inability to love him passionately. 'Only let me win you,' he had said, 'and I will submit to all that.' But now her lack of warmth seemed to irritate him, and he conducted himself towards her with a resentfulness which led to her passing many hours with him in painful silence. The heir-presumptive to the title was a remote relative, whom Lord Uplandtowers did not exclude from the dislike he entertained towards many persons and things besides, and he had set his mind upon a lineal successor. He blamed her much that there was no promise of this, and asked her what she was good for.

On a particular day in her gloomy life a letter, addressed to her as Mrs Willowes, reached Lady Uplandtowers from an unexpected quarter. A sculptor in Pisa, knowing nothing of her second marriage, informed her that the long-delayed life-size statue of Mr Willowes, which, when her husband left that city, he had been directed to retain till it was sent for, was still in his studio. As his commission had not wholly been paid, and the statue was taking up room he could ill spare, he should be glad to have the debt cleared off, and directions where to forward the figure. Arriving at a time when the Countess was beginning to have little secrets (of a harmless kind, it is true) from her husband, by reason of their growing estrangement, she replied to this letter without saying a word to Lord Uplandtowers, sending off the balance that was owing to the sculptor, and telling him to despatch the statue to her without delay.

It was some weeks before it arrived at Knollingwood Hall, and, by a singular coincidence, during the interval she received the first absolutely conclusive tidings of her Edmond's death. It had taken place years before, in a foreign land, about six months after their parting, and had been induced by the sufferings he had already undergone, coupled with much depression of spirit, which had caused him to succumb to a slight ailment. The news was sent her in a brief and formal letter from some relative of Willowes's in another part of England.

Her grief took the form of passionate pity for his misfortunes, and of reproach to herself for never having been able to conquer her aversion to his latter image by recollection of what Nature had originally made him. The sad spectacle that had gone from earth had never been her Edmond at all to her. O that she could have met him as he was at first! Thus Barbara thought. It was only a few days later that a waggon with two horses, containing an immense packing-case, was seen at breakfast time both by Barbara and her husband to drive round to the back of the house, and by and by they were informed that a case labelled 'Sculpture' had arrived for her ladyship.

'What can that be?' said Lord Uplandtowers.

'It is the statue of poor Edmond, which belongs to me, but has never been sent till now,' she answered.

'Where are you going to put it?' asked he.

'I have not decided,' said the Countess. 'Anywhere, so that it will not annoy you.'

'Oh, it won't annoy me,' says he.

When it had been unpacked in a back room of the house, they went to examine it. The statue was a full-length figure, in the purest Carrara marble,* representing Edmond Willowes in all his original beauty, as he had stood at parting from her when about to set out on his travels; a specimen of manhood almost perfect in every line and contour. The work had been carried out with absolute fidelity.

'Phoebus-Apollo,* sure,' said the Earl of Uplandtowers, who had never seen Willowes, real or represented, till now.

Barbara did not hear him. She was standing in a sort of trance before the first husband, as if she had no consciousness of the other husband at her side. The mutilated features of Willowes had disappeared from her mind's eye; this perfect being was really the man she had loved, and not that later pitiable figure; in whom tenderness and truth should have seen this image always, but had not done so.

It was not till Lord Uplandtowers said roughly, 'Are you going to stay here all the morning worshipping him?' that she roused herself.

Her husband had not till now the least suspicion that Edmond Willowes originally looked thus, and he thought how deep would have been his jealousy years ago if Willowes had been known to him. Returning to the Hall in the afternoon he found his wife in the gallery, whither the statue had been brought.

She was lost in reverie before it, just as in the morning.

'What are you doing?' he asked.

She started and turned. 'I am looking at my husb– my statue, to see if it is well done,' she stammered. 'Why should I not?'

'There's no reason why,' he said. 'What are you going to do with the monstrous thing? It can't stand here for ever.'

'I don't wish it,' she said. 'I'll find a place.'

In her boudoir there was a deep recess, and while the Earl was absent from home for a few days in the following week, she hired joiners from the village, who under her directions enclosed the recess with a panelled door. Into the tabernacle thus formed she had the statue placed, fastening the door with a lock, the key of which she kept in her pocket.

When her husband returned he missed the statue from the gallery, and, concluding that it had been put away out of deference to his feelings, made no remark. Yet at moments he noticed something on his lady's face which he had never noticed there before. He could not construe it; it was a sort of silent ecstasy, a reserved beatification. What had become of the statue he could not divine, and growing more and more curious, looked about here and there for it till, thinking of her private room, he went towards that spot. After knocking he heard the shutting of a door, and the click of a key; but when he entered his wife was sitting at work, on what was in those days called knotting.* Lord Uplandtowers' eye fell upon the newly-painted door where the recess had formerly been.

'You have been carpentering in my absence then, Barbara,' he said carelessly.

'Yes, Uplandtowers.'

'Why did you go putting up such a tasteless enclosure as that – spoiling the handsome arch of the alcove?'

'I wanted more closet-room; and I thought that as this was my own apartment – '

'Of course,' he returned. Lord Uplandtowers knew now where the statue of young Willowes was.

One night, or rather in the smallest hours of the morning, he missed the Countess from his side. Not being a man of nervous imaginings he fell asleep again before he had much considered the matter, and the next morning had forgotten the incident. But a few nights later the same circumstances occurred. This time he fully roused himself; but before he had moved to search for her she returned to the chamber in her dressing-gown, carrying a candle, which she extinguished as she approached, deeming him asleep. He could discover from her breathing that she was strangely moved; but not on this occasion either did he reveal that he had seen her. Presently, when she had lain down, affecting to wake, he asked her some trivial questions. 'Yes, *Edmond*,' she replied absently.

Lord Uplandtowers became convinced that she was in the habit of leaving the chamber in this queer way more frequently than he had observed, and he determined to watch. The next midnight he feigned deep sleep, and shortly after perceived her stealthily rise and let herself out of the room in the dark. He slipped on some clothing and followed. At the further end of the corridor, where the clash of flint and steel would be out of the hearing of one in the bedchamber, she struck a light. He stepped aside into an empty room till she had lit a taper and had passed on to her boudoir. In a minute or two he followed. Arrived at the door of the boudoir, he beheld the door of the private recess open, and Barbara within it, standing with her arms clasped tightly round the neck of her Edmond, and her mouth on his.

The shawl which she had thrown round her nightclothes had slipped from her shoulders, and her long white robe and pale face lent her the blanched appearance of a second statue embracing the first. Between her kisses, she apostrophized it in a low murmur of infantine tenderness:

'My only love – how could I be so cruel to you, my perfect one – so good and true – I am ever faithful to you, despite my seeming infidelity! I always think of you – dream of you – during the long hours of the day, and in the night-watches! O Edmond, I am always yours!' Such words as these, intermingled with sobs, and streaming tears, and dishevelled hair, testified to an intensity of feeling in his wife which Lord Uplandtowers had not dreamed of her possessing.

'Ha, ha!' says he to himself 'This is where we evaporate – this is where my hopes of a successor in the title dissolve – ha! ha! This must be seen to, verily!'

Lord Uplandtowers was a subtle man when once he set himself to strategy; though in the present instance he never thought of the simple stratagem of constant tenderness. Nor did he enter the room and surprise his wife as a blunderer would have done, but went back to his chamber as silently as he had left it. When the Countess returned thither, shaken by spent sobs and sighs, he appeared to be soundly sleeping as usual. The next day he began his countermoves by making inquiries as to the whereabouts of the tutor who had travelled with his wife's first husband; this gentleman, he found, was now master of a grammar-school at no great distance from Knollingwood. At the first convenient moment Lord Uplandtowers went thither and obtained an interview with the said gentleman. The schoolmaster was much gratified by a visit from such an influential neighbour, and was ready to communicate anything that his lordship desired to know.

After some general conversation on the school and its progress, the visitor observed that he believed the schoolmaster had once travelled a good deal with the unfortunate Mr Willowes, and had been with him on the occasion of his accident. He, Lord Uplandtowers, was interested in knowing what had really happened at that time, and had often thought of inquiring. And then the Earl not only heard by word of mouth as much as he wished to know, but, their chat becoming more intimate, the schoolmaster drew upon paper a sketch of the disfigured head, explaining with bated breath various details in the representation.

'It was very strange and terrible!' said Lord Uplandtowers, taking the sketch in his hand. 'Neither nose nor ears, nor lips scarcely!'

A poor man in the town nearest to Knollingwood Hall, who combined the art of sign-painting with ingenious mechanical occupations, was sent for by Lord Uplandtowers to come to the Hall on a day in that week when the Countess had gone on a short visit to her parents. His employer made the man understand that the business in which his assistance was demanded was to be considered private, and money insured the observance of this request. The lock of the cupboard was picked, and the ingenious mechanic and painter, assisted by the schoolmaster's sketch, which Lord Uplandtowers had put in his pocket, set to work upon the god-like countenance of the statue under my lord's direction. What the fire had maimed in the original the chisel maimed in the copy. It was a fiendish disfigurement, ruthlessly carried out, and was rendered still more shocking by being tinted to the hues of life, as life had been after the wreck.

Six hours after, when the workman was gone, Lord Uplandtowers looked upon the result, and smiled grimly, and said:

'A statue should represent a man as he appeared in life, and that's as he appeared. Ha! ha! But 'tis done to good purpose, and not idly.'

He locked the door of the closet with a skeleton key, and went his way to fetch the Countess home.

That night she slept, but he kept awake. According to the tale, she murmured soft words in her dream; and he knew that the tender converse of her imaginings was held with one whom he had supplanted but in name. At the end of her dream the Countess of Uplandtowers awoke and arose, and then the enactment of former nights was repeated. Her husband remained still and listened. Two strokes sounded from the clock in the pediment without, when, leaving the chamber-door ajar, she passed along the corridor to the other end, where, as usual, she obtained a light. So deep was the silence that he could even from his bed hear her softly blowing the tinder to a glow after striking the steel. She moved on into the boudoir, and he heard, or fancied he heard, the turning of the key in the closet-door. The next moment there came from that direction a loud and prolonged shriek, which resounded to the furthest corners of the house. It was repeated, and there was the noise of a heavy fall.

Lord Uplandtowers sprang out of bed. He hastened along the dark corridor to the door of the boudoir, which stood ajar, and, by the light of the candle within, saw his poor young Countess lying in a heap in her nightdress on the floor of the closet. When he reached her side he found that she had fainted, much to the relief of his fears that matters were worse. He quickly shut up and locked in the hated image which had done the mischief, and lifted his wife in his arms, where in a few instants she opened her eyes. Pressing her face to his without saying a word, he carried her back to her room, endeavouring as he went to disperse her terrors by a laugh in her ear, oddly compounded of causticity, predilection, and brutality.

'Ho – ho – ho!' says he. 'Frightened, dear one, hey? What a baby 'tis! Only a joke, sure, Barbara – a splendid joke! But a baby should not go to closets at midnight to look for the ghost of the dear departed! If it do it must expect to be terrified at his aspect – ho – ho – ho!'

When she was in her bed-chamber, and had quite come to herself, though her nerves were still much shaken, he spoke to her more sternly. 'Now, my lady, answer me: do you love him – eh?'

'No – no!' she faltered, shuddering, with her expanded eyes fixed on her husband. 'He is too terrible – no, no!'

'You are sure?'

'Quite sure!' replied the poor broken-spirited Countess.

But her natural elasticity asserted itself. Next morning he again inquired of her: 'Do you love him now?' She quailed under his gaze, but did not reply.

'That means that you do still, by God!' he continued.

'It means that I will not tell an untruth, and do not wish to incense my lord,' she answered, with dignity.

'Then suppose we go and have another look at him?' As he spoke, he suddenly took her by the wrist, and turned as if to lead her towards the ghastly closet.

'No – no! O – no!' she cried, and her desperate wriggle out of his hand revealed that the fright of the night had left more impression upon her delicate soul than superficially appeared.

'Another dose or two, and she will be cured,' he said to himself.

It was now so generally known that the Earl and Countess were not in accord, that he took no great trouble to disguise his deeds in relation to this matter. During the day he ordered four men with ropes and rollers to attend him in the boudoir. When they arrived, the closet was open, and the upper part of the statue tied up in canvas. He had it taken to the sleeping-chamber. What followed is more or less matter of conjecture. The story, as told to me, goes on to say that, when Lady Uplandtowers retired with him that night, she saw facing the foot of the heavy oak four-poster, a tall dark wardrobe, which had not stood there before; but she did not ask what its presence meant.

'I have had a little whim,' he explained when they were in the dark.

'Have you?' says she.

'To erect a little shrine, as it may be called.'

'A little shrine?'

'Yes; to one whom we both equally adore – eh? I'll show you what it contains.'

He pulled a cord which hung covered by the bed-curtains, and the doors of the wardrobe slowly opened, disclosing that the shelves within had been removed throughout, and the interior adapted to receive the ghastly figure, which stood there as it had stood in the boudoir, but with a wax candle burning on each side of it to throw the cropped and distorted features into relief. She clutched him, uttered a low scream, and buried her head in the bedclothes. 'O, take it away – please take it away!' she implored.

'All in good time; namely, when you love me best,' he returned calmly. 'You don't quite yet – eh?'

'I don't know – I think – O Uplandtowers, have mercy – I cannot bear it – O, in pity, take it away!'

'Nonsense; one gets accustomed to anything. Take another gaze.'

In short, he allowed the doors to remain unclosed at the foot of the bed, and the wax-tapers burning; and such was the strange fascination of the grisly exhibition that a morbid curiosity took possession of the Countess as she lay, and, at his repeated request, she did again look out from the coverlet, shuddered, hid her eyes, and looked again, all the while begging him to take it away, or it would drive her out of her senses. But he would not do so yet, and the wardrobe was not locked till dawn.

The scene was repeated the next night. Firm in enforcing his ferocious correctives, he continued the treatment till the nerves of the poor lady were quivering in agony under the virtuous tortures inflicted by her lord, to bring her truant heart back to faithfulness.

The third night, when the scene had opened as usual, and she lay staring with immense wild eyes at the horrid fascination, on a sudden she gave an unnatural laugh; she laughed more and more, staring at the image, till she literally shrieked with laughter: then there was silence, and he found her to have become insensible. He thought she had fainted, but soon saw that the event was worse: she was in an epileptic fit. He started up, dismayed by the sense that, like many other subtle personages, he had been too exacting for his own interests. Such love as he was capable of, though rather a selfish gloating than a cherishing solicitude, was fanned into life on the instant. He closed the wardrobe with the pulley, clasped her in his arms, took her gently to the window, and did all he could to restore her.*

It was a long time before the Countess came to herself, and when she did so, a considerable change seemed to have taken place in her emotions. She flung her arms around him, and with gasps of fear abjectly kissed him many times, at last bursting into tears. She had never wept in this scene before.

'You'll take it away, dearest – you will!' she begged plaintively.

'If you love me.'

'I do – oh, I do!'

'And hate him, and his memory?'

'Yes – yes!'

'Thoroughly?'

'I cannot endure recollection of him!' cried the poor Countess slavishly. 'It fills me with shame – how could I ever be so depraved! I'll never behave badly again, Uplandtowers; and you will never put the hated statue again before my eyes?'

He felt that he could promise with perfect safety. 'Never,' said he.

'And then I'll love you,' she returned eagerly, as if dreading lest the scourge should be applied anew. 'And I'll never, never dream of thinking a single thought that seems like faithlessness to my marriage vow.'

The strange thing now was that this fictitious love wrung from her by terror took on, through mere habit of enactment, a certain quality of reality. A servile mood of attachment to the Earl became distinctly visible in her contemporaneously with an actual dislike for her late husband's memory. The mood of attachment grew and continued when the statue was removed. A permanent revulsion was operant in her, which intensified as time wore on. How fright could have effected such a change of idiosyncrasy learned physicians alone can say; but I believe such cases of reactionary instinct are not unknown.

The upshot was that the cure became so permanent as to be itself a new disease. She clung to him so tightly that she would not willingly be out of his sight for a moment. She would have no sitting-room apart from his, though she could not help starting when he entered suddenly to her. Her eyes were well-nigh always fixed upon him. If he drove out, she wished to go with him; his slightest civilities to other women made her frantically jealous; till at length her very fidelity became a burden to him, absorbing his time, and curtailing his liberty, and causing him to curse and swear. If he ever spoke sharply to her now, she did not revenge herself by flying off to a mental world of her own, all that affection for another, which had provided her with a resource, was now a cold black cinder.

From that time the life of this scared and enervated lady – whose existence might have been developed to so much higher purpose but for the ignoble ambition of her parents and the conventions of the time – was one of obsequious amativeness towards a perverse and cruel man. Little personal events came to her in quick succession – half a dozen, eight, nine, ten such events, – in brief, she bore him no less than eleven children in the nine following years, but half of them came prematurely into the world, or died a few days old; only one, a girl, attained to maturity; she in after years became the wife of the Honourable Mr Beltonleigh, who was created Lord d'Almaine, as may be remembered.

There was no living son and heir. At length, completely worn out in mind and body, Lady Uplandtowers was taken abroad by her husband, to try the effect of a more genial climate upon her wasted frame. But nothing availed to strengthen her, and she died at Florence, a few months after her arrival in Italy.

Contrary to expectation, the Earl of Uplandtowers did not marry again. Such affection as existed in him – strange, hard, brutal as it was – seemed untransferable, and the title, as is known, passed at his death to his nephew. Perhaps it may not be so generally known that, during the enlargement of the Hall for the sixth Earl, while digging in the grounds for the new foundations, the broken fragments of a marble statue were unearthed. They were submitted to various antiquaries, who said that, so far as the damaged pieces would allow them to form an opinion, the statue seemed to be that of a mutilated Roman satyr;* or, if not, an allegorical figure of Death. Only one or two old inhabitants guessed whose statue those fragments had composed.

I should have added that, shortly after the death of the Countess, an excellent sermon was preached by the Dean of Melchester, the subject of which, though names were not mentioned, was unquestionably suggested by the aforesaid events. He dwelt upon the folly of indulgence in sensuous love for a handsome form merely; and showed that the only rational and virtuous growths of that affection were those based upon intrinsic worth. In the case of the tender but somewhat shallow lady whose life I have related, there is no doubt that an infatuation for the person of young Willowes was the chief feeling that induced her to marry him; which was the more deplorable in that his beauty, by all tradition, was the least of his recommendations, every report bearing out the inference that he must have been a man of steadfast nature, bright intelligence, and promising life.

To the eyes of a man viewing it from behind, the nut-brown hair was a wonder and a mystery. Under the black beaver hat surmounted by its tuft of black feathers, the long locks, braided and twisted and coiled like the rushes of a basket, composed a rare, if somewhat barbaric, example of ingenious art. One could understand such weavings and coilings being wrought to last intact for a year, or even a calendar month; but that they should be all demolished regularly at bedtime, after a single day of permanence, seemed a reckless waste of successful fabrication.

And she had done it all herself, poor thing. She had no maid, and it was almost the only accomplishment she could boast of. Hence the unstinted pains.

She was a young invalid lady – not so very much of an invalid – sitting in a wheeled chair, which had been pulled up in the front part of a green enclosure, close to a bandstand where a concert was going on, during a warm June afternoon. It had place in one of the minor parks or private gardens that are to be found in the suburbs of London, and was the effort of a local association to raise money for some charity. There are worlds within worlds in the great city, and though nobody outside the immediate district had ever heard of the charity, or the band, or the garden, the enclosure was filled with an interested audience sufficiently informed on all these.

As the strains proceeded many of the listeners observed the chaired lady, whose back hair, by reason of her prominent position, so challenged inspection. Her face was not easily discernible, but the aforesaid cunning tress-weavings, the white ear and poll,* and the curve of a cheek which was neither flaccid nor sallow, were signals that led to the expectation of good beauty in front. Such expectations are not infrequently disappointed as soon as the disclosure comes; and in the present case, when the lady, by a turn of the head, at length revealed herself, she was not so handsome as the people behind her had supposed, and even hoped – they did not know why.

For one thing (alas! the commonness of this complaint), she

was less young than they had fancied her to be. Yet attractive her face unquestionably was, and not at all sickly. The revelation of its details came each time she turned to talk to a boy of twelve or thirteen who stood beside her, and the shape of whose hat and jacket implied that he belonged to a well-known public school.* The immediate bystanders could hear that he called her 'Mother'.

When the end of the recital was reached, and the audience withdrew, many chose to find their way out by passing at her elbow. Almost all turned their heads to take a full and near look at the interesting woman, who remained stationary in the chair till the way should be clear enough for her to be wheeled out without obstruction. As if she expected their glances, and did not mind gratifying their curiosity, she met the eyes of several of her observers by lifting her own, showing these to be soft, brown, and affectionate orbs, a little plaintive in their regard.

She was conducted out of the gardens, and passed along the pavement till she disappeared from view, the schoolboy walking beside her. To inquiries made by some persons who watched her away, the answer came that she was the second wife of the incumbent of a neighbouring parish, and that she was lame. She was generally believed to be a woman with a story – an innocent one, but a story of some sort or other.

In conversing with her on their way home the boy who walked at her elbow said that he hoped his father had not missed them.

'He have been so comfortable these last few hours that I am sure he cannot have missed us,' she replied.

'*Has*, dear mother – not *have!*' exclaimed the public-school boy, with an impatient fastidiousness that was almost harsh. 'Surely you know that by this time!'

His mother hastily adopted the correction, and did not resent his making it, or retaliate, as she might well have done, by bidding him to wipe that crumby mouth of his, whose condition had been caused by surreptitious attempts to eat a piece of cake without taking it out of the pocket wherein it lay concealed. After this the pretty woman and the boy went onward in silence.

That question of grammar bore upon her history, and she fell into reverie, of a somewhat sad kind to all appearance. It might have been assumed that she was wondering if she had done wisely in shaping her life as she had shaped it, to bring out such a result as this.

In a remote nook in North Wessex, forty miles from London, near the thriving county-town of Aldbrickham, there stood a pretty village with its church and parsonage, which she knew well enough, but her son had never seen. It was her native village, Gaymead, and the first event bearing upon her present situation had occurred at that place when she was only a girl of nineteen.

How well she remembered it, that first act in her little tragi-comedy, the death of her reverend husband's first wife. It happened on a spring evening, and she who now and for many years had filled that first wife's place was then parlour-maid in the parson's house.

When everything had been done that could be done, and the death was announced, she had gone out in the dusk to visit her parents, who were living in the same village, to tell them the sad news. As she opened the white swing-gate and looked towards the trees which rose westward, shutting out the pale light of the evening sky, she discerned, without much surprise, the figure of a man standing in the hedge, though she roguishly exclaimed as a matter of form, 'O, Sam, how you frightened me!'

He was a young gardener of her acquaintance. She told him the particulars of the late event, and they stood silent, these two young people, in that elevated, calmly philosophic mind which is engendered when a tragedy has happened close at hand, and has not happened to the philosophers themselves. But it had its bearing upon their relations.

'And will you stay on now at the Vicarage, just the same?' asked he.

She had hardly thought of that. 'O yes – I suppose!' she said. 'Everything will be just as usual, I imagine?'

He walked beside her towards her mother's. Presently his arm stole round her waist. She gently removed it; but he placed it there again, and she yielded the point. 'You see, dear Sophy, you don't know that you'll stay on; you may want a home; and I shall be ready to offer one some day, though I may not be ready just yet.'

'Why, Sam, how can you be so fast! I've never even said I liked 'ee; and it is all your own doing, coming after me!'

'Still, it is nonsense to say I am not to have a try at you like the rest.' He stooped to kiss her a farewell, for they had reached her mother's door.

'No, Sam; you shan't!' she cried, putting her hand over his mouth. 'You ought to be more serious on such a night as this.' And she bade him adieu without allowing him to kiss her or to come indoors.

The vicar just left a widower was at this time a man about forty years of age, of good family, and childless. He had led a secluded existence in this college living,* partly because there were no resident landowners; and his loss now intensified his habit of withdrawal from outward observation. He was seen still less than heretofore, kept himself still less in time with the rhythm and racket of the movements called progress in the world without. For many months after his wife's decease the economy of his household remained as before; the cook, the housemaid, the parlour-maid, and the man out-of-doors performed their duties or left them undone, just as Nature prompted them – the vicar knew not which. It was then represented to him that his servants seemed to have nothing to do in his small family of one. He was struck with the truth of this representation, and decided to cut down his establishment. But he was forestalled by Sophy, the parlour-maid, who said one evening that she wished to leave him.

'And why?' said the parson.

'Sam Hobson has asked me to marry him, sir.'

'Well – do you want to marry?'

'Not much. But it would be a home for me. And we have heard that one of us will have to leave.'

A day or two after she said: 'I don't want to leave just yet, sir, if you don't wish it. Sam and I have quarrelled.'

He looked up at her. He had hardly ever observed her before, though he had been frequently conscious of her soft presence in the room. What a kitten-like, flexuous, tender creature she was! She was the only one of the servants with whom he came into immediate and continuous relation. What should he do if Sophy were gone?

Sophy did not go, but one of the others did, and things went on quietly again.

When Mr Twycott, the vicar, was ill, Sophy brought up his meals to him, and she had no sooner left the room one day than he heard a noise on the stairs. She had slipped down with the tray, and so twisted her foot that she could not stand. The village surgeon was called in; the vicar got better, but Sophy was incapacitated for a long time; and she was informed that she must never again walk much or engage in any occupation which required her to stand long on her feet. As soon as she was comparatively well she spoke to him alone. Since she was forbidden to walk and bustle about, and, indeed, could not do so, it became her duty to leave. She could very well work at something sitting down, and she had an aunt a seamstress.

The parson had been very greatly moved by what she had suffered on his account, and he exclaimed, 'No, Sophy; lame or not lame, I cannot let you go. You must never leave me again!'

He came close to her, and, though she could never exactly tell how it happened, she became conscious of his lips upon her cheek. He then asked her to marry him. Sophy did not exactly love him, but she had a respect for him which almost amounted to veneration. Even if she had wished to get away from him she hardly dared refuse a personage so reverend and august in her eyes, and she assented forthwith to be his wife.

Thus it happened that one fine morning, when the doors of the church were naturally open for ventilation, and the singing birds fluttered in and alighted on the tie-beams* of the roof, there was a marriage-service at the communion-rails, which hardly a soul knew of. The parson and a neighbouring curate had entered at one door, and Sophy at another, followed by two necessary persons, whereupon in a short time there emerged a newly-made husband and wife.

Mr Twycott knew perfectly well that he had committed social suicide by this step, despite Sophy's spotless character, and he had taken his measures accordingly. An exchange of livings had been arranged with an acquaintance who was incumbent of a church in the south of London, and as soon as possible the couple removed thither, abandoning their pretty country home, with trees and shrubs and glebe, for a narrow, dusty house in a long, straight street, and their fine peal of bells for the wretchedest one-tongued clangour that ever tortured mortal ears. It was all on her account. They were, however, away from every one who had known her former position; and also under less observation from without than they would have had to put up with in any country parish.

Sophy the woman was as charming a partner as a man could

possess, though Sophy the lady had her deficiencies. She showed a natural aptitude for little domestic refinements, so far as related to things and manners; but in what is called culture she was less intuitive. She had now been married more than fourteen years, and her husband had taken much trouble with her education; but she still held confused ideas on the use of 'was' and 'were', which did not beget a respect for her among the few acquaintances she made. Her great grief in this relation was that her only child, on whose education no expense had been and would be spared, was now old enough to perceive these deficiencies in his mother, and not only to see them but to feel irritated at their existence.

Thus she lived on in the city, and wasted hours in braiding her beautiful hair, till her once apple cheeks waned to pink of the very faintest. Her foot had never regained its natural strength after the accident, and she was mostly obliged to avoid walking altogether. Her husband had grown to like London for its freedom and its domestic privacy; but he was twenty years his Sophy's senior, and had latterly been seized with a serious illness. On this day, however, he had seemed to be well enough to justify her accompanying her son Randolph to the concert.

The next time we get a glimpse of her is when she appears in the mournful attire of a widow.

Mr Twycott had never rallied, and now lay in a well-packed cemetery to the south of the great city, where, if all the dead it contained had stood erect and alive, not one would have known him or recognized his name. The boy had dutifully followed him to the grave, and was now again at school.

Throughout these changes Sophy had been treated like the child she was in nature though not in years. She was left with no control over anything that had been her husband's beyond her modest personal income. In his anxiety lest her inexperience should be overreached he had safeguarded with trustees all he possibly could. The completion of the boy's course at the public school, to be followed in due time by Oxford and ordination, had been all previsioned and arranged, and she really had nothing to occupy her in the world but to eat and drink, and make a business of indolence, and go on weaving and coiling the nut-brown hair, merely keeping a home open for the son whenever he came to her during vacations.

Foreseeing his probable decease long years before her, her husband in his lifetime had purchased for her use a semi-detached villa in the same long, straight road whereon the church and parsonage faced, which was to be hers as long as she chose to live in it. Here she now resided, looking out upon the fragment of lawn in front, and through the railings at the ever-flowing traffic; or, bending forward over the window-sill on the first floor, stretching her eyes far up and down the vista of sooty trees, hazy air, and drab house-façades, along which echoed the noises common to a suburban main thoroughfare.

Somehow, her boy, with his aristocratic school-knowledge, his grammars, and his aversions, was losing those wide infantine sympathies, extending as far as to the sun and moon themselves, with which he, like other children, had been born, and which his mother, a child of nature herself, had loved in him; he was reducing their compass to a population of a few thousand wealthy and titled people, the mere veneer of a thousand million or so of others who did not interest him at all. He drifted further and further away from her. Sophy's *milieu** being a suburb of minor tradesmen and under-clerks, and her almost only companions the two servants of her own house, it was not surprising that after her husband's death she soon lost the little artificial tastes she had acquired from him, and became – in her son's eyes – a mother whose mistakes and origin it was his painful lot as a gentleman to blush for. As yet he was far from being man enough – if he ever would be – to rate these sins of hers at their true infinitesimal value beside the yearning fondness that welled up and remained penned in her heart till it should be more fully accepted by him, or by some other person or thing. If he had lived at home with her he would have had all of it; but he seemed to require so very little in present circumstances, and it remained stored.

Her life became insupportably dreary; she could not take walks, and had no interest in going for drives, or, indeed, in travelling anywhere. Nearly two years passed without an event, and still she looked on that suburban road, thinking of the village in which she had been born, and whither she would have gone back – O how gladly! – even to work in the fields.

Taking no exercise she often could not sleep, and would rise in the night or early morning to look out upon the then vacant thoroughfare, where the lamps stood like sentinels waiting for some procession to go by. An approximation to such a procession was indeed made early every morning about one o'clock, when the country vehicles passed up with loads of vegetables for Covent Garden market.* She often saw them creeping along at this silent and dusky hour – waggon after waggon, bearing green bastions of cabbages nodding to their fall, yet never falling, walls of baskets enclosing masses of beans and peas, pyramids of snow-white turnips, swaying howdahs* of mixed produce – creeping along behind aged night-horses, who seemed ever patiently wondering between their hollow coughs why they had always to work at that still hour when all other sentient creatures were privileged to rest. Wrapped in a cloak, it was soothing to watch and sympathize with them when depression and nervousness hindered sleep, and to see how the fresh green-stuff brightened to life as it came opposite the lamp, and how the sweating animals steamed and shone with their miles of travel.

They had an interest, almost a charm, for Sophy, these semirural people and vehicles moving in an urban atmosphere, leading a life quite distinct from that of the daytime toilers on the same road. One morning a man who accompanied a waggon-load of potatoes gazed rather hard at the house-fronts as he passed, and with a curious emotion she thought his form was familiar to her. She looked out for him again. His being an old-fashioned conveyance, with a yellow front, it was easily recognizable, and on the third night after she saw it a second time. The man alongside was, as she had fancied, Sam Hobson, formerly gardener at Gaymead, who would at one time have married her.

She had occasionally thought of him, and wondered if life in a cottage with him would not have been a happier lot than the life she had accepted. She had not thought of him passionately, but her now dismal situation lent an interest to his resurrection – a tender interest which it is impossible to exaggerate. She went back to bed, and began thinking. When did these market-gardeners, who travelled up to town so regularly at one or two in the morning, come back? She dimly recollected seeing their empty waggons, hardly noticeable amid the ordinary day-traffic, passing down at some hour before noon.

It was only April, but that morning, after breakfast, she had the window opened, and sat looking out, the feeble sun shining full upon her. She affected to sew, but her eyes never left the street. Between ten and eleven the desired waggon, now unladen, reappeared on its return journey. But Sam was not looking round him then, and drove on in a reverie.

'Sam!' cried she.

Turning with a start, his face lighted up. He called to him a little boy to hold the horse, alighted, and came and stood under the window.

'I can't come down easily, Sam, or I would!' she said. 'Did you know I lived here?'

'Well, Mrs Twycott, I knew you lived along here somewhere. I have often looked out for 'ee.'

He briefly explained his own presence on the scene. He had long since given up his gardening in the village near Aldbrickham, and was now manager at a market-gardener's on the south side of London, it being part of his duty to go up to Covent Garden with waggon-loads of produce two or three times a week. In answer to her curious inquiry, he admitted that he had come to this particular district because he had seen in the Aldbrickham paper, a year or two before, the announcement of the death in South London of the aforetime vicar of Gaymead, which had revived an interest in her dwelling-place that he could not extinguish, leading him to hover about the locality till his present post had been secured.

They spoke of their native village in dear old North Wessex, the spots in which they had played together as children. She tried to feel that she was a dignified personage now, that she must not be too confidential with Sam. But she could not keep it up, and the tears hanging in her eyes were indicated in her voice.

'You are not happy, Mrs Twycott, I'm afraid?' he said.

'O, of course not! I lost my husband only the year before last.'

'Ah! I meant in another way. You'd like to be home again?'

'This is my home – for life. The house belongs to me. But I understand – ' She let it out then. 'Yes, Sam. I long for home – *our* home! I *should* like to be there, and never leave it, and die there.' But she remembered herself. 'That's only a momentary feeling. I have a son, you know, a dear boy. He's at school now.'

'Somewhere handy, I suppose? I see there's lots on 'em along this road.'

'O no! Not in one of these wretched holes! At a public school
– one of the most distinguished in England.'

'Chok' it all! of course! I forget, ma'am, that you've been a
lady for so many years.'

'No, I am not a lady,' she said sadly. 'I never shall be. But
he's a gentleman, and that – makes it – O how difficult for
me!'

The acquaintance thus oddly reopened proceeded apace. She
often looked out to get a few words with him, by night or by
day. Her sorrow was that she could not accompany her one old
friend on foot a little way, and talk more freely than she could
do while he paused before the house. One night, at the beginning
of June, when she was again on the watch after an absence of
some days from the window, he entered the gate and said softly,
'Now, wouldn't some air do you good? I've only half a load this
morning. Why not ride up to Covent Garden with me? There's
a nice seat on the cabbages, where I've spread a sack. You can
be home again in a cab before anybody is up.'

She refused at first, and then, trembling with excitement,
hastily finished her dressing, and wrapped herself up in cloak
and veil, afterwards sidling downstairs by the aid of the handrail, in a way she could adopt on an emergency. When she had
opened the door she found Sam on the step, and he lifted her
bodily on his strong arm across the little forecourt into his
vehicle. Not a soul was visible or audible in the infinite length
of the straight, flat highway, with its ever-waiting lamps converging to points in each direction. The air was fresh as country
air at this hour, and the stars shone, except to the north-
eastward, where there was a whitish light – the dawn. Sam
carefully placed her in the seat, and drove on.

They talked as they had talked in old days, Sam pulling
himself up now and then, when he thought himself too familiar.
More than once she said with misgiving that she wondered if
she ought to have indulged in the freak. 'But I am so lonely in
my house,' she added, 'and this makes me so happy!'

'You must come again, dear Mrs Twycott. There is no time o'
day for taking the air like this.'

It grew lighter and lighter. The sparrows became busy in the
streets, and the city waxed denser around them. When they
approached the river it was day, and on the bridge they beheld

the full blaze of morning sunlight in the direction of St Paul's, the river glistening towards it, and not a craft stirring.

Near Covent Garden he put her into a cab, and they parted, looking into each other's faces like the very old friends they were. She reached home without adventure, limped to the door, and let herself in with her latch-key unseen.

The air and Sam's presence had revived her: her cheeks were quite pink – almost beautiful. She had something to live for in addition to her son. A woman of pure instincts, she knew there had been nothing really wrong in the journey, but supposed it conventionally to be very wrong indeed.

Soon, however, she gave way to the temptation of going with him again, and on this occasion their conversation was distinctly tender, and Sam said he never should forget her, notwithstanding that she had served him rather badly at one time. After much hesitation he told her of a plan it was in his power to carry out, and one he should like to take in hand, since he did not care for London work: it was to set up as a master greengrocer down at Aldbrickham, the county-town of their native place. He knew of an opening – a shop kept by aged people who wished to retire.

'And why don't you do it, then, Sam?' she asked with a slight heartsinking.

'Because I'm not sure if – you'd join me. I know you wouldn't – couldn't! Such a lady as ye've been so long, you couldn't be a wife to a man like me.'

'I hardly suppose I could!' she assented, also frightened at the idea.

'If you could,' he said eagerly, 'you'd on'y have to sit in the back parlour and look through the glass partition when I was away sometimes – just to keep an eye on things. The lameness wouldn't hinder that. . . . I'd keep you as genteel as ever I could, dear Sophy – if I might think of it!' he pleaded.

'Sam, I'll be frank,' she said, putting her hand on his. 'If it were only myself I would do it, and gladly, though everything I possess would be lost to me by marrying again.'

'I don't mind that! It's more independent.'

'That's good of you, dear, dear Sam. But there's something else. I have a son. . . . I almost fancy when I am miserable sometimes that he is not really mine, but one I hold in trust for my late husband. He seems to belong so little to me personally, so entirely to his dead father. He is so much educated and I so little that I do not feel dignified enough to be his mother. . . . Well, he would have to be told.'

'Yes. Unquestionably.' Sam saw her thought and her fear. 'Still, you can do as you like, Sophy – Mrs Twycott,' he added. 'It is not you who are the child, but he.'

'Ah, you don't know! Sam, if I could, I would marry you, some day. But you must wait a while, and let me think.'

It was enough for him, and he was blithe at their parting. Not so she. To tell Randolph seemed impossible. She could wait till he had gone up to Oxford, when what she did would affect his life but little. But would he ever tolerate the idea? And if not, could she defy him?

She had not told him a word when the yearly cricket-match came on at Lord's* between the public schools, though Sam had already gone back to Aldbrickham. Mrs Twycott felt stronger than usual: she went to the match with Randolph, and was able to leave her chair and walk about occasionally. The bright idea occurred to her that she could casually broach the subject while moving round among the spectators, when the boy's spirits were high with interest in the game, and he would weigh domestic matters as feathers in the scale beside the day's victory. They promenaded under the lurid July sun, this pair, so wide apart, yet so near, and Sophy saw the large proportion of boys like her own, in their broad white collars and dwarf hats, and all around the rows of great coaches under which was jumbled the *débris* of luxurious luncheons; bones, pie-crusts, champagne-bottles, glasses, plates, napkins, and the family silver; while on the coaches sat the proud fathers and mothers; but never a poor mother like her. If Randolph had not appertained to these, had not centred all his interests in them, had not cared exclusively for the class they belonged to, how happy would things have been! A great huzza at some small performance with the bat burst from the multitude of relatives, and Randolph jumped wildly into the air to see what had happened. Sophy fetched up the sentence that had been already shaped; but she could not get it out. The occasion was, perhaps, an inopportune one. The contrast between her story and the display of fashion to which Randolph had grown to regard himself as akin would be fatal. She awaited a better time.

It was on an evening when they were alone in their plain

suburban residence, where life was not blue but brown, that she ultimately broke silence, qualifying her announcement of a probable second marriage by assuring him that it would not take place for a long time to come, when he would be living quite independently of her.

The boy thought the idea a very reasonable one, and asked if she had chosen anybody? She hesitated; and he seemed to have a misgiving. He hoped his stepfather would be a gentleman? he said.

'Not what you call a gentleman,' she answered timidly. 'He'll be much as I was before I knew your father'; and by degrees she acquainted him with the whole. The youth's face remained fixed for a moment; then he flushed, leant on the table, and burst into passionate tears.

His mother went up to him, kissed all of his face that she could get at, and patted his back as if he were still the baby he once had been, crying herself the while. When he had somewhat recovered from his paroxysm he went hastily to his own room and fastened the door.

Parleyings were attempted through the keyhole, outside which she waited and listened. It was long before he would reply, and when he did it was to say sternly at her from within: 'I am ashamed of you! It will ruin me! A miserable boor! a churl! a clown! It will degrade me in the eyes of all the gentlemen of England!'

'Say no more – perhaps I am wrong! I will struggle against it!' she cried miserably.

Before Randolph left her that summer a letter arrived from Sam to inform her that he had been unexpectedly fortunate in obtaining the shop. He was in possession; it was the largest in the town, combining fruit with vegetables, and he thought it would form a home worthy even of her some day. Might he not run up to town to see her?

She met him by stealth, and said he must still wait for her final answer. The autumn dragged on, and when Randolph was home at Christmas for the holidays she broached the matter again. But the young gentleman was inexorable.

It was dropped for months; renewed again; abandoned under his repugnance; again attempted; and thus the gentle creature reasoned and pleaded till four or five long years had passed. Then the faithful Sam revived his suit with some peremptoriness.

Sophy's son, now an undergraduate, was down from Oxford one Easter, when she again opened the subject. As soon as he was ordained, she argued, he would have a home of his own, wherein she, with her bad grammar and her ignorance, would be an encumbrance to him. Better obliterate her as much as possible.

He showed a more manly anger now, but would not agree. She on her side was more persistent, and he had doubts whether she could be trusted in his absence. But by indignation and contempt for her taste he completely maintained his ascendency; and finally taking her before a little cross and altar that he had erected in his bedroom for his private devotions, there bade her kneel, and swear that she would not wed Samuel Hobson without his consent. 'I owe this to my father!' he said.

The poor woman swore, thinking he would soften as soon as he was ordained and in full swing of clerical work. But he did not. His education had by this time sufficiently ousted his humanity to keep him quite firm; though his mother might have led an idyllic life with her faithful fruiterer and greengrocer, and nobody have been anything the worse in the world.

Her lameness became more confirmed as time went on, and she seldom or never left the house in the long southern thoroughfare, where she seemed to be pining her heart away. 'Why mayn't I say to Sam that I'll marry him? Why mayn't I?' she would murmur plaintively to herself when nobody was near.

Some four years after this date a middle-aged man was standing at the door of the largest fruiterer's shop in Aldbrickham. He was the proprietor, but today, instead of his usual business attire, he wore a neat suit of black; and his window was partly shuttered. From the railway-station a funeral procession was seen approaching: it passed his door and went out of the town towards the village of Gaymead. The man, whose eyes were wet, held his hat in his hand as the vehicles moved by; while from the mourning coach a young smooth-shaven priest in a high waistcoat looked black as a cloud at the shopkeeper standing there.

ON THE WESTERN CIRCUIT*

The man who played the disturbing part in the two quiet feminine lives hereunder depicted – no great man, in any sense, by the way – first had knowledge of them on an October evening, in the city of Melchester. He had been standing in the Close, vainly endeavouring to gain amid the darkness a glimpse of the most homogeneous pile of mediaeval architecture in England, which towered and tapered from the damp and level sward in front of him. While he stood the presence of the Cathedral walls was revealed rather by the ear than by the eyes; he could not see them, but they reflected sharply a roar of sound which entered the Close by a street leading from the city square, and, falling upon the building, was flung back upon him.

He postponed till the morrow his attempt to examine the deserted edifice, and turned his attention to the noise. It was compounded of steam barrel-organs,* the clanging of gongs, the ringing of hand-bells, the clack of rattles, and the undistinguishable shouts of men. A lurid light hung in the air in the direction of the tumult. Thitherward he went, passing under the arched gateway, along a straight street, and into the square.

He might have searched Europe over for a greater contrast between juxtaposed scenes. The spectacle was that of the eighth chasm of the Inferno* as to colour and flame, and, as to mirth, a development of the Homeric heaven.* A smoky glare, of the complexion of brass-filings, ascended from the fiery tongues of innumerable naphtha lamps affixed to booths, stalls, and other temporary erections which crowded the spacious market-square. In front of this irradiation scores of human figures, more or less in profile, were darting athwart and across, up, down, and around, like gnats against a sunset.

Their motions were so rhythmical that they seemed to be moved by machinery. And it presently appeared that they were moved by machinery indeed; the figures being those of the patrons of swings, see-saws, flying-leaps, above all of the three steam roundabouts which occupied the centre of the position. It was from the latter that the din of steam-organs came.

Throbbing humanity in full light was, on second thoughts, better than architecture in the dark. The young man, lighting a short pipe, and putting his hat on one side and one hand in his pocket, to throw himself into harmony with his new environment, drew near to the largest and most patronized of the steam circuses, as the roundabouts were called by their owners. This was one of brilliant finish, and it was now in full revolution. The musical instrument around which and to whose tones the riders revolved, directed its trumpet-mouths of brass upon the young man, and the long plate-glass mirrors set at angles, which revolved with the machine, flashed the gyrating personages and hobby-horses kaleidoscopically into his eyes.

It could now be seen that he was unlike the majority of the crowd. A gentlemanly young fellow, one of the species found in large towns only, and London particularly, built on delicate lines, well, though not fashionably dressed, he appeared to belong to the professional class; he had nothing square or practical about his look, much that was curvilinear and sensuous. Indeed, some would have called him a man not altogether typical of the middle-class male of a century wherein sordid ambition is the master-passion that seems to be taking the time-honoured place of love.

The revolving figures passed before his eyes with an unexpected and quiet grace in a throng whose natural movements did not suggest gracefulness or quietude as a rule. By some contrivance there was imparted to each of the hobby-horses a motion which was really the triumph and perfection of roundabout inventiveness – a galloping rise and fall, so timed that, of each pair of steeds, one was on the spring while the other was on the pitch. The riders were quite fascinated by these equine undulations in this most delightful holiday-game of our times. There were riders as young as six, and as old as sixty years, with every age between. At first it was difficult to catch a personality, but by and by the observer's eyes centred on the prettiest girl out of the several pretty ones revolving.

It was not that one with the light frock and light hat whom he had been at first attracted by; no, it was the one with the black cape, grey skirt, light gloves and – no, not even she, but the one behind her; she with the crimson skirt, dark jacket, brown hat and brown gloves. Unmistakably that was the prettiest girl.

Having finally selected her, this idle spectator studied her as well as he was able during each of her brief transits across his visual field. She was absolutely unconscious of everything save the act of riding: her features were rapt in an ecstatic dreaminess; for the moment she did not know her age or her history or her lineaments, much less her troubles. He himself was full of vague latter-day glooms and popular melancholies, and it was a refreshing sensation to behold this young thing then and there, absolutely as happy as if she were in a Paradise.

Dreading the moment when the inexorable stoker, grimily lurking behind the glittering rococo-work,* should decide that this set of riders had had their pennyworth, and bring the whole concern of steam-engine, horses, mirrors, trumpets, drums, cymbals, and such-like to pause and silence, he waited for her every reappearance, glancing indifferently over the intervening forms, including the two plainer girls, the old woman and child, the two youngsters, the newly-married couple, the old man with a clay pipe, the sparkish youth with a ring, the young ladies in the chariot, the pair of journeyman-carpenters, and others, till his select country beauty followed on again in her place. He had never seen a fairer product of nature, and at each round she made a deeper mark in his sentiments. The stoppage then came, and the sighs of the riders were audible.

He moved round to the place at which he reckoned she would alight; but she retained her seat. The empty saddles began to refill, and she plainly was deciding to have another turn. The young man drew up to the side of her steed, and pleasantly asked her if she had enjoyed her ride.

'O yes!' she said, with dancing eyes. 'It has been quite unlike anything I have ever felt in my life before!'

It was not difficult to fall into conversation with her. Unreserved – too unreserved – by nature, she was not experienced enough to be reserved by art, and after a little coaxing she answered his remarks readily. She had come to live in Melchester from a village on the Great Plain, and this was the first time that she had ever seen a steam-circus; she could not understand how such wonderful machines were made. She had come to the city on the invitation of Mrs Harnham, who had taken her into her household to train her as a servant, if she showed any aptitude. Mrs Harnham was a young lady who before she married had been Miss Edith White, living in the country near the speaker's cottage; she was now very kind to her through knowing her in childhood so well. She was even taking the trouble to educate her. Mrs Harnham was the only friend she had in the world, and being without children had wished to have her near her in preference to anybody else, though she had only lately come; allowed her to do almost as she liked, and to have a holiday whenever she asked for it. The husband of this kind young lady was a rich wine-merchant of the town, but Mrs Harnham did not care much about him. In the daytime you could see the house from where they were talking. She, the speaker, liked Melchester better than the lonely country, and she was going to have a new hat for next Sunday that was to cost fifteen and ninepence.

Then she inquired of her acquaintance where he lived, and he told her in London, that ancient and smoky city, where everybody lived who lived at all, and died because they could not live there. He came into Wessex two or three times a year for professional reasons; he had arrived from Wintoncester yesterday, and was going on into the next county in a day or two. For one thing he did like the country better than the town, and it was because it contained such girls as herself.

Then the pleasure-machine started again, and, to the light-hearted girl, the figure of the handsome young man, the market-square with its lights and crowd, the houses beyond, and the world at large, began moving round as before, countermoving in the revolving mirrors on her right hand, she being as it were the fixed point in an undulating, dazzling, lurid universe, in which loomed forward most prominently of all the form of her late interlocutor. Each time that she approached the half of her orbit that lay nearest him they gazed at each other with smiles, and with that unmistakable expression which means so little at the moment, yet so often leads up to passion, heart-ache, union, disunion, devotion, overpopulation, drudgery, content, resignation, despair.

When the horses slowed anew he stepped to her side and proposed another heat. 'Hang the expense for once,' he said. 'I'll pay!'

She laughed till the tears came.

'Why do you laugh, dear?' said he.

'Because – you are so genteel that you must have plenty of money, and only say that for fun!' she returned.

'Ha-ha!' laughed the young man in unison, and gallantly producing his money she was enabled to whirl on again.

As he stood smiling there in the motley crowd, with his pipe in his hand, and clad in the rough pea-jacket* and wideawake* that he had put on for his stroll, who would have supposed him to be Charles Bradford Raye, Esquire, stuff-gownsman,* educated at Wintoncester,* called to the Bar at Lincoln's-Inn,* now going the Western Circuit, merely detained in Melchester by a small arbitration after his brethren had moved on to the next county-town?

The square was overlooked from its remoter corner by the house of which the young girl had spoken, a dignified residence of considerable size, having several windows on each floor. Inside one of these, on the first floor, the apartment being a large drawing-room, sat a lady, in appearance from twenty-eight to thirty years of age. The blinds were still undrawn, and the lady was absently surveying the weird scene without, her cheek resting on her hand. The room was unlit from within, but enough of the glare from the market-place entered it to reveal the lady's face. She was what is called an interesting creature rather than a handsome woman; dark-eyed, thoughtful, and with sensitive lips.

A man sauntered into the room from behind and came forward.

'O, Edith, I didn't see you,' he said. 'Why are you sitting here in the dark?'

'I am looking at the fair,' replied the lady in a languid voice.

'Oh? Horrid nuisance every year! I wish it could be put a stop to.'

'I like it.'

'H'm. There's no accounting for taste.'

For a moment he gazed from the window with her, for politeness' sake, and then went out again.

In a few minutes she rang.

'Hasn't Anna come in?' asked Mrs Harnham.

'No m'm.'

'She ought to be in by this time. I meant her to go for ten minutes only.'

'Shall I go and look for her, m'm?' said the housemaid alertly.

'No. It is not necessary: she is a good girl and will come soon.'

However, when the servant had gone Mrs Harnham arose, went up to her room, cloaked and bonneted herself, and proceeded downstairs, where she found her husband.

'I want to see the fair,' she said; 'and I am going to look for Anna. I have made myself responsible for her, and must see she comes to no harm. She ought to be indoors. Will you come with me?'

'Oh, she's all right. I saw her on one of those whirligig things, talking to her young man as I came in. But I'll go if you wish, though I'd rather go a hundred miles the other way.'

'Then please do so. I shall come to no harm alone.'

She left the house and entered the crowd which thronged the market-place, where she soon discovered Anna, seated on the revolving horse. As soon as it stopped Mrs Harnham advanced and said severely, 'Anna, how can you be such a wild girl? You were only to be out for ten minutes.'

Anna looked blank, and the young man, who had dropped into the background, came to help her alight.

'Please don't blame her,' he said politely. 'It is my fault that she has stayed. She looked so graceful on the horse that I induced her to go round again. I assure you that she has been quite safe.'

'In that case I'll leave her in your hands,' said Mrs Harnham, turning to retrace her steps.

But this for the moment it was not so easy to do. Something had attracted the crowd to a spot in their rear, and the wine-merchant's wife, caught by its sway, found herself pressed against Anna's acquaintance without power to move away. Their faces were within a few inches of each other, his breath fanned her cheek as well as Anna's. They could do no other than smile at the accident; but neither spoke, and each waited passively. Mrs Harnham then felt a man's hand clasping her fingers, and from the look of consciousness on the young fellow's face she knew the hand to be his: she also knew that from the position of the girl he had no other thought than that the imprisoned hand was Anna's. What prompted her to refrain from undeceiving him she could hardly tell. Not content with holding the hand, he playfully slipped two of his fingers inside her glove, against her palm. Thus matters continued till the pressure lessened; but several minutes passed before the crowd thinned sufficiently to allow Mrs Harnham to withdraw.

'How did they get to know each other, I wonder?' she mused as she retreated. 'Anna is really very forward – and he very wicked and nice.'

She was so gently stirred with the stranger's manner and voice, with the tenderness of his idle touch, that instead of re-entering the house she turned back again and observed the pair from a screened nook. Really she argued (being little less impulsive than Anna herself) it was very excusable in Anna to encourage him, however she might have contrived to make his acquaintance; he was so gentlemanly, so fascinating, had such beautiful eyes. The thought that he was several years her junior produced a reasonless sigh.

At length the couple turned from the roundabout towards the door of Mrs Harnham's house, and the young man could be heard saying that he would accompany her home. Anna, then, had found a lover, apparently a very devoted one. Mrs Harnham was quite interested in him. When they drew near the door of the wine-merchant's house, a comparatively deserted spot by this time, they stood invisible for a little while in the shadow of a wall, where they separated, Anna going on to the entrance, and her acquaintance returning across the square.

'Anna,' said Mrs Harnham, coming up. 'I've been looking at you! That young man kissed you at parting, I am almost sure.'

'Well,' stammered Anna; 'he said, if I didn't mind – it would do me no harm, and, and, him a great deal of good!'

'Ah, I thought so! And he was a stranger till to-night?'

'Yes ma'am.'

'Yet I warrant you told him your name and everything about yourself?'

'He asked me.'

'But he didn't tell you his?'

'Yes ma'am, he did!' cried Anna victoriously. 'It is Charles Bradford, of London.'

'Well, if he's respectable, of course I've nothing to say against your knowing him,' remarked her mistress, prepossessed, in spite of general principles, in the young man's favour. 'But I must reconsider all that, if he attempts to renew your acquaint-ance. A country-bred girl like you, who has never lived in Melchester till this month, who had hardly ever seen a black-coated man till you came here, to be so sharp as to capture a young Londoner like him!'

'I didn't capture him. I didn't do anything,' said Anna, in confusion.

When she was indoors and alone Mrs Harnham thought what a well-bred and chivalrous young man Anna's companion had seemed. There had been a magic in his wooing touch of her hand; and she wondered how he had come to be attracted by the girl.

The next morning the emotional Edith Harnham went to the usual weekday service in Melchester cathedral. In crossing the Close through the fog she again perceived him who had interested her the previous evening, gazing up thoughtfully at the high-piled architecture of the nave: and as soon as she had taken her seat he entered and sat down in a stall opposite hers.

He did not particularly heed her; but Mrs Harnham was continually occupying her eyes with him, and wondered more than ever what had attracted him in her unfledged maidservant. The mistress was almost as unaccustomed as the maiden herself to the end-of-the-age young man, or she might have wondered less. Raye, having looked about him awhile, left abruptly, without regard to the service that was proceeding; and Mrs Harnham – lonely, impressionable creature that she was – took no further interest in praising the Lord. She wished she had married a London man who knew the subtleties of love-making as they were evidently known to him who had mistakenly caressed her hand.

The calendar* at Melchester had been light, occupying the court only a few hours; and the assizes at Casterbridge, the next county-town on the Western Circuit, having no business for Raye, he had not gone thither. At the next town after that they did not open till the following Monday, trials to begin on Tuesday morning. In the natural order of things Raye would have arrived at the latter place on Monday afternoon; but it was not till the middle of Wednesday that his gown and grey wig, curled in tiers, in the best fashion of Assyrian bas-reliefs,* were seen blowing and bobbing behind him as he hastily walked up the High Street from his lodgings. But though he entered the assize building there was nothing for him to do, and sitting at the blue baize table in the well of the court, he mended pens with a mind far away from the case in progress. Thoughts of unpremeditated conduct, of which a week earlier he would not have believed himself capable, threw him into a mood of dissatisfied depression.

He had contrived to see again the pretty rural maiden Anna, the day after the fair, had walked out of the city with her to the earthworks of Old Melchester, and feeling a violent fancy for her, had remained in Melchester all Sunday, Monday, and Tuesday; by persuasion obtaining walks and meetings with the girl six or seven times during the interval; had in brief won her, body and soul.

He supposed it must have been owing to the seclusion in which he had lived of late in town that he had given way so unrestrainedly to a passion for an artless creature whose inexperience had, from the first, led her to place herself unreservedly in his hands. Much he deplored trifling with her feelings for the sake of a passing desire; and he could only hope that she might not live to suffer on his account.

She had begged him to come to her again; entreated him; wept. He had promised that he would do so, and he meant to carry out that promise. He could not desert her now. Awkward as such unintentional connections were, the interspace of a hundred miles – which to a girl of her limited capabilities was like a thousand – would effectually hinder this summer fancy from greatly encumbering his life; while thought of her simple love might do him the negative good of keeping him from idle pleasures in town when he wished to work hard. His circuit journeys would take him to Melchester three or four times a year; and then he could always see her.

The pseudonym, or rather partial name, that he had given her as his before knowing how far the acquaintance was going to carry him, had been spoken on the spur of the moment, without any ulterior intention whatever. He had not afterwards disturbed Anna's error, but on leaving her he had felt bound to give her an address at a stationer's not far from his chambers, at which she might write to him under the initials 'C. B.'

In due time Raye returned to his London abode, having called at Melchester on his way and spent a few additional hours with his fascinating child of nature. In town he lived monotonously every day. Often he and his rooms were enclosed by a tawny fog from all the world besides, and when he lighted the gas to read or write by, his situation seemed so unnatural that he would look into the fire and think of that trusting girl at Melchester again and again. Often, oppressed by absurd fondness for her, he would enter the dim religious nave of the Law Courts by the north door, elbow other juniors habited like himself, and like him unretained; edge himself into this or that crowded court where a sensational case was going on, just as if he were in it, though the police officers at the door knew as well as he knew himself that he had no more concern with the business in hand than the patient idlers at the gallery-door outside, who had waited to enter since eight in the morning because, like him, they belonged to the classes that live on expectation. But he would do these things to no purpose, and think how greatly the characters in such scenes contrasted with the pink and breezy Anna.

An unexpected feature in that peasant maiden's conduct was that she had not as yet written to him, though he had told her she might do so if she wished. Surely a young creature had never before been so reticent in such circumstances. At length he sent her a brief line, positively requesting her to write. There was no answer by the return post, but the day after a letter in a neat feminine hand, and bearing the Melchester postmark, was handed to him by the stationer.

The fact alone of its arrival was sufficient to satisfy his imaginative sentiment. He was not anxious to open the epistle, and in truth did not begin to read it for nearly half-an-hour, anticipating readily its terms of passionate retrospect and tender adjuration. When at last he turned his feet to the fireplace and unfolded the sheet, he was surprised and pleased to find that neither extravagance nor vulgarity was there. It was the most charming little missive he had ever received from woman. To be sure the language was simple and the ideas were slight; but it was so self-possessed; so purely that of a young girl who felt her womanhood to be enough for her dignity that he read it through twice. Four sides were filled, and a few lines written across, after the fashion of former days; the paper, too, was common, and not of the latest shade and surface. But what of those things? He had received letters from women who were fairly called ladies, but never so sensible, so human a letter as this. He could not single out any one sentence and say it was at all remarkable or clever; the *ensemble** of the letter it was which won him; and beyond the one request that he would write or come to her again soon there was nothing to show her sense of a claim upon him.

To write again and develop a correspondence was the last thing Raye would have preconceived as his conduct in such a situation; yet he did send a short, encouraging line or two, signed with his pseudonym, in which he asked for another letter, and cheeringly promised that he would try to see her again on some near day, and would never forget how much they had been to each other during their short acquaintance.

To return now to the moment at which Anna, at Melchester, had received Raye's letter.

It had been put into her own hand by the postman on his morning rounds. She flushed down to her neck on receipt of it, and turned it over and over. 'It is mine?' she said.

'Why, yes, can't you see it is?' said the postman, smiling as he guessed the nature of the document and the cause of the confusion.

'O yes, of course!' replied Anna, looking at the letter, forcedly tittering, and blushing still more.

Her look of embarrassment did not leave her with the postman's departure. She opened the envelope, kissed its contents, put away the letter in her pocket, and remained musing till her eyes filled with tears.

A few minutes later she carried up a cup of tea to Mrs Harnham in her bed-chamber. Anna's mistress looked at her, and said: 'How dismal you seem this morning, Anna. What's the matter?'

'I'm not dismal, I'm glad; only I – ' She stopped to stifle a sob.

'Well?'

'I've got a letter – and what good is it to me, if I can't read a word in it!'

'Why, I'll read it, child, if necessary.'

'But this is from somebody – I don't want anybody to read it but myself!' Anna murmured.

'I shall not tell anybody. Is it from that young man?'

'I think so.' Anna slowly produced the letter, saying: 'Then will you read it to me, ma'am?'

This was the secret of Anna's embarrassment and fluttering. She could neither read nor write. She had grown up under the care of an aunt by marriage, at one of the lonely hamlets on the

Great Mid-Wessex Plain where, even in days of national education,* there had been no school within a distance of two miles. Her aunt was an ignorant woman; there had been nobody to investigate Anna's circumstances, nobody to care about her learning the rudiments; though, as often in such cases, she had been well fed and clothed and not unkindly treated. Since she had come to live at Melchester with Mrs Harnham, the latter, who took a kindly interest in the girl, had taught her to speak correctly, in which accomplishment Anna showed considerable readiness, as is not unusual with the illiterate; and soon became quite fluent in the use of her mistress's phraseology. Mrs Harnham also insisted upon her getting a spelling and copy book, and beginning to practise in these. Anna was slower in this branch of her education, and meanwhile here was the letter.

Edith Harnham's large dark eyes expressed some interest in the contents, though, in her character of mere interpreter, she threw into her tone as much as she could of mechanical passiveness. She read the short epistle on to its concluding sentence, which idly requested Anna to send him a tender answer.

'Now – you'll do it for me, won't you, dear mistress?' said Anna eagerly. 'And you'll do it as well as ever you can, please? Because I couldn't bear him to think I am not able to do it myself. I should sink into the earth with shame if he knew that!'

From some words in the letter Mrs Harnham was led to ask questions, and the answers she received confirmed her suspicions. Deep concern filled Edith's heart at perceiving how the girl had committed her happiness to the issue of this new-sprung attachment. She blamed herself for not interfering in a flirtation which had resulted so seriously for the poor little creature in her charge; though at the time of seeing the pair together she had a feeling that it was hardly within her province to nip young affection in the bud. However, what was done could not be undone, and it behoved her now, as Anna's only protector, to help her as much as she could. To Anna's eager request that she, Mrs Harnham, should compose and write the answer to this young London man's letter, she felt bound to accede, to keep alive his attachment to the girl if possible; though in other circumstances she might have suggested the cook as an amanuensis.

A tender reply was thereupon concocted, and set down in

Edith Harnham's hand. This letter it had been which Raye had received and delighted in. Written in the presence of Anna it certainly was, and on Anna's humble note-paper, and in a measure indited* by the young girl; but the life, the spirit, the individuality, were Edith Harnham's.

'Won't you at least put your name yourself?' she said. 'You can manage to write that by this time?'

'No, no,' said Anna, shrinking back. 'I should do it so bad. He'd be ashamed of me, and never see me again!'

The note, so prettily requesting another from him, had, as we have seen, power enough in its pages to bring one. He declared it to be such a pleasure to hear from her that she must write every week. The same process of manufacture was accordingly repeated by Anna and her mistress, and continued for several weeks in succession; each letter being penned and suggested by Edith, the girl standing by; the answer read and commented on by Edith, Anna standing by and listening again.

Late on a winter evening, after the dispatch of the sixth letter, Mrs Harnham was sitting alone by the remains of her fire. Her husband had retired to bed and she had fallen into that fixity of musing which takes no count of hour or temperature. The state of mind had been brought about in Edith by a strange thing which she had done that day. For the first time since Raye's visit Anna had gone to stay over a night or two with her cottage friends on the Plain, and in her absence had arrived, out of its time, a letter from Raye. To this Edith had replied on her own responsibility, from the depths of her own heart, without waiting for her maid's collaboration. The luxury of writing to him what would be known to no consciousness but his was great, and she had indulged herself therein.

Why was it a luxury?

Edith Harnham led a lonely life. Influenced by the belief of the British parent that a bad marriage with its aversions is better than free womanhood with its interests, dignity, and leisure, she had consented to marry the elderly wine-merchant as a *pis aller*,* at the age of seven-and-twenty – some three years before this date – to find afterwards that she had made a mistake. That contract had left her still a woman whose deeper nature had never been stirred.

She was now clearly realizing that she had become possessed to the bottom of her soul with the image of a man to whom she was hardly so much as a name. From the first he had attracted her by his looks and voice; by his tender touch; and, with these as generators, the writing of letter after letter and the reading of their soft answers had insensibly developed on her side an emotion which fanned his; till there had resulted a magnetic reciprocity between the correspondents, notwithstanding that one of them wrote in a character not her own. That he had been able to seduce another woman in two days was his crowning though unrecognized fascination for her as the she-animal.*

They were her own impassioned and pent-up ideas – lowered to monosyllabic phraseology in order to keep up the disguise – that Edith put into letters signed with another name, much to the shallow Anna's delight, who, unassisted, could not for the world have conceived such pretty fancies for winning him, even had she been able to write them. Edith found that it was these, her own foisted-in sentiments, to which the young barrister mainly responded. The few sentences occasionally added from Anna's own lips made apparently no impression upon him.

The letter-writing in her absence Anna never discovered; but on her return the next morning she declared she wished to see her lover about something at once, and begged Mrs Harnham to ask him to come.

There was a strange anxiety in her manner which did not escape Mrs Harnham, and ultimately resolved itself into a flood of tears. Sinking down at Edith's knees, she made confession that the result of her relations with her lover it would soon become necessary to disclose.

Edith Harnham was generous enough to be very far from inclined to cast Anna adrift at this conjuncture. No true woman ever is so inclined from her own personal point of view, however prompt she may be in taking such steps to safeguard those dear to her. Although she had written to Raye so short a time previously, she instantly penned another Anna-note hinting clearly though delicately the state of affairs.

Raye replied by a hasty line to say how much he was concerned at her news: he felt that he must run down to see her almost immediately.

But a week later the girl came to her mistress's room with another note, which on being read informed her that after all he could not find time for the journey. Anna was broken with grief; but by Mrs Harnham's counsel strictly refrained from hurling at him the reproaches and bitterness customary from young women so situated. One thing was imperative: to keep the young man's romantic interest in her alive. Rather therefore did Edith, in the name of her *protégée*,* request him on no account to be distressed about the looming event, and not to inconvenience himself to hasten down. She desired above everything to be no weight upon him in his career, no clog upon his high activities. She had wished him to know what had befallen: he was to dismiss it again from his mind. Only he must write tenderly as ever, and when he should come again on the spring circuit it would be soon enough to discuss what had better be done.

It may well be supposed that Anna's own feelings had not been quite in accord with these generous expressions; but the mistress's judgment had ruled, and Anna had acquiesced. 'All I want is that *niceness* you can so well put into your letters, my dear, dear mistress, and that I can't for the life o' me make up out of my own head; though I mean the same thing and feel it exactly when you've written it down!'

When the letter had been sent off, and Edith Harnham was left alone, she bowed herself on the back of her chair and wept.

'I wish his child was mine – I wish it was!' she murmured. 'Yet how can I say such a wicked thing!'

The letter moved Raye considerably when it reached him. The intelligence itself had affected him less than her unexpected manner of treating him in relation to it. The absence of any word of reproach, the devotion to his interests, the self-sacrifice apparent in every line, all made up a nobility of character that he had never dreamt of finding in womankind.

'God forgive me!' he said tremulously. 'I have been a wicked wretch. I did not know she was such a treasure as this!'

He reassured her instantly; declaring that he would not of course desert her, that he would provide a home for her somewhere. Meanwhile she was to stay where she was as long as her mistress would allow her.

But a misfortune supervened in this direction. Whether an inkling of Anna's circumstances reached the knowledge of Mrs Harnham's husband or not cannot be said, but the girl was compelled, in spite of Edith's entreaties, to leave the house. By her own choice she decided to go back for a while to the cottage on the Plain. This arrangement led to a consultation as to how the correspondence should be carried on; and in the girl's inability to continue personally what had been begun in her name, and in the difficulty of their acting in concert as heretofore, she requested Mrs Harnham – the only well-to-do friend she had in the world – to receive the letters and reply to them off-hand, sending them on afterwards to herself on the Plain, where she might at least get some neighbour to read them to her, if a trustworthy one could be met with. Anna and her box then departed for the Plain.

Thus it befell that Edith Harnham found herself in the strange position of having to correspond, under no supervision by the real woman, with a man not her husband, in terms which were virtually those of a wife, concerning a corporeal condition that was not Edith's at all; the man being one for whom, mainly through the sympathies involved in playing this part, she secretly cherished a predilection, subtle and imaginative truly, but strong and absorbing. She opened each letter, read it as if intended for herself, and replied from the promptings of her own heart and no other.

Throughout this correspondence, carried on in the girl's absence, the high-strung Edith Harnham lived in the ecstasy of fancy; the vicarious intimacy engendered such a flow of passionateness as was never exceeded. For conscience' sake Edith at first sent on each of his letters to Anna, and even rough copies of her replies; but later on these so-called copies were much abridged, and many letters on both sides were not sent on at all.

Though sensuous, and, superficially at least, infested with the self-indulgent vices of artificial society, there was a substratum of honesty and fairness in Raye's character. He had really a tender regard for the country girl, and it grew more tender than ever when he found her apparently capable of expressing the deepest sensibilities in the simplest words. He meditated, he wavered; and finally resolved to consult his sister, a maiden lady much older than himself, of lively sympathies and good intent. In making this confidence he showed her some of the letters.

'She seems fairly educated,' Miss Raye observed. 'And bright in ideas. She expresses herself with a taste that must be innate.'

'Yes. She writes very prettily, doesn't she, thanks to these elementary schools?'

'One is drawn out towards her, in spite of one's self, poor thing.'

The upshot of the discussion was that though he had not been directly advised to do it, Raye wrote, in his real name, what he would never have decided to write on his own responsibility; namely that he could not live without her, and would come down in the spring and shelve her looming difficulty by marrying her.

This bold acceptance of the situation was made known to Anna by Mrs Harnham driving out immediately to the cottage on the Plain. Anna jumped for joy like a little child. And poor, crude directions for answering appropriately were given to Edith Harnham, who on her return to the city carried them out with warm intensifications.

'O!' she groaned, as she threw down the pen. 'Anna – poor good little fool – hasn't intelligence enough to appreciate him! How should she? While I – don't bear his child!'

It was now February. The correspondence had continued altogether for four months; and the next letter from Raye contained incidentally a statement of his position and prospects. He said that in offering to wed her he had, at first, contemplated the step of retiring from a profession which hitherto had brought him very slight emolument, and which, to speak plainly, he had thought might be difficult of practice after his union with her. But the unexpected mines of brightness and warmth that her letters had disclosed to be lurking in her sweet nature had led him to abandon that somewhat sad prospect. He felt sure that, with her powers of development, after a little private training in the social forms of London under his supervision, and a little help from a governess if necessary, she would make as good a professional man's wife as could be desired, even if he should rise to the woolsack.* Many a Lord Chancellor's wife had been less intuitively a lady than she had shown herself to be in her lines to him.

'O – poor fellow, poor fellow!' mourned Edith Harnham.

Her distress now raged as high as her infatuation. It was she who had wrought him to this pitch – to a marriage which meant his ruin; yet she could not, in mercy to her maid, do anything to hinder his plan. Anna was coming to Melchester that week, but she could hardly show the girl this last reply from the young man; it told too much of the second individuality that had usurped the place of the first.

Anna came, and her mistress took her into her own room for

privacy. Anna began by saying with some anxiety that she was glad the wedding was so near.

'O Anna!' replied Mrs Harnham. 'I think we must tell him all – that I have been doing your writing for you? – lest he should not know it till after you become his wife, and it might lead to dissension and recriminations – '

'O mis'ess, dear mis'ess – please don't tell him now!' cried Anna in distress. 'If you were to do it, perhaps he would not marry me; and what should I do then? It would be terrible what would come to me! And I am getting on with my writing, too. I have brought with me the copybook you were so good as to give me, and I practise every day, and though it is so, so hard, I shall do it well at last, I believe, if I keep on trying.'

Edith looked at the copybook. The copies had been set by herself, and such progress as the girl had made was in the way of grotesque facsimile of her mistress's hand. But even if Edith's flowing caligraphy were reproduced the inspiration would be another thing.

'You do it so beautifully,' continued Anna, 'and say all that I want to say so much better than I could say it, that I do hope you won't leave me in the lurch just now!'

'Very well,' replied the other. 'But I – but I thought I ought not to go on!'

'Why?'

Her strong desire to confide her sentiments led Edith to answer truly:

'Because of its effect upon me.'

'But it *can't* have any!'

'Why, child?'

'Because you are married already!' said Anna with lucid simplicity.

'Of course it can't,' said her mistress hastily; yet glad, despite her conscience, that two or three outpourings still remained to her. 'But you must concentrate your attention on writing your name as I write it here.'

Soon Raye wrote about the wedding. Having decided to make the best of what he feared was a piece of romantic folly, he had acquired more zest for the grand experiment. He wished the ceremony to be in London, for greater privacy. Edith Harnham would have preferred it at Melchester; Anna was passive. His reasoning prevailed, and Mrs Harnham threw herself with mournful zeal into the preparations for Anna's departure. In a last desperate feeling that she must at every hazard be in at the death of her dream, and see once again the man who by a species of telepathy had exercised such an influence on her, she offered to go up with Anna and be with her through the ceremony – 'to see the end of her,' as her mistress put it with forced gaiety; an offer which the girl gratefully accepted; for she had no other friend capable of playing the part of companion and witness, in the presence of a gentlemanly bridegroom, in such a way as not to hasten an opinion that he had made an irremediable social blunder.

It was a muddy morning in March when Raye alighted from a four-wheel cab at the door of a registry office in the S.W. district of London, and carefully handed down Anna and her companion Mrs Harnham. Anna looked attractive in the somewhat fashionable clothes which Mrs Harnham had helped her to buy, though not quite so attractive as, an innocent child, she had appeared in her country gown on the back of the wooden horse at Melchester Fair.

Mrs Harnham had come up this morning by an early train, and a young man – a friend of Raye's – having met them at the door, all four entered the registry office together. Till an hour before this time Raye had never known the wine-merchant's wife, except at that first casual encounter, and in the flutter of the performance before them he had little opportunity for more than a brief acquaintance. The contract of marriage at a registry is soon got through; but somehow, during its progress, Raye discovered a strange and secret gravitation between himself and Anna's friend.

The formalities of the wedding – or rather ratification of a previous union – being concluded, the four went in one cab to Raye's lodgings, newly taken in a new suburb in preference to a house, the rent of which he could ill afford just then. Here Anna cut the little cake which Raye had bought at a pastrycook's on his way home from Lincoln's Inn the night before. But she did not do much besides. Raye's friend was obliged to depart almost immediately, and when he had left the only ones virtually present were Edith and Raye, who exchanged ideas with much animation. The conversation was indeed theirs only, Anna being as a domestic animal who humbly heard but understood not.*

Raye seemed startled in awakening to this fact, and began to feel dissatisfied with her inadequacy.

At last, more disappointed than he cared to own, he said, 'Mrs Harnham, my darling is so flurried that she doesn't know what she is doing or saying. I see that after this event a little quietude will be necessary before she gives tongue to that tender philosophy which she used to treat me to in her letters.'

They had planned to start early that afternoon for Knollsea, to spend the few opening days of their married life there, and as the hour for departure was drawing near Raye asked his wife if she would go to the writing-desk in the next room and scribble a little note to his sister, who had been unable to attend through indisposition, informing her that the ceremony was over, thanking her for her little present, and hoping to know her well now that she was the writer's sister as well as Charles's.

'Say it in the pretty poetical way you know so well how to adopt,' he added, 'for I want you particularly to win her, and both of you to be dear friends.'

Anna looked uneasy, but departed to her task, Raye remaining to talk to their guest. Anna was a long while absent, and her husband suddenly rose and went to her.

He found her still bending over the writing-table, with tears brimming up in her eyes; and he looked down upon the sheet of note-paper with some interest, to discover with what tact she had expressed her goodwill in the delicate circumstances. To his surprise she had progressed but a few lines, in the characters and spelling of a child of eight, and with the ideas of a goose.

'Anna,' he said. staring; 'what's this?'

'It only means – that I can't do it any better!' she answered, through her tears.

'Eh? Nonsense!'

'I can't!' she insisted, with miserable, sobbing hardihood. 'I – I – didn't write those letters, Charles! I only told *her* what to write! And not always that! But I am learning, O so fast, my dear, dear husband! And you'll forgive me, won't you, for not telling you before?' She slid to her knees, abjectly clasped his waist and laid her face against him.

He stood a few moments, raised her, abruptly turned, and shut the door upon her, rejoining Edith in the drawing-room. She saw that something untoward had been discovered, and their eyes remained fixed on each other.

'Do I guess rightly?' he asked, with wan quietude. '*You* were her scribe through all this?'

'It was necessary,' said Edith.

'Did she dictate every word you ever wrote to me?'

'Not every word.'

'In fact, very little?'

'Very little.'

'You wrote a great part of those pages every week from your own conceptions, though in her name!'

'Yes.'

'Perhaps you wrote many of the letters when you were alone, without communication with her?'

'I did.'

He turned to the bookcase, and leant with his hand over his face; and Edith, seeing his distress, became white as a sheet.

'You have deceived me – ruined me!' he murmured.

'O, don't say it!' she cried in her anguish, jumping up and putting her hand on his shoulder. 'I can't bear that!'

'Delighting me deceptively! Why did you do it – *why* did you!'

'I began doing it in kindness to her! How could I do otherwise than try to save such a simple girl from misery? But I admit that I continued it for pleasure to myself.'

Raye looked up. 'Why did it give you pleasure?' he asked.

'I must not tell,' said she.

He continued to regard her, and saw that her lips suddenly began to quiver under his scrutiny, and her eyes to fill and droop. She started aside, and said that she must go to the station to catch the return train: could a cab be called immediately?

But Raye went up to her, and took her unresisting hand. 'Well, to think of such a thing as this!' he said. 'Why, you and I are friends – lovers – devoted lovers – by correspondence!'

'Yes; I suppose.'

'More.'

'More?'

'Plainly more. It is no use blinking that. Legally I have married her – God help us both! – in soul and spirit I have married you, and no other woman in the world!'

'Hush!'

'But I will not hush! Why should you try to disguise the full truth, when you have already owned half of it? Yes, it is between you and me that the bond is – not between me and her! Now I'll say no more. But, O my cruel one, I think I have one claim upon you!'

She did not say what, and he drew her towards him, and bent over her. 'If it was all pure invention in those letters,' he said emphatically, 'give me your cheek only. If you meant what you said, let it be lips. It is for the first and last time, remember!'

She put up her mouth, and he kissed her long. 'You forgive me?' she said, crying.

'Yes.'

'But you are ruined!'

'What matter!' he said, shrugging his shoulders. 'It serves me right!'

She withdrew, wiped her eyes, entered and bade good-bye to Anna, who had not expected her to go so soon, and was still wrestling with the letter. Raye followed Edith downstairs, and in three minutes she was in a hansom driving to the Waterloo station.

He went back to his wife. 'Never mind the letter, Anna, today,' he said gently. 'Put on your things. We, too, must be off shortly.'

The simple girl, upheld by the sense that she was indeed married, showed her delight at finding that he was as kind as ever after the disclosure. She did not know that before his eyes he beheld as it were a galley, in which he, the fastidious urban, was chained to work for the remainder of his life, with her, the unlettered peasant, chained to his side.

Edith travelled back to Melchester that day with a face that showed the very stupor of grief, her lips still tingling from the desperate pressure of his kiss. The end of her impassioned dream had come. When at dusk she reached the Melchester station her husband was there to meet her, but in his perfunctoriness and her preoccupation they did not see each other, and she went out of the station alone.

She walked mechanically homewards without calling a fly. Entering, she could not bear the silence of the house, and went up in the dark to where Anna had slept, where she remained thinking awhile. She then returned to the drawing-room, and not knowing what she did, crouched down upon the floor.

'I have ruined him!' she kept repeating. 'I have ruined him; because I would not deal treacherously towards her!'

In the course of half-an-hour a figure opened the door of the apartment.

'Ah – who's that?' she said, starting up, for it was dark.

'Your husband – who should it be?' said the worthy merchant.

'Ah – my husband! – I forgot I had a husband!' she whispered to herself.

'I missed you at the station,' he continued. 'Did you see Anna safely tied up? I hope so, for 'twas time.'

'Yes – Anna is married.'

Simultaneously with Edith's journey home Anna and her husband were sitting at the opposite windows of a second-class carriage which sped along to Knollsea. In his hand was a pocket-book full of creased sheets closely written over. Unfolding them one after another he read them in silence, and sighed.

'What are you doing, dear Charles?' she said timidly from the other window, and drew nearer to him as if he were a god.

'Reading over all those sweet letters to me signed "Anna",' he replied with dreary resignation.

'Talking of Exhibitions, World's Fairs, and what not,' said the old gentleman, 'I would not go round the corner to see a dozen of them nowadays. The only exhibition that ever made, or ever will make, any impression upon my imagination was the first of the series, the parent of them all, and now a thing of old times – the Great Exhibition of 1851, in Hyde Park, London.* None of the younger generation can realize the sense of novelty it produced in us who were then in our prime. A noun substantive went so far as to become an adjective in honour of the occasion. It was "exhibition" hat, "exhibition" razor-strop, "exhibition" watch; nay, even "exhibition" weather, "exhibition" spirits, sweethearts, babies, wives – for the time.

'For South Wessex, the year formed in many ways an extra-ordinary chronological frontier or transit-line, at which there occurred what one might call a precipice in Time. As in a geological "fault", we had presented to us a sudden bringing of ancient and modern into absolute contact, such as probably in no other single year since the Conquest* was ever witnessed in this part of the country.'

These observations led us onward to talk of the different personages, gentle and simple, who lived and moved within our narrow and peaceful horizon at that time; and of three people in particular, whose queer little history was oddly touched at points by the Exhibition, more concerned with it than that of anybody else who dwelt in those outlying shades of the world, Stickleford, Mellstock, and Egdon. First in prominence among these three came Wat Ollamoor – if that were his real name – whom the seniors in our party had known well.

He was a woman's man, they said, – supremely so – externally little else. To men he was not attractive; perhaps a little repulsive at times. Musician, dandy, and company-man in practice; veter-inary surgeon in theory, he lodged awhile in Mellstock village, coming from nobody knew where; though some said his first appearance in this neighbourhood had been as fiddle-player in a show at Greenhill Fair.*

Many a worthy villager envied him his power over unsophisticated maidenhood – a power which seemed sometimes to have
a touch of the weird and wizardly in it. Personally he was not
ill-favoured, though rather un-English, his complexion being a
rich olive, his rank hair dark and rather clammy – made still
clammier by secret ointments, which, when he came fresh to a
party, caused him to smell like 'boys'-love' (southernwood)
steeped in lamp-oil. On occasion he wore curls – a double row
– running almost horizontally around his head. But as these
were sometimes noticeably absent, it was concluded that they
were not altogether of Nature's making. By girls whose love for
him had turned to hatred he had been nicknamed 'Mop', from
this abundance of hair, which was long enough to rest upon his
shoulders; as time passed the name more and more prevailed.

His fiddling possibly had the most to do with the fascination
he exercised, for, to speak fairly, it could claim for itself a most
peculiar and personal quality, like that in a moving preacher.
There were tones in it which bred the immediate conviction that
indolence and averseness to systematic application were all that
lay between 'Mop' and the career of a second Paganini.*

While playing he invariably closed his eyes; using no notes,
and, as it were, allowing the violin to wander on at will into the
most plaintive passages ever heard by rustic man. There was a
certain lingual character in the supplicatory expressions he
produced, which would well-nigh have drawn an ache from the
heart of a gate-post. He could make any child in the parish, who
was at all sensitive to music, burst into tears in a few minutes by
simply fiddling one of the old dance-tunes he almost entirely
affected – country jigs, reels, and 'Favourite Quick Steps'* of
the last century – some mutilated remains of which even now
reappear as nameless phantoms in new quadrilles and gallops,
where they are recognized only by the curious, or by such old-
fashioned and far-between people as have been thrown with
men like Wat Ollamoor in their early life.

His date was a little later than that of the old Mellstock quire-
band* which comprised the Dewys, Mail, and the rest – in fact,
he did not rise above the horizon thereabout till those well-
known musicians were disbanded as ecclesiastical functionaries.
In their honest love of thoroughness they despised the new
man's style. Theophilus Dewy (Reuben the tranter's younger
brother) used to say there was no 'plumness'* in it – no bowing,

no solidity – it was all fantastical. And probably this was true. Anyhow, Mop had, very obviously, never bowed a note of church-music from his birth; he never once sat in the gallery of Mellstock church where the others had tuned their venerable psalmody so many hundreds of times; had never, in all likelihood, entered a church at all. All were devil's tunes in his repertory. 'He could no more play the "Wold Hundredth"* to his true time than he could play the brazen serpent,'* the tranter would say. (The brazen serpent was supposed in Mellstock to be a musical instrument particularly hard to blow.)

Occasionally Mop could produce the aforesaid moving effect upon the souls of grown-up persons, especially young women of fragile and responsive organization. Such an one was Car'line Aspent. Though she was already engaged to be married before she met him, Car'line, of them all, was the most influenced by Mop Ollamoor's heart-stealing melodies, to her discomfort, nay, positive pain and ultimate injury. She was a pretty, invocating, weak-mouthed girl, whose chief defect as a companion with her sex was a tendency to peevishness now and then. At this time she was not a resident in Mellstock parish where Mop lodged, but lived some miles off at Stickleford, further down the river.

How and where she first made acquaintance with him and his fiddling is not truly known, but the story was that it either began or was developed on one spring evening, when, in passing through Lower Mellstock, she chanced to pause on the bridge near his house to rest herself, and languidly leaned over the parapet. Mop was standing on his door-step, as was his custom, spinning the insidious thread of semi- and demi-semiquavers from the E string of his fiddle for the benefit of passers-by, and laughing as the tears rolled down the cheeks of the little children hanging around him. Car'line pretended to be engrossed with the rippling of the stream under the arches, but in reality she was listening, as he knew. Presently the aching of the heart seized her simultaneously with a wild desire to glide airily in the mazes of an infinite dance. To shake off the fascination she resolved to go on, although it would be necessary to pass him as he played. On stealthily glancing ahead at the performer, she found to her relief that his eyes were closed in abandonment to instrumentation, and she strode on boldly. But when closer her step grew timid, her tread convulsed itself more and more accordantly with the time of the melody, till she very nearly danced along. Gaining another glance at him when immediately opposite, she saw that *one* of his eyes was open, quizzing her as he smiled at her emotional state. Her gait could not divest itself of its compelled capers till she had gone a long way past the house; and Car'line was unable to shake off the strange infatuation for hours.

After that day, whenever there was to be in the neighbourhood a dance to which she could get an invitation, and where Mop Ollamoor was to be the musician, Car'line contrived to be present, though it sometimes involved a walk of several miles; for he did not play so often in Stickleford as elsewhere.

The next evidences of his influence over her were singular enough, and it would require a neurologist to fully explain them. She would be sitting quietly, any evening after dark, in the house of her father, the parish-clerk, which stood in the middle of Stickleford village street, this being the highroad between Lower Mellstock and Moreford, five miles eastward. Here, without a moment's warning, and in the midst of a general conversation between her father, sister, and the young man before alluded to, who devotedly wooed her in ignorance of her infatuation, she would start from her seat in the chimney-corner as if she had received a galvanic shock, and spring convulsively towards the ceiling; then she would burst into tears, and it was not till some half-hour had passed that she grew calm as usual. Her father, knowing her hysterical tendencies, was always excessively anxious about this trait in his youngest girl, and feared the attack to be a species of epileptic fit. Not so her sister Julia. Julia had found out what was the cause. At the moment before the jumping, only an exceptionally sensitive ear situated in the chimney-nook could have caught from down the flue the beat of a man's footstep along the highway without. But it was in that footfall, for which she had been waiting, that the origin of Car'line's involuntary springing lay. The pedestrian was Mop Ollamoor, as the girl well knew; but his business that way was not to visit her; he sought another woman whom he spoke of as his Intended, and who lived at Moreford, two miles further on. On one, and only one, occasion did it happen that Car'line could not control her utterance; it was when her sister alone chanced to be present. 'O – O – O – !' she cried. 'He's going to *her*, and not coming to *me!*'

To do the fiddler justice he had not at first thought greatly of, or spoken much to, this girl of impressionable mould. But he had soon found out her secret, and could not resist a little by-play with her too easily hurt heart, as an interlude between his more serious love-makings at Moreford. The two became well acquainted, though only by stealth, hardly a soul in Stickleford except her sister, and her lover Ned Hipcroft, being aware of the attachment. Her father disapproved of her coldness to Ned; her sister, too, hoped she might get over this nervous passion for a man of whom so little was known. The ultimate result was that Car'line's manly and simple wooer Edward found his suit becoming practically hopeless. He was a respectable mechanic, in a far sounder position than Mop the nominal horse-doctor; but when, before leaving her, Ned put his flat and final question, would she marry him, then and there, now or never, it was with little expectation of obtaining more than the negative she gave him. Though her father supported him and her sister supported him, he could not play the fiddle so as to draw your soul out of your body like a spider's thread, as Mop did, till you felt as limp as withywind* and yearned for something to cling to. Indeed, Hipcroft had not the slightest ear for music; could not sing two notes in tune, much less play them.

The No he had expected and got from her, in spite of a preliminary encouragement, gave Ned a new start in life. It had been uttered in such a tone of sad entreaty that he resolved to persecute her no more; she should not even be distressed by a sight of his form in the distant perspective of the street and lane. He left the place, and his natural course was to London.

The railway to South Wessex* was in process of construction, but it was not as yet opened for traffic; and Hipcroft reached the capital by a six days' trudge on foot, as many a better man had done before him. He was one of the last of the artisan class who used that now extinct method of travel to the great centres of labour, so customary then from time immemorial.

In London he lived and worked regularly at his trade. More fortunate than many, his disinterested willingness recommended him from the first. During the ensuing four years he was never out of employment. He neither advanced nor receded in the modern sense; he improved as a workman, but he did not shift one jot in social position. About his love for Car'line he maintained a rigid silence. No doubt he often thought of her; but being always occupied, and having no relations at Stickleford, he held no communication with that part of the country, and showed no desire to return. In his quiet lodging in Lambeth he moved about after working-hours with the facility of a woman, doing his own cooking, attending to his stocking-heels, and shaping himself by degrees to a life-long bachelorhood. For this conduct one is bound to advance the canonical reason that time could not efface from his heart the image of little Car'line Aspent – and it may be in part true; but there was also the inference that his was a nature not greatly dependent upon the ministrations of the other sex for its comforts.

The fourth year of his residence as a mechanic in London was the year of the Hyde Park Exhibition already mentioned, and at the construction of this huge glass-house,* then unexampled in the world's history, he worked daily. It was an era of great hope and activity among the nations and industries. Though Hipcroft was, in his small way, a central man in the movement, he plodded on with his usual outward placidity. Yet for him, too, the year was destined to have its surprises, for when the bustle of getting the building ready for the opening day was past, the ceremonies had been witnessed, and people were flocking thither from all parts of the globe, he received a letter from Car'line. Till that day the silence of four years between himself and Stickleford had never been broken.

She informed her old lover, in an uncertain penmanship which suggested a trembling hand, of the trouble she had been put to in ascertaining his address, and then broached the subject which had prompted her to write. Four years ago, she said with the greatest delicacy of which she was capable, she had been so foolish as to refuse him. Her wilful wrong-headedness had since been a grief to her many times, and of late particularly. As for Mr Ollamoor, he had been absent almost as long as Ned – she did not know where. She would gladly marry Ned now if he were to ask her again, and be a tender little wife to him till her life's end.

A tide of warm feeling must have surged through Ned Hipcroft's frame on receipt of this news, if we may judge by the issue. Unquestionably he loved her still, even if not to the exclusion of every other happiness. This from his Car'line, she who had been dead to him these many years, alive to him again as of old, was in itself a pleasant, gratifying thing. Ned had grown so resigned to, or satisfied with, his lonely lot, that he probably would not have shown much jubilation at anything. Still, a certain ardour of preoccupation, after his first surprise, revealed how deeply her confession of faith in him had stirred him. Measured and methodical in his ways, he did not answer the letter that day, nor the next, nor the next. He was having 'a good think'. When he did answer it, there was a great deal of sound reasoning mixed in with the unmistakable tenderness of his reply; but the tenderness itself was sufficient to reveal that he was pleased with her straightforward frankness; that the anchorage she had once obtained in his heart was renewable, if it had not been continuously firm.

He told her – and as he wrote his lips twitched humorously over the few gentle words of raillery he indited* among the rest of his sentences – that it was all very well for her to come round at this time of day. Why wouldn't she have him when he wanted her? She had no doubt learned that he was not married, but suppose his affections had since been fixed on another? She ought to beg his pardon. Still, he was not the man to forget her. But considering how he had been used, and what he had suffered, she could not quite expect him to go down to Stickleford and fetch her. But if she would come to him, and say she was sorry, as was only fair; why, yes, he would marry her, knowing what a good little woman she was at the core. He added that the request for her to come to him was a less one to make than it would have been when he first left Stickleford, or even a few months ago; for the new railway into South Wessex was now open, and there had just begun to be run wonderfully contrived special trains, called excursion-trains, on account of the Great Exhibition; so that she could come up easily alone.

She said in her reply how good it was of him to treat her so generously, after her hot and cold treatment of him; that though she felt frightened at the magnitude of the journey, and was never as yet in a railway train, having only seen one pass at a distance, she embraced his offer with all her heart; and would, indeed, own to him how sorry she was, and beg his pardon, and try to be a good wife always, and make up for lost time.

The remaining details of when and where were soon settled, Car'line informing him, for her ready identification in the crowd, that she would be wearing 'my new sprigged-laylock cotton gown', and Ned gaily responding that, having married her the morning after her arrival, he would make a day of it by taking her to the Exhibition. One early summer afternoon, accordingly, he came from his place of work, and hastened towards Waterloo Station to meet her. It was as wet and chilly as an English June day can occasionally be, but as he waited on the platform in the drizzle he glowed inwardly, and seemed to have something to live for again.

The 'excursion-train' – an absolutely new departure in the history of travel – was still a novelty on the Wessex line, and probably everywhere.* Crowds of people had flocked to all the stations on the way up to witness the unwonted sight of so long a train's passage, even where they did not take advantage of the opportunity it offered. The seats for the humbler class of travellers in these early experiments in steam-locomotion, were open trucks, without any protection whatever from the wind and rain; and damp weather having set in with the afternoon, the unfortunate occupants of these vehicles were, on the train drawing up at the London terminus, found to be in a pitiable condition from their long journey; blue-faced, stiff-necked, sneezing, rain-beaten, chilled to the marrow, many of the men being hatless; in fact, they resembled people who had been out all night in an open boat on a rough sea, rather than inland excursionists for pleasure. The women had in some degree protected themselves by turning up the skirts of their gowns over their heads, but as by this arrangement they were additionally exposed about the hips, they were all more or less in a sorry plight.

In the bustle and crush of alighting forms of both sexes which followed the entry of the huge concatenation into the station, Ned Hipcroft soon discerned the slim little figure his eye was in search of, in the sprigged lilac, as described. She came up to him with a frightened smile – still pretty, though so damp, weather-beaten, and shivering from long exposure to the wind.

'O Ned!' she sputtered, 'I – I – ' He clasped her in his arms and kissed her, whereupon she burst into a flood of tears.

'You are wet, my poor dear! I hope you'll not get cold,' he said. And surveying her and her multifarious surrounding packages, he noticed that by the hand she led a toddling child – a little girl of three or so – whose hood was as clammy and tender face as blue as those of the other travellers.

'Who is this – somebody you know?' asked Ned curiously.

'Yes, Ned. She's mine.'

'Yours?'

'Yes – my own.'

'Your own child?'

'Yes!'

'But who's the father?'

'The young man I had after you courted me.'

'Well – as God's in – '

'Ned, I didn't name it in my letter, because, you see, it would have been so hard to explain! I thought that when we met I could tell you how she happened to be born, so much better than in writing! I hope you'll excuse it this once, dear Ned, and not scold me, now I've come so many, many miles!'

'This means Mr Mop Ollamoor, I reckon!' said Hipcroft, gazing palely at them from the distance of the yard or two to which he had withdrawn with a start.

Car'line gasped. 'But he's been gone away for years!' she supplicated. 'And I never had a young man before! And I was so onlucky to be catched the first time he took advantage o' me, though some of the girls down there go on like anything!'

Ned remained in silence, pondering.

'You'll forgive me, dear Ned?' she added, beginning to sob outright. 'I haven't taken 'ee in after all, because – because you can pack us back again, if you want to; though 'tis hundreds o' miles, and so wet, and night a-coming on, and I with no money!'

'What the devil can I do!' Hipcroft groaned.

A more pitiable picture than the pair of helpless creatures presented was never seen on a rainy day, as they stood on the great, gaunt, puddled platform, a whiff of drizzle blowing under the roof upon them now and then; the pretty attire in which they had started from Stickleford in the early morning bemuddled and sodden, weariness on their faces, and fear of him in their eyes; for the child began to look as if she thought she too had done some wrong, remaining in an appalled silence till the tears rolled down her chubby cheeks.

'What's the matter, my little maid?' said Ned mechanically.

'I do want to go home!' she let out, in tones that told of a bursting heart. 'And my totties* be cold, an' I shan't have no bread an' butter no more!'

'I don't know what to say to it all!' declared Ned, his own eye moist as he turned and walked a few steps with his head down;

then regarded them again point-blank. From the child escaped troubled breaths and silently welling tears.

'Want some bread and butter, do 'ee?' he said, with factitious hardness.

'Ye – e – s!'

'Well, I dare say I can get 'ee a bit! Naturally, you must want some. And you, too, for that matter, Car'line.'

'I do feel a little hungered. But I can keep it off,' she murmured.

'Folk shouldn't do that,' he said gruffly. . . . 'There, come along!' He caught up the child, as he added, 'You must bide here tonight, anyhow, I s'pose! What can you do otherwise? I'll get 'ee some tea and victuals; and as for this job, I'm sure I don't know what to say! This is the way out.'

They pursued their way, without speaking, to Ned's lodgings, which were not far off. There he dried them and made them comfortable, and prepared tea; they thankfully sat down. The ready-made household of which he suddenly found himself the head imparted a cosy aspect to his room, and a paternal one to himself. Presently he turned to the child and kissed her now blooming cheeks; and, looking wistfully at Car'line, kissed her also.

'I don't see how I can send you back all them miles,' he growled, 'now you've come all the way o' purpose to join me. But you must trust me, Car'line, and show you've real faith in me. Well, do you feel better now, my little woman?'

The child nodded beamingly, her mouth being otherwise occupied.

'I did trust you, Ned, in coming; and I shall always!'

Thus, without any definite agreement to forgive her, he tacitly acquiesced in the fate that Heaven had sent him; and on the day of their marriage (which was not quite so soon as he had expected it could be, on account of the time necessary for banns) he took her to the Exhibition when they came back from church, as he had promised. While standing near a large mirror in one of the courts devoted to furniture, Car'line started, for in the glass appeared the reflection of a form exactly resembling Mop Ollamoor's – so exactly, that it seemed impossible to believe anybody but that artist in person to be the original. On passing round the objects which hemmed in Ned, her, and the child from a direct view, no Mop was to be seen. Whether he were

really in London or not at that time was never known; and
Car'line always stoutly denied that her readiness to go and meet
Ned in town arose from any rumour that Mop had also gone
thither; which denial there was no reasonable ground for
doubting.

And then the year glided away, and the Exhibition folded
itself up and became a thing of the past. The park trees that had
been enclosed for six months were again exposed to the winds
and storms, and the sod grew green anew. Ned found that
Car'line resolved herself into a very good wife and companion,
though she had made herself what is called cheap to him; but in
that she was like another domestic article, a cheap tea-pot,
which often brews better tea than a dear one. One autumn
Hipcroft found himself with but little work to do, and a prospect
of less for the winter. Both being country born and bred, they
fancied they would like to live again in their natural atmosphere.
It was accordingly decided between them that they should leave
the pent-up London lodging, and that Ned should seek out
employment near his native place, his wife and her daughter
staying with Car'line's father during the search for occupation
and an abode of their own.

Tinglings of pride pervaded Car'line's spasmodic little frame
as she journeyed down with Ned to the place she had left two
or three years before, in silence and under a cloud. To return to
where she had once been despised, a smiling London wife with
a distinct London accent, was a triumph which the world did
not witness every day.

The train did not stop at the petty roadside station that lay
nearest to Stickleford, and the trio went on to Casterbridge. Ned
thought it a good opportunity to make a few preliminary
inquiries for employment at workshops in the borough where
he had been known; and feeling cold from her journey, and it
being dry underfoot and only dusk as yet, with a moon on the
point of rising, Car'line and her little girl walked on toward
Stickleford, leaving Ned to follow at a quicker pace, and pick
her up at a certain half-way house, widely known as an inn.

The woman and child pursued the well-remembered way
comfortably enough, though they were both becoming wearied.
In the course of three miles they had passed Heedless-William's
Pond, the familiar landmark by Bloom's End, and were drawing
near the Quiet Woman, a lone roadside hostel on the lower

verge of the Egdon Heath, since and for many years abolished. In stepping up towards it Car'line heard more voices within than had formerly been customary at such an hour, and she learned that an auction of fat stock had been held near the spot that afternoon. The child would be the better for a rest as well as herself, she thought, and she entered.

The guests and customers overflowed into the passage, and Car'line had no sooner crossed the threshold than a man whom she remembered by sight came forward with a glass and mug in his hands towards a friend leaning against the wall; but, seeing her, very gallantly offered her a drink of the liquor, which was gin-and-beer hot, pouring her out a tumblerful and saying, in a moment or two: 'Surely, 'tis little Car'line Aspent that was – down at Stickleford?'

She assented, and, though she did not exactly want this beverage, she drank it since it was offered, and her entertainer begged her to come in further and sit down. Once within the room she found that all the persons present were seated close against the walls, and there being a chair vacant she did the same. An explanation of their position occurred the next moment. In the opposite corner stood Mop, rosining his bow and looking just the same as ever. The company had cleared the middle of the room for dancing, and they were about to dance again. As she wore a veil to keep off the wind she did not think he had recognized her, or could possibly guess the identity of the child; and to her satisfied surprise she found that she could confront him quite calmly – mistress of herself in the dignity her London life had given her. Before she had quite emptied her glass the dance was called, the dancers formed in two lines, the music sounded, and the figure began.

Then matters changed for Car'line. A tremor quickened itself to life in her, and her hand so shook that she could hardly set down her glass. It was not the dance nor the dancers, but the notes of that old violin which thrilled the London wife, these having still all the witchery that she had so well known of yore, and under which she had used to lose her power of independent will. How it all came back! There was the fiddling figure against the wall; the large, oily, mop-like head of him, and beneath the mop the face with closed eyes.

After the first moments of paralyzed reverie the familiar tune in the familiar rendering made her laugh and shed tears simultaneously. Then a man at the bottom of the dance, whose partner had dropped away, stretched out his hand and beckoned to her to take the place. She did not want to dance; she entreated by signs to be left where she was, but she was entreating of the tune and its player rather than of the dancing man. The saltatory tendency which the fiddler and his cunning instrument had ever been able to start in her was seizing Car'line just as it had done in earlier years, possibly assisted by the gin-and-beer hot. Tired as she was she grasped her little girl by the hand, and plunging in at the bottom of the figure, whirled about with the rest. She found that her companions were mostly people of the neighbouring hamlets and farms – Bloom's End, Mellstock, Lewgate, and elsewhere; and by degrees she was recognized as she convulsively danced on, wishing that Mop would cease and let her heart rest from the aching he caused, and her feet also.

After long and many minutes the dance ended, when she was urged to fortify herself with more gin-and-beer; which she did, feeling very weak and overpowered with hysteric emotion. She refrained from unveiling, to keep Mop in ignorance of her presence, if possible. Several of the guests having left, Car'line hastily wiped her lips and also turned to go; but, according to the account of some who remained, at that very moment a five-handed reel was proposed, in which two or three begged her to join.

She declined on the plea of being tired and having to walk to Stickleford, when Mop began aggressively tweedling 'My Fancy-Lad',* in D major, as the air to which the reel was to be footed. He must have recognized her, though she did not know it, for it was the strain of all seductive strains which she was least able to resist – the one he had played when she was leaning over the bridge at the date of their first acquaintance. Car'line stepped despairingly into the middle of the room with the other four.

Reels were resorted to hereabouts at this time by the more robust spirits, for the reduction of superfluous energy which the ordinary figure-dances were not powerful enough to exhaust. As everybody knows, or does not know, the five reelers stood in the form of a cross, the reel being performed by each line of three alternately, the persons who successively came to the middle place dancing in both directions. Car'line soon found herself in this place, the axis of the whole performance, and could not get out of it, the tune turning into the first part without giving her opportunity. And now she began to suspect that Mop did know her, and was doing this on purpose, though whenever she stole a glance at him his closed eyes betokened obliviousness to everything outside his own brain. She continued to wend her way through the figure of 8 that was formed by her course, the fiddler introducing into his notes the wild and agonizing sweetness of a living voice in one too highly wrought; its pathos running high and running low in endless variation, projecting through her nerves excruciating spasms, a sort of blissful torture. The room swam, the tune was endless; and in about a quarter of an hour the only other woman in the figure dropped out exhausted, and sank panting on a bench.

The reel instantly resolved itself into a four-handed one. Car'line would have given anything to leave off; but she had, or fancied she had, no power, while Mop played such tunes; and thus another ten minutes slipped by, a haze of dust now clouding the candles, the floor being of stone, sanded. Then another dancer fell out – one of the men – and went into the passage in a frantic search for liquor. To turn the figure into a three-handed reel was the work of a second, Mop modulating at the same time into 'The Fairy Dance',* as better suited to the contracted movement, and no less one of those foods of love* which, as manufactured by his bow, had always intoxicated her.

In a reel for three there was no rest whatever, and four or five minutes were enough to make her remaining two partners, now thoroughly blown, stamp their last bar, and, like their predecessors, limp off into the next room to get something to drink. Car'line, half-stifled inside her veil, was left dancing alone, the apartment now being empty of everybody save herself, Mop, and their little girl.

She flung up the veil, and cast her eyes upon him, as if imploring him to withdraw himself and his acoustic magnetism from the atmosphere. Mop opened one of his own orbs, as though for the first time, fixed it peeringly upon her, and smiling dreamily, threw into his strains the reserve of expression which he could not afford to waste on a big and noisy dance. Crowds of little chromatic subtleties, capable of drawing tears from a statue, proceeded straightway from the ancient fiddle, as if it were dying of the emotion which had been pent up within it

ever since its banishment from some Italian or German city
where it first took shape and sound. There was that in the look
of Mop's one dark eye which said: 'You cannot leave off, dear,
whether you would or no!' and it bred in her a paroxysm of
desperation that defied him to tire her down.

She thus continued to dance alone, defiantly as she thought,
but in truth slavishly and abjectly, subject to every wave of the
melody, and probed by the gimlet-like gaze of her fascinator's
open eye; keeping up at the same time a feeble smile in his face,
as a feint to signify it was still her own pleasure which led her
on. A terrified embarrassment as to what she could say to him if
she were to leave off, had its unrecognized share in keeping her
going. The child, who was beginning to be distressed by the
strange situation, came up and whimpered: 'Stop, mother, stop,
and let's go home!' as she seized Car'line's hand.

Suddenly Car'line sank staggering to the floor; and rolling
over on her face, prone she remained. Mop's fiddle thereupon
emitted an elfin shriek of finality; stepping quickly down from
the nine-gallon beer-cask which had formed his rostrum, he
went to the little girl, who disconsolately bent over her mother.

The guests who had gone into the back-room for liquor and
change of air, hearing something unusual, trooped back hitherward, where they endeavoured to revive poor, weak Car'line by
blowing her with the bellows and opening the window. Ned,
her husband, who had been detained in Casterbridge, as aforesaid, came along the road at this juncture, and hearing excited
voices through the open casement, and to his great surprise, the
mention of his wife's name, he entered amid the rest upon the
scene. Car'line was now in convulsions, weeping violently, and
for a long time nothing could be done with her. While he was
sending for a cart to take her onward to Stickleford Hipcroft
anxiously inquired how it had all happened; and then the
assembly explained that a fiddler formerly known in the locality
had lately visited his old haunts, and had taken upon himself
without invitation to play that evening at the inn and raise a
dance.

Ned demanded the fiddler's name, and they said Ollamoor.

'Ah!' exclaimed Ned, looking round him. 'Where is he, and
where – where's my little girl?'

Ollamoor had disappeared, and so had the child. Hipcroft
was in ordinary a quiet and tractable fellow, but a determination

which was to be feared settled in his face now. 'Blast him!' he cried. 'I'll beat his skull in for'n, if I swing for it tomorrow!'

He had rushed to the poker which lay on the hearth, and hastened down the passage, the people following. Outside the house, on the other side of the highway, a mass of dark heathland rose sullenly upward to its not easily accessible interior, a ravined plateau, whereon jutted into the sky, at the distance of a couple of miles, the fir-woods of Mistover backed by the Yalbury coppices – a place of Dantesque* gloom at this hour, which would have afforded secure hiding for a battery of artillery, much less a man and a child.

Some other men plunged thitherward with him, and more went along the road. They were gone about twenty minutes altogether, returning without result to the inn. Ned sat down in the settle, and clasped his forehead with his hands.

'Well – what a fool the man is, and hev been all these years, if he thinks the child his, as a' do seem to!' they whispered. 'And everybody else knowing otherwise!'

'No, I don't think 'tis mine!' cried Ned hoarsely, as he looked up from his hands. 'But she *is* mine, all the same! Ha'n't I nussed her? Ha'n't I fed her and teached her? Ha'n't I played wi' her? O, little Carry – gone with that rogue – gone!'

'You ha'n't lost your mis'ess, anyhow,' they said to console him. 'She's throwed up the sperrits, and she is feeling better, and she's more to 'ee than a child that isn't yours.'

'She isn't! She's not so particular much to me, especially now she's lost the little maid! But Carry's the whole world to me!'

'Well, ver' like you'll find her tomorrow.'

'Ah – but shall I? Yet he *can't* hurt her – surely he can't! Well – how's Car'line now? I am ready. Is the cart here?'

She was lifted into the vehicle, and they sadly lumbered on toward Stickleford. Next day she was calmer; but the fits were still upon her; and her will seemed shattered. For the child she appeared to show singularly little anxiety, though Ned was nearly distracted by his passionate paternal love for a child not his own. It was nevertheless quite expected that the impish Mop would restore the lost one after a freak of a day or two; but time went on, and neither he nor she could be heard of, and Hipcroft murmured that perhaps he was exercising upon her some unholy musical charm, as he had done upon Car'line herself. Weeks passed, and still they could obtain no clue either to the fiddler's whereabouts or to the girl's; and how he could have induced her to go with him remained a mystery.

Then Ned, who had obtained only temporary employment in the neighbourhood, took a sudden hatred toward his native district, and a rumour reaching his ears through the police that a somewhat similar man and child had been seen at a fair near London, he playing a violin, she dancing on stilts, a new interest in the capital took possession of Hipcroft with an intensity which would scarcely allow him time to pack before returning thither. He did not, however, find the lost one, though he made it the entire business of his over-hours to stand about in by-streets in the hope of discovering her, and would start up in the night, saying, 'That rascal's torturing her to maintain him!' To which his wife would answer peevishly, 'Don't 'ee raft* yourself so, Ned! You prevent my getting a bit o' rest! He won't hurt her!' and fall asleep again.

That Carry and her father had emigrated to America was the general opinion; Mop, no doubt, finding the girl a highly desirable companion when he had trained her to keep him by her earnings as a dancer. There, for that matter, they may be perfoming in some capacity now, though he must be an old scamp verging on three-score-and-ten, and she a woman of four-and-forty.

AN IMAGINATIVE WOMAN

When William Marchmill had finished his inquiries for lodgings at the well-known watering-place of Solentsea in Upper Wessex, he returned to the hotel to find his wife. She, with the children, had rambled along the shore, and Marchmill followed in the direction indicated by the military-looking hall-porter.

'By Jove,* how far you've gone! I am quite out of breath,' Marchmill said, rather impatiently, when he came up with his wife, who was reading as she walked, the three children being considerably further ahead with the nurse.

Mrs Marchmill started out of the reverie into which the book had thrown her. 'Yes,' she said, 'you've been such a long time. I was tired of staying in that dreary hotel. But I am sorry if you have wanted me, Will?'

'Well, I have had trouble to suit myself. When you see the airy and comfortable rooms heard of, you find they are stuffy and uncomfortable. Will you come and see if what I've fixed on will do? There is not much room, I am afraid; but I can light on nothing better. The town is rather full.'

The pair left the children and nurse to continue their ramble, and went back together.

In age well-balanced, in personal appearance fairly matched, and in domestic requirements conformable, in temper this couple differed, though even here they did not often clash, he being equable, if not lymphatic,* and she decidedly nervous and sanguine. It was to their tastes and fancies, those smallest, greatest particulars, that no common denominator could be applied. Marchmill considered his wife's likes and inclinations somewhat silly; she considered his sordid and material. The husband's business was that of a gunmaker in a thriving city northwards, and his soul was in that business always; the lady was best characterized by that superannuated phrase of elegance 'a votary of the muse'.* An impressionable, palpitating creature was Ella, shrinking humanely from detailed knowledge of her husband's trade whenever she reflected that everything he manufactured had for its purpose the destruction of life. She could only recover her equanimity by assuring herself that some, at least, of his weapons were sooner or later used for the extermination of horrid vermin and animals almost as cruel to their inferiors in species as human beings were to theirs.

She had never antecedently regarded this occupation of his as any objection to having him for a husband. Indeed, the necessity of getting life-leased at all cost, a cardinal virtue which all good mothers teach, kept her from thinking of it at all till she had closed with William, had passed the honeymoon, and reached the reflecting stage. Then, like a person who has stumbled upon some object in the dark, she wondered what she had got; mentally walked round it,* estimated it; whether it were rare or common; contained gold, silver, or lead; were a clog or a pedestal, everything to her or nothing.

She came to some vague conclusions, and since then had kept her heart alive by pitying her proprietor's* obtuseness and want of refinement, pitying herself, and letting off her delicate and ethereal emotions in imaginative occupations, day-dreams, and night-sighs, which perhaps would not much have disturbed William if he had known of them.

Her figure was small, elegant, and slight in build, tripping, or rather bounding, in movement. She was dark-eyed, and had that marvellously bright and liquid sparkle in each pupil which characterizes persons of Ella's cast of soul, and is too often a cause of heartache to the possessor's male friends, ultimately sometimes to herself. Her husband was a tall, long-featured man, with a brown beard; he had a pondering regard; and was, it must be added, usually kind and tolerant to her. He spoke in squarely shaped sentences, and was supremely satisfied with a condition of sublunary things which made weapons a necessity.

Husband and wife walked till they had reached the house they were in search of, which stood in a terrace facing the sea, and was fronted by a small garden of wind-proof and salt-proof evergreens, stone steps leading up to the porch. It had its number in the row, but, being rather larger than the rest, was in addition sedulously distinguished as Coburg House by its landlady, though everybody else called it 'Thirteen, New Parade'. The spot was bright and lively now; but in winter it became necessary to place sandbags against the door, and to stuff up the keyhole against the wind and rain, which had worn the paint so thin that the priming and knotting showed through.

The householder, who had been watching for the gentleman's return, met them in the passage, and showed the rooms. She informed them that she was a professional man's widow, left in needy circumstances by the rather sudden death of her husband, and she spoke anxiously of the conveniences of the establishment.

Mrs Marchmill said that she liked the situation and the house; but, it being small, there would not be accommodation enough, unless she could have all the rooms.

The landlady mused with an air of disappointment. She wanted the visitors to be her tenants very badly, she said, with obvious honesty. But unfortunately two of the rooms were occupied permanently by a bachelor gentleman. He did not pay season prices, it was true; but as he kept on his apartments all the year round, and was an extremely nice and interesting young man, who gave no trouble, she did not like to turn him out for a month's 'let', even at a high figure. 'Perhaps, however,' she added, 'he might offer to go for a time.'

They would not hear of this, and went back to the hotel, intending to proceed to the agent's to inquire further. Hardly had they sat down to tea when the landlady called. Her gentleman, she said, had been so obliging as to offer to give up his rooms for three or four weeks rather than drive the new-comers away.

'It is very kind, but we won't inconvenience him in that way,' said the Marchmills.

'O, it won't inconvenience him, I assure you!' said the landlady eloquently. 'You see, he's a different sort of young man from most – dreamy, solitary, rather melancholy – and he cares more to be here when the south-westerly gales are beating against the door, and the sea washes over the Parade, and there's not a soul in the place, than he does now in the season. He'd just as soon be where, in fact, he's going temporarily, to a little cottage on the Island opposite, for a change.' She hoped therefore that they would come.

The Marchmill family accordingly took possession of the house next day, and it seemed to suit them very well. After luncheon Mr Marchmill strolled out towards the pier, and Mrs Marchmill, having despatched the children to their outdoor amusements on the sands, settled herself in more completely, examining this and that article; and testing the reflecting powers of the mirror in the wardrobe door.

In the small back sitting-room, which had been the young bachelor's, she found furniture of a more personal nature than in the rest. Shabby books, of correct rather than rare editions, were piled up in a queerly reserved manner in corners, as if the previous occupant had not conceived the possibility that any incoming person of the season's bringing could care to look inside them. The landlady hovered on the threshold to rectify anything that Mrs Marchmill might not find to her satisfaction.

'I'll make this my own little room,' said the latter, 'because the books are here. By the way, the person who has left seems to have a good many. He won't mind my reading some of them, Mrs Hooper, I hope?'

'O dear no, ma'am. Yes, he has a good many. You see, he is in the literary line himself somewhat. He is a poet – yes, really a poet – and he has a little income of his own, which is enough to write verses on, but not enough for cutting a figure, even if he cared to.'

'A poet! O, I did not know that.'

Mrs Marchmill opened one of the books, and saw the owner's name written on the title-page. 'Dear me!' she continued; 'I know his name very well – Robert Trewe – of course I do; and his writings! And it is *his* rooms we have taken, and *him* we have turned out of his home?'

Ella Marchmill, sitting down alone a few minutes later, thought with interested surprise of Robert Trewe. Her own latter history will best explain that interest. Herself the only daughter of a struggling man of letters, she had during the last year or two taken to writing poems, in an endeavour to find a congenial channel in which to let flow her painfully embayed* emotions, whose former limpidity and sparkle seemed departing in the stagnation caused by the routine of a practical household and the gloom of bearing children to a commonplace father. These poems, subscribed with a masculine pseudonym, had appeared in various obscure magazines, and in two cases in rather prominent ones. In the second of the latter the page which bore her effusion at the bottom, in smallish print, bore at the top, in large print, a few verses on the same subject by this very man, Robert Trewe. Both of them had, in fact, been struck by a tragic incident reported in the daily papers, and had used it simultaneously as an inspiration, the editor remarking in a note upon the coincidence, and that the excellence of both poems prompted him to give them together.

After that event Ella, otherwise 'John Ivy', had watched with much attention the appearance anywhere in print of verse bearing the signature of Robert Trewe, who, with a man's unsusceptibility on the question of sex, had never once thought of passing himself off as a woman. To be sure, Mrs Marchmill had satisfied herself with a sort of reason for doing the contrary in her case; since nobody might believe in her inspiration if they found that the sentiments came from a pushing tradesman's wife, from the mother of three children by a matter-of-fact small-arms manufacturer.

Trewe's verse contrasted with that of the rank and file of recent minor poets in being impassioned rather than ingenious, luxuriant rather than finished. Neither *symboliste* nor *décadent*,* he was a pessimist in so far as that character applies to a man who looks at the worst contingencies as well as the best in the human condition. Being little attracted by excellences of form and rhythm apart from content, he sometimes, when feeling outran his artistic speed, perpetrated sonnets in the loosely rhymed Elizabethan fashion,* which every right-minded reviewer said he ought not to have done.

With sad and hopeless envy Ella Marchmill had often and often scanned the rival poet's work, so much stronger as it always was than her own feeble lines. She had imitated him, and her inability to touch his level would send her into fits of despondency. Months passed away thus, till she observed from the publishers' list that Trewe had collected his fugitive pieces into a volume, which was duly issued, and was much or little praised according to chance, and had a sale quite sufficient to pay for the printing.

This step onward had suggested to John Ivy the idea of collecting her pieces also, or at any rate of making up a book of her rhymes by adding many in manuscript to the few that had seen the light, for she had been able to get no great number into print. A ruinous charge was made for costs of publication; a few reviews noticed her poor little volume; but nobody talked of it, nobody bought it, and it fell dead in a fortnight – if it had ever been alive.

The author's thoughts were diverted to another groove just then by the discovery that she was going to have a third child, and the collapse of her poetical venture had perhaps less effect upon her mind than it might have done if she had been domestically unoccupied. Her husband had paid the publisher's bill with the doctor's, and there it all had ended for the time. But, though less than a poet of her century, Ella was more than a mere multiplier of her kind, and latterly she had begun to feel the old afflatus* once more. And now by an odd conjunction she found herself in the rooms of Robert Trewe.

She thoughtfully rose from her chair and searched the apartment with the interest of a fellow-tradesman. Yes, the volume of his own verse was among the rest. Though quite familiar with its contents, she read it here as if it spoke aloud to her, then called up Mrs Hooper, the landlady, for some trivial service, and inquired again about the young man.

'Well, I'm sure you'd be interested in him, ma'am, if you could see him, only he's so shy that I don't suppose you will.' Mrs Hooper seemed nothing loth to minister to her tenant's curiosity about her predecessor. 'Lived here long? Yes, nearly two years. He keeps on his rooms even when he's not here: the soft air of this place suits his chest, and he likes to be able to come back at any time. He is mostly writing or reading, and doesn't see many people, though, for the matter of that, he is such a good, kind young fellow that folks would only be too glad to be friendly with him if they knew him. You don't meet kind-hearted people every day.'

'Ah, he's kind-hearted . . . and good.'

'Yes; he'll oblige me in anything if I ask him. "Mr Trewe," I say to him sometimes, "you are rather out of spirits." "Well, I am, Mrs Hooper," he'll say, "though I don't know how you should find it out." "Why not take a little change?" I ask. Then in a day or two he'll say that he will take a trip to Paris, or Norway, or somewhere; and I assure you he comes back all the better for it.'

'Ah, indeed! His is a sensitive nature, no doubt.'

'Yes. Still he's odd in some things. Once when he had finished a poem of his composition late at night he walked up and down the room rehearsing it; and the floors being so thin – jerry-built houses, you know, though I say it myself – he kept me awake up above him till I wished him further. . . . But we get on very well.'

This was but the beginning of a series of conversations about the rising poet as the days went on. On one of these occasions Mrs Hooper drew Ella's attention to what she had not noticed before: minute scribblings in pencil on the wall-paper behind the curtains at the head of the bed.

'O! let me look,' said Mrs Marchmill, unable to conceal a rush of tender curiosity as she bent her pretty face close to the wall.

'These,' said Mrs Hooper, with the manner of a woman who knew things, 'are the very beginnings and first thoughts of his verses. He has tried to rub most of them out, but you can read them still. My belief is that he wakes up in the night, you know, with some rhyme in his head, and jots it down there on the wall lest he should forget it by the morning. Some of these very lines you see here I have seen afterwards in print in the magazines. Some are newer; indeed, I have not seen that one before. It must have been done only a few days ago.'

'O yes! . . .'

Ella Marchmill flushed without knowing why, and suddenly wished her companion would go away, now that the information was imparted. An indescribable consciousness of personal interest rather than literary made her anxious to read the inscription alone; and she accordingly waited till she could do so, with a sense that a great store of emotion would be enjoyed in the act.

Perhaps because the sea was choppy outside the Island, Ella's husband found it much pleasanter to go sailing and steaming about without his wife, who was a bad sailor, than with her. He did not disdain to go thus alone on board the steamboats of the cheap-trippers, where there was dancing by moonlight, and where the couples would come suddenly down with a lurch into each other's arms; for, as he blandly told her, the company was too mixed for him to take her amid such scenes. Thus, while this thriving manufacturer got a great deal of change and sea-air out of his sojourn here, the life, external at least, of Ella was monotonous enough, and mainly consisted in passing a certain number of hours each day in bathing and walking up and down a stretch of shore. But the poetic impulse having again waxed strong, she was possessed by an inner flame which left her hardly conscious of what was proceeding around her.

She had read till she knew by heart Trewe's last little volume of verses, and spent a great deal of time in vainly attempting to rival some of them, till, in her failure, she burst into tears. The personal element in the magnetic attraction exercised by this circumambient,* unapproachable master of hers was so much stronger than the intellectual and abstract that she could not understand it. To be sure, she was surrounded noon and night by his customary environment, which literally whispered of him to her at every moment; but he was a man she had never seen, and that all that moved her was the instinct to specialize a waiting emotion on the first fit thing that came to hand did not, of course, suggest itself to Ella.

In the natural way of passion under too pratical conditions which civilization has devised for its fruition, her husband's love for her had not survived, except in the form of fitful friendship, any more than, or even so much as, her own for him; and, being a woman of very living ardours, that required sustenance of some sort, they were beginning to feed on this chancing material, which was, indeed, of a quality far better than chance usually offers.

One day the children had been playing hide-and-seek in a closet, whence, in their excitement, they pulled out some clothing. Mrs Hooper explained that it belonged to Mr Trewe, and hung it up in the closet again. Possessed of her fantasy, Ella went later in the afternoon, when nobody was in that part of the house, opened the closet, unhitched one of the articles, a mackintosh, and put it on, with the waterproof cap belonging to it.

'The mantle of Elijah!'* she said. 'Would it might inspire me to rival him, glorious genius that he is!'

Her eyes always grew wet when she thought like that, and she turned to look at herself in the glass. *His* heart had beat inside that coat, and *his* brain had worked under that hat at levels of thought she would never reach. The consciousness of her weakness beside him made her feel quite sick. Before she had got the things off her the door opened, and her husband entered the room.

'What the devil – '

She blushed, and removed them.

'I found them in the closet here,' she said, 'and put them on in a freak. What have I else to do? You are always away!'

'Always away? Well . . .'

That evening she had a further talk with the landlady, who might herself have nourished a half-tender regard for the poet, so ready was she to discourse ardently about him.

'You are interested in Mr Trewe, I know, ma'am,' she said; 'and he has just sent to say that he is going to call tomorrow afternoon to look up some books of his that he wants, if I'll be in, and he may select them from your room?'

'O yes!'

'You could very well meet Mr Trewe then, if you'd like to be in the way!'

She promised with secret delight, and went to bed musing of him.

Next morning her husband observed: 'I've been thinking of what you said, Ell: that I have gone about a good deal and left you without much to amuse you. Perhaps it's true. Today, as there's not much sea, I'll take you with me on board the yacht.'

For the first time in her experience of such an offer Ella was not glad. But she accepted it for the moment. The time for setting out drew near, and she went to get ready. She stood reflecting. The longing to see the poet she was now distinctly in love with overpowered all other considerations.

'I don't want to go,' she said to herself. 'I can't bear to be away! And I won't go.'

She told her husband that she had changed her mind about wishing to sail. He was indifferent, and went his way.

For the rest of the day the house was quiet, the children having gone out upon the sands. The blinds waved in the sunshine to the soft, steady stroke of the sea beyond the wall; and the notes of the Green Silesian band,* a troop of foreign gentlemen hired for the season, had drawn almost all the residents and promenaders away from the vicinity of Coburg House. A knock was audible at the door.

Mrs Marchmill did not hear any servant go to answer it, and she became impatient. The books were in the room where she sat; but nobody came up. She rang the bell.

'There is some person waiting at the door,' she said.

'O no, ma'am! He's gone long ago. I answered it,' the servant replied, and Mrs Hooper came in herself.

'So disappointing!' she said. 'Mr Trewe not coming after all!'

'But I heard him knock, I fancy!'

'No; that was somebody inquiring for lodgings who came to the wrong house. I forgot to tell you that Mr Trewe sent a note just before lunch to say I needn't get any tea for him, as he should not require the books, and wouldn't come to select them.'

Ella was miserable, and for a long time could not even re-read his mournful ballad on 'Severed Lives',* so aching was her erratic little heart, and so tearful her eyes. When the children came in with wet stockings, and ran up to her to tell her of their adventures, she could not feel that she cared about them half as much as usual.

'Mrs Hooper, have you a photograph of – the gentleman who lived here?' She was getting to be curiously shy in mentioning his name.

'Why, yes. It's in the ornamental frame on the mantelpiece in your own bedroom, ma'am.'

'No; the Royal Duke and Duchess are in that.'

'Yes, so they are; but he's behind them. He belongs rightly to that frame, which I bought on purpose; but as he went away he said: "Cover me up from those strangers that are coming, for God's sake. I don't want them staring at me, and I am sure they won't want me staring at them." So I slipped in the Duke and Duchess temporarily in front of him, as they had no frame, and Royalties are more suitable for letting furnished than a private young man. If you take 'em out you'll see him under. Lord, ma'am, he wouldn't mind if he knew it! He didn't think the next tenant would be such an attractive lady as you, or he wouldn't have thought of hiding himself, perhaps.'

'Is he handsome?' she asked timidly.

'*I* call him so. Some, perhaps, wouldn't.'

'Should I?' she asked, with eagerness.

'I think you would, though some would say he's more striking than handsome; a large-eyed thoughtful fellow, you know, with a very electric flash in his eye when he looks round quickly, such as you'd expect a poet to be who doesn't get his living by it.'

'How old is he?'

'Several years older than yourself, ma'am; about thirty-one or two, I think.'

Ella was, as a matter of fact, a few months over thirty herself; but she did not look nearly so much. Though so immature in nature, she was entering on that tract of life in which emotional women begin to suspect that last love may be stronger than first love; and she would soon, alas, enter on the still more melancholy tract when at least the vainer ones of her sex shrink from receiving a male visitor otherwise than with their backs to the window or the blinds half down. She reflected on Mrs Hooper's remark, and said no more about age.

Just then a telegram was brought up. It came from her husband, who had gone down the Channel as far as Budmouth with his friends in the yacht, and would not be able to get back till next day.

After her light dinner Ella idled about the shore with the children till dusk, thinking of the yet uncovered photograph in her room, with a serene sense of something ecstatic to come. For, with the subtle luxuriousness of fancy in which this young woman was an adept, on learning that her husband was to be absent that night she had refrained from incontinently rushing upstairs and opening the picture-frame, preferring to reserve the inspection till she could be alone, and a more romantic tinge be imparted to the occasion by silence, candles, solemn sea and stars outside, than was afforded by the garish afternoon sunlight.

The children had been sent to bed, and Ella soon followed, though it was not yet ten o'clock. To gratify her passionate curiosity she now made her preparations, first getting rid of superfluous garments and putting on her dressing-gown, then arranging a chair in front of the table and reading several pages of Trewe's tenderest utterances. Next she fetched the portrait-frame to the light, opened the back, took out the likeness, and set it up before her.

It was a striking countenance to look upon. The poet wore a luxuriant black moustache and imperial,* and a slouched hat which shaded the forehead. The large dark eyes described by the landlady showed an unlimited capacity for misery; they looked out from beneath well-shaped brows as if they were reading the universe in the microcosm of the confronter's face, and were not altogether overjoyed at what the spectacle portended.

Ella murmured in her lowest, richest, tenderest tone: 'And it's *you* who've so cruelly eclipsed me these many times!'

As she gazed long at the portrait she fell into thought, till her eyes filled with tears, and she touched the cardboard with her lips. Then she laughed with a nervous lightness, and wiped her eyes.

She thought how wicked she was, a woman having a husband and three children, to let her mind stray to a stranger in this unconscionable manner. No, he was not a stranger! She knew his thoughts and feelings as well as she knew her own; they were, in fact, the self-same thoughts and feelings as hers, which her husband distinctly lacked; perhaps luckily for himself, considering that he had to provide for family expenses.

'He's nearer my real self, he's more intimate with the real me than Will is, after all, even though I've never seen him,' she said.

She laid his book and picture on the table at the bedside, and when she was reclining on the pillow she re-read those of Robert Trewe's verses which she had marked from time to time as most touching and true. Putting these aside she set up the photograph on its edge upon the coverlet, and contemplated it as she lay. Then she scanned again by the light of the candle the half-obliterated pencillings on the wallpaper beside her head. There they were – phrases, couplets, *bouts-rimés*,* beginnings and middles of lines, ideas in the rough, like Shelley's scraps,* and the least of them so intense, so sweet, so palpitating, that it seemed as if his very breath, warm and loving, fanned her cheeks from those walls, walls that had surrounded his head times and times as they surrounded her own now. He must often have put up his hand so – with the pencil in it. Yes, the writing was sideways, as it would be if executed by one who extended his arm thus.

These inscribed shapes of the poet's world,

> Forms more real than living man,
> Nurslings of immortality,*

were, no doubt, the thoughts and spirit-strivings which had come to him in the dead of night, when he could let himself go and have no fear of the frost of criticism. No doubt they had often been written up hastily by the light of the moon, the rays of the lamp, in the blue-grey dawn, in full daylight perhaps never. And now her hair was dragging where his arm had lain when he secured the fugitive fancies; she was sleeping on a poet's lips,* immersed in the very essence of him, permeated by his spirit as by an ether.

While she was dreaming the minutes away thus, a footstep

came upon the stairs, and in a moment she heard her husband's heavy step on the landing immediately without.

'Ell, where are you?'

What possessed her she could not have described, but, with an instinctive objection to let her husband know what she had been doing, she slipped the photograph under the pillow just as he flung open the door with the air of a man who had dined not badly.

'O, I beg pardon,' said William Marchmill. 'Have you a headache? I am afraid I have disturbed you.'

'No, I've not got a headache,' said she. 'How is it you've come?'

'Well, we found we could get back in very good time after all, and I didn't want to make another day of it, because of going somewhere else tomorrow.'

'Shall I come down again?'

'O no. I'm as tired as a dog. I've had a good feed, and I shall turn in straight off. I want to get out at six o'clock tomorrow if I can. . . . I shan't disturb you by my getting up; it will be long before you are awake.' And he came forward into the room.

While her eyes followed his movements, Ella softly pushed the photograph further out of sight.

'Sure you're not ill?' he asked, bending over her.

'No, only wicked!'

'Never mind that.' And he stooped and kissed her. 'I wanted to be with you tonight.'

Next morning Marchmill was called at six o'clock; and in waking and yawning she heard him muttering to himself: 'What the deuce is this that's been crackling under me so?' Imagining her asleep he searched round him and withdrew something. Through her half-opened eyes she perceived it to be Mr Trewe.

'Well, I'm damned!' her husband exclaimed.

'What, dear?' said she.

'O, you are awake? Ha! ha!'

'What *do* you mean?'

'Some bloke's photograph – a friend of our landlady's, I suppose. I wonder how it came here; whisked off the mantel-piece by accident perhaps when they were making the bed.'

'I was looking at it yesterday, and it must have dropped in then.'

'O, he's a friend of yours? Bless his picturesque heart!'

OUTSIDE THE GATES OF THE WORLD

Ella's loyalty to the object of her admiration could not endure to hear him ridiculed. 'He's a clever man!' she said, with a tremor in her gentle voice which she herself felt to be absurdly uncalled for. 'He is a rising poet – the gentleman who occupied two of these rooms before we came, though I've never seen him.'

'How do you know, if you've never seen him?'

'Mrs Hooper told me when she showed me the photograph.'

'O, well, I must up and be off. I shall be home rather early. Sorry I can't take you today, dear. Mind the children don't go getting drowned.'

That day Mrs Marchmill inquired if Mr Trewe were likely to call at any other time.

'Yes,' said Mrs Hooper. 'He's coming this day week to stay with a friend near here till you leave. He'll be sure to call.'

Marchmill did return quite early in the afternoon; and, opening some letters which had arrived in his absence, declared suddenly that he and his family would have to leave a week earlier than they had expected to do – in short, in three days.

'Surely we can stay a week longer?' she pleaded. 'I like it here.'

'I don't. It is getting rather slow.'

'Then you might leave me and the children!'

'How perverse you are, Ell! What's the use? And have to come to fetch you! No: we'll all return together; and we'll make out our time in North Wales or Brighton a little later on. Besides, you've three days longer yet.'

It seemed to be her doom not to meet the man for whose rival talent she had a despairing admiration, and to whose person she was now absolutely attached. Yet she determined to make a last effort; and having gathered from her landlady that Trewe was living in a lonely spot not far from the fashionable town on the Island opposite, she crossed over in the packet from the neighbouring pier the following afternoon.

What a useless journey it was! Ella knew but vaguely where the house stood, and when she fancied she had found it, and ventured to inquire of a pedestrian if he lived there, the answer returned by the man was that he did not know. And if he did live there, how could she call upon him? Some women might have the assurance to do it, but she had not. How crazy he would think her. She might have asked him to call upon her, perhaps; but she had not the courage for that, either. She lingered mournfully about the picturesque seaside eminence till it was time to return to the town and enter the steamer for recrossing, reaching home for dinner without having been greatly missed.

At the last moment, unexpectedly enough, her husband said that he should have no objection to letting her and the children stay on till the end of the week, since she wished to do so, if she felt herself able to get home without him. She concealed the pleasure this extension of time gave her; and Marchmill went off the next morning alone.

But the week passed, and Trewe did not call.

On Saturday morning the remaining members of the March-mill family departed from the place which had been productive of so much fervour in her. The dreary, dreary train; the sun shining in moted beams upon the hot cushions; the dusty permanent way;* the mean rows of wire – these things were her accompaniment: while out of the window the deep blue sea-levels disappeared from her gaze, and with them her poet's home. Heavy-hearted, she tried to read, and wept instead.

Mr Marchmill was in a thriving way of business, and he and his family lived in a large new house, which stood in rather extensive grounds a few miles outside the midland city wherein he carried on his trade. Ella's life was lonely here, as the suburban life is apt to be, particularly at certain seasons; and she had ample time to indulge her taste for lyric and elegiac composition. She had hardly got back when she encountered a piece by Robert Trewe in the new number of her favourite magazine, which must have been written almost immediately before her visit to Solentsea, for it contained the very couplet she had seen pencilled on the wall-paper by the bed, and Mrs Hooper had declared to be recent. Ella could resist no longer, but seizing a pen impulsively, wrote to him as a brother-poet, using the name of John Ivy, congratulating him in her letter on his triumphant executions in metre and rhythm of thoughts that moved his soul, as compared with her own brow-beaten efforts in the same pathetic trade.

To this address there came a response in a few days, little as she had dared to hope for it – a civil and brief note, in which the young poet stated that, though he was not well acquainted with Mr Ivy's verse, he recalled the name as being one he had seen attached to some very promising pieces; that he was glad to gain Mr Ivy's acquaintance by letter, and should certainly look with much interest for his productions in the future.

There must have been something juvenile or timid in her own epistle, as one ostensibly coming from a man, she declared to herself; for Trewe quite adopted the tone of an elder and superior in this reply. But what did it matter? He had replied; he had written to her with his own hand from that very room she knew so well, for he was now back again in his quarters.

The correspondence thus begun was continued for two months or more, Ella Marchmill sending him from time to time some that she considered to be the best of her pieces, which he very kindly accepted, though he did not say he sedulously read them, nor did he send her any of his own in return. Ella would have been more hurt at this than she was if she had not known that Trewe laboured under the impression that she was one of his own sex.

Yet the situation was unsatisfactory. A flattering little voice told her that, were he only to see her, matters would be otherwise. No doubt she would have helped on this by making a frank confession of womanhood, to begin with, if something had not happened, to her delight, to render it unnecessary. A friend of her husband's, the editor of the most important newspaper in their city and county, who was dining with them one day, observed during their conversation about the poet that his (the editor's) brother the landscape-painter was a friend of Mr Trewe's, and that the two men were at that very moment in Wales together.

Ella was slightly acquainted with the editor's brother. The next morning down she sat and wrote, inviting him to stay at her house for a short time on his way back, and requesting him to bring with him, if practicable, his companion Mr Trewe, whose acquaintance she was anxious to make. The answer arrived after some few days. Her correspondent and his friend Trewe would have much satisfaction in accepting her invitation on their way southward, which would be on such and such a day in the following week.

Ella was blithe and buoyant. Her scheme had succeeded; her beloved though as yet unseen one was coming. 'Behold, he standeth behind our wall; he looked forth at the windows, showing himself through the lattice,' she thought ecstatically. 'And, lo, the winter is past, the rain is over and gone, the flowers appear on the earth, the time of the singing of birds is come, and the voice of the turtle is heard in our land.'*

But it was necessary to consider the details of lodging and feeding him. This she did most solicitously, and awaited the pregnant day and hour.

It was about five in the afternoon when she heard a ring at the door and the editor's brother's voice in the hall. Poetess as she was, or as she thought herself, she had not been too sublime that day to dress with infinite trouble in a fashionable robe of rich material, having a faint resemblance to the *chiton** of the Greeks, a style just then in vogue among ladies of an artistic and romantic turn, which had been obtained by Ella of her Bond Street dressmaker when she was last in London. Her visitor entered the drawing-room. She looked towards his rear; nobody else came through the door. Where, in the name of the God of Love, was Robert Trewe?

'O, I'm sorry,' said the painter, after their introductory words had been spoken. 'Trewe is a curious fellow, you know, Mrs Marchmill. He said he'd come; then he said he couldn't. He's rather dusty. We've been doing a few miles with knapsacks, you know; and he wanted to get on home.'

'He – he's not coming?'

'He's not; and he asked me to make his apologies.'

'When did you p-p-part from him?' she asked, her nether lip starting off quivering so much that it was like a *tremolo*-stop* opened in her speech. She longed to run away from this dreadful bore and cry her eyes out.

'Just now, in the turnpike-road yonder there.'

'What! he has actually gone past my gates?'

'Yes. When we got to them – handsome gates they are, too, the finest bit of modern wrought-iron work I have seen – when we came to them we stopped, talking there a little while, and then he wished me good-bye and went on. The truth is, he's a little bit depressed just now, and doesn't want to see anybody. He's a very good fellow, and a warm friend, but a little uncertain and gloomy sometimes; he thinks too much of things. His poetry is rather too erotic and passionate, you know, for some tastes; and he has just come in for a terrible slating from the —— *Review* that was published yesterday; he saw a copy of it at the station by accident. Perhaps you've read it?'

'No.'

'So much the better. O, it is not worth thinking of; just one of those articles written to order, to please the narrow-minded set of subscribers upon whom the circulation depends. But he's upset by it. He says it is the misrepresentation that hurts him so; that, though he can stand a fair attack, he can't stand lies that he's powerless to refute and stop from spreading. That's just Trewe's weak point. He lives so much by himself that these things affect him much more than they would if he were in the bustle of fashionable or commercial life. So he wouldn't come here, making the excuse that it all looked so new and monied – if you'll pardon – '

'But – he must have known – there was sympathy here! Has he never said anything about getting letters from this address?'

'Yes, yes, he has, from John Ivy – perhaps a relative of yours, he thought, visiting here at the time?'

'Did he – like Ivy, did he say?'

'Well, I don't know that he took any great interest in Ivy.'

'Or in his poems?'

'Or in his poems – so far as I know, that is.'

Robert Trewe took no interest in her house, in her poems, or in their writer. As soon as she could get away she went into the nursery and tried to let off her emotion by unnecessarily kissing the children, till she had a sudden sense of disgust at being reminded how plain-looking they were, like their father.

The obtuse and single-minded landscape-painter never once perceived from her conversation that it was only Trewe she wanted, and not himself. He made the best of his visit, seeming to enjoy the society of Ella's husband, who also took a great fancy to him, and showed him everywhere about the neighbourhood, neither of them noticing Ella's mood.

The painter had been gone only a day or two when, while sitting upstairs alone one morning, she glanced over the London paper just arrived, and read the following paragraph:–

SUICIDE OF A POET

Mr Robert Trewe, who has been favourably known for some years as one of our rising lyrists, committed suicide at his lodgings at Solentsea on Saturday evening last by shooting himself in the right temple with a revolver. Readers hardly need to be reminded that Mr Trewe has recently attracted the attention of a much wider public than had hitherto known him, by his new volume of verse, mostly of

AN IMAGINATIVE WOMAN   369

an impassioned kind, entitled 'Lyrics to a Woman Unknown', which
has been already favourably noticed in these pages for the extraordinary gamut of feeling it traverses, and which has been made the
subject of a severe, if not ferocious, criticism in the —— *Review*. It is
supposed, though not certainly known, that the article may have
partially conduced to the sad act, as a copy of the review in question
was found on his writing-table; and he has been observed to be in a
somewhat depressed state of mind since the critique appeared.

Then came the report of the inquest, at which the following letter was read, it having been addressed to a friend at a
distance: –

Dear——, – Before these lines reach your hands I shall be delivered
from the inconveniences of seeing, hearing, and knowing more of the
things around me. I will not trouble you by giving my reasons for
the step I have taken, though I can assure you they were sound and
logical. Perhaps had I been blessed with a mother, or a sister, or a
female friend of another sort tenderly devoted to me, I might have
thought it worth while to continue my present existence. I have long
dreamt of such an unattainable creature, as you know; and she, this
undiscoverable, elusive one, inspired my last volume; the imaginary
woman alone, for, in spite of what has been said in some quarters,
there is no real woman behind the title. She has continued to the last
unrevealed, unmet, unwon. I think it desirable to mention this in
order that no blame may attach to any real woman as having been
the cause of my decease by cruel or cavalier treatment of me. Tell my
landlady that I am sorry to have caused her this unpleasantness; but
my occupancy of the rooms will soon be forgotten. There are ample
funds in my name at the bank to pay all expenses.

                                                R. TREWE

Ella sat for a while as if stunned, then rushed into the
adjoining chamber and flung herself upon her face on the bed.
Her grief and distraction shook her to pieces; and she lay in
this frenzy of sorrow for more than an hour. Broken words
came every now and then from her quivering lips: 'O, if he had
only known of me – known of me – me! ... O, if I had only
once met him – only once; and put my hand upon his hot
forehead – kissed him – let him know how I loved him – that I
would have suffered shame and scorn, would have lived and
died, for him! Perhaps it would have saved his dear life! ... But

no – it was not allowed! God is a jealous God; and that happiness was not for him and me!'

All possibilities were over; the meeting was stultified. Yet it was almost visible to her in her fantasy even now, though it could never be substantiated –

> The hour which might have been, yet might not be,
> Which man's and woman's heart conceived and bore,
> Yet whereof life was barren.*

She wrote to the landlady at Solentsea in the third person, in as subdued a style as she could command, enclosing a postal order for a sovereign, and informing Mrs Hooper that Mrs Marchmill had seen in the papers the sad account of the poet's death, and having been, as Mrs Hooper was aware, much interested in Mr Trewe during her stay at Coburg House, she would be obliged if Mrs Hooper could obtain a small portion of his hair before his coffin was closed down, and send it her as a memorial of him, as also the photograph that was in the frame.

By the return-post a letter arrived containing what had been requested. Ella wept over the portrait and secured it in her private drawer; the lock of hair she tied with white ribbon and put in her bosom, whence she drew it and kissed it every now and then in some unobserved nook.

'What's the matter?' said her husband, looking up from his newspaper on one of these occasions. 'Crying over something? A lock of hair? Whose is it?'

'He's dead!' she murmured.

'Who?'

'I don't want to tell you, Will, just now, unless you insist!' she said, a sob hanging heavy in her voice.

'O, all right.'

'Do you mind my refusing? I will tell you some day.'

'It doesn't matter in the least, of course.'

He walked away whistling a few bars of no tune in particular; and when he had got down to his factory in the city the subject came into Marchmill's head again.

He, too, was aware that a suicide had taken place recently at the house they had occupied at Solentsea. Having seen the volume of poems in his wife's hand of late, and heard fragments of the landlady's conversation about Trewe when they were her tenants, he all at once said to himself, 'Why of course it's he! . . . How the devil did she get to know him? What sly animals women are!'

Then he placidly dismissed the matter, and went on with his daily affairs. By this time Ella at home had come to a determination. Mrs Hooper, in sending the hair and photograph, had informed her of the day of the funeral; and as the morning and noon wore on an overpowering wish to know where they were laying him took possession of the sympathetic woman. Caring very little now what her husband or any one else might think of her eccentricities, she wrote Marchmill a brief note, stating that she was called away for the afternoon and evening, but would return on the following morning. This she left on his desk, and having given the same information to the servants, went out of the house on foot.

When Mr Marchmill reached home early in the afternoon the servants looked anxious. The nurse took him privately aside, and hinted that her mistress's sadness during the past few days had been such that she feared she had gone out to drown herself. Marchmill reflected. Upon the whole he thought that she had not done that. Without saying whither he was bound he also started off, telling them not to sit up for him. He drove to the railway-station, and took a ticket for Solentsea.

It was dark when he reached the place, though he had come by a fast train, and he knew that if his wife had preceded him thither it could only have been by a slower train, arriving not a great while before his own. The season at Solentsea was now past: the parade was gloomy, and the flys were few and cheap. He asked the way to the Cemetery, and soon reached it. The gate was locked, but the keeper let him in, declaring, however, that there was nobody within the precincts. Although it was not late, the autumnal darkness had now become intense; and he found some difficulty in keeping to the serpentine path which led to the quarter where, as the man had told him, the one or two interments for the day had taken place. He stepped upon the grass, and, stumbling over some pegs, stooped now and then to discern if possible a figure against the sky. He could see none; but lighting on a spot where the soil was trodden, beheld a crouching object beside a newly made grave. She heard him, and sprang up.

'Ell, how silly this is!' he said indignantly. 'Running away from home – I never heard such a thing! Of course I am not jealous of this unfortunate man; but it is too ridiculous that you, a married woman with three children and a fourth coming, should go losing your head like this over a dead lover! ... Do you know you were locked in? You might not have been able to get out all night.'

She did not answer.

'I hope it didn't go far between you and him, for your own sake.'

'Don't insult me, Will.'

'Mind, I won't have any more of this sort of thing; do you hear?'

'Very well,' she said.

He drew her arm within his own, and conducted her out of the Cemetery. It was impossible to get back that night; and not wishing to be recognized in their present sorry condition he took her to a miserable little coffee-house close to the station, whence they departed early in the morning, travelling almost without speaking, under the sense that it was one of those dreary situations occurring in married life which words could not mend, and reaching their own door at noon.

The months passed, and neither of the twain ever ventured to start a conversation upon this episode. Ella seemed to be only too frequently in a sad and listless mood, which might almost have been called pining. The time was approaching when she would have to undergo the stress of childbirth for a fourth time, and that apparently did not tend to raise her spirits.

'I don't think I shall get over it this time!' she said one day.

'Pooh! what childish foreboding! Why shouldn't it be as well now as ever?'

She shook her head. 'I feel almost sure I am going to die; and I should be glad, if it were not for Nelly, and Frank, and Tiny.'

'And me!'

'You'll soon find somebody to fill my place,' she murmured, with a sad smile. 'And you'll have a perfect right to; I assure you of that.'

'Ell, you are not thinking still about that – poetical friend of yours?'

She neither admitted nor denied the charge. 'I am not going to get over my illness this time,' she reiterated. 'Something tells me I shan't.'

This view of things was rather a bad beginning, as it usually is; and, in fact, six weeks later, in the month of May, she was lying in her room, pulseless and bloodless, with hardly strength enough left to follow up one feeble breath with another, the infant for whose unnecessary life she was slowly parting with her own being fat and well. Just before her death she spoke to Marchmill softly:

'Will, I want to confess to you the entire circumstances of that – about you know what – that time we visited Solentsea. I can't tell what possessed me – how I could forget you so, my husband! But I had got into a morbid state: I thought you had been unkind; that you had neglected me; that you weren't up to my intellectual level, while he was, and far above it. I wanted a fuller appreciator, perhaps, rather than another lover – '

She could get no further then for very exhaustion; and she went off in sudden collapse a few hours later, without having said anything more to her husband on the subject of her love for the poet. William Marchmill, in truth, like most husbands of several years' standing, was little disturbed by retrospective jealousies, and had not shown the least anxiety to press her for confessions concerning a man dead and gone beyond any power of inconveniencing him more.

But when she had been buried a couple of years it chanced one day that, in turning over some forgotten papers that he wished to destroy before his second wife entered the house, he lighted on a lock of hair in an envelope, with the photograph of the deceased poet, a date being written on the back in his late wife's hand. It was that of the time they spent at Solentsea.

Marchmill looked long and musingly at the hair and portrait, for something struck him. Fetching the little boy who had been the death of his mother, now a noisy toddler, he took him on his knee, held the lock of hair against the child's head, and set up the photograph on the table behind, so that he could closely compare the features each countenance presented. By a known but inexplicable trick of Nature there were undoubtedly strong traces of resemblance to the man Ella had never seen; the dreamy and peculiar expression of the poet's face sat, as the transmitted idea, upon the child's, and the hair was of the same hue.

'I'm damned if I didn't think so!' murmured Marchmill. 'Then she *did* play me false with that fellow at the lodgings! Let me see: the dates – the second week in August . . . the third week in May. . . . Yes . . . yes . . . Get away, you poor little brat! You are nothing to me!'

APPENDIX I
GENERAL PREFACE TO THE WESSEX
EDITION OF 1912

In accepting a proposal for a definite edition of these productions in prose and verse I have found an opportunity of classifying the novels under heads that show approximately the author's aim, if not his achievement, in each book of the series at the date of its composition. Sometimes the aim was lower than at other times; sometimes, where the intention was primarily high, force of circumstances (among which the chief were the necessities of magazine publication) compelled a modification, great or slight, of the original plan. Of a few, however, of the longer novels, and of many of the shorter tales, it may be assumed that they stand today much as they would have stood if no accidents had obstructed the channel between the writer and the public. That many of them, if any, stand as they would stand if written *now* is not to be supposed.

In the classification of these fictitious chronicles – for which the name of 'The Wessex Novels' was adopted, and is still retained – the first group is called 'Novels of Character and Environment', and contains those which approach most nearly to uninfluenced works; also one or two which, whatever their quality in some few of their episodes, may claim a verisimilitude in general treatment and detail.

The second group is distinguished as 'Romances and Fantasies', a sufficiently descriptive definition. The third class – 'Novels of Ingenuity' – show a not infrequent disregard of the probable in the chain of events, and depend for their interest mainly on the incidents themselves. They might also be characterized as 'Experiments', and were written for the nonce simply; though despite the artificiality of their fable some of their scenes are not without fidelity to life.

It will not be supposed that these differences are distinctly perceptible in every page of every volume. It was inevitable that blendings and alternations should occur in all. Moreover, as it was not thought desirable in every instance to change the arrangement of the shorter stories to which readers have grown accustomed, certain of these may be found under headings to which an acute judgment might deny appropriateness.

It has sometimes been conceived of novels that evolve their action on a circumscribed scene – as do many (though not all) of these – that they cannot be so inclusive in their exhibition of human nature as novels wherein the scenes cover large extents of country, in which events figure amid towns and cities, even wander over the four quarters of the globe. I am not concerned to argue this point further than to suggest that the conception is an untrue one in respect of the elementary passions. But I would state that the geographical limits of the stage here trodden were not absolutely forced upon the writer by circumstances; he forced them upon himself from judgment. I considered that our magnificent heritage from the Greeks in dramatic literature found sufficient room for a large proportion of its action in an extent of their country not much larger than the half-dozen counties here reunited under the old name of Wessex, that the domestic emotions have throbbed in Wessex nooks with as much intensity as in the palaces of Europe, and that, anyhow, there was quite enough human nature in Wessex for one man's literary purpose. So far was I possessed by this idea that I kept within the frontiers when it would have been easier to overlap them and give more cosmopolitan features to the narrative.

Thus, though the people in most of the novels (and in much of the shorter verse) are dwellers in a province bounded on the north by the Thames, on the south by the English Channel, on the east by a line running from Hayling Island to Windsor Forest, and on the west by the Cornish coast, they were meant to be typically and essentially those of any and every place where

> Thought's the slave of life, and life time's fool

– beings in whose hearts and minds that which is apparently local should be really universal.

But whatever the success of this intention, and the value of these novels as delineations of humanity, they have at least a humble supplementary quality of which I may be justified in reminding the reader, though it is one that was quite unintentional and unforeseen. At the dates represented in the various narrations things were like that in Wessex: the inhabitants lived in certain ways, engaged in certain occupations, kept alive certain customs, just as they are shown doing in these pages. And in particularizing such I have often been reminded of Boswell's remarks on the trouble to which he was put and the pilgrimages he was obliged to make to authenticate some detail, though the labour was one which would bring him no praise. Unlike his achievement, however, on which an error would as he says have brought discredit, if these country customs and vocations, obsolete and obsolescent, had been detailed wrongly, nobody would have discovered such errors to the end of Time. Yet I have instituted inquiries to correct tricks of memory, and striven against temptations to exaggerate, in order to preserve for my own satisfaction a fairly true record of a vanishing life.

It is advisable also to state here, in response to inquiries from readers interested in landscape, prehistoric antiquities, and especially old English architecture, that the description of these backgrounds has been done from the real – that is to say, has something real for its basis, however illusively treated. Many features of the first two kinds have been given under their existing names; for instance, the Vale of Blackmoor or Blakemore, Hambledon Hill, Bulbarrow, Nettlecombe Tout, Dogbury Hill, High-Stoy, Bubb-Down Hill, The Devil's Kitchen, Cross-in-Hand, Long-Ash Lane, Benvill Lane, Giant's Hill, Crimmer-crock Lane, and Stonehenge. The rivers Froom, or Frome, and Stour, are, of course, well known as such. And the further idea was that large towns and points tending to mark the outline of Wessex – such as Bath, Plymouth, The Start, Portland Bill, Southampton, etc. – should be named clearly. The scheme was not greatly elaborated, but, whatever its value, the names remain still.

In respect of places described under fictitious or ancient names in the novels – for reasons that seemed good at the time of writing them – and kept up in the poems – discerning people have affirmed in print that they clearly recognize the originals: such as Shaftesbury in 'Shaston', Sturminster Newton in 'Stour-castle', Dorchester in 'Casterbridge', Salisbury Plain in 'The Great Plain', Cranborne Chase in 'The Chase', Beaminster in 'Emminster', Bere Regis in 'Kingsbere', Woodbury Hill in 'Greenhill', Wool Bridge in 'Wellbridge', Harfoot or Harput Lane in 'Stagfoot Lane', Hazlebury in 'Nuttlebury', Bridport in 'Port Bredy', Maiden Newton in 'Chalk Newton', a farm near

Nettlecombe Tout in 'Flintcomb-Ash', Sherborne in 'Sherton Abbas', Milton Abbey in 'Middleton Abbey', Cerne Abbas in 'Abbot's Cernel', Evershot in 'Evershed', Taunton in 'Toneborough', Bournemouth in 'Sandbourne', Winchester in 'Wintoncester', Oxford in 'Christminster', Reading in 'Aldbrickham', Newbury in 'Kennetbridge', Wantage in 'Alfredston', Basingstoke in 'Stoke Barehills', and so on. Subject to the qualifications above given, that no detail is guaranteed – that the portraiture of fictitiously named towns and villages was only suggested by certain real places, and wantonly wanders from inventorial descriptions of them – I do not contradict these keen hunters for the real; I am satisfied with their statements as at least an indication of their interest in the scenes.

Thus much for the novels. Turning now to the verse – to myself the more individual part of my literary fruitage – I would say that, unlike some of the fiction, nothing interfered with the writer's freedom in respect of its form or content. Several of the poems – indeed many – were produced before novel-writing had been thought of as a pursuit; but few saw the light till all the novels had been published. The limited stage to which the majority of the latter confine their exhibitions has not been adhered to here in the same proportion, the dramatic part especially having a very broad theatre of action. It may thus relieve the circumscribed areas treated in the prose, if such relief be needed. To be sure, one might argue that by surveying Europe from a celestial point of vision – as in *The Dynasts* – that continent becomes virtually a province – a Wessex, an Attica, even a mere garden – and hence is made to conform to the principle of the novels, however far it outmeasures their region. But that may be as it will.

The few volumes filled by the verse cover a producing period of some eighteen years first and last, while the seventeen or more volumes of novels represent correspondingly about four-and-twenty years. One is reminded by this disproportion in time and result how much more concise and quintessential expression becomes when given in rhythmic form than when shaped in the language of prose.

One word on what has been called the present writer's philosophy of life, as exhibited more particularly in this metrical section of his compositions. Positive views on the Whence and the Wherefore of things have never been advanced by this pen as a consistent philosophy. Nor is it likely, indeed, that imaginative writings extended over more than forty years would exhibit a coherent scientific theory of the universe even if it had been attempted – of that universe concerning which Spencer owns to the 'paralysing thought' that possibly there exists no comprehension of it anywhere. But such objectless consistency never has been attempted, and the sentiments in the following pages have been stated truly to be mere impressions of the moment, and not convictions or arguments.

That these impressions have been condemned as 'pessimistic' – as if that were a very wicked adjective – shows a curious muddle-mindedness. It must be obvious that there is a higher characteristic of philosophy than pessimism, or than meliorism, or even than the optimism of these critics – which is truth. Existence is either ordered in a certain way, or it is not so ordered, and conjectures which harmonize best with experience are removed above all comparison with other conjectures which do not so harmonize. So that to say one view is worse than other views without proving it erroneous implies the possibility of a false view being better or more expedient than a true view; and no pragmatic proppings can make that *idolum specus* stand on its feet, for it postulates a prescience denied to humanity.

And there is another consideration. Differing natures find their tongue in the presence of differing spectacles. Some natures become vocal at tragedy, some are made vocal by comedy, and it seems to me that to whichever of these aspects of life a writer's instinct for expression the more readily responds, to that he should allow it to respond. That before a contrasting side of things he remains undemonstrative need not be assumed to mean that he remains unperceiving.

It was my hope to add to these volumes of verse as many more as would make a fairly comprehensive cycle of the whole. I had wished that those in dramatic, ballad, and narrative form should include most of the cardinal situations which occur in social and public life, and those in lyric form a round of emotional experiences of some completeness. But

The petty done, the undone vast!

The more written the more seems to remain to be written; and the night cometh. I realize that these hopes and plans, except possibly to the extent of a volume or two, must remain unfulfilled.

T.H.

October 1911

PREFACES TO THE SHORT STORIES

Preface to *Wessex Tales*

An apology is perhaps needed for the neglect of contrast which is shown by presenting two stories of hangmen and one of a military execution in such a small collection as the following. But as to the former, in the neighbourhood of county-towns hanging matters used to form a large proportion of the local tradition; and though never personally acquainted with any chief operator at such scenes, the writer of these pages had as a boy the privilege of being on speaking terms with a man who applied for the office, and who sank into an incurable melancholy because he failed to get it, some slight mitigation of his grief being to dwell upon striking episodes in the lives of those happier ones who had held it with success and renown. His tale of disappointment used to cause his listener some wonder why his ambition should have taken such an unfortunate form, by limiting itself to a profession of which there could be only one practitioner in England at one time, when it might have aimed at something that would have afforded him more chances – such as the office of a judge, a bishop, or even a Member of Parliament – but its nobleness was never questioned. In those days, too, there was still living an old woman who, for the cure of some eating disease, had been taken in her youth to have her 'blood turned' by a convict's corpse, in the manner described in 'The Withered Arm'.

Since writing this story some years ago I have been reminded by an aged friend who knew 'Rhoda Brook' that, in relating her dream, my forgetfulness has weakened the facts out of which the tale grew. In reality it was while lying down on a hot afternoon that the incubus oppressed her and she flung it off, with the results upon the body of the original as described. To my mind the occurrence of such a vision in the daytime is more impressive than if it had happened in a midnight dream. Readers are therefore asked to correct the misrelation, which affords an instance of how our imperfect memories insensibly formalize the fresh originality of living fact – from whose shape they slowly depart, as machine-made castings depart by degrees from the sharp hand-work of the mould.

Among the many devices for concealing smuggled goods in caves and pits of the earth, that of planting an apple-tree in a tray or box which was placed over the mouth of the pit is, I believe, unique, and it is detailed in 'The Distracted Preacher' precisely as described by an old carrier of 'tubs' – a man who was afterwards in my father's employ for over thirty years. I never gathered from his reminiscences what means were adopted for lifting the tree, which, with its roots, earth, and receptacle, must have been of considerable weight. There is no doubt, however, that the thing was done through many years. My informant often spoke, too, of the horribly suffocating sensation produced by the pair of spirit-tubs slung upon the chest and back, after stumbling with the burden of them for several miles inland over a rough country and in darkness. He said that though years of his youth and young manhood were spent in this irregular business, his profits from the same, taken all together, did not average the wages he might have earned in a steady employment, whilst the fatigues and risks were excessive.

I may add that the action of this story is founded on certain smuggling exploits that occurred between 1825 and 1830, and were brought to a close in the latter year by the trial of the chief actors at the Assizes before Baron Bolland for their desperate armed resistance to the Custom-house officers during the landing of a cargo of spirits. This happened only a little time after the doings recorded in the narrative, in which some incidents that came out at the trial are also embodied.

In the culminating affray the character called Owlett was badly wounded, and several of the Preventive-men would have lost their lives through being overpowered by the far more numerous body of smugglers, but for the forbearance and manly conduct of the latter. This served them in good stead at their trial, in which the younger Erskine prosecuted, their defence being entrusted to Erle. Baron Bolland's summing up was strongly in their favour; they were merely ordered to enter into their own recognizances for good behaviour and discharged. (See also as to facts the note at the end of the tale.)

However, the stories are but dreams, and not records. They were first collected and published under their present title, in two volumes, in 1888.

T.H.

April 1896–May 1912

Preface to *A Group of Noble Dames*

The pedigrees of our county families, arranged in diagrams on the pages of county histories, mostly appear at first sight to be as barren of any touch of nature as a table of logarithms. But given a clue – the faintest tradition of what went on behind the scenes, and this dryness as of dust may be transformed into a palpitating drama. More, the careful comparison of dates alone – that of birth with marriage, of marriage with death, of one marriage, birth, or death with a kindred marriage, birth, or death – will often effect the same transformation, and anybody practised in raising images from such genealogies finds himself unconsciously filling into the framework the motives, passions, and personal qualities which would appear to be the single explanation possible of some extraordinary conjunction in times, events, and personages that occasionally marks these reticent family records.

Out of such pedigrees and supplementary material most of the following stories have arisen and taken shape.

I would make this preface an opportunity of expressing my sense of the courtesy and kindness of several bright-eyed Noble Dames yet in the flesh, who, since the first publication of these tales in periodicals, six or seven years ago, have given me interesting comments and conjectures on such of the narratives as they have recognized to be connected with their own families, residences, or traditions; in which they have shown a truly philosophic absence of prejudice in their regard of those incidents whose relation has tended more distinctly to dramatize than to eulogize their ancestors. The outlines they have also given of other singular events in their family histories for use in a second 'Group of Noble Dames' will, I fear, never reach the printing-press through me; but I shall store them up in memory of my informants' good nature.

The tales were first collected and published in their present form in 1891.

T.H.
June 1896

Preface to *Life's Little Ironies*

Of the following collection the first story, 'An Imaginative Woman', which has hitherto stood in *Wessex Tales*, has been brought into this volume as being more nearly its place, turning as it does upon a trick of Nature, so to speak, a physical possibility that may attach to a wife of vivid imaginings, as is well known to medical practitioners and other observers of such manifestations.

The two stories named 'A Tradition of Eighteen Hundred and Four' and 'The Melancholy Hussar of the German Legion', which were formerly printed in this series, have been transferred to *Wessex Tales*, where their more naturally belong.

The present narratives and sketches, though separately published at various antecedent dates, were first collected and issued in a volume in 1894.

T.H.
May 1912

Preface to *'A Changed Man' and Other Tales*

I reprint in this volume, for what they may be worth, a dozen minor novels that have been published in the periodical press at various dates in the past, in order to render them accessible to readers who desire to have them in the complete series issued by my publishers. For aid in reclaiming some of the narratives I express my thanks to the proprietors and editors of the newspapers and magazines in whose pages they first appeared.

T.H.
August 1913

NOTES

The Distracted Preacher

Written in London in the early months of 1879, the story was first published, as 'The Distracted Young Preacher', in the *New Quarterly Magazine* (April 1879); in America, it appeared as a serial in *Harper's Weekly* (19 April – 17 May 1879). The title was changed to 'The Distracted Preacher' when the story appeared in *Wessex Tales* in 1888; a note on the ending was added in the 1912 Wessex edition. Other textual changes were relatively minor and involved mainly topographical details: the original 'Nether-Mynton' changed to 'Nether Moynton' in the 1896 Osgood-McIlvaine edition, while the 1879 'Lulworth' became 'Lullstead' in 1888, 'Lulstead Cove' in 1896, and finally 'Lulwind Cove' in 1912.

p. 3 **Wesleyan:** mainstream Methodist. Methodism is a Protestant tradition originating from an 18th-century revivalist movement in the Church of England led by John (1703–91) and Charles (1707–88) Wesley. After John Wesley's death, his followers did not maintain the Anglican connection and formed a separate church, which later underwent several divisions and transformations.

pp. 3–183: cf. Preface to *Wessex Tales*, pp. 382–3.

p. 3 **church in the morning and chapel in the evening:** non-Anglican places of worship were known as chapels, as opposed to Anglican churches.

p. 3 **Episcopalians:** technically, members of any church ruled by bishops, but normally used about members of the Anglican Communion; here: members of the Church of England.

p. 3 **Dissenters:** (in England) members of any Protestant church other than the Church of England.

p. 8 **nave:** the hub of a wheel.

p. 8 **smugglers' liquor:** smuggling was widespread in eighteenth- and nineteenth-century Dorset. Hardy knew about it from his parents, as the family home at Higher Bockhampton had itself been used, in the early years of the century, as a hiding-place for contraband spirits. He also heard smuggling stories from an employee of his father's, James Selby (cf. Preface to *Wessex Tales*, p. 381), from the ex-coastguard George Nicholls, and from his Swanage landlord, Captain Joseph Masters.

p. 9 from which she took mouthfuls, conveying each to the keg by putting her pretty lips to the hole: the serial version is characteristically more reticent: 'which she poured on the hole'.

p. 10 shining light: John 5:35.

p. 11 from Abigail to Zenobia: in the Old Testament, Abigail was the beautiful and prudent wife of Nabal, a wealthy shepherd at Carmel in Judea. When Nabal refused to invite David to his sheep-shearing, she decided to go and ask David not to take revenge on her husband. After Nabal's death she became David's wife (1 Samuel 25:3–42). Zenobia was a third-century queen of Palmyra (in present-day Syria) who conquered several Roman provinces in the eastern part of the empire before being subjugated by the emperor Aurelian. The two women represent two opposing ideals of womanhood.

p. 13 tutelary saints: guardian saints, not venerated in most Protestant churches; cf. John Wesley's 'Articles of Religion', XIV: 'Of Purgatory: The Romish doctrine concerning purgatory, pardons, worshipping, and adoration, as well of images as of relics, and also invocation of saints, is a foul thing, vainly invented, and grounded upon no arrant of Scripture, but repugnant to the word of God'.

p. 15 Owlett: allusion to Hewlett, an actual 1820s Dorset smuggler; possibly also to 'owler' – wool smuggler.

p. 19 Seven Sleepers: seven young Christians from Ephesus (in present-day Turkey) said to have been walled up in a cave when taking refuge during the Decian persecutions (*c*.250) and to have been awakened under the emperor Theodosius II (d.450) as a proof of the resurrection of the dead.

p. 19 Romans for Corinthians: abbreviated titles for St Paul's Epistle to the Romans and his two Epistles to the Corinthians.

p. 22 aspen: tremulous, quivering.

p. 24 lint: soft frayed linen used as tinder.

p. 28 Preventive-men: officers of the Coast Guard whose duty it was to prevent smuggling.

p. 28 **stray-line:** submerged or floating line fastened at one end only.

p. 28 **'Render unto Caesar the things that are Caesar's':** cf. Matthew 22:21, Mark 12:17, Luke 20:25.

p. 32 **Round Pound:** there are about 1800 round barrows (Bronze Age gravemounds) scattered around Dorset.

p. 33 **chine hoops:** bands of metal or wood surrounding the projecting rim at the head of a cask.

p. 34 **mixen:** manure-heap.

p. 35 **Latimer:** actual name of an early 19th-century Customs-officer in Dorset.

p. 37 **tole:** (dial.) entice, decoy.

p. 38 **chimmers:** (dial.) chambers, bedrooms.

p. 38 **myrmidons:** in Greek mythology, Myrmidons were humans created by Zeus out of ants after the people of the island of Aegina were destroyed by a plague; they were devoted followers of Achilles; here, subordinates who carry out orders implacably.

p. 39 **knee-naps:** leather knee-covers.

p. 40 **road-scrapings:** heaps of manure collected from the roads.

p. 46 **strakes:** sections of the iron rim of a wheel.

p. 50 **clitches:** crooks of arm or leg.

p. 52 **hairbreadth escapes:** *Othello*, I, iii, 135.

p. 55 **assizes:** (in England before 1971) periodical sessions of the High Court of Justice held outside London.

p. 56 *de rigueur:* (French) proper and necessary according to fashion or custom.

p. 56 **true incidents:** cf. Preface to *Wessex Tales*, pp. 382–3.

Fellow-Townsmen

The story, written in London in the early months of 1880, first appeared in the *New Quarterly Magazine* in April 1880; in America, it was serialized in *Harper's Weekly* (17 April–15 May 1880) and published in a separate volume at the end of April the same year. The opening pages were rewritten before the story was collected in *Wessex Tales* in 1888. In the rather more sentimental magazine version, Barnet, having gone

'in a ruffled and recalcitrant state of mind' and with a 'violent banging
of the front door', visits the Downes at home to seek 'a relief to the
lurid picture which his own home so constantly presented'; later, he
goes back home, but once on his own doorstep he changes his mind
and goes to see Lucy. The character of the earlier relations between
Barnet and Lucy is, in the magazine version, made to appear even more
vague than in the story as it stands now – Lucy stresses that 'there had
been nothing said by [Barnet] which gave [her] any right to send [him]
a letter' and that '[he] had made [her] no promises, and [she] did not
feel that [he] had broken any'; consequently there is no suggestion on
her part that Barnet married his wife for money rather than for love.

p. 57 **greensward:** expanse of grassy turf.

p. 57 **flax-merchant:** flax was grown around Bridport for the needs of
the town's traditional rope-making industry.

p. 63 **Raffaelesque:** characteristic of the works of the Italian painter
Raphael (Raffaello Sanzio, 1483–1520), particularly of his peaceful,
serene representations of the Virgin and Child.

p. 63 **images on the retina:** the retina is a layer of nervous tissue at the
back of an eyeball; it includes light-sensitive cells which remain
activated for a brief moment after the stimulus is withdrawn.

p. 65 **'Ambition pricked me on':** cf. Shakespeare's *1 Henry IV*, V, i,
129–30 ('honour pricks me on').

p. 67 **coddle:** over-protective doctor who indulges his patients.

p. 68 **Tophet:** place near Jerusalem where sacrificial burnings were
carried out to pagan gods; cf. Jeremiah 7:31–32.

p. 69 **'Not poppy nor mandragora':** *Othello*, III, iii, 334.

p. 70 **Xantippe:** the wife of the ancient Greek philosopher Socrates; a
nagging, quarrelsome woman.

p. 71 *politesse du coeur:* kind-heartedness and empathy.

p. 72 **Libyan bay which sheltered the shipwrecked Trojans:** when
shipwrecked at sea, the Trojan warrior Aeneas and his companions
landed on the coast of Libya, where they were received by Dido, the
Queen of Carthage; cf. Virgil, *Aeneid*, I, 157–79.

p. 75 **bear-garden:** place set apart for bear-baiting and other rough
sports; a scene of strife and tumult.

p. 76 numerous faded portraits by Sir Joshua Reynolds: Sir Joshua Reynolds (1723–92) was one of the greatest British painters; his technical experiments involved frequent use of unsuitable, perishable painting materials, such as bitumen.

p. 76 octavo volume of Domestic Medicine: William Buchan's *Domestic Medicine, or the Family Physician* (1769), reissued several times throughout the 19th century.

p. 78 'my wife was dead, and she is alive again': cf. Luke 15:24, 32.

p. 86 Palladian: Neo-Classical; the Palladian style, named after the Italian architect and writer Andrea Palladio (1508–80), was dominant in British architecture throughout the 18th century.

p. 86 coped: having the top or upper surface sloping down on each side.

p. 88 smoke-jacks: devices fixed in a chimney to turn a roasting-spit.

p. 89 balusters: short posts supporting a handrail.

p. 90 whimsical god at other times known as blind Circumstance: a characteristic idea of Hardy's; cf. e.g., 'Hap'.

p. 94 durable stone and triple brass: cf. Shakespeare, Sonnet 65, 1–2 ('Since brass, nor stone, nor earth, nor boundless sea / But sad mortality o'ersways their power').

p. 94 a railway had invaded the town: a branch of the Great Western line, opened in 1857, linked Bridport to Maiden Newton.

p. 94 some facetious restorer: ironically, St Mary's, Bridport, was restored in 1858–60 by the Dorchester architect John Hicks, with whom Hardy was at the time apprenticed; Hicks's idea of restoration was one of modernization rather than preservation, a view Hardy was later to come to deplore.

p. 94 home-along: homewards.

p. 95 poll: top of the head.

p. 96 East Street: inconsistent; cf. 'a small street on the right' (p. 59), clearly off East Street.

The Honourable Laura

The story was written in Wimborne in the autumn of 1881; it had been contracted, at £7 per 2,000 words, with the fiction agency of Tillotson & Son, who subsequently published it, under the original title

'Benighted Travellers', first in the *Christmas Leaves* supplement to *Bolton Weekly Journal and District News* on 17 December 1881, and later in numerous other provincial papers. In America, it appeared in *Harper's Weekly* on 10 and 17 December 1881. The present title was adopted when the story appeared in *A Group of Noble Dames* in 1891; the textual changes in this edition as well as subsequently were relatively small, involving mainly the names of characters and details of location. Thus, in the magazine version, the heroine's name is Lucetta (changed in the 1891 text to avoid confusion with the character in *The Mayor of Casterbridge*) and her father is not referred to by name, while the action takes place in a non-specific setting of 'one of the most picturesque glens in Great Britain' rather than on the coast of North Devon.

p. 105 **basket-carriage:** carriage with a wicker body.

p. 109 **City Road:** in London, leading from Finsbury Square to Islington High Street.

p. 109 **plied:** tried to persuade.

p. 111 **Adonis:** in Greek mythology, a beautiful youth, a favourite of the goddess Aphrodite.

p. 113 **Recitativo:** (Italian) style of accompanied solo song, emphasizing the rhythms and accents of spoken language.

p. 120 **familiar words of Brabantio, 'She has deceived her father, and may thee':** *Othello*, I, iii, 293.

The Three Strangers

The story was written in 1882–3 in Wimborne. Completed in January 1883, it was published the following March in *Longman's Magazine* and serialized in America in *Harper's Weekly* (3–10 March); in 1888, it was included in *Wessex Tales*. Hardy's revisions of the text were relatively small; in 1888, he moved the location of the home of the escaped convict from the original Anglebury (Wareham) to Shottsford, which may have been meant to suggest that the clockmaker's poverty was linked to the agricultural unrest in the Vale of Blackmoor in the 1820s. In the 1896 Osgood-McIlvaine edition, the convict's name, 'Sommers', was changed to 'Summers', perhaps to add an element of warmth.

p. 125 **coombs:** valleys or hollows in the side of a hill.

p. 125 **ewe-leases:** pastures for sheep.

p. 125 **to isolate a Timon or a Nebuchadnezzar:** Timon, the misanthropic hero of *Timon of Athens*, exiled himself from the city when, having lost his fortune, he was denied financial support by those who had previously profited from his generosity; Nebuchadnezzar was a king of Babylon, whom God exiled from his kingdom into the wilderness for several years as a punishment for his sins – cf. Daniel 4:19–37.

p. 125 **'conceive and meditate of pleasant things':** source not identified.

p. 126 **the clothyard shafts of Senlac and Crecy:** yard-long longbow arrows used at the battles of Senlac (i.e. Hastings, 1066) and Crécy (1346).

p. 126 **back-brand:** large log placed at the back of the fire.

p. 126 **'like the laughter of the fool':** cf. Ecclesiastes 7:6.

p. 126 *pourparlers:* (French) preliminary discussions prior to official negotiations.

p. 127 *bonhomie:* (French) geniality, good-natured friendliness.

p. 127 **toping:** drinking, esp. excessively.

p. 127 **the fiddler was a boy of those parts:** as a young boy, Hardy often accompanied his father on his musical ourings; memories of these occasions were to remain for him, throughout his life, a major source of inspiration.

p. 127 **tweedle-dee:** high-pitched musical sound.

p. 127 **serpent:** old bass wind instrument made from leather-covered wood, roughly in the form of an S.

p. 129 **pent-roof:** roof sloping in one direction only.

p. 131 **vamp:** upper front part of a boot or a shoe.

p. 132 **grog-blossoms:** pimples on the nose caused by excessive drinking.

p. 133 **gone the way of all flesh:** died (proverbial; cf. Dekker and Webster, *Westward Ho!*, II, ii, 204).

p. 133 **small (mead):** weak, light in alcohol.

p. 133 **metheglin:** spiced or medicated mead.

p. 133 **comb-washings:** drainings of the honeycomb.

p. 134 **het:** (dial.) hot.

p. 134 **famine or sword:** cf. Isaiah 51:19.

p. 135 **Daze:** (dial.) damn.

p. 136 **'O my trade it is the rarest one ...':** later included in *Wessex Poems* (1898) as 'The Stranger's Song'.

p. 136 **Belshazzar's Feast:** Belshazzar was the son of Nebuchadnezzar; a feast at his palace was interrupted when a mysterious hand wrote on a wall words 'Mene, Mene, Tekel, Upharsin', interpreted by the prophet Daniel as indicating Belshazzar's impending death and the fall of his kingdom – cf. Daniel 5:1–31.

p. 137 **sheep-stealing:** in England, sheep-stealing remained a capital offence until 1832.

p. 138 **Prince of Darkness:** *King Lear*, III, iv, 134; cf. also Matthew 12:24 ('Beelzebub the prince of the devils').

p. 138 **'... circulus, cujus centrum diabolus':** circle in the middle of which is the devil; source not identified, possibly used in exorcisms.

p. 139 **the lion and the unicorn:** in heraldry, supporters of the British royal coat of arms, the lion representing England, and the unicorn Scotland.

p. 140 **skimmer-cake:** small pudding made from the remnants of another and cooked upon a skimmer.

p. 141 **cretaceous:** dating back to the last period of the Mesozoic era, when extensive deposits of chalk were formed.

p. 142 **horn:** side of a lantern, made of horn.

p. 145 **raze out the written troubles:** *Macbeth*, V, iii, 44.

p. 145 **a matron in the sere and yellow leaf:** cf. *Macbeth*, V, iii, 25.

The Romantic Adventures of a Milkmaid

The story was written in Wimborne in the winter of 1882–3; despatched to the publishers on 25 February, it first appeared in the *Graphic* Summer Number on 25 June 1883. In America, the story was serialized in *Harper's Weekly* between 23 June and 4 August of the same year; in an unsuccessful attempt to avoid piracy, *Harper's* brought out, also in June 1883, a cheap edition in volume form. Although very popular in America, where it went through several editions in the next few decades, the story was never taken very seriously by Hardy himself;

he dismissed it as 'written only with a view of fleeting life in a periodical', and did not have it collected until it appeared, revised, in *'A Changed Man' and Other Tales* (1913). In the 1913 text, substantially the same as the 1914 Wessex version reprinted here, the scene was moved from its original Dorset location to Devon, possibly to avoid confusion with the setting of *Tess of the d'Urbervilles*; other revisions involved greater explicitness in the description of von Xanten's suicide attempt at the beginning of the story and in Margery's admission of her attraction to him in the final chapter. In a note made in 1927, Hardy explained that his original intention was that Margery should at the end of the story, rather than be re-united with Jim, instead join the Baron on his yacht and leave England to return no more; the closing pages as they stand were written to comply with the requirements of magazine publication.

p. 146 **barton(-gate):** farmyard (gate).

p. 148 **tacker-haired:** (dial.) with wiry black hair.

p. 148 **Italian elevation made familiar by Inigo Jones and his school:** Inigo Jones (1573–1652) was an English architect and theatrical designer responsible for the introduction of Palladianism (cf. note to 'Fellow-Townsmen' p. 389) to England.

p. 148 **greensward:** cf. note to 'Fellow-Townsmen' p. 388.

p. 151 **hinder:** rear, hind.

p. 153 **foot-post:** postman who travels on foot.

p. 154 **(living too) rithe:** (dial.) fast, wildly.

p. 154 **croud:** coo; sound produced by birds such as doves or pigeons.

p. 155 *proh pudor!*: (Latin) for shame!

p. 155 **Yeomanry:** (in Britain 1761–1907) volunteer mounted troops of the home defence army.

p. 156 **country dances like the "New-Rigged-Ship", and "Fellow-my-Lover", and "Haste-to-the-Wedding", and the "College Hornpipe", and the "Favourite Quickstep", and "Captain White's" dance:** traditional and folk dances popular in the South-West of England in the early 19th century; tunes of some of them ('The New-Rigged-Ship', 'Haste-to-the-Wedding') are to be found in the Hardy family music notebooks.

p. 156 Chaucer: Geoffrey Chaucer (1343?–1400), English poet, author of *The Canterbury Tales.*

p. 157 at Lord Toneborough's, ... who, I suppose, wishes to please the yeomen because his brother is going to stand for the county: as a result of the gradual extension of franchise throughout the 19th century, the continued political influence of landed aristocracy depended more and more on maintaining a good relationship with local voters.

p. 157 Almack's: London club and assembly rooms founded in 1764 by William Almack in King Street, St James's, venue of exclusive balls throughout the 19th century.

p. 157 Scythian: relating to Scythia, an ancient region of southern Europe and Asia, north of the Black Sea.

p. 158 polka: lively dance of Czech origin.

p. 158 It arrived in London only some few months ago: fashionable throughout Europe after having been presented in Paris in 1840, the polka was first brought to London in 1844.

p. 158 Rubicon: symbol of a decision or move committing one to a particular course of action. The Rubicon was a small stream in northern Italy which in Roman times separated Cisalpine Gaul from Italy; Julius Caesar's crossing of it was a violation of the law and thus a proclamation of war on the Roman Senate.

p. 163 touchwood: readily inflammable wood made soft by fungi, used as tinder.

p. 167 steam: the steam-engine, invented by James Watt in 1769, was in the first half of the 19th century transforming transport and industry throughout Britain.

p. 168 Angel Gabriel: one of the archangels, the messenger of Divine comfort (cf. Daniel 8:15–27, 9:21–27, and Luke 1:11–20, 26–38).

p. 169 Rhadamanthus: in Greek mythology, son of Zeus and Europa, one of the judges of the dead in the lower world, and symbol of inflexible integrity and impartiality.

p. 169 granddame: grandmother.

p. 173 Fidgets: condition or mood of impatient uneasiness or restlessness; here, expression of annoyance.

p. 174 **guinea-gold:** 22-carat gold of which guinea coins were minted.

p. 174 **Talleyrand:** Charles Maurice Talleyrand-Périgord (1754–1838), French statesman, foreign minister under Napoleon and during the Congress of Vienna, renowned for his cool, calculating political manoeuvring.

p. 179 **queer:** bad, worthless.

p. 179 **calcinations:** here: desiccated objects found in quicklime.

p. 179 **Pompeian remains:** Pompeii was an ancient city in Italy, southeast of Naples, buried by an eruption of Vesuvius in 79 BC; excavations of its well-preserved remains began in 1748.

p. 182 **St Swithin's:** 15 July; according to folk belief, if it rains on St Swithin's day, rain will continue for 40 days.

p. 182 **the Jacques of this forest and stream:** melancholy courtier of the exiled duke in *As You Like It* (cf. II, i, 25–43).

p. 186 **that of Prospero over the gentle Ariel:** cf. *Tempest*, I, ii, 190–307.

p. 189 **rendlewood:** barked oak.

p. 189 **I've suffered horseflesh:** I've suffered terribly (?).

p. 189 **flick-flack:** nonsense, thoughtless talk.

p. 190 **wind-quarter:** direction.

p. 190 **Hobbema and his school:** Meindert Hobbema (1638–1709), Dutch painter of peaceful rural landscapes.

p. 191 **'the cankered heaps of strange-achieved gold':** *2 Henry IV*, IV, iii, 200–1.

p. 195 **'a painless sympathy':** source not identified.

p. 196 **the orange-flower and the sad cypress were intertwined:** the orange-flower is a symbol of purity and marriage, and the cypress of death (cf. *Twelfth Night*, II, iv, 50–1: 'Come away, come away death / And in sad cypress let me be laid').

p. 199 **deedy:** active, energetic.

p. 199 **special licence:** permit to marry without banns being asked.

p. 199 **Lambeth:** here: Lambeth Palace, official London residence of the Archbishop of Canterbury.

p. 202 **blaze out:** shine in society, brag, boast.

p. 204 **footy:** (dial.) mean, base.

p. 205 **there was neither vell or mark:** (dial.) there was no trace.

p. 205 **three-cunning:** (dial.) intensely knowing, sensitive.

p. 205 **drawlatcheting:** (dial.) walking lazily, loitering, dawdling.

p. 206 **jawed:** scolded, lectured.

p. 207 **skirring:** moving rapidly with a whirring sound.

p. 210 **gone to the Table:** taken Communion.

p. 210 **avast:** (used by sailors) hold, stop.

p. 210 **'Talian iron:** hollow cylindrical heater used for crimping laces, frills, etc.

p. 211 **I've pulled grass from my husband's grave to cure it – wove the blades into true lover's knots; took off my shoes upon the sod:** superstitious ways of ensuring that one's dead lover is not forgotten.

p. 212 **young Queen Victoria's uniform:** Victoria ascended to the throne in 1837, at the age of 18.

p. 212 *coup*: (French) unusual and successful move or action.

p. 213 **Pandaemonium:** palace of Satan; cf. Milton, *Paradise Lost*, 1, 756–7.

p. 215 **spencer:** short close-fitting jacket.

p. 216 **over-right:** right opposite.

p. 216 *nonchalance*: calm and casual attitude.

p. 217 **larry:** scolding, lecture, lesson.

p. 219 **slummocky:** slovenly, untidy.

p. 219 **like hell-and-skimmer:** very fast.

p. 219 **cust:** (dial.) cursed.

p. 220 **teave:** (dial.) throw oneself about as in a passion or in a fever.

p. 226 **Margery did not explain:** cf. similar motif in *Under the Greenwood Tree*, V, 2.

p. 227 **'la jalousie rétrospective,' as George Sand calls it:** (French) jealousy in retrospect; cf. George Sand, *Elle et lui*, ch. XII ('l'horrible jalousie rétrospective, la pire de toutes, parce qu'elle se prend à tout sans pouvoir s'assurer de rien, rongea le coeur et brisa le cerveau du malhereux artiste'). George Sand (1804–76) was a major 19th-century French woman novelist.

A Tryst at an Ancient Earthwork

The background of the story, written in Dorchester in 1884–5, relates directly to Hardy's interest in local history and archaeology; it was through his membership of the Dorset Natural History and Antiquarian Field Club that he met the local antiquary Edward Cunnington, whose dubious research methods, already criticized by Hardy in a paper he delivered to the Club in May 1884, are the direct source of the anecdote told here. In a characteristically evasive way, Hardy decided to have the story published in America rather than in Britain; it first appeared, as 'Ancient Earthworks and What Two Enthusiastic Scientists Found Therein', in the *Detroit Post* on 15 March 1885. The story was not reprinted in Britain until a revised version, with some changes of wording and a few additions, came out, as 'Ancient Earthworks at Casterbridge', in the *English Illustrated Magazine* in December 1893; the final title was eventually arrived at, and more minor changes introduced, before the story was eventually collected in 'A Changed Man' and Other Tales (1913).

p. 220 antediluvian: belonging to the period before the biblical Flood.

p. 228 cephalopod: any mollusc with a distinct tentacled head.

p. 228 striae: superficial furrows, grooves, or ridges.

p. 229 Ptolemy: (c.100–c.170) a Greek astronomer and geographer working in Alexandria, best known for his geocentric theory of the universe; his *Geography*, which includes a reference to 'Dunium', was a standard source of information until the 16th century.

p. 229 Durotriges: ancient British tribe living in Dorset before the conquest of Britain by the Romans.

p. 230 To turn aside, as did Christian's companion, from such a Hill Difficulty: in John Bunyan's allegorical story *The Pilgrim's Progress*, the central character, Christian, approaches Hill Difficulty accompanied by two other pilgrims, Formalist and Hypocrisy; rather than following Christian uphill, the two choose sideway roads, which turn out to lead them, respectively, to Danger and Destruction.

p. 230 counterscarp: outer side of the ditch of a fort.

p. 231 Thor: ancient Norse god of thunder, war, and agriculture.

p. 231 Jotun-land: in Norse mythology, the country of the giants.

p. 232 Vespasian: (9–79) Roman emperor, who consolidated Roman rule in Britain and Germany.

p. 233 architraves: main beams resting across the tops of columns; here, mouldings around doorways, window openings, etc.

p. 233 Belgae: ancient Celtic inhabitants of modern-day Belgium and France.

p. 234 loving-kindness: a characteristic Hardy concept; cf., e.g., 'A Plaint to Man'.

p. 234 Icening Way: Icknield Way; prehistoric trackway across England from Norfolk through Wiltshire to Devon.

p. 236 tesserae: small square tiles of stone or glass used in mosaics.

p. 236 Mercury: in Roman mythology, the god of trade and messenger of the gods.

p. 237 Roman Forum: main forum, or public square, of ancient Rome, situated between the Capitoline and the Palatine Hills.

The Withered Arm

The story was written in Dorchester in the autumn of 1887; rejected by *Longman's Magazine* as too gloomy, it was later sold, for £24, to *Blackwood's Edinburgh Magazine*, which published it in January 1888. It was then collected in *Wessex Tales*. The textual changes in that and later editions were relatively minor; some of the more significant of them involved introducing phrasings which stressed the subjectivity of Rhoda's dream-vision.

The anecdote told in the story reflects the folk beliefs and superstitions common in nineteenth-century Dorset and thus well-known to Hardy (cf. Preface to *Wessex Tales*, pp. 381–2); Hardy indeed insisted that the story was 'largely based on fact' and that its 'cardinal incidents [were] true'. The use of the motif of hanging can be related to the popular accounts of crimes and executions which Hardy heard in his childhood and youth and which fuelled his interest in death and the macabre; one of such stories, told by his father, concerned a young man sentenced to death in circumstances similar to those described in the story.

p. 239 The Withered Arm: cf. *Richard III*, III, iv, 67–9 ('Then be your eyes the witness of their evil: / See how I am bewitch'd! Behold, mine arm / Is like a blasted sapling wither'd up!').

p. 239 water-meadows: meadows periodically overflowed by a stream.

p. 239 tisty-tosty: (dial.) round, plump and comely.

p. 239 barton: cf. note to 'The Romantic Adventures of a Milkmaid', p. 393.

p. 239 laved: baled, drew water.

p. 239 what the Turk: what on earth.

p. 240 milchers: cows kept for milk.

p. 244 gownd: gown.

p. 244 whewed: whistled, rustled.

p. 245 chimmer: cf. note to 'The Distracted Preacher', p. 387.

p. 247 like a guilty thing: cf. *Hamlet*, I, i, 129.

p. 250 Trendle: perhaps allusion to the Anglo-Saxon word 'trendle' (meaning 'circle') and its possible mystical connotations.

p. 252 Wessex King Ina, presented to after-ages as Lear: Ina (d.726) was an Anglo-Saxon king of Wessex; Hardy's source for the identification of Ina with Lear has not been found.

p. 252 sharp sand: hard, grainy sand used for making mortar.

p. 253 opaline: opalescent, iridescent.

p. 253 garniture: decoration, trimmings; here, landscape.

p. 253 overlooked: bewitched with the evil eye.

p. 256 those days, when men were executed for horse-stealing, arson, and burglary: in England, horse-stealing and burglary remained capital offences until 1832; capital punishment for arson, though by the mid-century regularly commuted to deportation, remained on the statute-book until 1861.

p. 256 assize: cf. note to 'The Distracted Preacher', p. 387.

p. 258 Amazon: member of a mythical race of female warriors, renowned for their riding skills; here, mare.

p. 259 Enclosure Acts: (in Britain after 1730) Acts of Parliament permitting erection of fences or hedges to enclose open fields in order to create private holdings and thus to facilitate agricultural work, mainly sheep-farming.

p. 259 rights of commonage: rights to use common land, esp. as pastures.

p. 259 turbary: concerning the right of digging turf on common ground.

p. 260 hang-fair: public execution.

p. 261 Davies: the real name of a 19th-century Dorchester hangman, personally known to the Hardy family.

p. 262 a-scram: (dial.) shrunken, withered.

p. 263 glum: (dial.) gloom.

p. 263 ashlar: large square-cut stone.

p. 265 of a painless decline: a last-minute change: Lodge was originally to have committed suicide.

Barbara of the House of Grebe

The story was written in Dorchester at the turn of 1889–90, part of a collection of six tales, 'A Group of Noble Dames', which Hardy had in 1889 promised to the *Graphic*. Judged by the editors as too drastic in its exploration of the darker sides of human psychology and sexuality to be acceptable for magazine publication, the story was heavily bowdlerized before it finally appeared, as 'Barbara (Daughter of Sir John Grebe)' in the Christmas number of the *Graphic* on 1 December 1890. The most important change was the excision of the most part of the account of the psychological torture of Barbara by Lord Upland-towers; other changes involved softening the descriptions of the disfigurement of Willowes's appearance and of the physicality of Barbara's consequent impulses of horror, as well as removing the stress on Uplandtowers's obsession with the idea of fathering an heir. No bowdlerizations were required for the first publication of the collection in America, where the six stories were serialized in *Harper's Weekly* between 29 November and 20 December 1890. In Britain, the story was restored to its original form when *A Group of Noble Dames*, now expanded to ten stories, appeared in 1891; later textual changes were negligible.

The story is loosely based on the life of Barbara Webb (1762–1819), wife of the fifth Earl of Shaftesbury.

p. 267 **Great Western Highway:** from London to Bristol.

p. 267 **Civil War:** the conflict between Charles I and Parliament (1642–9).

pp. 267–8 **Hundred of Cockdene:** in Britain, a hundred is a subdivision of a county or shire.

p. 268 **one of the Drenkhards:** based on the family of the Trenchards of Wolfeton House, near Charminster, Dorset.

p. 268 **congeries:** disorderly collection, mass or heap.

p. 268 **John of Gaunt:** Duke of Lancaster (1340–99), son of Edward III.

p. 272 **Maundeville, and Mohun, and Syward, and Peverell, and Culliford, and Talbot, and Plantagenet, and York, and Lancaster:** the first six were old Norman families in Dorset; the Plantagenets were the royal house of England from 1154 to 1485; the conflict between its two branches, the Yorkists and the Lancastrians, led to the Wars of the Roses (1455–85).

p. 272 **haunches:** sides of an arch between the crown and the pier.

p. 272 **as described to us sometimes by our worthy President:** reference to the framework within which the story is told; a supposed meeting of the South-Wessex Field and Antiquarian Club.

p. 273 **murrey:** mulberry-coloured, deep red or purple.

p. 273 **drab:** dull yellowish-brown cloth.

p. 273 *sang froid*: (French) composure, coolness.

p. 274 **the King and Court at Versailles:** Versailles, near Paris, was before the French Revolution (1789) the seat of the kings of France.

p. 274 **Mont Cenis:** pass over the Graian Alps between Lanslebourg (France) and Susa (Italy).

p. 275 *mésalliance*: (French) marriage with a person of a lower social position.

p. 276 **Carnival:** celebrations of the time preceding the beginning of Lent.

p. 282 *écorché*: (French) anatomical figure without the skin, showing the muscular structure of the body.

p. 282 **Adonis:** cf. note to 'The Honourable Laura', p. 390.

p. 284 **lion-and-unicorn**: cf. note to 'The Three Strangers', p. 392.

p. 284 **the happy times in which we live**: the 19th century was in Britain a period of unprecedented dynamism in church building and church restoration, aimed to keep pace with the rapid growth of the population and with the movement of people from rural to urban areas.

p. 286 **whose ancestor had run scores of Saracens through and through in fighting for the site of the Holy Sepulchre**: i.e. took part in the crusades (military expeditions by Western Christians against Muslim powers in order to take possession of the Holy Land). There were eight major crusades between 1095 and 1291.

p. 287 **purest Carrara marble**: marble from Carrara (town in northwestern Italy) is believed to be the finest in the world.

p. 288 **Phoebus-Apollo**: in Greek mythology, the god of the sun.

p. 289 **knotting**: knitting of knots for fancy-work, similar to tatting.

pp. 292–4 **When she was in her bed-chamber ... all he could to restore her**: the whole passage was removed from the British serial version.

p. 296 **satyr**: in Roman mythology, one of a class of woodland gods, with a goat's ears, tail, legs, and budding horns.

The Son's Veto
The story, thought by Hardy to be his best, was written in Dorchester and London in the spring of 1891 and published in the Christmas number of the *Illustrated London News* on 1 December that year. It was collected, with minor revisions, in *Life's Little Ironies* (1894).

p. 297 **poll**: here, nape of the neck.

p. 298 **public school**: (in England) private fee-paying secondary school, esp. for boarders; here, possibly Harrow.

p. 300 **college living**: parish whose vicar was appointed by an Oxford or Cambridge college.

p. 301 **tie-beams**: rods or beams holding parts of a structure together.

p. 303 *milieu*: (French) environment or social surroundings.

p. 304 **Covent Garden market**: fruit and vegetable market in central London. Hardy saw carts delivering goods to Covent Garden when he stayed in London in 1888.

p. 304 **howdahs:** seats for riding on the back of an elephant or a camel, usually with a canopy.

p. 308 **Lord's:** England's most important cricket ground, at St John's Wood, London, headquarters of the Marylebone Cricket Club, and traditional venue for numerous events, including the annual match between the public schools of Eton and Harrow.

p. 308 *débris:* (French) scattered fragments, esq. of something wrecked or destroyed.

On the Western Circuit

The story was written in Dorchester and London in the summer of 1891; it was published in the *English Illustrated Magazine* in December that year, having first appeared, in America, in *Harper's Weekly* on 28 November. Editorial requirements demanded some major bowdlerizations: in the magazine version, references to Raye's seduction of Anna and her resulting pregnancy are all carefully excised; Mrs Harnham is a widow rather than a wife, with an uncle replacing her wine-merchant husband. These changes were reinstated when the story was collected, in 1894, in *Life's Little Ironies*; at the same time, Hardy added a number of comments stressing, in remarkably explicit terms, the sexual nature of Mrs Harnham's attraction to Raye.

p. 311 **Western Circuit:** (before 1971) one of the territorial subdivisions of the High Court of Justice, consisting of the counties of south-western England.

p. 311 **barrel-organs:** mechanical musical instruments in which a rotating pin-studded cylinder acts on a series of pipe-valves, strings, or metal tongues.

p. 311 **eighth chasm of the Inferno:** for those who have committed fraud; cf. Dante, *La Divina Commedia*, I, xviii–xxx.

p. 311 **Homeric heaven:** cf. Homer, *Iliad*, I, 595–604.

p. 313 **rococo-work:** elaborate ornamentation in the light, playful style characteristic of the early 18th century.

p. 315 **pea-jacket:** short double-breasted overcoat of coarse woollen cloth.

p. 315 **wideawake:** soft felt hat with a low crown and wide brim.

p. 315 **stuff-gownsman:** (in England) barrister who is not a Queen's (King's) Counsel.

p. 315 educated at Wintoncester: Winchester College, the oldest of English public schools (founded in 1382).

p. 315 called to the Bar at Lincoln's-Inn: in England, to qualify as a barrister one has to complete a course of training in one of the four Inns of Court in London: Gray's Inn, Lincoln's Inn, Inner Temple, or Middle Temple.

p. 318 calendar: list of prisoners for trial at the assizes (cf. note to 'The Distracted Preacher', p. 387).

p. 318 in the best fashion of Assyrian bas-reliefs: reminiscent of ancient sculptures from Mesopotamia, like those exhibited in the British Museum.

p. 320 *ensemble*: (French) here: overall effect.

p. 322 days of national education: Elementary Education Act (1870) established the principle of the responsibility of the state for the provision of elementary education, which was subsequently made compulsory (1880) and free (1891).

p. 323 indited: put into words.

p. 323 *pis aller*: (French) course of action followed as a last resort.

p. 324 That he had been able to seduce another woman in two days was his crowning though unrecognized fascination for her as the she-animal: perhaps the most important of the additions introduced into the text of the story prior to its publication in *Life's Little Ironies*, this sentence reflects Hardy's search for a more direct and explicit treatment of the theme of Mrs Harnham's sexuality.

p. 325 *protégée:* (French) woman remaining under someone's protection, patronage, or tutelage.

p. 327 woolsack: (in Britain) the seat of the Lord Chancellor in the House of Lords, formerly made of a large square sack of wool; the symbol of his office, the highest in British judicature.

p. 329 as a domestic animal who humbly heard but understood not: source not identified.

The Fiddler of the Reels

The story was written in Dorchester in the winter of 1892–3, commissioned to be published, in May 1893, in the Exhibition Number of *Scribner's Magazine*, marking the Chicago World Fair. It was collected the following year, with minor revisions only, in *Life's Little Ironies*.

p. 334 **Great Exhibition of 1851, in Hyde Park, London:** organized by the Society of Arts, under the presidency of Prince Albert, between May and October 1851.

p. 334 **Conquest:** conquest of England by the Normans in 1066.

p. 334 **Greenhill Fair:** annual entertainment and sheep fair held on Woodbury Hill in September.

p. 335 **Paganini:** Niccolò Paganini (1782–1840), Italian violinist and composer renowned for his technical virtuosity.

p. 335 **'Favourite Quick Steps':** popular 18th-century dance tunes.

p. 335 **old Mellstock quire-band:** cf. *Under the Greenwood Tree*.

p. 335 **plumness:** solidity.

p. 336 **'Wold Hundredth':** (dial.) mid-16th-century tune to the metrical translation of Psalm C by Nahum Tate and Nicholas Brady; one of Hardy's favourite melodies.

p. 336 **brazen serpent:** cf. note to 'The Three Strangers', p. 39, as well as Numbers 21:9 and 2 Kings 18:4.

p. 338 **withywind:** bindweed.

p. 338 **railway to South Wessex:** Dorchester was first reached by railway in 1847.

p. 339 **this huge glass-house:** Crystal Palace, built in Hyde Park in 1851 to house the London Exhibition; taken down and re-erected in south London in 1852–4, it was destroyed by fire in 1936.

p. 340 **indited:** here: wrote.

p. 341 **novelty on the Wessex line, and probably everywhere:** special excursion trains were run on most lines from June 1851 to serve those wishing to visit the Exhibition.

p. 342 **totties:** (dial.) feet, toes.

p. 346 **'My Fancy Lad':** one of Hardy's favourite tunes in his childhood.

p. 347 **'The Fairy Dance':** another of Hardy's favourite tunes.

p. 347 **foods of love:** cf. *Twelfth Night*, I, i, 1 ('If music be the food of love, play on').

p. 349 Dantesque: characteristic of the works of the Italian poet Dante Alighieri (1265–1321), particularly *La Divina Commedia*.

p. 350 raft: (dial.) disturb, alarm.

An Imaginative Woman

The story was written mainly in Dorchester in the summer of 1893; it was offered, for £100, to the literary agent William Morris Colles, who arranged for it to be published in the *Pall Mall Magazine* in April 1894. it was first collected, with minor revisions, in 1896, when, in the collected Osgood-McIlvaine Hardy, it was added to *Wessex Tales*; in the 1912 Wessex edition, it was transferred to *Life's Little Ironies*.

To a degree greater than most of Hardy's other stories, 'An Imaginative Woman' can be seen as relating to the circumstances of Hardy's own personal life, with the vision of the unfulfilled romantic potential of a relationship between Ella Marchmill and Robert Trewe reflecting his perception of his friendship with Florence Henniker. This may explain why Hardy claimed, in his autobiography, to have 'found and touched up' the story only in December 1893, although it had in fact been despatched to Colles on 14 September the same year; the rather secretive man that he was becoming in his old age, Hardy did not want the story to be associated too directly with Mrs Henniker, whom he first met in May 1893 and with whom he may have hoped in the following months, when they met several times and remained in permanent correspondence, to develop a more intimate relationship. Hardy may also have been influenced by Flaubert's *Madame Bovary* and Mary Braddon's *The Doctor's Wife*.

p. 351 Jove: Jupiter, king of the gods in Roman mythology; here, an exclamation of surprise.

p. 351 lymphatic: inactive, sluggish.

p. 351 'a votary of the muse': cf. Browning, 'The Two Poets of Croisic', XXXI, 1–2 ('silence and solitude / Befit the votary of the Muse').

p. 352 mentally walked round it: cf. Psalm 48:12 ('Walk about Zion, and go round about her; tell the towers thereof') and *The Return of the Native*, I, 7 ('she had mentally walked round love, told the towers thereof').

p. 352 proprietor's: until the Married Women's Property Acts (1882, 1884), a woman was legally a 'chattel', or property, of her husband.

p. 354 embayed: enclosed as in a bay, shut in.

p. 355 neither _symboliste_ nor _décadent_: in France in the 1880s and 90s the spirit of _décadence_ (sense of exhaustion and futility, disillusionment with the world, distaste for moral and religious restraint) led to the development of symbolism, a poetic movement stressing the fluidity and musicality of poetic form, the departure from realism, the role of subjective impressions, intuition, etc.; its main representatives were Stéphane Mallarmé and Paul Verlaine.

p. 355 sonnets in the loosely rhymed Elizabethan fashion: possibly using rhyming scheme _abab bcbc cdcd ee_, as in Spenser's _Amoretti_ and Hardy's 'Her Reproach', or _abab cdcd efef gg_, as in the sonnets of Shakespeare and in Hardy's 'From Her in the Country'.

p. 356 afflatus: divine impulse of creative power or inspiration.

p. 358 circumambient: surrounding.

p. 358 mantle of Elijah: when the prophet Elijah was instructed by God to anoint Elisha to be his successor, he 'cast his mantle upon him' (1 Kings 19:19).

p. 359 Green Silesian band: Silesia, now in Poland, was in the 19th century an Eastern province of Germany.

p. 360 'Severed Lives': possibly an allusion to Dante Gabriel Rossetti's 'Severed Selves' (_The House of Life_, XL).

p. 361 imperial: small part of the beard left growing beneath the lower lip. as worn by Emperor Napoleon III.

p. 362 _bouts-rimés_: (French) pairs of words with rhyming endings.

p. 362 Shelley's scraps: Percy Bysshe Shelley (1792–1822) was one of England's greatest Romantic poets.

p. 362 'Forms more real than living man ...': Shelley, _Prometheus Unbound_, I, 748–9.

p. 362 she was sleeping on a poet's lips: cf. ibid., I, 737 ('On a poet's lips I slept').

p. 365 permanent way: finished roadbed of a railway.

pp. 366–7 'Behold, he standeth ... through the lattice' ... 'And, lo, the winter is past ... is heard in our land': Song of Solomon 2:9, 11–12.

p. 367 _chiton_: in ancient Greece and Rome, a loose woollen tunic worn knee length by men and full length by women.

p. 367 *tremolo*-stop: in an organ, mechanical device producing a tremolous or vibrating effect.

p. 370 'The hour which might have been ...': D. G. Rossetti, 'Stillborn Love' (*The House of Life*, LV), 1–3.

GLOSSARY OF PLACE NAMES
IN HARDY'S WESSEX

ALDBRICKHAM, Reading.

ANGLEBURY, Wareham.

BLOOM'S END, see EGDON HEATH.

BUDMOUTH, Weymouth

CASTERBRIDGE, Dorchester. The MUSEUM is the Dorset County Museum. The prison was rebuilt in 1884–5, but the stone portal of the original building (1790–2) has been preserved; the hangman's cottage nearby still remains. The White Hart is still to be visited. The MAI-DUN is Maiden Castle, one and a half miles south-west of Dorchester.

CHENE, Canford Magna. The manor-house was rebuilt in 1825–36, but the 15th-century John of Gaunt's kitchen still survives.

CLIFF-MARTIN, Combe Martin. The PROSPECT HOTEL is imaginary; its location, however, can be identified as the coast of Woody Bay. The 'nearest railway-town' is Lynton, on the Barnstaple and Lynton railway, now closed.

COCKDENE, Cogdean.

DAGGER'S GRAVE, see LULWIND COVE.

DOWNSTAPLE, Barnstaple.

EAST SHALDON, see SHALDON.

EGDON HEATH, a composite of numerous heaths between Stinsford and Bournemouth. Rushy Pond and Heedless William's Pond are both in its western part, near Higher Bockhampton, as are BLOOM'S END (difficult to identify precisely), the fir-woods of MISTOVER, and the site of the QUIET WOMAN inn (modelled on the old Duck Dairy Farm, between Stinsford and Tincleton, now rebuilt). The 'YALBURY coppices' are Yellowham Wood.

EXONBURY, Exeter. The ASSEMBLY ROOMS are imaginary.

GAYMEAD, variously identified as Theale, Shinfield, or Sulhampstead Abbots.

GREAT (MID-WESSEX) PLAIN, Salisbury Plain.

GREENHILL, Woodbury Hill, near Bere Regis.

HAVENPOOL, Poole.

HIGHER CROWSTAIRS, probably on Hog Hill, near Charminster, three miles north-west of Dorchester.

HOLMSTOKE, East Stoke. Farmer Lodge's house is difficult to identify; it may be Hethfelton House, some two miles north-west of the village; the GREAT WEIR could then be Stony Weir on the Frome. The location of Conjuror Trendle's house is not clear. The old church of St Mary is now a ruin.

IDMOUTH, Sidmouth.

KINGSBERE, Bere Regis.

KNOLLINGWOOD, Wimborne St Giles. The HALL is St Giles House.

KNOLLSEA, Swanage.

LEWGATE, see MELLSTOCK.

LORNTON, Horton. The inn, now refurbished, is still there to be visited. The (GREAT) FOREST is the New Forest, and the CHASE is Cranborne Chase.

LOWER MELLSTOCK, see MELLSTOCK.

LOWER WESSEX, Devon.

LULWIND COVE, Lulworth Cove. DAGGER'S GRAVE is Dagger's Gate, a crossroads nearby.

MELCHESTER, Salisbury. The Early English Gothic cathedral (1220–58) is indeed 'the most homogeneous pile of mediaeval architecture in England'. OLD MELCHESTER, with its earthworks, is Old Sarum.

MELLSTOCK, Stinsford. LOWER MELLSTOCK is Lower Bockhampton; LEWGATE is Higher Bockhampton.

MID-WESSEX, Wiltshire.

MISTOVER, see EGDON HEATH.

MOREFORD, Moreton.

NETHER-MOYNTON, Owermoigne. The parish church was rebuilt in 1883, but the old Perpendicular tower still remains.

NORTH WESSEX, Berkshire.

OUTER WESSEX, Somerset.

PORT-BREDY, Bridport. St Mary's church, the townhall, the Bull Hotel (BLACK-BULL HOTEL), and the Congregational church (built in 1859) are all actual buildings, still to be seen in the town. CHÂTEAU RINGDALE is imaginary. The harbour is that of West Bay; the HARBOUR INN is the Bridport Arms.

QUIET WOMAN, see EGDON HEATH.

RINGSWORTH, Ringstead Bay.

SHALDON/EAST SHALDON, East Chaldon/Chaldon Herring.

SHALDON DOWN, Chaldon Down.

SHERTON ABBAS, Sherborne.

SHOTTSFORD/SHOTTSFORD FORUM, Blandford Forum.

SILVERTHORN, Silverton. MOUNT LODGE, ROOK'S GATE, and CHIL-LINGTON WOOD are all imaginary. The 'next county' is Somerset (OUTER WESSEX), and its county town is Taunton (TONEBOROUGH).

SOLENTSEA, Southsea. NEW PARADE might be St Helen's Parade. The CEMETERY may be the one in Highland Road. The 'Island opposite' is the Isle of Wight; the 'fashionable town' there is Ryde.

SOUTH WESSEX, Dorset.

STICKLEFORD, Tincleton. The 'petty roadside station that lay nearest Stickleford' is at Moreton.

TIVWORTHY, Tiverton.

TONEBOROUGH, Taunton. ST MARY'S church is that of St Mary Magdalen.

UPPER WESSEX, Hampshire.

WARBORNE, Wimborne Minster.

WARM'LL, Warmwell.

WINTONCESTER, Winchester.

YALBURY see EGDON HEATH.

YEWSHOLT, Farrs, one and a half miles west of Wimborne. The house is still there to be seen.

HARDY AND HIS CRITICS

It is something of an irony of circumstance that the short stories of Thomas Hardy, although acclaimed by some critics as ranking among the best achievements of the genre in the English language, do not seem to have earned their author a reputation, as a writer of short fiction, comparable to those enjoyed by Henry James or Rudyard Kipling. Hardy's achievement in the field of the novel has for over a century now been beyond dispute; the last fifty years have witnessed a recognition of his influence as a major force in the development of modern English poetry – and yet his short stories, though duly respected as part of the Hardy canon and in consequence regularly reprinted and anthologized, tend on the whole to be treated in a rather cursory manner, relegated to chapters on 'minor works' or mentioned in passing if they happen to exemplify particular points raised in the analysis of Hardy's major novels or, less often, his poetry. As a result, Hardy's short stories, though reasonably well-known, or rather well-known-about, still remain, in comparison with the rest of his *oeuvre*, relatively under-researched; they have to date generated only one full-length critical study, and their major place in the development of the short story as a genre has been recognized, rather significantly, only by critics who are, like John Bayley or Harold Orel, Hardy specialists in their own right.

The traditional perception of Hardy's stories as footnotes to – or perhaps spill-overs from – his major fiction goes back to the time of their first publication: as could in fact well have been expected, most of the early reviews placed the stories against the background of Hardy's novels in an attempt to look for analogies, similarities, or contrasts. Thus, in the case of *Wessex Tales* (1888), the comparisons tended to be favourable: the *Literary World* praised the stories for their 'genuine local colouring, painted with all the charm of Mr Hardy's best style'[1], while the *Glasgow Herald* saw them as illustrating Hardy's 'dramatic faculty of grouping characters' and his 'imaginative power of eliciting deepest tragedy from people and circumstances among whom and in which one would least anticipate it'[2]. The reviewer of the *Athenaeum* was alone in complaining that *Wessex Tales* did not display Hardy's usual 'power of humour [and] ... his talent for telling a story'[3]; the predominant view was expressed by the *Westminster Review*, which described the stories as 'homely and rugged, but never commonplace, intensely real, yet highly idyllic and poetical'[4]. Singled out for praise were 'The Distracted Preacher' and 'The Three Strangers', the former as a 'thrilling smuggler's story of daring ingenuity mingled with much which is irresistibly comic, and led up to by a gradual unfolding and mutual recognition of character on the part of the two chief actors which make the whole stand out before us with striking reality'[5], the latter for 'the tension of its wild emotion, raising common scenes and common speakers, in the midst of their ludicrous humours, to the heights of tragedy'[6] – in a word, the main merit of the stories was judged to consist in recapturing the method and spirit of many of the earlier novels, such as, for instance, *Far from the Madding Crowd* and *The Return of the Native*.

Critical opinion was far less favourable to *A Group of Noble Dames* (1891) – although the *World* hailed the stories as marking 'the Victorian return to the great tragic motives of the Periclean and Elizabethan dramatists'[7], and the *Literary World* found the overall quality of the stories 'impossible to deny'[8], other views were more critical. The *Saturday Review* called the collection 'a literary freak'[9]; the *Spectator*, while appreciating the realism of Hardy's descriptions of rural life, complained of his 'low view of women' and 'a certain nauseous element' about the stories[10]; finally, the *National Review* criticized Hardy's unnecessary coarseness, targeting in particular 'Barbara of the House of Grebe', which it described as 'revolting in its forced and hysterical materialism'[11]. Many of the critical opinions and attitudes expressed in these reviews were indeed to be voiced over and over again in the early and mid-1890s, during the controversies surrounding the publication of *Tess of the d'Urbervilles* and, in particular, *Jude the Obscure*.

Between these two, however, came *Life's Little Ironies* (1894). The critics were rather more favourable to Hardy this time: the *Athenaeum* praised his 'magnificently sombre pictures of Wessex life'[12], while the *Bookman* commended the stories for their 'delicacy of diction, the sweetness of simple English, the purity and charm of style'[13]; the new collection was also praised in the *Academy* by the doyen of Victorian literary taste, George Saintsbury[14]. The power of Hardy's writing was recognized by the *Spectator*, which, however, sounded a characteristic note of reservation in stressing the 'dreary feeling of inevitableness as [the reader] follows the chain being remorselessly forged for its victims' and stating that Hardy's women characters suffered from 'a touch of vulgarity'[15]. The more directly outspoken voice of Mrs Grundy was in evidence too: the *Literary World*, for instance, criticized 'On the Western Circuit' as 'dangerous for a girl to read'[16].

The nineteen years that elapsed before the publication of Hardy's next, and last, volume of short stories, *'A Changed Man' and Other Tales* (1913), changed both the tastes of the English reading public and the place occupied in the literary world by Hardy himself – the controversies surrounding his works well behind him, Hardy, the last of the great Victorians, was becoming very much a national institution, the Grand Old Man of English letters. No wonder then that the tone of the reviews of his new collection of stories was almost unanimously respectful and sometimes even laudatory; the *Nation* declared that 'nobody but Mr Hardy possess[ed] the secret of this thin, fine atmosphere of reticent tragedy . . . as spiritually delicate as the air of a chalk down'[17], while the *Daily Mail* praised the 'tragic sense of an epic range as deep and wide as the sense of fate in Aeschylus or of historical doom in the sagas'[18]. Only the *Times Literary Supplement*, though generally appreciative, worried about Hardy's unwillingness to 'humour and pacify, to make happy, his puppets'[19].

In the earliest book-length studies of Hardy's work, the discussion of his short stories centred, again, on their significance *vis-à-vis* his novels. Thus, according to Annie Macdonell (1894), the essence of Hardy's artistic achievement lay exactly in his ability to restrict the scope of his tales to achieve compactness of form:

It is not only that he has learnt not to be discursive, where order, clearness, deftness, are the first qualities, where fine cut and finish tell more than wealth of material. His scheme, conscious or unconscious, has affected his choice of subject, his style, and his tone. Some of the plots of his shorter tales might, of course, have been elaborated into novels, but a further elaboration does not pressingly suggest itself. As you look, you feel that a small canvas is the more fitting. He has seen that the chief use of short stories is to skim the surface of life and when he has struck a tragic note in these, he has restrained his expression as far as possible. What is food for light satire or laughter, and incidents that draw a sigh rather than a wail, are the materials he moulds best and most frequently into this form.[20]

Although Lascelles Abercrombie's (1912) interpretation of Hardy's fictional method takes a diametrically opposite view, he none the less recognizes the artistic respectability of the short stories as significant constituents of Hardy's Wessex world:

> In Hardy's hands, fiction has done, in the scale of the novel, what previously it could only do with certainty and ease in the scale of the short story; the power of making a human action render, with astonishing impressiveness, and by means of a most exact formality, some metaphysic of existence. . . . To exercise this power his fiction requires expatiation rather than concentration. But, though his short stories are a decoration for his main literary structure, they are entirely appropriate decoration. They give us, in varying forms and manners, his characteristic vision of life; what we miss in them is the subtle declaration of what that vision profoundly *means* to his inmost emotion. If they do not add much power to the effect of his writings as a whole, they nevertheless perfectly fit in with it.[21]

In the 1920s and 1930s the consensus of critical opinion turned sharply against Hardy's stories, very much in line with the general direction of the Modernist response to all things Victorian. Although some critics, such as Patrick Braybrooke (1928)[22] and Fergal McGrath (1928)[23], wrote about his short fiction with appreciation –

> [Hardy's] short stories have all the power of his novels, wealth of description, quaint lore of the Wessex countryside, shrewd psychology. In addition, they are comparatively free from one of the great blemishes of his novels, the intruding presence of the 'Fate motif'.[24]

– the prevalent view was that Hardy's stories were simply bad literature. Thus, 'The Romantic Adventures of a Milkmaid' was described, in 1922, as 'the most arrant pot-boiler that was ever turned out by tired and harassed writer of novels'[25]; 'Barbara of the House of Grebe' was first savagely (and very amusingly as it happens) parodied by George Moore (1924)[26], and then declared, by T. S. Eliot (1934) to have been written 'solely to provide a satisfaction for some morbid emotion'[27]; finally, in 1938, all the stories were ruthlessly denied what would have amounted to an official stamp of approval when William Rutland, in a book that was to become for many years the most authoritative study of Hardy's work, said that 'on a general review of them, one is tempted to say that the distinguishing characteristics of Hardy's short stories are improbability and unpleasantness'[28].

The revival of interest in and study of Hardy that began in 1940 with the publication of the Hardy Centennial Edition of the *Southern Review* did not for several years result in a major revaluation of the short stories; significantly, some of the best Hardy critics from that period ignored the stories altogether[29], while others, rather characteristically, offered broad generalizations and/or sympathetic summaries of their personal favourites, without, however, attempting much in terms of closer textual analysis, interpretation, or classification of Hardy's short fiction. This was the case even though some of the stories were judged very highly indeed; when Albert J. Guerard (1949) declared 'The Fiddler of the Reels' 'one of the finest short stories in the language'[30], he did so very much as an aside, taking the story as an illustration of the main line of his argument about Hardy's vision of the world of Wessex rather than as a subject of study in its own right.

It was not until the 1960s that Hardy's stories began to attract more serious critical attention, with some of the most interesting work concentrating on the question of their place in the broader tradition of short fiction. Thus, Richard C. Carpenter (1964) addressed the question of whether Hardy's short stories could be legitimately called short stories at all:

> In essence Hardy's short stories belong to the oral tradition of the *tale*, rather than to the compressed and consciously artistic form which we have come to think of as the 'short story' since Poe and Chekhov. He is clearly not scrupulous about the construction of the story, but lets it meander about where it will; character is not developed; he seems unaware of any need for unity of effect; and his purpose is seldom thematic beyond indicating the irony of existence.

Oftentimes, as for example in 'The Withered Arm' . . ., there seems to be nearly enough material for a novel; what Hardy is doing resembles a plot synopsis, with dramatic scenes interspersed. On the other hand, like the bards in whose tradition he is working, Hardy has a keen sense of the fundamental qualities of a story, which, as James said, must be *interesting* first of all. He deals with the bases of human action, with love and jealousy, ambition and frustration, the power of fear and hate. His view is radically ironic, his humour wry and folklike so that we come away from his best tales as we come away from the ballad: we feel that we have come to grips with life, and death, in a powerfully monitory way.[31]

T. O. Beachcroft (1968), in turn, offered the first attempt to consider Hardy's short stories in the context of the historical development of the genre; in his view, Hardy's stories, though overshadowed by the novels and poems, are, alongside Robert Louis Stevenson's, among the best produced in the late nineteenth century. Interestingly, though Hardy 'has the kind of imagination that looks back to his own young days'[32], the modernity of his themes and the poetic quality of his vision make him a startlingly modern writer:

A writer of a later generation to whom these stories are surprisingly close is D. H. Lawrence. In 'The Son's Veto' we have a working-class girl giving comfort to a clergyman whose former wife has been ill and childless; then a self-conscious class struggle between a son and his mother; finally, the suggestion that Sam, the country worker, is leading a better, more genuine life than the young public school priest. . . .

Hardy has other resemblances to Lawrence as a short-story writer. Although they both wrote a large number of short stories, and among them some very fine ones, they neither of them seem to be greatly concerned with the short story as a form, but were apt to let short stories range and sprawl as they would. Both made a large contribution to literature through novels and poetry. In fact some of Hardy's best story conceptions take the form of short poems. As so often with Hardy, one is amazed that with such a perfect mastery of condensed form in his power he cared at times so little for the craftsmanship of the story.[33]

The poetic quality of Hardy's short stories was further explored by Jean Brooks (1971):

The result of lack of space to develop the delicate counterpoint between narrative and poetic impulses can be seen in many of Hardy's tales. . . . Many tales suffer from an overbalance of [his characteristic vision of life] or [of his inmost emotion]. Sometimes it is an excess of poetic feeling. 'A Tryst at an Ancient Earthwork' builds up a powerful mood picture of Maiden Castle that recalls Egdon Heath in *The Return of the Native*. But its 'obtrusive personality' overpowers the slight incident of the scholar's discovery, and probable theft, of a Roman statuette. On the other hand, the slow-paced evocation of night, storm and pastoral setting that begins 'The Three Strangers' contributes to its meaning. The ironic but unlikely conjunction of life and death embodied in the meeting of hangman and intended victim gains imaginative belief from the echoes of Christian ritual – the shepherd's cottage at the cross-roads, the christening, the three strangers, the three knocks, the victim's drink at the door, the ritual withdrawal in a 'remote circle' from the *cinder*-grey stranger, 'whom some of them seemed to take for the Prince of Darkness himself' – blended with the sharp details of the pastoral world that is at once part of the myth and a guarantee of authenticity in the world of sense experience; 'the tails of little birds trying to roost on some scraggy thorn were blown inside-out like umbrellas', and the earthy Wessex humour of the guests. The swift telling of the tale, with its skilful use of primary narrative effects of suspense, surprise, expectation, ritual repetition, false inference, and true conclusion, all converging on a single dramatic crisis, makes a satisfactory poetic image of life such as one finds in poems of situation like 'Life and Death in Sunrise', 'At the Railway Station, Upway', and the title poems of *Satires of Circumstance*.

The most obvious lack of balance comes in those tales where plot dominates. The power of events and the effects of time are among Hardy's major themes. An extended form, almost a skeleton novel, is used to develop the consequences of missed chances, possibilities of rechoice, the righting or consolidation of old wrongs, the maturing of ambition, revenge, compassion, or indifference, and the quirks of fate that complete a design in an unexpected manner. But the sensational happenings and coincidences that embody Hardy's essence of the cosmic Absurd become less credible in a crowded synopsis unprepared for by poetic atmosphere. The sudden deaths of Mrs Downes [*sic*!] and Mrs Barnet . . . are little more than improbable plot devices to set in motion the endeavour 'to rectify early deviations of the heart by harking back to the old point'.[34]

The first full typology of Hardy's stories was proposed in 1977 by Norman Page:

More generally, four types of stories may be distinguished: (1) those revealing a humorous and affectionate observation of rustic life (e.g., 'A Few Crusted Characters' (1891, *LLI*: the date given is that of first publication, the initials those of the volume in which the story was collected) and 'The Distracted Preacher' (1879, *WT*)); (2) tales on romantic or supernatural themes, often reminiscent of balladry and folk-tales (e.g., 'The Withered Arm' (1888, *WT*) and 'The Fiddler of the Reels' (1893, *LLI*)); (3) realistic and often ironic or tragic stories of modern life, usually later in date of composition than most of those in the previous two categories (e.g., 'On the Western Circuit' (1891, *LLI*) and 'An Imaginative Woman' (1894, *LLI*)); (4) historical tales, set in the Napoleonic period ('A Tradition of 1804' (1882, *WT*), 'The Melancholy Hussar of the German Legion' (1890, *LLI*)) or earlier (*A Group of Noble Dames*). Though there is inevitably some overlapping between these groups, each of them may be related to a distinctive element in Hardy's work as a whole. (1) has obvious affinities with the rustic portions of the Wessex novels, (2) with the many poems of ballad type in the *Collected Poems*, (3) with the late novels, especially *Tess of the d'Urbervilles* and *Jude the Obscure*, and (4) with *The Trumpet-Major* and *The Dynasts*. The last of these groups is probably the least interesting: stories like 'A Tradition of 1804' seem to resemble a discarded episode from one of the longer works cited, and with the exception of the powerful story 'Barbara of the House of Grebe', *A Group of Noble Dames* shows neither Hardy's characteristic preoccupations nor his imagination as fully engaged. As always, he conveys a sense of the past most successfully when he is not explicitly working with historical or pseudo-historical material.

The examples in the first of the four groups are not without interest, but add little to the knowledge of Hardy that is derived from the major fiction. Such stories as 'The Distracted Preacher', in which observation and recollection are shaped into rustic romance, with a stimulating touch of astringency, belong to the world of *Under the Greenwood Tree* and to comparable passages in some of the other novels. But the second and third groups contain stories that are not only successful in their own right but constitute an extension of Hardy's art, taking up (it is true) elements that exist elsewhere but developing them with the clarity and concentration demanded by the genre. It is here that we find the by no means negligible best of Hardy's work in the short-story medium, though it has so far been accorded little recognition.[35]

Page then goes on to discuss in greater detail four stories representing, two each, these two most successful strands in Hardy's short fiction – 'The Romantic Adventures of a Milkmaid' and 'The Fiddler of the Reels' from the second group, and 'On the Western Circuit' and 'An Imaginative Woman' from the third.

That those four stories should have been singled out as particularly significant examples of Hardy's achievement in the genre is indeed symptomatic of the direction that the study of Hardy's tales, very much in line with broader developments in modern literary criticism, seems to have taken over the last twenty years. The attention of most critics shifted, some time in the 1970s, from the 'old-time Hardy favourites' such as 'The Three Strangers' or 'The Distracted Preacher' – fully realistic, related to the traditional Wessex background, classically structured and neat in execution – to stories reflecting the alternative side of Hardy, his interest in the unusual, the bizarre, the grotesque, the unexplained, the subjective. This is indeed why Walter Allen's (1981) comments on Hardy's stories ('they are at their best when at their furthest remove from the modern short story'[36]) sound so curiously old-fashioned now; the impression is enhanced when Allen's reading of Hardy is compared to that suggested, also in 1981, by Rosemary Sumner. This is, for instance, what she has to say about 'The Fiddler of the Reels':

'The Fiddler of the Reels' is a powerful evocation of a state of being in which all conscious control and even identity is dissipated. Mop playing the fiddle manipulates and controls every movement and Car'line responds involuntarily but with a kind of willingness which indicates the sexual attraction she feels. The power of this story lies in the vividness of Hardy's evocation of Car'line's experience. By focusing on the music and the dancing and using these as a symbolic expression of sexual domination, he achieves an effect of extreme concentration. It is a rare example of Hardy using the brevity of the short story form to advantage.

The theoretical basis of the story – Hardy's interest in hypnotic states, in the effect of music on a susceptible person, and in the control and manipulation of one person by another – are all completely embodied in the central characters, so that the reader is far more aware of the lived experience of Car'line, of her hypnotised state, her compulsive response to the music and her physical exhaustion than of the possibility of a 'neurological explanation' which Hardy suggests would be available if we cared to look for it. This is rare in those short stories which deal with unusual psychological states. In most of them, the *idea* of the psychological oddity is conveyed clearly, but a feeling of what it is like to experience such a state is not usually adequately suggested.[37]

This is followed by a discussion, far too long to be quoted here, of 'Barbara of the House of Grebe', another of the short stories to have been radically re-evaluated over the last two decades; the point of the argument is succinctly summarized in the conclusion:

['Barbara of the House of Grebe'] shows that even when writing sensationally and superficially, Hardy still has extraordinary insight into how the mind works, and even foresees how men will use such knowledge in the future. It may seem extraordinary to suggest that Hardy's interest in psychology has led him to foresee the development of aversion therapy long before it was practised, but this story, and the introduction to it in *A Group of Noble Dames*, seem to me fully to justify such a claim.[38]

An attempt at a thorough and comprehensive analysis of the entire course of Hardy's career as a writer of short fiction arrived, finally, with the publication of Kristin Brady's study *The Short Stories of Thomas Hardy: Tales of Past and Present* (1982). Very full and immensely informative as well as thoroughly readable, the book comes close to being a definitive study of the subject; it offers a clear account of the relevant aspects of the historical, personal, and literary background of Hardy's work as well as some very interesting readings of all the individual stories. Kristin Brady's most important contribution lies in defining what she sees as unifying principles underlying Hardy's arrangement of his stories into collections; unlike any of her predecessors, she analyses *Wessex Tales*, *A Group of Noble Dames*, and *Life's Little Ironies* as separate, distinct unities defined by a particular type of narratorial perspective:

Within the broad spectrum of Hardy's experiments in the short story are certain subjects, themes, image patterns, and techniques which are frequently repeated. This fact has led some critics to accuse Hardy of tedious self-duplication, and others to use these similarities as a basis for analysing his work along specific categorical guidelines, yoking together stories from different periods and volumes, and ignoring Hardy's conscious arrangement of them in *Wessex Tales*, *A Group of Noble Dames*, and *Life's Little Ironies*. Such a method illuminates similarities among all the stories, but arbitrarily removes them both from their chronological context and from the thematic context which Hardy himself chose to give them. . . . Hardy's own organization of the stories, on the other hand, is based not only on subject matter, setting, and theme, but also on an equally important, but less obvious division – that of narrative voice. The *Noble Dames* stories, filtered through the narrow and distorted perspective of the Antiquarian Club, are different in quite essential ways from the traditional stories in *Wessex Tales*, whose meaning and complexity are based on the clarity and breadth of perspective that characterize the pastoral voice. . . .

The labels I have attached to the three short-story volumes – parstoral histories, ambivalent exempla, and tragedies of circumstance – are merely descriptive of the types of story which emerge from their three different narrative modes. The pastoral perspective draws together the stories of *Wessex Tales*, the subjective perspective of the Antiquarian Club gives the *Noble Dames* stories their two levels of moral interpretation, and the ironic perspective of the voice in *Life's Little Ironies* uncovers the tragedy in conventionally farcical situations. This unity of perspective in each volume serves the double purpose of drawing together disparate kinds of material, and making each book as a whole greater than the sum of its parts. The stories are, of course, self-contained, and most of them are rich enough to merit attention in their own right, but even the greatest of them – 'The Three Strangers', 'The Withered Arm', 'A Tragedy of Two Ambitions', 'On the Western Circuit', and 'The Fiddler of the Reels' – acquire a broader range of meaning when seen in the context of their respective volumes. Because none of the *Noble Dames* stories by itself is superlatively good, the similarities and differences among them are especially important, and the two stories which open the volume add substantially to the value of the rest by setting up the pattern of repetition and contrast which structures the book. Most of the stories in *A Group of Noble Dames*, it must be remembered, were never published separately, and therefore have a special claim to be considered as parts of a single, larger work.[39]

Finally, Kristin Brady arrives at her definition of the place that Hardy's tales occupy in the tradition of the short story as a genre:

> Those who have spoken in favour of the short stories have tended, like Irving Howe, to argue that Hardy has 'little to do with the main line of the modern short story' represented by 'Chekhov, Joyce and Hemingway,' and that his work ought to be considered as an example of an older form, the tale – 'a more easy-paced and amiable mode of narrative.'[40] Hardy, however, wrote tales that are consciously crafted and uniquely modern. The stories of *Wessex Tales*, through their use of a pastoral voice, are mimetic reworkings of the old traditional tale. While the oral tale, as Howe says, 'stops, starts up again and wanders, seemingly unconcerned with the effects of accumulation or foreshortening',[41] Hardy's pastoral histories, even the longer ones, are tightly controlled narratives, whose digressions are themselves part of the overall pattern of meaning. The *Noble Dames* stories, with their personal narrators, seem to imitate the oral tale more exactly, but their structure and meaning depend upon a concept that is distinctly literary: the discrepancy between the narrator's point of view and that elicited from the reader by the story itself. The narratives in *Life's Little Ironies* are not oral tales at all in Howe's sense, and their clever inversion of sentimental plots suggests an awareness of literary technique frequently associated with, though certainly not unique to, the 'modern' era. In their way, they are as original in form and style as the stories of a Chekhov, a Joyce, or a Hemingway.
>
> All of Hardy's short-story volumes demonstrate a degree of self-consciousness in narrative strategy which makes them distinct from the 'tale' in its simplest sense. Yet Hardy uses this term indiscriminately to describe his stories, perhaps because all of them, including those in *Life's Little Ironies*, are told in a voice that approximates to the spoken word. In the pastoral, the ambivalent, and the ironic voices of each of the volumes is a unique rhetoric which defines the meaning of each story. . . . Perhaps the genre of Hardy's short stories can best be described by expanding upon A. F. Cassis's observation that Hardy follows two distinct narrative traditions: 'the tradition of the conscious, artistic literary short story, that of the *écrivain*, and the tradition of the *raconteur*, the narrator who simulates a spoken story in print.'[42] In *Wessex Tales* and the *Noble Dames* stories, the *raconteur* is more visible, while in *Life's Little Ironies* it is the

écrivain who is more prominent, but in all of the best stories there is a joining of these two roles which produces a quality that is both oral and literary. It is this double dimension in the narrative voice of Hardy's short stories which makes them, like their author, both profoundly traditional and recognizably 'modern'. They are tales of the past and of the present.[43]

Ironically, the very comprehensiveness and exhaustiveness of Kristin Brady's study seems to have led, in the years following the publication of her book, to a considerable change of the character of critical debate on Hardy's short fiction; rather than attempting to offer alternative visions of Hardy the short-story writer, most critics seem to have accepted Brady's conclusions and turned instead to close readings and interpretations of individual stories, frequently as illustrations of points made in their discussions of very specific and narrowly-defined (if significant and potentially interesting) dimensions of Hardy's *oeuvre* as a whole. This unwillingness to propose an alternative overall interpretation of Hardy's short stories transpires even from two important books on the development of the short story written in the 1980s by two Hardy specialists; though both Harold Orel (1986)[44] and John Bayley (1988)[45] treat Hardy far more attentively than most of the earlier historians of the genre, they do not provide broader critical generalizations, opting instead either for a more fact-based historical approach (Orel), or for a dense and penetrating reading of a few selected stories (Bayley).

In terms of its major thematic concerns, the focus of most of the recent critical work on Hardy's short fiction is still on its open-endedness, indeterminacies, and 'instabilities'[46]. This is, for example, what T. R. Wright (1989) says about the stories in his chapter on 'Diabolical Dames and Grotesque Desires':

Hardy's short stories are often dismissed as melodramtic and clumsy because they are full of such abnormal characters and perverse situations.... Yet Hardy can be seen to be challenging the liberal humanist notion of coherent personality, deliberately focusing on the incoherence of human behaviour, in particular the irrationality of desire. The short stories demonstrate a particular interest in the 'uncanny' in Freud's famous definition, 'that class of the frightening which leads back to what is known of old and long familiar', combining the 'strange' with the 'commonplace', breaking down that 'distinction between imagination and reality' upon which sanity is based and shedding doubt on the stable certainties of the rational world.[47]

And later:

> None of these stories ... concerns itself very deeply with character-isation in the conventional sense, which may explain their relative unpopularity. What they do show, in a complex and powerful manner, is the perennial perversity of desire: its refusal to accommodate itself to morality, to marriage, to any of the means by which people try to bring their lives under some form of control. The world Hardy depicts in his short stories is anarchic and fundamentally cruel, for desire is seen to bring in its wake suffering, sadness and a total disregard for the conventions by which society struggles to survive. To repress it is dangerous and debilitating, yet to indulge it is to make the everyday world which we call 'real' meaningless and absurd.[48]

In a rather similar vein, Roger Ebbatson (1993) studies the ways in which three of Hardy's short stories – characteristically, 'On the Western Circuit', 'An Imaginative Woman', and 'Barbara of the House of Grebe' – investigate, through their uses of symbolism and through their manipulation of the narrative voice, the complex nature of human sexuality, particularly in relation to creativity and power. Ebbatson's interpretations are far too complex to be adequately represented by short excerpts; however, even a brief passage is enough to demonstrate the character of his approach to Hardy, by no means uncontroversial, but for that very reason most stimulating and pointing towards the future:

> 'On the Western Circuit' may itself be read as a kind of letter, an open letter from author to reader. A story in which a woman impersonating a second woman addresses a man known by pseudonymous initials problematizes the very act of interpretation upon which the reader is engaged. The meaning can lie only in the text, but that text, like the letters it purports to describe, remains opaque. The final recognition of the lovers is also inevitably a moment of concealment, a blindness in which the reader is implicated. 'On the Western circuit' is a text which registers a seeping away of bodily passion into verbal expression; the body and its drives are marginalized, energy and sexuality contained by, and tamed into, textuality. Edith's displacement of desire into an endlessly inventive discursivity, a bodiless

speech, acts out that primacy of textuality. Her writing is a bid for authority and a threat to the patriarchal mediation of power wielded by Harnham and Raye. In her dangerous inventiveness Edith begins to challenge the construction of womanhood epitomized by Anna's seduction. In a sense, her writings cover up the gap which the (absent) seduction makes in the text. In this story Hardy produces his *dénouement* through a scrupulously ironized reversal in which speech stands revealed as belated supplement to writing.[49]

References

1. 'Mr Hardy's *Wessex Tales*', *Literary World*, XXXVIII (27 July 1888), p. 76, in Helmut E. Gerber and W. Eugene Davis (eds), *Thomas Hardy: An Annotated Bibliography of Writings about Him*, 2 vols. (De Kalb, Ill.: Northern Illinois University Press, 1973–83). Unless indicated otherwise, all quotations from early newspaper and magazine reviews of Hardy's short stories are taken from excerpts reprinted in Gerber and Davis.
2. 'Novels and Stories', *Glasgow Herald*, 25 May 1888, p. 10.
3. 'Novels of the Week', *Athenaeum*, 30 June 1888, pp. 825–6.
4. 'Belles Lettres', *Westminster Review*, CXXX (July 1888), p. 115.
5. 'Books: Mr Hardy's Wessex Stories', *Spectator*, LXI (28 July 1888), pp. 1037–8.
6. Edmund Gosse, 'Thomas Hardy', *Speaker*, II (13 Sept 1890), p. 295, in R. G. Cox (ed.), *Thomas Hardy: The Critical Heritage* (London: Routledge and Kegan Paul, 1970), p. 171.
7. P. and Q., 'Pages in Waiting', *World*, 8 July 1891, pp. 30–1.
8. 'A Group of Noble Dames', *Literary World*, XLIII (12 June 1891), pp. 556–8.
9. 'New Books and Reprints', *Saturday Review*, LXXI (20 June 1891), pp. 757–8.
10. Untitled review, *Spectator*, LXVII (1 Aug 1891), pp. 163–4.
11. 'Contemporary Literature', *National Review*, XVII (Aug 1891), p. 845.
12. 'Novels of the Week', *Athenaeum*, 24 March 1894, p. 367.
13. Walter Raymond, 'Mr Thomas Hardy's New Book', *Bookman*, VI (April 1894), pp. 18–19.
14. Cf. George Saintsbury, 'New Novels', *Academy*, XLV (2 June 1894), p. 453.
15. 'Books: *Life's Little Ironies*', *Spectator*, LXXI (21 April 1894), pp. 537–9.

16. 'Table Talk', *Literary World*, XLIX (11 May 1894), p. 437.

17. 'Mr Hardy's Evolution', *Nation*, XIV (8 Nov 1913), pp. 262–4.

18. 'The Epic Range of Thomas Hardy', *Daily Mail*, 24 Oct 1913, p. 2.

19. 'A Happy Surprise: Mr Hardy's Short Stories', *Times Literary Supplement*, 30 Oct 1913, p. 479.

20. Annie Macdonell, *Thomas Hardy*, Contemporary Writers (London: Hodder and Stoughton, 1894), p. 76.

21. Lascelles Abercrombie, *Thomas Hardy: A Critical Study* (London: Martin Secker, 1912), pp. 78–9.

22. Cf. Patrick Braybrooke, *Thomas Hardy and His Philosophy* (London: Daniel, 1928).

23. Cf. Fergal McGrath, 'Reviews', *Studies*, XVII (Sept 1928), pp. 504–5.

24. Ibid., p. 504.

25. Joseph Warren Beach, *The Technique of Thomas Hardy* (New York: Russell and Russell, 1922), p. 125.

26. Cf. George Moore, *Conversations in Ebury Street* (London: Heinemann, 1924).

27. T. S. Eliot, *After Strange Gods* (London: Faber, 1934), p. 58.

28. William R. Rutland, *Thomas Hardy: A Study of His Writings and Their Background* (Oxford: Basil Blackwell, 1938), p. 218.

29. Cf. Harvey Curtis Webster, *On a Darkling Plain: The Art and Thought of Thomas Hardy* (Chicago: University of Chicago Press, 1947).

30. Albert J. Guerard, *Thomas Hardy: The Novels and Stories* (London: Oxford University Press, 1949), p. 21.

31. Richard C. Carpenter, *Thomas Hardy*, Twayne's English Authors (New York: Twayne, 1964), pp. 69–70.

32. T. O. Beachcroft, *The Modest Art: A Survey of the Short Story in English* (London: Oxford University Press, 1968), p. 112.

33. Ibid., p. 117.

34. Jean Brooks, *Thomas Hardy: The Poetic Structure* (London: Elek Books, 1961), pp. 143–4.

35. Norman Page, *Thomas Hardy* (London: Routledge and Kegan Paul, 1977), pp. 123–4.

36. Walter Allen, *The Short Story in English* (Oxford: Oxford University Press, 1981), p. 13.

37. Rosemary Sumner, *Thomas Hardy: Psychological Novelist* (London: Macmillan, 1981), p. 22.

38. Ibid., p. 28.

39. Kristin Brady, *The Short Stories of Thomas Hardy: Tales of Past and Present* (London: Macmillan, 1982), pp. 197–8.

40. Irving Howe, *Thomas Hardy* (London: Weidenfeld and Nicolson, 1968), p. 76.

41. Ibid., p. 79.

42. A. F. Cassis, 'A Note on the Structure of Hardy's Short Stories', *Colby Library Quarterly*, X (March 1974), p. 287.

43. Brady (1982), pp. 199–201.

44. Cf. Harold Orel, *The Victorian Short Story: Development and Triumph of a Literary Genre* (Cambridge: Cambridge University Press, 1986).

45. Cf. John Bayley, *The Short Story: Henry James to Elizabeth Bowen* (Brighton: Harvester Press, 1988).

46. Ibid., p. 149.

47. T. R. Wright, *Hardy and the Erotic* (Basingstoke: Macmillan, 1989), pp. 89–90.

48. Ibid., pp. 104–5.

49. Roger Ebbatson, *Hardy: The Margin of the Unexpressed* (Sheffield: Sheffield Academic Press, 1993), pp. 81–2.

SUGGESTIONS FOR FURTHER READING

The best modern biography of Hardy is by Michael Millgate; his *Thomas Hardy: A Biography* (Oxford: Oxford University Press, 1982) is thoroughly researched and yet remarkably lucid and readable. Michael Millgate has also edited Hardy's autobiography, *The Life and Work of Thomas Hardy by Thomas Hardy* (London: Macmillan, 1984). For readers interested in the Wessex background of Hardy's fiction, Denys Kay-Robinson's *The Landscape of Thomas Hardy* (Exeter: Webb and Bower, 1984) offers a useful and entertaining introduction.

Critical works on Hardy are legion. The best introductory studies of Hardy's entire *oeuvre*, including his fiction and poetry as well as *The Dynasts*, are Irving Howe's *Thomas Hardy* (London: Weidenfeld and Nicolson, 1968), Norman Page's *Thomas Hardy* (London: Routledge and Kegan Paul, 1977), and Merryn Williams's *A Preface to Hardy* (2nd ed., London: Longman, 1993). Among other works, worth mentioning are J. Hillis Miller's *Thomas Hardy: Distance and Desire* (Cambridge, Mass.: Harvard University Press, 1970) and Michael Millgate's *Thomas Hardy: His Career as a Novelist* (London: Bodley Head, 1971); neither of these, however, devotes much space to the short stories.

As a result, for readers interested in Hardy's short fiction, Kristin Brady's *The Short Stories of Thomas Hardy: Tales of Past and Present* (London: Macmillan, 1982) remains indispensable; the only full-length study of the short stories so far, it is both insightful and subtle and at the same time thoroughly informative, likely to remain the definitive book on the subject for many years to come. For other books including material on Hardy's short fiction, see the section on 'Hardy and His Critics' earlier in this volume.

ACKNOWLEDGEMENTS

The editors and publishers wish to thank the following for permission to use copyright material:

HarperCollins Publishers Ltd for material from Jean Brooks, *Thomas Hardy: The Poetic Structure* (Elek Books, 1961), pp. 143–4;

Routledge for material from Norman Page, *Thomas Hardy* (Routledge and Kegan Paul, 1977), pp. 123–4;

Macmillan Ltd for material from Kristin Brady, *The Short Stories of Thomas Hardy: Tales of Past and Present* (1982), pp. 197–201.

Every effort has been made to trace all the copyright holders but if any have been inadvertently overlooked the publishers will be pleased to make the necessary arrangement at the first opportunity.